COLOR INSIDE THE LINES

BILL FISHER

A BRIEF INTRODUCTION

During 2020, millions of Americans paused to thank our Greatest Generation for preserving the hard-won freedoms guaranteed by our Founding Generation. We joined people around the world to commemorate the 75th Anniversary of VE and VJ Day, the Alliance's victories over the Axis powers in World War II.

To soldier up for the conflict, our military transformed the nation's multiethnic pool of raw recruits into cohesive, codependent fighting forces. With no time for distractions, Army recruits stifled old prejudices and formed new kinships. Long after the war, most acknowledged owing eternal debts of gratitude to those with whom they served. However, the Army had not yet evolved to become the colorblind meritocracy we have today, and adopted a policy of racial segregation for African Americans.

Contemporary publishers understood that images of the Army's multicultural bands of brothers would forever shape perceptions of the war. Contemporary *Negro* publishers understood that images of segregated units would forever distort perceptions of the Tanned Yanks' contributions. They lobbied the Army, as early as the day after the attack on Pearl Harbor, to end its policy of racial segregation. The top brass refused, insisting that their multicultural Army *was not a laboratory for social experiments.*

During the previous war, the Army had credentialed only one *Negro* war correspondent. At the start of WWII, the War Department's public affairs bureau acknowledged that mainstream newspaper reporters accustomed to ignoring *colored news* at home would ignore *colored news* overseas. To provide news coverage of segregated units, the bureau accredited three dozen war correspondents for the *Chicago Defender*, the *Pittsburg Courier*, the *Baltimore Afro American,* the *Norfolk Journal and Guide,* and two London-based news services. Many of these journalists risked their lives to ensure that the *first drafts of history* written on the war included participation by segregated air, ground, armored and services units.

The fictitious *Washington Record* employs this novel's protagonist, Jack Savoy, as the weekly newspaper's war correspondent. Neither Jack nor his employers are intentional representations or composites of contemporary reporters, editors or publishers. The work of African American correspondents in World War II and the civil rights activism of their publishers inspire this novel of historical fiction.

Chapter 1

· ·

Last Year

"**W**hat're you doing in here?"
            "Good morning, Captain."
            "Why are you in my jeep?"

"Are you Captain Ed Gale? I'm Jack Savoy, a reporter from the *Washington Record*."

"Oh, so you work for the colored newspaper that trashed FDR and General Marshall right after *Pearl*. Get out of my jeep."

"My paper is against segregation in the Army, not the president nor the Army chief of staff."

"There's no time for dealing with *the colored thing* now. We're at war. Look, *if you're really a war correspondent*, I'll transport you, but not in my command jeep. Hell, there's no war here."

"Well, this is *a military action*."

"Wrong. The battle for New Guinea is a military action. Protecting colored people in Detroit is a *civil action*. Now, get out and find a seat on one of the trucks."

Jack held out a folded blank sheet of paper. "I have permission from your press officer."

"Keep it. I have enough paper. By *press officer* you mean Lieutenant Stanley? Stan's also the *weather* officer who promised me, in writing, clear visibility this morning. Savoy, what kind of accent is that? Oh, you have a trace of a French accent but you don't speak much French. No kidding?"

A sergeant slid into the driver's seat and started the engine. "Good morning, Captain. Who's the hitchhiker?"

"Good morning, Tommy. It looks like we'll have to move out in the dark this time. Lingering overcast skies and fog coming in from the lake, the opposite of what Stan promised. Oh, and that colored Canuck back there obstructing your rear view claims he's a *war correspondent*—with no uniform. Jack Savoy, this steady Mackinaw man is my lead driver, Sergeant Tom Weeks. Keep out of his way and keep your hands off my radio."

"It's a pleasure to meet you, Mister Savoy."

"The pleasure's mine, Sergeant Weeks."

"Oh, don't get all emotional. Tommy, we need to push off. You got any questions, Savoy?"

"Yeah, what's a *jeep*?"

Both soldiers laughed. Capt. Gale replied, "This four-wheel drive is a *Willy's Quad,* made in Ohio, of all places. Ford's also making some here. GIs love them, and call them *jeeps.* So far, the nickname has stuck."

"Like the cartoon," added Sgt. Weeks. "They can go anywhere, do anything. But I ain't in love just yet."

"One more question? What about armed resistance today?"

"*What a-boot it,* Savoy? That's what you get when you ask to ride the point. You'll be the first one to know. Let's go Tommy." The captain reached back for his microphone. "Rally-Two to all drivers, we're rolling."

A chorus of confirmations followed. Sgt. Weeks explained, "They don't get many chances to use their radios." He pulled off slowly and led the small convoy of three jeeps and four trucks away from the castle-like structure that served as their downtown headquarters.

Capt. Gale turned around to face Jack. "To answer your question, we have to anticipate armed resistance. The protestors threatened to retaliate if the mayor called in the National Guard. How seriously you take them depends on how seriously you measure their resolve."

Jack imagined vigilantes hiding behind every tree. The captain asked, "How're we doing, Tommy?"

"It's still pretty dark out here, Sir. There's just enough mist hitting the windshield to be annoying. I'm okay though."

"Yeah, but we should've seen some daylight by now." Capt. Gale plucked the face of his wristwatch. "This thing can't be right. Savoy, what time do you have?"

"It's half past six, Captain. Glad I could be useful."

The captain ignored Jack's quip and rekeyed his microphone. "Rally-Three, this is Rally Two. How're we holding up back there, Sam?"

"Rally-Two, all's well. Sir, I think our first turn's coming up, Rally Three, out."

Scrambling to unfold his map, the captain confirmed, "That was quick. Okay Tommy, after the turn, let them reform."

The veteran sergeant patiently indulged his young commanding officer. He eased the convoy into a turn just as he had a hundred times before. Afterward, he slowed, waiting for the headlights to realign behind him.

Suddenly, bright flashes lit up the dark road as gunfire erupted, shattering the morning calm.

Capt. Gale shouted, "Stop the jeep, muzzle flashes dead ahead!"

Startled, Sgt. Weeks slammed the brake, jerking his company commander forward in the shotgun seat. The drivers behind them skidded in sequence, each veering off several feet to avoid a string of collisions. All stopped, their tight, single-file formation had devolved into a jagged line of old relics leftover from the previous war.

Trapped in the back seat, Jack agonized over the eternity that passed before the captain climbed out of the canvassed-topped jeep. The moment his egress was clear, Jack bolted for cover.

Master Sergeant Sam Ellis was already out of the second jeep, walking back and forth shouting orders. "Everybody out and take cover." Boots skidded on the damp pavement as infantrymen bailed from the trucks.

More shots rang out.

A third jeep raced up to the point, screeching to a stop alongside the command vehicle. Sgt. Ellis shouted. "Corporal, get that damn jeep back in line!" Without waiting for concurrence from a young lieutenant riding shotgun, the driver returned his platoon leader to the rear. Capt. Gale, brandishing a 45-automatic, took cover behind the command vehicle, right next to Jack.

All eyes followed Sgt. Ellis as he spoke in a series of crusty growls. "Get me some eyes on the shooters. Don't shoot back unless I say so. I rode in with 60 Wolverines and I plan to ride out with at least 50."

Jack was thankful for the nervous laughter that followed. The untested weekend warriors carried dated, but effective, heavy Garand rifles. He feared the collateral damage from two platoons of sweaty trigger fingers. Looking for something to do, he raised his compact Kodak Medalist, which, without a flash, was a useless prop.

The captain, anxious to contribute something to the veteran sergeant's monologue, admonished Jack. "Put that camera away and keep your head down. I shouldn't have brought you with us until we got a handle on this thing, and verified that you're really a war correspondent."

"Again, Captain? Really?"

Truthfully, the captain's instincts were correct. Jack had lied to Lieutenant Stanley. His application for press credentials was still under review at the War Department. To add depth to his ongoing series about racial unrest in Detroit, he wanted to write one installment from the National Guard's perspective. He gambled, reasonably, that Army reservists would not yet have the 1942 edition of the *War Correspondents Field Manual* just published in January by General George Marshall.

When the shooting stopped, Sgt. Ellis returned to the point and deferred to Capt. Gale." It's all over, with no casualties, Sir. What do you want me to do?"

Eager to resume command, the captain stood up and responded with practiced stoicism. "Don't chase them. Just call it in to the State boys. Get the company boxed up again, so we can move out. We're running late."

Sgt. Ellis responded to the captain's rediscovered command voice without a hint of the condescension a less seasoned NCO might be unable to suppress. "Yes sir. Alright everybody, let's saddle up!"

As he climbed into the back seat again, Jack had second thoughts about riding in the convoy's lead vehicle. Sgt. Weeks was already behind the wheel, offering a bit of advice. "Don't take him too personal, Jack. He's better than most. He's just wants to get into the war."

Jack leaned over, trying to reduce his tall silhouette. He bumped his head against the radio mounted in the left rear corner, producing a short screeching sound. The captain stuck his head inside to admonish him. "What did I tell you about my radio, Savoy?" With his nerves tightly wound, Jack flinched at the harmless, crackle of an incoming transmission.

"Rally Two, this is Rally One, over."

Smiling with satisfaction at Jack's discomfort, Capt. Gale reached back for the microphone. "Go ahead, Rally One, this is Rally Two, over."

An authoritative voice demanded to know, "Ed, what's going on out there? We have reports of shots fired."

After the captain made his detailed report of the brief incident, he turned back to Jack. "Relax, Savoy. We can't have the men seeing our fearless war reporter bailing from the command jeep."

Then he paused to look toward the eastern sky. Concerned about the effects that the lingering darkness might also have on his inexperienced troops, he rekeyed his microphone. "Rally One, what's holding up daybreak, over." He regretted using those words, but could not pull them back off the air.

A static filled pause followed a long moment of stunned silence. Then, the voice managed a stuttered request for clarification. "Uh, Rally Two, could you say again, over?"

Shaking his head after his poor choice of words, the captain signed off. "Disregard last transmission, Rally Two, out." As he got back in the passenger seat, he glanced back to see if Jack had taken any pleasure in his gaffe. He saw only a distracted reporter fussing with his camera as though he had not heard a word.

The driver rescued his commander by redirecting his attention to the unscheduled smoking break that had ensued among the troops. With a letup in the drizzle, metallic clicks of Zippo lighters and tobacco smoke filled the air. Sgt. Weeks lamented, "Sir, nothing else smells like a *Lucky*."

Shifting his focus back to the vulnerability of his stalled convoy, Capt. Gale extended his right arm through the opening to make a circular motion with his index finger. "All right Tommy let's get this gypsy caravan back underway."

As the convoy continued, Jack organized his thoughts about the minutemen he had interviewed the night before. Most had expressed a desire to transfer over to the 32nd Infantry Division, the Wisconsin and Michigan men who recently deployed to Australia. General Douglas McArthur had already thrown them into the battle for New Guinea. They had big shoes to fill. During the previous war, their fathers, uncles and neighbors that served in the old 32nd had broken through every enemy line they faced and never surrendered ground. Their French allies called them *Les Teribles.*

Capt. Gale was determined to ship out to New Guinea *at the earliest.* "Savoy, tell me, if we need every swinging dick overseas, why am I still in Detroit in May 1942."

Still focused on real and imagined snipers, Jack had not expected a question. With his eyes fixed on the trunk of a large elm, he mumbled without thinking. "Instead of policing the protestors who were harassing Negroes, the city cops bagged 200 Negroes."

The captain retorted, "I thought they arrested *both white and colored.*"

Hearing the aggravation in the captain's voice, Jack replayed his own words, realizing that it was too late to retreat to the conservative high ground. "I've been here the whole time Ed. They only arrested two or three white protestors."

"Why were 200 Negroes arrested? What were they doing?"

"Certainly, a few were grandstanding. Others were counter-protesting, but most were just trying to protect the families. You know, doing what the coppers were supposed to do."

The captain collected himself and spoke with a slow, deliberate cadence. "Well, I guess I'm asking you, *as an objective war correspondent,* why you think I'm still here instead of with the 32nd."

Jack empathized with him more than the captain could know. He had sought an overseas assignment himself after the attack on Pearl Harbor and Germany's subsequent war declaration. However, Jack was claiming to be a war correspondent already, and would blow his cover by complaining about the delay in getting his press accreditation.

In November 1941, Jack had been the only Negro reporter in America working at a metropolitan daily newspaper. A month after the *Oakland Chronicle* denied his request for an overseas reassignment, he had been on a train bound for an interview with a Negro weekly in Washington DC. When he detoured to Detroit to check on his younger brother, local racial tensions were drawing national attention. Jack agreed to remain in town, hoping to demonstrate his dexterity to the managing editor of the *Record*.

Recognizing that an angry captain could create problems for him, Jack thought carefully this time before answering. "After FDR integrated the war production plants, workers of all races flocked to Detroit for the new jobs. To accommodate some, the city built segregated public housing. Unfortunately, there's not much land left in the city without race covenants attached."

When the captain said nothing, Jack concluded, "The city put the new *Sojourner Truth* apartments on redlined land, yet still designated it for Negroes. Things took an ugly turn. The whole nation is watching this unusual deployment, so I guess the Army Guard picked someone to lead with a steady hand and a reasonable disposition. The mayor wants you and the state police to keep the peace while the rioting gets sorted out."

Aware of Jack's transparent pandering, the captain processed the information in silence, as though hearing the pretext for his mission for the very first time. He remained quiet as his convoy rumbled toward the southeastern corner of *Conant Gardens*, North Detroit's affluent, predominantly Negro community. Despite the early hour, curious residents stared through windows as the Army trucks passed by. After another orderly turn, the convoy lined up along Nevada Avenue in front of the rail yard opposite *Sojourner Truth*.

Seeing a throng of restless protestors already wrapped around the perimeter of the complex, the captain said, "Jack, you go ahead and move freely. Don't go far. If you run into trouble, haul your ass back here to me."

After the captain walked away, Sgt. Ellis went over to speak with Jack alone. "We can get somebody to drive you, Savoy." When Jack waived him off, the sergeant growled, "Then what happens when somebody refuses to buy the load of bullshit you've been selling?"

Despite the old veteran's stern face, Jack laughs. "Sam, I'll be fine."

"Okay, but don't get your ass blown off on my watch. I don't need the extra paperwork." With another growl, he returned to his duties, assigning men to various points along Conant, Fenelon Street and Nevada Avenue.

Jack jotted down a few more notes and strolled along well-lit Nevada Avenue. Reporters, some with the luxury of flash photography, scurried about, pursuing various angles of the developing story. Onlookers milled around the fringes, contemplating their next moves. After days of dispersing protesters, state policemen were everywhere, patrolling on foot, horseback, motorcycles and automobiles. Jack paused to get a picture of several guardsmen carrying rifles with fixed bayonets.

Suddenly, he spun around, sensing someone looming much too close, but relaxed at the sound of a familiar voice. "You know what I say, Red? They think this new place is too good for us. Brick buildings with sunny windows—they can't stand the thought of us owning it."

Jack tried to keep his younger sibling focused. "It's public housing, Serge. No one *owns it.* Is it time to go yet?"

"We'll walk over to the far side of *Black Jack High*, taking side streets to dodge the checkpoints."

Jack made eye contact with Sergeant Ellis. Seeing Jack and Serge headed for the perimeter of the heavily guarded zone, the sergeant frowned, but returned to his duties.

Serge was still talking. "Red, Sojourner Truth could be a model for housing Afro-Americans coming north for jobs. The only way protesters can stop us here is by going to jail."

"They might just do that yet." Jack warned.

"They ain't the types. All eyes are upon us. This is the front line of the new movement, plain and simple." Serge laughed at Jack's obvious discomfort. "A few months ago, my big brother was the only so-called *American Negro* working for a big city daily in this country."

Jack interjected, "I'd be overseas now if the *Oakland Chronicle* had just given me the reassignment I requested."

"And now maybe you'll understand that you're no longer a *Noir Canadien.* You're a Naturalized US citizen of the *Negro persuasion.* They don't dice up colored people in the States. You're a Negro working for a Negro paper run by Negro civil rights activists."

Jack assured him, "I'm fine with that. Hopefully, I'll soon be a war correspondent, and later, a foreign news correspondent reporting from postwar Europe."

"And you want it so much that you're willing to work with a troublemaker like me *on a civil rights story*. Who'd have believed it?"

Jack said, "First of all, don't act as though I haven't written in support of civil rights, both here and Canada. Second, I came here because Mamie wants to know how her estranged grandson makes a living working for civil rights. I had no idea this thing would blow up while I was here."

"It had to blow up, Red. Now keep in mind, the Negro editors are out front on segregation. The newspapers have the ink and the readers. So, you're in the hot seat, not me." Serge laughed again, slapping his brother's back.

On their way to John Pershing High School, Jack and Serge passed small groups of people drifting toward Sojourner Truth. Although most appeared calm and bound for work or school, the potential for trouble was apparent.

A block after flashing a revoked press card at a police checkpoint, the crowds thinned until they were virtually alone on the street. Serge walked up to a towering man he introduced only as *Ham from the Council.* As Jack shook the catcher's mitt he extended, Ham warned, "We have to be careful we don't get caught up in a messy triangle. I heard that some of the educated Negroes in Conant Gardens may be aligned with the white protestors."

"What?"

Serge confirmed, "He's right. They don't want a colored public housing project near them either. We got us a real mixed bag."

Just as daylight finally began filtering through, a dozen figures emerged from the shadows. Ham guessed, "These boys must be the volunteer bodyguards coming from the *Black Bottom.*"

Jack pulled a small notebook from his breast pocket. Ham froze in midstride. Squinting at the approaching figures, Serge asked, "Are they carrying guns? That's not the plan."

Twin shotgun blasts revealed the faces of a small angry mob. "That ain't them," Serge shouted from farther away. Jack turned to ask him for guidance, but Serge was already running and Ham was several yards ahead of him. Jack broke into a headlong sprint behind them. Someone in the mob fired again.

Certain the shooters were merely firing into the air, Jack looked for a place to rest, regretting the full breakfast he had eaten earlier. He found a place to catch his breath just as Serge and Ham disappeared around a corner. After several deep breaths, Jack followed them. Assuming his companions chose the same route, Jack ran out toward the perceived safety of a lighted side street.

However, an authoritative voice stopped him in midstride. "Hold on there, Mister. Are you chasing these boys?"

Jack surveyed the scene in front of him. Within the space of a few minutes, Ham was on the ground, blood seeping from a fresh gash on his forehead. A city policeman gripped the back of his collar with one hand, a bloodied baton with the other. Another policeman pinned Serge against a car, pressing a baton against his chest.

Seeing Serge so detained reminded Jack of a precarious scene from ten years earlier. He remembered loaded shotguns and men with too much whiskey, rope and warped perceptions of right and wrong. He averted his eyes as though they might have revealed his role in what occurred that night so long ago.

The policeman with two stripes on his sleeve tried again. "Did you hear what I said? We caught these boys running, and wondered if they were running from you."

Jack repeated the words, emphasizing their absurdity, "You *caught them running?*" He flashed his former employer's press pass. "I'm Jack Savoy, officer, a reporter covering the public housing opening. These men have been helping me get around. Someone started shooting at us over by the high school, and we all ran."

Serge's jailor said innocently, "We didn't hear any shots." Pages from Serge's copy of the *Chicago Defender* newspaper scatter over the ground.

The officer holding down Ham looked around suspiciously. He asked, "Did one of those boys from the Gardens shoot at you? We can take care of that."

The notion that the officer would invent an excuse to harass the peaceful residents of *Conant Gardens* left Jack speechless. Serge snickered, earning him a stiff shove. Hearing footsteps approaching, everyone turned to see the angry pursuers emerge from the alley. Shotguns were nowhere in sight. The corporal jumped up and held out his arms as though corralling horses and asked, "Whoa now, what's this all about, Jake?"

A man in the group stepped forward, spat and wedged a well-chawed tobacco wad between his cheek and gum. "We ain't for sure. Con, they're here for some kind of powwow."

Con nodded his understanding. Wondering what the policeman could possibly *understand* from Jake's cryptic summary, Jack shot his brother a puzzled glance. Serge shook his head almost imperceptibly.

The officer pressing Serge against the car glared at Jack. "No, he won't say anything. That's how I know we got ourselves a couple of *race men*. Our local boys would be shucking and buck dancing by now. These cool customers won't talk until they see the *N-Double-A* lawyer down at the station tomorrow."

"What do you mean, a*t the station tomorrow?"* Incredulous to hear that the police would hold two innocent men overnight, Jack's face contorted into an expression of pained agony.

Con became agitated. "Hold on now, *Mister Savoy*, boys from the *Bottoms* came up here and started all the trouble around here. We had that situation under control. Now, the Army and the State boys are in control of the area over there. This is still ours and this little misunderstanding is nothing we can't fix ourselves."

Another man in the crowd raised his hand like a schoolboy. "Con, is it true? Will the Army be escorting niggers into the new place today? The japs ain't been paid back yet for Pearl."

Another, deviously smiling man spoke up, "But if y'all got more important things to do, we got this little situation under control. Ain't that right, Mister *Newspaperman*?"

The leader silenced him with a wave of his hand. "Con, we don't know that reporter. That big buck there with the new red tattoo is in the *colored people's association*. Now, that wavy haired mongrel against the truck—he's had his black ass in the thick of it all along."

Suddenly, Jake looked confused. He requested a closer look at the detainees. When Con permitted him to examine Serge, Jake walked over and studied his face like an anthropologist.

Next, Jake walked over to stare at Jack. Growing wide-eyed and standing close enough to spray tobacco spit into Jack's face, he shouted, "Well I'll be goddamned. Hey, Con. Did you get a *good look* at this boy? Now look at that one."

Con obliged, and asked to see Jack's press pass again. Speaking to Jack in a different tone of voice, he asked, "Just what the hell is going on here, boy?" Jack pretended to search his pockets for the expired pass. Con grabbed his arm. "What's the holdup on that other truck? I want to keep this one separated."

Now in custody himself, Jack cringed at the sound of a noisy engine approaching. Fearing another city police wagon had arrived, he became tense, imagining the worst. However, his spirits soared when Con flinched at the harmless crackle of an incoming radio transmission.

The sound of the keyed microphone and the familiar crusty growl were unmistakable. "Rally Two this is Rally Three. I found him."

Chapter 2

· ·

A Year Later

"Let's move along now."
"What?"
"Young man, we already talked about this."
"Oh."

As my southbound train prepares to roll out of Baltimore's Penn Station, a Pullman porter reminds me that I must leave the dining car and move to another car where I *may read undisturbed*. A few minutes later, I settle into my new surroundings amid a chorus of groans from other relocated ticketholders. I do not doubt that a few are getting a rude introduction to the *Jim Crow* rules of the South. Most, however, quietly take seats in the *colored car*, aware that protesting is a waste of energy and emotion.

I am relieved to be on the last leg of my return trip from Nova Scotia, aboard a train that has crept painfully through the busy northeast corridor of a nation at war.

After reading a lengthy account in the *New York Times* about Allied naval successes in the Pacific, I open a March 1943 issue of the *Baltimore Afro American*. The newspaper leads with war correspondent Ollie Stewart's eyewitness account of action in North Africa. His description of a Negro support unit's rescue of a downed pilot fuels my desire to go overseas and my frustration over the continued delay.

Almost a year ago, after I finished my stringer work in Detroit, I arrived in Washington hoping to find my war correspondent's credentials approved, my new job secured and a date set for my departure overseas. I was disappointed. For the next several months, I received just enough work at the *Record* to live without spending the cash I had saved from selling my belongings in Oakland.

While I waited, shortly after ringing in the 1943 New Year in Washington, I learned that Mamie had died. After confirming that my brothers were not available to accompany me, I returned to Canada alone to bury our grandmother. I settled a few minor debts attached to her real estate, teaming up with crafty Uncle Louis to negotiate settlements for pennies on the dollar. Still, I was concerned that purchasing tickets back to Washington would leave me with almost no cash.

With no definite job offers in DC, I spent a week rethinking my career plans and improving the family gravesite where we also buried our maternal great grandparents as well as Lieutenant and Mrs. Jack Savoy, Sr. At one point, I contemplated repatriation in Canada. After all, I had come into valuable real estate that my French relations had coveted for decades. Even selling it directly to my uncle would enable me to live comfortably in Nova Scotia.

In the end, however, I decided to finish what I had started. I would get concurrences from Charles and Serge on the sale, and distribute reasonable shares. Unfortunately, until then I would be quite broke.

After riding in the dining car through New England, sustained only by coffee with extra cream and sugar, an older Pullman porter heard my stomach growl outside Manhattan. Without a word, he brought me a steaming hot plate of ham, eggs and toast. Without a word, I shoved aside my fifth cup of coffee and devoured his charitable gift.

When my train pulls into Washington, I step off the platform and regain my sea legs by walking briskly through cavernous Union Station. At the exit, I waive off a cab driver and walk a block to board the northbound streetcar that, at ten cents, is well within my current budget.

I take a seat in the rear *colored section*, just in case. The remaining coins in my pocket jingle, reminding me that tonight I must negotiate my way back into my boarding house. Otherwise, I will have to impose on Charles and Anne.

On U Street, I step down from the westbound electric powered conveyance with two suitcases in tow. I spend one of my few remaining nickels on a phone call to the War Department's public affairs bureau. I leave yet another five-cent message that Owen Todd will surely ignore.

I use another precious nickel to call Charles, but Anne tells me my middle brother is still asleep. I tell her not to wake him, refusing to impose on what might be their last time together before his armored unit ships overseas.

I take a deep breath to steady my nerves and walk toward the Lomax Publishing Building. Out of options and with no real plan, I intend to blindside the managing editor of the *Washington Record* by reporting for a job he has not formally offered. Worse, the war correspondent's job requires the press credentials Owen has promised since December 1941. I only hope the managing editor still wants me overseas half as much as I still want to go.

Ted Lomax graciously meets me in the lobby. "Jack, we were all sorry to hear about your grandmother. I hope our floral arrangement arrived on time. I know you just got back in DC, but have you heard from Owen? Walt's cut my budget for stringers."

Although tempted to tell him that approval of my application is imminent, I decide to answer truthfully. "No, there's still no word from him yet."

Ted grimaces. "Come on Jack, still nothing? I know we're not General Marshall's best friends, but we aren't his worst enemies either. Why are his people doing this to us? At least, I assume the problem lies with us. I mean, you're clean, aren't you?" I do not respond, refusing to comment on the absurdity. Expressing his exasperation with the continued delay, Ted throws up both hands, but still invites me upstairs to sit in on his meetings with senior staff. He also promises that we will meet today with his older brother, publisher and president, Walter Lomax. "Jack, you look like you could use a break. I'll see what I can do."

Upstairs, I find space for my luggage behind the receptionist's desk. Inside the conference room, Connie Howard, Ted's star reporter and *de facto* city editor, is in rare form.

"Jack, did I just see you get off a streetcar? Are you sure about giving up your Canadian citizenship now? They've integrated their army, commissioned colored pilots. Maybe you should go back home and get us some exclusives on that?"

While Connie couches her *tongue in cheek* suggestion as an opportunity for me, I know that returning to Canada would put me out of sight and out of the Lomax brothers' minds. Now that the military services have accredited a few female war correspondents, Connie would campaign in my absence for the very job I am here to claim. "Or you could go back to Detroit, Jack. Things are heating up out there again."

As the morning progresses, I get no farther than Ted's smoke-filled conference room. During his various meetings, I pass the time trading views on the war and looking through Ted's interior window at the open bay that serves as a newsroom floor. Ted indulges good-natured sparring between senior editors. After allowing them to haggle over the remaining space on tomorrow's front page, Ted silences the gladiators by issuing final instructions.

"We're all set with lead-ins for the top local articles. Below the fold, lead into the colored fighter pilots and the *Zoot Suits* in LA. Then, add the follow-up to Roosevelt's Casablanca conference. Hold the last column for the London news services and anything on the fighting in the Solomon Islands."

Miffed to have even a single word of their hard work *buried* inside, they lodge feeble protests before adjourning. One makes a final effort. "I knew you'd lead with the Tuskegee pilots. Although, who knows what's next for them? This Camp Huachuca piece on the colored infantry division has the real legs."

"And it'll be fine inside."

As they leave, Ted shakes his head and smiles. A cloud of tobacco smoke escapes behind them through the opened door and fresher air filters in. Two other people walk in and quickly focus their attention on me. Ted introduces me as *his choice* to become the *Record's* new war correspondent.

Connie, the only woman who has come into the room and the only woman listed on the newspaper's masthead, returns and issues a warning to Ted. "I heard the War Department just approved a guy named Tubbs as a second war correspondent for the *Afro American.* Your brother's head is going to explode."

Acknowledging her warning, Ted lets out his trademark low whistle, his upbeat mood suddenly turning sour. "Did you say Tubbs from the *Journal and Guide*?"

Connie answers coyly, "Yeah, that's him. You should know him, another *Morehouse man*. I wonder if he'll go to the Pacific since Ollie's in North Africa."

Ted responds to the question Connie has not asked. "I know who won't be going."

Chester Franklin walks in and clears his throat. "Ted, when's Jack going to replace me overseas?" Chet is a senior statesman among Negro war correspondents. During the previous war, he traveled to France at his own expense. Through his friendship with Emmitt Scott, a special adjutant to the Secretary of War, he met Ralph Tyler, the only person of color officially accredited as a war correspondent.

With Tyler's guidance, Chet interviewed Negro troops, compiling stories about the French-led 369th US Colored Regiment. He was not the only American Negro writer in Europe, but Chet began a lifetime friendship with war hero Walter Lomax.

Rather than fashion a response to Chet's question, Ted redirects his question to me. Before I can respond, they all turn away and peer through the glass window, distracted by something I had not noticed—*complete silence* in a newsroom working against deadline. Earlier, we had to shout above the noise. Suddenly, the seasoned veterans seated around the conference table flinch as a booming bass voice pierces the deafening silence.

"Where the hell is Ted?" The blast detonates out in the newsroom once more, louder this time. "Somebody go find Ted, Goddammit!"

Ted, a man once known for his fearless investigative reporting, looks sheepishly across the table at me. "That's just Walt," he confirms for my benefit. "Why can't he just walk over here and knock on the door?" Even as he asks his rhetorical question, Ted jumps to his feet. I am surprised to see the man who once stared down lynch mobs scurry out to answer his older brother's summons.

The low hum resumes on the newsroom floor, making it difficult to hear Ted's words, but the secondary explosion they detonate rings true enough. "That's bullshit Ted!"

A door slams against its frame as though punctuating the publisher's tirade. Through the window, I see them and two other men walking across the floor in single file. Both brothers stop just outside the open door. The others walk in silently and take seats.

I can hear them clearly now. "Ted, how can the *Afro* have two—and we have none? The *Courier* has Rouzeau and even the *Harlem Advocate* has Ron Maxwell. The colored wire services in London are churning out releases. You mean to tell me we can't get one goddam reporter overseas?"

After another muffled remark from Ted, Walter's voice becomes lower but no less vitriolic. "Jack who? Jack Savoy? Oh yeah, I thought he left, pending accreditation. Why's he back here?" The edge comes off the publisher's voice as he addresses his secretary. "June, get Owen Todd on the phone and put him through to Ted's conference room."

June Carter's response confirms my worst fear. "Ted's already put me on it. I've been trying all morning, Walt. Except for that cryptic message he left yesterday about the moratorium, Mister Todd hasn't returned my calls."

Through the doorway, I look up into the deep-set eyes of a predator, sweeping the room as though probing a herd for exploitable weaknesses. Another person walks past the rangy boss and sits at the table.

The publisher snarls at his sibling once more. "What cryptic message is she talking about? Ted, how could Ike have a moratorium for us and not have one for the *Afro*? We can't wait until the war is over. How could you make a deal with a file clerk like Todd to select this kid anyway?"

Even with empty pockets, I feel an urge to walk out. With two major mainstream newspapers in DC, plus the *Baltimore Afro American's* new Washington edition, the *Record* is far from the only game in town. Besides, if Owen has told an ill-advised lie about a moratorium from the Supreme Allied Commander, I suspect I may not be long for the door anyway.

Surprisingly, Ted defends me and his longtime colleague. "Walt, you know Owen's in public affairs working behind the scenes to get our reporters overseas." Ted's voice is steadier but still respectful of his brother's authority. "As for Jack, I checked him out myself."

The publisher stalks into the room and acknowledges greetings until pausing just above me. Ted follows him in and takes a seat near the head of the table. When I rise to introduce myself, the Midwesterner laughs derisively.

"So, you're my brother's latest indulgence?" I do not ask him to elaborate. "Is that your stuff stacked behind my secretary's desk? Why didn't you take it to your room? What was your hurry?" Well, at least now I know why no one has ever met the *first Negro reporter at a major daily*. You're hiding inside a white French Canadian."

Nervous laughter fills the room. People have warned me about Lomax's abrasive style and his use of measured intimidation. Seeing the ease with which he manipulates these old veterans, I suspect those warnings could be-understated. Maintaining a smile, my response is void of emotion. "Well, that's why my brothers call me *Red*."

The publisher joins the others in chuckling good-naturedly and finally sticks out a clammy hand. "So, tell me *Mister Caribbean Canadian* or whatever you people up there say, why have you left a big city daily to work for a colored weekly, eh? Are you slumming, crusading or are you just a Trojan horse from that new five-sided bunker across the river? Or are you just unemployed? No shame in it."

I ignore all the possible implications of his questions, and do my best to get a grip on the cold fish Lomax extends. "It's an honor to meet you Mister Lomax."

The publisher scoffs. "Call me *Walt*. All these other hacks do. Now Jack to be fair, I've read your clips and the copy you wrote for us—crisp, thorough, fluid. Now, I have to say that your journalistic voice is a bit *colorblind* for us. Funny thing though. When Murphy said he met you over at the *Afro,* I wondered exactly when that meeting took place."

I say nothing as Lomax appraises me like a used car. "What's the matter, caught *Red-handed*? Look, Jack, we're a very small community. I know you gotta eat, and hedge your bets, but don't meet with my competitor behind my back and then ask Ted for stringer gigs. Answer one question sans bullshit. Can Owen Todd get you credentialed, I mean, *for us?*"

After Owen's elusiveness, I have lost any measure of goodwill I may have established with the people seated around the conference table. Now Walt knows about my overtures to his biggest competitor. I feel vulnerable and exposed. Ted glares at me, clearly feeling betrayed by my clandestine meeting with the *Afro's* president. I answer his brother's question. "I know he can."

Looking satisfied, I suspect because he has come between me and his brother, Walt flops into the chair left vacant at the head of the table and fires his pipe with a gold-plated lighter. As he speaks, he scans issues of the *Pittsburg Courier*, the *Afro* and the *Chicago Defender* scattered across the table. "I can't imagine why Owen left that bogus message about a moratorium. How about you Jack? Why is your friend lying to us?"

Walt's frustration is understandable. Two years have passed since Chet returned home after falling ill in the North African desert. The War Department has denied every request for a replacement, forcing the *Record* to rely on reprints and pooled copy from two London-based Negro news services.

I share Walt's disappointment in Owen. I have packed everything I own and stacked it behind a desk in an alcove. I avoid answering Walt's questions while trying to sound reassuring and buy more time. Instead, I admit, "Honestly, I don't know."

Walt throws his head back, groans and flashes a pained expression. He says, "Look Savoy, you're certain he can get your deal done but uncertain about his motives. I know you took a chance showing up here today without credentials. It's ballsy, like walking out on the *Chronicle* with no fallback position."

When I merely nod, but say nothing more, Walt continues. "If we knew last year what we know now, I probably would have hired you sight unseen." I search Ted's face for an explanation, but rather than address the delay his brother's words suggest, he looks away.

Walt reminds me, "The Army won't transport you, house you or protect you until they accredit you. Until then, you're just another reporter—and I don't need another reporter. And by the way Jack, you could have been a little less extravagant with my money in Detroit."

He has answered his own question about my reasons for secretly interviewing at the *Afro*, but I hold my tongue, considering no one over there mentioned plans for sending Vince Tubbs overseas. Then, Walt suddenly softens, and muses, "You know, people might share things with a *French Canadian* they would never say in front of me."

Still, I say nothing. Walt finally utters the *magic words*. "Today is Thursday. We'll pay you for a month, and give you an expense account and an advance. Get your friend to finalize your accreditation any way you can. But Jack..."

"Yes Walt?" My spirit soars, but I have already guessed that Lomax will offset his expression of generosity with something at least mildly degrading.

"If I see you again sneak out to use that phone booth across the street, you'd better reemerge as Superman."

Just as another wave of laughter breaks the tension. Ted, now steely eyed, asks, "Well, I guess we're so despised over there that Jack is the only boy we're likely to get, right Jack? Just say it. Are we over a barrel?"

I respond truthfully. "I don't know anything about that, Ted."

Before Ted can fire off his retort, Walt shifts our focus. "Ted, he's either a fantastic liar or he honestly has no idea what you're talking about. Let's get on track. I need to talk to your team. The people who do the real work can get along without you prima donnas for another hour." Walt yells out to June. "Tell Doris to come in here."

A woman walks in with folders in hand, leaving the odor of mimeograph fluid in her wake. Chet, a veteran reporter for two wars, pulls out a chair for her midway between the Lomax brothers.

Walt continues, "All the colored papers push for integration, and we've been way out-front towing the line." Several people around the table groan in agreement.

"But we've got a competitor moving into our territory." Walt pauses, looking from one person to the next, and back at me with a wink. "If the Allies plan to win this world war with logistics, then let's get our boys involved with logistics. It'll be easier."

Looking suddenly confused, Ted interjects, "I don't understand, Walt."

His brother is dismissive. "Sure, you do, Ted. We've stuck our necks out long enough fighting against segregation. The Army will never integrate. I'm tired of begging. Let's be smart and concentrate on something we can get, like the skills needed to get postwar technical jobs for our boys."

I flinch. Already concerned about the stigma of working for the Lomax brothers, I do not want to confine my work to promoting technical training instead of writing the gripping combat stories Americans crave. Ted speaks up, "Walt, are you suggesting we spin our wheels looking for colored technicians and editorializing about the need for more?"

Walt snaps back. "That's the job and our new editorial direction, Ted. Negro combat troops may never get overseas. Jack can cover Negroes in engineering, signals, ordinance...."

Interrupting, Connie dryly adds, "Sanitation, transportation, labor units."

Walt again snaps back at her. "Miss Howard, they can't all be fighter pilots. According to Judge Hastie's survey, four out of five don't even expect to get a better job after the war." Walt looks around at his senior staff, annoyed. "Jack, do you understand my point?"

When I hesitate to respond, Walt's nostrils flare as though irritated by the stench of my anxiety. I look over at Ted. He averts his glance and takes a pack of cigarettes from his shirt pocket. Then everyone else lights up. I do not want to alienate Ted, but Walt has committed to hiring me. Besides, they all have made me for an out-of-work reporter chasing a lead gone cold. In full self-preservation mode, I acquiesce. "Walt, I think you're right on point."

Ted becomes incredulous. "Really Jack, you're folding just like that?" He rises to his feet, as if to make a speech. "We have to challenge second class accommodations, and keep the combat units in the public eye. The same lynch mobs that hunted down Negro GIs in the States are hunting our boys over there. Hell, they'll lock them up and hang them, just to keep things in perspective. If that's not why Jack is going over there, then maybe I should be working someplace else."

Walt laughs. "Then, why'd you select this guy? He wants to work for the *Times* or like he's back in high school working for Bill Walker at the *Cleveland Call and Post*. Jack doesn't feel what you feel, and he ain't going to write like that. Are you, Jack?"

I say something about racism in Canada. Walt howls and dismisses my remark with a shrug. "I always do my homework, Jack. I know you were there when Bob Taft tested the waters."

After several minutes of similar exchanges, I fear becoming collateral damage in a battle between the Lomax brothers. I scramble to break the icy chill. "May I say something that could be helpful?" Walter nods but Ted growls something indecipherable.

"Look, no one wants the Army and this crazy country *desegregated* any more than I do. Please believe that. I can file stories from any angle and write features regularly. You both know I'm no stranger to meeting *daily* deadlines while also writing copy for weekend editions." I emphasize the word *daily*, and eyes roll.

Walt appears to be tiring. He tables the discussion for later. "I think it's about time we broke for lunch. Let's get back here in an hour." Everyone files out of the room.

As I pass the front desk, June has a message. "Jack, you had a call from Mister Todd. He didn't want to be patched through, but wanted to know if you could meet him for lunch today at Union Station."

Both Lomax brothers have already stopped in midstride. Walt answers for me. "June, you call Todd back yourself and tell him Jack will be right there. Grab a cab, Jack—unless you're flying today."

Skepticism remains in Ted's voice. "Keep all your receipts, and don't let me find out you're carrying Owen's water. I know him and I'm beginning to know you. June, put him in the Whitelaw and set him up with an expense account—*for one week at a time.* Jack, don't let Owen off the hook on your credentials. Get it done." Walt nods his concurrence.

Before following Ted into Walt's office, Chet says, "Hot dog, Jack. I think you did it. You know, I've seen the photos from your 35-millimeter Kodak. It isn't much, but it's as much as you can get away with. It's against the rules for a reporter to carry one overseas, but we'll tell you later how to sneak pics back to us."

When I turn back to June, she smiles as though acknowledging the small victory I desperately needed. "I'll make your reservation at the Whitelaw, and send your bags over. Just so you know, the Whitelaw is a *colored hotel* just around the corner. Will that be okay?"

Having stayed in one during my previous visit, I am aware that most Negroes visiting Washington stay at one of the boarding houses that thrive in this segregated southern city. "June, are you asking me if *I belong* in a colored hotel?"

She flashes an indulgent smile. "Jack, I know *exactly where* you belong. I was asking where you think you belong." With no interest in discussing the matter further, she whisks debris off the front of my suit. "This needs to go to the cleaners. Drop it off across the street before they close and tell them you work here."

I tuck the envelope inside my breast pocket. She turns me around to give my back the onceover. When I turn back, my spirits soar at the sight of a stack of bills inside an open leather pouch.

"I'm sure you're fine with cash. It's an advance on your first two weeks' salary. Always keep an envelope for your receipts. Give those to me. Please thank Mister Todd for me. He's been so patient. I could never have put together your application package without him."

Chapter 3

. . . .

Owen Todd

"Why, it's Jack Savoy—as I live and breathe."
I have not seen Owen Todd since he moved to the Capital *to ensure that Negroes get a fair hand out of the New Deal.* He was just one of many who placed successful careers on hold to follow Judge William Hastie to work for a wildly popular president. However, no one had expected a man with Owen's education and reputation to settle for a low-level administrative job.

During our telephone conversations, I had begun to detect subtle changes in his once powerful delivery. Certain that nothing could damage my mentor's self-esteem I attributed the change to poor long-distance telephone connections.

However, the hollow monotone I hear behind me in Union Station today struggles to generate the qualities that once riveted me, one of only a few dozen students of color at Oberlin College during the Depression years, to the lectures of the only faculty member of color on campus in 1934.

I respond before I have completely turned around. "How've you been, professor?" When our eyes meet, I no longer see the rigid face of the celebrated journalist who once influenced me so profoundly. That face is lost in the inflexible smile of a compromising chameleon. He clasps my hand as though it holds a tie-breaking vote and I attempt to return the force of his spirited Washington grip.

There is an uncertainty about him that belies his attempt to project happiness. "I've been marvelous. But I swear Jack, you haven't changed a bit."

Instead of comfortably attired in his familiar bowtie and tweed jacket, I see a department store mannequin wallpapered into the uniform of a Washington bureaucrat. Owen still has his smooth, freckled, medium brown complexion and middle-aged boyish charm. However, his eyes seem empty. His hand remains locked in a pumping motion. "Hungry? You look like man who could make it rain."

I have too much to lose to engage in overdone bluster, so I get right to the point. "Come on Owen, I look like last night's garbage wrapped in last week's newspaper. I need to know how you've been doing in the *rainmaking* department. Where do I stand on my accreditation?"

I inform Owen that half the people at Lomax Publishing always doubted his ability to deliver, and now his unexplained silence has shaken the confidence of the other half. Owen merely gestures toward the back of the diner. "I have a table over in the corner that'll be the perfect spot for us to talk about that."

I walk past men in business attire, surprised to see white and colored people in the South sitting together at a diner. Some sip coffee, and smoke, while reading neatly folder newspapers. Others sit in rigid etiquette, handling napkins and utensils as though seated in the city's finest restaurant.

After weaving through the throng, we reach a quiet table secured with an opened newspaper, a half-smoked cigarette smoldering in an ashtray and a trench coat draped across one of the chairs.

Before Owen removes the newspaper, I manage to scan stories about General Patton commanding a corps in El Guettar, the siege of Stalingrad and aerial dogfights over the Solomon Islands. I lament that none of the stories carry my by-line.

Owen begins, "Sit down Jack. I thought this would be an appropriate venue. You can thank Teddy Roosevelt for this. He threatened to pull funding for construction if they segregated this lunchroom."

Trying to express the urgency of my situation, I mention that, "It's all right nice. I was down here just this morning, but couldn't afford to feed in here a few hours ago. Speaking of the Roosevelt's, Ted said FDR took down the *colored* and *white* restroom signs in the new building. That shows some spunk."

Hearing Ted's name brings Owen's first genuine smile. "Yeah, he sure did. By the way, some are calling the new building *The Pentagon*." He adds, "You know, most white people in DC won't care when segregation ends."

With Ted's cynicism fresh in mind, perhaps compounded by my own frustration, I cut Owen off far more harshly than I should. "So then, in the meantime, I have to hike 15 blocks from the Lincoln Memorial to the *colored* restrooms in the Archives building."

With a sigh, Owen laments, "And there you go, Jack. Pardon me if I failed to guess which mask you were wearing today. Am I talking to the Jack who worked for Hoover's reelection, or the Jack who took his conservative editorials to interview with the *Chronicle*? Or are you the Jack who took my 17-year-old niece to a Klan rally in Indiana ten years ago?"

Owen throws up a hand before I can respond. "You became a civil rights reporter in Detroit, to impress the Lomax brothers no doubt. A person might say you'll be whoever you need to be."

"Do you mean a person like a tough civil rights reporter who takes a job pushing paper for the chief architect of a segregated Army?" I immediately regret taking the cheap shot at my mentor, who has been like a godfather deserving my respect and appreciation. "I'm sorry, Owen. I had no right to say that. I need to relax."

However, my blunt quip seems to settle him down. He assures me that, "I'm used to it, but as long as I know why I'm here, that's all that matters to me. You're going to work for two civil rights crusaders. Don't worry about me. You need to figure out who you're going to be."

I do not think we have time for this game. "I never pretend to be anyone other than myself. I let people think whatever they want. I don't know why Americans think I'm obligated to disclose my ancestry, or that it's any of their business. Right now, I just need to be an objective journalist."

Owen matches my energy level. "Jack, don't kid yourself, my coworkers aren't looking at you as an objective reporter, and that's not what Ted wants you to be. Just so you know I've got other things to do than making you a war correspondent." Anticipating my next comment, he adds, "I know you think Ted sent me your stuff in January 1942. The truth is I never got your package until he had a chance to look you over."

His disturbing revelation of Ted's role in the delay catches me by surprise. I wait for him to expand, but he offers nothing more. "I just thought you deserved to know." Though I have other questions about the delay, he drifts even further off topic saying, "Jack, I never congratulated you on your citizenship."

My mind is racing, but I remember that I never thanked Owen for his help. "I appreciated your affidavit." However, I am still regaining my balance from learning that Ted is just as responsible as Owen is for my delayed accreditation.

Owen continues to dodge. "Now, one of your brothers did it the old-fashioned way, married a US citizen. The youngest still travels a lot." Owen allows his words to trail off. Suddenly he reminds me of the agents who oversaw my Naturalization process, from filing my oath to renouncing my Canadian allegiance, to petitioning for US citizenship.

I try to relax. "After two years of law school, Charles up and volunteered for the Army, the day after Pearl. He's home now spending time with his wife."

Owen asks, "What about the youngest?"

I ask impatiently, "Owen, why don't you just ask me whatever it is you want to know?"

"Okay Jack, I'll ask you directly. Has Serge been working with a new militant civil rights group?"

I smile at the characterization, remembering the docility with which Serge and Ham accepted their fates that night in Detroit. "I honestly don't think the Council on Racial Equality is a militant group. It didn't seem that way in Detroit. Is that what this is about?"

"You know exactly what this is about." Owen looks amused. "Remember, Jack, you *used* to be a Caribbean Canadian. Now, you're a *colored guy, a nigger* as some will say, working for a colored publisher, asking for press credentials." Owen laughs as he leans in closer. "It wasn't easy getting this done, but you're in."

Though leveraging this information has been like pulling a wisdom tooth, hearing them lifts the weight of uncertainty from my shoulders. For the moment, I forget his obsession with my civil rights pedigree and with my family. Stress evaporates from my body. Almost a full minute passes before I speak again.

"Look, Owen, I can't find the words. You don't know how badly I needed to hear that. I apologize if I don't always say enough about your support. If Serge shows up here to see us off, I'll try to get to the bottom of it."

"That's all I ask, Jack."

I want to move on, but have to ask, "Why did it take so long? Even if Ted dragged his feet, is there really so much contempt for a decorated war veteran like Walter Lomax?"

Owen starts talking slowly, "This thing with Ted's brother runs deep. He has been a constant problem. He cosigned Garvey's plan to ship a million Negroes to Liberia. At the Negro Editors' Conference, we held right after Pearl, Lomax called General Marshall a racist. When Marshall's men said the Army *wasn't a laboratory for social experiments,* Lomax wrote some scathing editorials, right after all those boys took it on the chin in Hawaii. My boss wanted to hang him for treason."

Against my better judgment, I defend Walt. "He's not the only publisher on the hook for sedition. He's far from the only publisher who criticizes the Army."

Owen waves off someone without looking up. He whispers, "You never read the editorial. Then Lomax also stood up for Randolph and Rustin when they grabbed FDR by the balls on war plants integration. We were all forced to take a bite off that *shit sandwich.* Hell, we've other things to discuss. Let's start with this obsession with integrating combat units."

When I reach inside my coat pocket, he stops me. "Do not take out a pad, Jack. I must be very careful. No one appreciates the job I'm doing. It pays to be invisible. And, Jack, just so you know, I ain't giving Lomax a correspondent to beat his drum all the way to Berlin."

I reassure him, "I plan to write the stories I find—with minimal editorializing, but you have to admit that it's bogus to pay for separate quarters, separate training and air fields just to keep apart white and colored." I continue, "And what about separate hospital wards with separate nurses?"

He flinches. "Jack. Look, that's a tough one, just the thought of colored girls putting their hands-on white soldiers. No one even talks about it. Maybe you could write something suggesting we use them to care for POWs."

I raise my voice, "No one would be satisfied with that." Then I immediately have second thoughts about it. "But at least the nurses would gain the same experience that white nurses get."

Those words perk him up. "That's the way you've got to sell it, Jack. Help your readers see it that way. By the way, you do know that the Canadians are integrating. Still sure you made the right choice?"

"Yes. All of Halifax was buzzing about that. It's going to shake up the whole Commonwealth. But I can tell you that racism had nothing to do with my decision to immigrate, at least not racism outside the extended French-Canadian Savoy clan."

Once we have finished eating, Owen asks, "Jack, do you think Lomax will endorse FDR again in '44?"

I shift forward, now assuming the posture of co-conspirator. "Walt will support the ticket—no matter what. He's concerned about being profitable, gaining market share—about survival. He's talking about dropping his campaign for integrated units and advocating instead for more Negro soldiers in technical roles—segregated or not."

"No kidding?" The notion seems to appeal to him.

"Yes. He wants me to lead the call for better training, deployments and complex duties. However, as you know, I'll also need battlefield stories for my postwar portfolio."

Owen appears to be intrigued. "Now that's great news, and important intelligence. And I haven't forgotten your career goals—which brings me to my proposal."

My stomach tightens. I have felt the spirit of *quid pro quo* since I first sat down. Owen says, "You'll have a lot to do before you leave, so we'll be in touch. You'll need inside scoops, and a few special favors won't hurt. Otherwise, you can't see ten yards in front of you. I can make that easier for you. And I could sure use someone to talk to other colored reporters—to kind of serve as my eyes and ears."

I stiffen and my instincts tell me to respectfully decline. "No Owen, I can't spy on anyone for you."

"No spying, Jack. Just let me know if anyone is about to self-destruct. For instance, you've heard of Ron Maxwell? He's over in Algeria circumventing Army censors."

"Yes. I know of him. He's with the *Amsterdam News*?"

"Ron's with the *Harlem Advocate* now, made it overseas as a favor for an old friend. I think it'll help if another colored reporter fresh from the States looks him in the eye and tells him his accreditation is at risk."

Despite my concern that I will regret making such a commitment, I rationalize, "That sounds pretty straightforward. Delivering a warning that will help another reporter may not be a lot to ask."

Owen continues, "Then, there's a personal matter. It has to do with my niece, Rachel. She's now an Army nurse." Just the mention of her name is unsettling. I have never told Owen that attending the Klan rally was Rachel's idea. It was the last place on earth I wanted to be that night. From far away, I hear Owen say, "Jack, I'd be grateful if you'd look in on her for me."

Rachel, Serge and I agreed a long time ago that Owen was better off not knowing the details of that night ten years ago. I do not know how much she eventually shared with her uncle. Though she spent a few more days, and nights, on campus, Rachel and I never exchanged another word about it. I struggle to speak in a neutral tone. "How can I possibly help her with anything?"

He responds matter-of-factly, "Do it through your press contact at Fifth Army—your friend from college, Tom James—now a major and press officer."

"Do what through him, Owen? What's going on with her?" In that moment, I reflect on my long friendship with Tom Nightwalker James. We once ran errands in Taft's presidential exploratory campaign office. The job had evolved from our work for Herbert Hoover's presidential reelection as kids in 1932. Tom approached Vice President Charles Curtis' staff with his membership in the Kaw Nation. I vaguely referenced my Canadian Cree lineage.

Owen says, "Jack, I just need you to very quietly and discreetly look in on Rachel. Find out if she's having any problems. If she's okay, give her my love. If there's a problem, tell Tom whatever you find out."

Though this request is both personal and disconcerting, I feel compelled to grant it, considering Rachel may well be Owen's only living family member. I ask, "How do I find her? North Africa is a big place."

"Rachel's at the Army general hospital in Casablanca. The trains are running now all along the Mediterranean coast. Once you talk to her, you can easily get back to Fifth Army HQ." He stands, putting on his coat. "Let's keep talking over the next few days."

"Owen, there's a lot of violence committed against soldiers of color, unfair punishment and demeaning trials. With Ted on my back, if I hear about it, I need to investigate it. If I find it, I'll have to write it."

Owen responds softly, "Jack, just get used to saying *colored* or *Negro*, please. Everyone'll appreciate it and you'll eliminate confusion. I must be honest with you though. I sold you using the term you prefer: *Canadian Caribbean*, even though just a trace of the Caribbean in you remains. I told them you were a guy less inclined to beat that drum. Of course, I can't stop you. So, write whatever the censors allow."

Again, it sounds like a warning. Appearing disappointed, Owen stands and extends a cold and clammy hand, which feels much like the deal I just made. Without saying anything further, he leaves ahead of me and makes his way out into the rolling sea of Washington mannequins.

I linger a while longer, thinking about our conversation and wondering how many pounds of flesh I will need to sell before this war is over. However, my adrenalin surges. I consider the advantages I may have over other reporters—even as the weight of added baggage strains my sense of integrity.

After supplementing the meager tip Owen has left on the table, I leave the dining room, walking behind a young white male patron. We both pause before walking through the door, inviting an elderly man to enter first. However, rather than accept deference to his age, he gestures for us to exit first. I believe it is his silent primer on entitlement in this genteel southern town.

I pause awkwardly at the door to acknowledge his gesture. "Thank you very much, sir."

Startled by my expression of basic human decency, the old man frowns and lifts his face to look at me. The wrinkles that cut deeply into his ebony skin appear to map the myriad journeys that have very likely brought him to this small space we now share. His soft eyes glisten, his curiosity morphs into familiarity.

As if to reassure me, he says. "Don't pay nobody no mind, *son*. You just go ahead and do whatever you gotta do."

Chapter 4

· ·

The Brothers Savoy

O
ne evening, as my time in Washington nears an end, I walk the
distance from Lomax Publishing to my brother's home two neigh-
borhoods to the east. As darkness falls, the U Street corridor, also
known as Washington's *Black Broadway,* gradually transforms into a
florescent entertainment strip.

Vehicles for hire stop in front of nightclubs to discharge women
adorned in reds, metallic sheens and pastels—escorted by soldiers in
uniforms of white, blue and shades of olive green.

Jazz musicians compete for their attention and the aromas of
southern cuisine drift out to the sidewalks, luring aficionados and
hearty appetites inside. Seemingly oblivious to differences of race,
partygoers of all races enjoy nightlife side-by-side.

I wonder whether these young men are concerned about bigotry
in the military or only with doing their duty and coming back alive.
Do they dream, as Walt does, of a postwar period with increased
rights and privileges? Tonight, they all look like confident young lions
strolling along the illuminated boulevard, wearing their uniforms as
only colored men will—projecting every bit of personality allowed
within the confines of service dress codes.

I have been promising to visit Charles before he ships out. However,
every workday has seemed longer than the day before. Long bumpy

train rides and fits of sleep have taken their toll. I have left work every night ready for nothing more than dinner, a bath and a comfortable bed.

The Whitelaw Hotel has never disappointed. I have been more than satisfied with everything, from the ornate moldings that frame the stained-glass ceiling to the floors waxed to a soft glow, and every knob and handle polished with equal aplomb. Each night, the comfortable bed calls out to me the second I walk through the door.

To lure me away this evening, Charles has issued an ultimatum and the promise of a home cooked meal that will rival anything I can find on U Street. He also has promised that Serge will be there. I have not seen either of my younger brothers in almost a year.

I walk past Griffith Stadium and see a long line across the avenue forming outside the Howard Theater. A signpost announces a performance by jazz greats Dizzy Gillespie and Earl Hines. It is a reminder that, though some of the world's best-known musicians routinely appear within walking distance of my hotel room, I have not taken in a single show.

Charles' house is further away than I anticipated, and as I finally climb the steps up to his door, I wonder for the first time if I will have the stamina for following troops in combat.

Serge is already there. Soon, our warm reunion devolves into something more recognizable. Serge, as always, fires the first salvo. "I'd like to propose a toast. Here's to the end of my big brother's indentured servitude at the *Chronicle*, and finding his true calling with two pillars like the Lomax brothers."

As he helps Anne set the dining room table, Charles pauses to dismiss Serge's jaded toast. "I know you can do better than that. It's our first dinner together as a family in years."

Serge has our grandmother's smile, but flashes that annoying smirk he dipped from some unsavory corner of the gene pool. He promises to try again. "Okay. I'll make a toast to family—to Mamie, our great-grandparents, our extended family in Africville and the house we called home."

Now in unanimous agreement, we toast the man the people of Halifax's Africville community called Papa Joe Domingo, his wife Souwanas and their daughter, the grandmother who raised her three grandsons.

I often think about the kidnapped Fulani child last sold in Jamaica. Known simply as *Joe,* he escaped the certain death that awaited slaves on the hazardous Domingo sugar plantation. Wearing a confiscated suit of clothing, he slowly made his way to Nova Scotia in 1840. He settled in Canada amid a community of former slaves, African sailors, colored soldiers who sided with Britain during the American Revolution, and other English loyalists of color.

Joe married a French and Algonquian Cree woman who gave birth to a daughter, our dearest Mamie, born with the features of their anonymous European lineages. Mamie married a French trader. Their daughter's subsequent marriage to another French trader inexplicably produced three sons who each inherited varying doses of Papa Joe's features. Years after our mother's sudden death, all three of us eventually immigrated to America, at Mamie's behest.

Serge, by far the most cerebral, met and followed his adopted hero, civil rights organizer Bayard Rustin. I know questioning him about his work at CORE will not go well. Charles desires to maintain an air of cordiality in his home around Anne. However, his wife may as well get used to our frequent rifts.

"Red, how much of your own money did you have to spend back home?"

I am pleased that someone else has raised the subject. "Everything I had, Charles. I don't have to do it right away, but I need everyone's concurrence to sell the house, and the old place on the edge of Africville."

Charles answers right away. "That's an easy one. You should have put them both on the market right away. I guess the Americans will let our baby brother into their country at some point."

Serge ignores the dig, and concurs. "Sell it all, Red, structures and land. Take out whatever we owe you, send me a few bucks and give Anne the rest to hold on to for me. I know Mamie loved her house and Papa Joe's place, but she knew the day would come when you'd have to turn it all over. What about the *white Savoy's?*"

I respond, "They won't contest. Uncle Louis offered a very fair price on both properties, *as is.* I could probably get his check before I leave. Let him handle the paperwork."

Charles ends the discussion. "*L'Oncle Louis* certainly has the money. Then that's that."

Pleased to get that issue out of the way so easily, I need to snatch the scab off an old wound. "Your toast reminds me of another question I have for you, Serge. Owen asked me about your involvement with *CORE*, saying they promote *direct action*. What does that mean? Did *Rustin the Quaker* have an epiphany while he was in prison?"

Charles attempts to circumvent our argument before it begins. "Oh no, not tonight fellas, okay? Didn't you two get a chance to fight in Detroit? Anne worked hard on what may be our last meal together for a long time. Can we have just one night without an argument?"

Charles' wife seconds her husband's suggestion. "I agree. Time is too short to waste. Besides, my pie is just about ready to eat."

My sister-in-law was born to sharecroppers who sent her to Washington as a child. After she graduated from a local teachers' college, she encouraged my brother to go back to school—then supported him through college and two years of law school. She is perfect for Charles, but the seriousness with which she takes herself contrasts sharply with the glib dispositions of the Savoy brothers.

I cut in. "That was a year ago. We went through a lot together in Detroit, even chased by an armed mob. If the National Guard hadn't come to our rescue, we might still be there. I'm just concerned that Serge could affect all of us."

Serge is dismissive. "You mean affect *your government-issued* press credentials don't you, Red? Come on. Owen Todd is afraid of his own shadow, a colored New Dealer working as a low-level Army clerk. Yes, let's all make sure we don't offend his Jim Crow sensibilities."

I defend my friend. "You don't know what you're talking about. Owen's working the only way he knows how—with results. How much have you accomplished with catchy slogans?"

Charles is determined. "Okay. That's it. We ain't here to watch you two go at it."

Anne poses a curious question to me. "Does that newspaper want you to write about pushing the Army to integrate?"

Before Serge can chime in with the retort, I know he has ready, I address my sister-in-law's question. "Anne, actually, it's no secret that the Army is already integrated."

Seeing her mouth agape, I continue quickly. "It's a melting pot of ethnic people who don't normally get along. They have our Indians and Indian Indians, Irish, Scotts-Irish, Arabs, Jews, Italians, Mexicans, South Americans, Eastern Europeans, people whose parents are from everywhere on earth. They do a lot of nicknaming but they work it out. In truth, they only segregate Negroes *and now domestic Japanese.* They'd rather build two versions of everything than make the other recruits sleep, train and eat with Negroes."

Her next question sounds logical, on its face. "So, they already know that asking whites and Negroes to get along would never work?"

This time, Serge answers before I can. "No Anne. They're afraid that it *would work.*" He does not stop there. "Regardless, the tanned Yanks are the future. When they get home, and people try to conduct business as usual, we can have ourselves a real civil rights movement."

"So, is that the last word, Serge?"

"Not quite, Charles. The Afro American publishers are out in front on desegregation. Red could help frame the thinking of a whole new generation, if he *wanted to.*"

I ignore him. "Anne was right when she said every minute should be cherished." I raise my glass. "I'd like to propose a toast to my brother and the sister we finally got: Lieutenant and Mrs. Charles Savoy. May God bless their marriage made in Heaven and preserve the love they share with us on Earth."

"Oh!"

"That was a good one, Jack."

"Great toast, Red."

The meal is nothing less than extraordinary, and we keep conversation to a bare minimum. Afterwards, I awkwardly wonder aloud how Charles remained slim enough to fit into a Sherman tank. It is the wrong joke at the wrong time.

Anne tries to mask her discomfort by offering a toast of her own. "May my husband and my brothers remember the love they shared in this house, and keep one another close wherever they go, and return to us—safely to me and a child who won't meet her father until he returns." Her voice waivers at the end and she hurries upstairs with her hands covering her eyes. Charles follows closely behind her, leaving us alone.

"So, should we leave?" I am annoyed that Serge's voice is void of emotion.

"No, you little shit. Don't light that cigarette in her dining room. If you must smoke, go outside. We should cut ourselves two healthy slices of that pie and pour two cups of coffee. Then we should sit here quietly, respect our brother's house, and show each other some civility."

He tries to deflect. "You got her started with that crack about the tank. So, tell me about Owen." He asks the question casually, but I know Serge is eager to hear. I hesitate to open up to him, but I need to *confide in someone.* "He wants me to look in on Rachel. She's at an Army hospital in Casablanca."

I watch my brother's jaw drop. "Oh no, Jack. I thought you'd seen the last of her. I know you were in love back then, but man, I'd assumed that was behind you. How do you make a relationship work with a woman who looks like her? I was almost murdered for just driving her around in Indiana."

I try to sound reassuring. "I didn't say anything about rekindling our romance. Believe me. I'm over her, Serge. What happened after that rally though was not her fault, and not yours. It's just that, of all the ways a colored man can die, being seen with a white woman—or someone who appears to be a white woman—is the quickest way to get killed."

Serge is more painfully specific. "Or it can be the quickest way to *become a killer.* You know, Red, I'm scared to ask, but have you asked yourself what an Afro nurse is doing stationed in an Army hospital in Morocco? We were under the impression that they were all still in Liberia or England or here in the States."

"I don't know what's going on. It could be anything—or nothing. Hold on to your seat though. There's more. It's hard to explain, but hear me out. Owen is feeling a paternal responsibility for the *colored* war correspondents. No, not for the bigger weeklies, they don't really need his help."

Serge fires back, "And just what does he think our reporters need that he could possibly supply? And we ain't done talking about Nurse Todd."

"I'm not sure what he needs me to do for them."

"He's nuts? Okay," Serge says dismissively. Confiding in my brother is always like traversing a slippery slope. However, Anne has preoccupied the far more stable Charles tonight.

"You know Owen and I are close. He's done a lot for me—maybe even *for us*." I try to appeal to his sense of family.

Serge remains unfazed. "What else does he *want from you*, Red?"

I regret inviting his scrutiny on this point but I have gone too far now to abort. "I told him flatly that I would not be his spy. I think he just wants me to be his eyes and ears overseas." The words are not the best I could have chosen. "It's not a lot to ask, if it keeps a few reporters out of trouble." However, saying it aloud, I realize that it does sound absurd.

Serge does not let up. "My God, Red, he wants you to spy on the other reporters?"

I try to assure him. "No, he doesn't. Besides I made it clear that I wouldn't."

"Oh Red, like hell he doesn't, and you know it. Don't do it—even if you must agree to it just to get what you want. He has no right to ask you to do any of this. Why, if they get wind of it, no one will ever trust you again."

"Come on Serge."

"No. You *come on*, Jack. They'll all find out, and it'll come across a lot worse than you think. Disassociate yourself from Owen. Too much of his stench may be already on you. And for God's sake, please don't get mixed up again with a girl who looks that white—even whiter than you. She's not why you agreed to this, is she? You're really over her, right?"

Before I can respond, I hear Charles and Anne returning as I had expected, grateful that we have served ourselves and remained in the house. "Now what's this I hear about a white girl? Jack?" We both ignore his question and spend the next hour discussing a range of issues. Anne asks, "Jack didn't you have a girlfriend out there in California?"

"It wasn't serious enough to make leaving an issue." I am curious to know how Anne will be filling her days with Charles away. "So, what's next for you Anne?"

She appears startled that I asked. "I'll try to stay busy teaching. Then there's volunteer work at our church. We're organizing a blood drive."

Serge asks, "Are they taking blood from all donors here? I heard that Afro-American donors were still being turned away."

"Yes, you can donate here but the Red Cross is still going to segregate it. We think that's silly, but at least it will be there for the colored units," adds Anne. She wants to change the subject. "And you're getting closer to getting that dream job, Jack."

It is the perfect segue for my announcement. "Well, in a few days, I head down to the Virginia coast to board a troop ship."

They immediately seek information I should not know and cannot disclose. "Where are you going? Oh, come on Red. It has to be Africa—probably Algeria."

"Then I guess it's on to Africa. Okay Serge, what's next for you, Moscow perhaps?" I feel the room grow tense.

He answers matter-of-factly. "That's right, Red. Whenever we show courage or forethought, the Commies must be behind us." I see that mischievous smile forming. "But, you know, we need men in the Army. That's where the vanguard is incubating—*where men ain't scared*. Why're you all looking at me so shocked? I don't want to be the only Savoy brother with no war stories."

He looks at each of us and laughs at our expressions of horror over the prospect of him in the Army. "What are you talking about Serge?"

Playfully, Serge responds, "I'd give anything to see how the Army plans to segregate a battlefield. I mean—will they segregate foxholes? Will they put up *white and colored only* signs?"

Anne voices the concern probably shared by all. "Please be careful, Serge. Being an activist in the army or in front of a factory sounds dangerous."

Charles wants to go back and close the door on Serge's notion. "Maybe you should join up back home. They're seeing the light. You're still a Canadian citizen. Man, if you only knew what we go through at, and around, Camp Claiborne. In the Army, we all belong to Uncle Sam. They mean that. If you rant about race, they'll lock you up for sure."

I chime in. "Look Serge, you need to stay out of the Army, here and in Canada. Half the guys won't even understand you. The other half will turn your ass in."

Serge has heard enough. "It's too late to worry about me. I've already been beaten, kidnapped and buckshot. Did Jack ever tell you about the night I had a noose around my neck?" Serge laughs at the uncomfortable silence that follows, basking in the shock he loves to inspire.

I use the quiet moment to consider his endless reminders about my *social responsibility*. He and Rachel use to have that in common. Lomax wants me to *pass for white* so I can spy. Owen just wants me to spy.

I believe that segregating Negro soldiers only validates pre-existing prejudices. I know that, if ordered to sleep next to Negro soldiers, white soldiers would have to comply. Americans would never forfeit the war just to preserve bigotry.

I also believe that the most important civil rights contribution I could make would be to journal, on the record, the contributions Negro soldiers, airmen and sailors make to the certain victory. I look up at the portrait of our great grandparents I have consulted throughout my life. Once again, I wonder if the enslaved Fulani and the outcast Algonquin Cree approve of my judgment.

Chapter 5

. . . .

Isaac Blue

L ast week, delayed by traffic between Washington and Norfolk, my bus
arrived late at the Hampton Roads, Virginia Port of Embarkation.
The cluster of facilities was imposing, a massive staging area born of
the need to support last year's Allied landings in Algeria and Morocco.

Unlike thousands of soldiers with no idea whether they were
awaiting passage to England, North Africa or the Middle East, I knew
my destination. I was to board a troop ship, sail from Virginia, join
a massive convoy and head across the Atlantic to Morocco. In the
scheduled blackout intended to render anchored vessels invisible to
Nazi U-boats prowling along the coast, I made my way to the docked
USS Dorothea Dix.

With a cursory glance at my orders and credentials, an embarkation
officer gestured for me to wait until two full battalions of recruits made
their way up the ship's gangway. After they disappeared into the ship,
a third battalion, this time Negro soldiers, moved up into position.
Their officers stepped aboard but no one issued instructions for them.

A half hour later, someone began directing the men up the gangway.
I searched their faces for signs of disgust. However, no one appeared
fazed by the unexplained delay. Rather they were jocular, filing on
board, as jokes whispered out of the corners of their mouths produced
smiles and suppressed laughter.

Once I was on the ship, someone *got me squared away*, billeted—against the Army's regulations—in segregated quarters with Negro non-commissioned officers. Sometime later, I felt the ship slipping into the U-boat infested waters of the Atlantic. We were on the way to war. However, we were restricted to separate accommodations, shifts and our side of hastily installed chicken-wire fencing.

I have never sailed on a ship, and with a week at sea under my belt, I still fear the ocean's power and vastness. Now recognized by most of the Merchant Marine crew as a war correspondent, I avoid contact with Army officers and enjoy nearly unfettered access to the outside decks. I try to conquer my fear of drowning by staring out into the water and far into the horizon.

The sea is only slightly restless tonight, but I hold tight to an interior rail, concerned as always with slipping or washing overboard. The smell of salt water fills my nostrils and the constant roar of the ocean reminds me how vulnerable I am to the power of Nature.

I ask a sailor, "Which do you think is worse, to get killed in an air raid or slammed by a torpedo? I guess the choice is burning in fire or drowning in the ocean." Having asked, I am embarrassed that my silly question reveals the difficulty I am having with managing my fear.

Since I cannot pull the words back out of the air, I decide not to hold back another gnawing concern. "I still don't see any other ships on this side. Does that mean we're on the edge of the convoy's flank? We could be a tempting target. What happened to the flotilla we joined after sailing from Virginia?"

Writing in his logbook, the young crewman looks up and responds matter-of-factly, removing the pipe he had clenched in his teeth. "Hampton Roads is still new. It supported the Allied landings in North Africa. Man, it was a mess then. Somehow, they managed to sort it out but communications are still kind of up in the air."

I do not find his words comforting. "Well now, that's not reassuring, is it?"

He tries to inject humor. "Can you swim, Mister Savoy? Okay, then take your chances in the water." His relaxed demeanor in the face of danger belies his years, and the sailor easily sees into my mortal fear. In a soothing tone, he adds, "Let these grunts worry about running the ports. Let others worry about the fighting. You worry about telling their stories to the readers back home. Let us worry about getting y'all there safely. Everybody's scared—including me."

Dressed in a navy pea coat, he had been enjoying a quiet smoke and making log entries when I approached him for an interview. He had patiently responded to a few questions as I jotted down notes in the small leather backed journal that has become my familiar appendage.

I learn that the young sailor has attained his confidence level after several trips across the Atlantic. He was on deck last year when the *Dix* served as a modified attack transport during the invasion of French Morocco.

I have heard about the diverse backgrounds of the Merchant Marines, their contributions to the war effort and legendary stoicism. Still, I had not expected to see a dozen Negroes among an integrated crew that performs seamlessly and efficiently in front of 3000 passengers who cannot sleep in the same quarters, eat on the same shifts or venture out on deck during the same exercise periods.

I have purchased and lugged aboard with me a used Royal portable typewriter on which I have been banging out five stories concurrently. I look forward to getting them through censors and on to Ted for publication.

Later, I fall asleep but dream that the ship is under attack. I hear the nerve shattering sounds of metal torn from the ship's superstructure by torpedo strikes. As I run, trying to escape death through columns of thick black smoke, I hear and feel the deck ripping apart beneath me.

I dive headlong into a lifeboat only to find myself awake and unharmed, with a tight grip on the edges of my mattress. Even after discovering that all is well, I refuse to release my grip on my personal territory in a section of the ship's hold designated for senior non-commissioned officers. We refer to it endearingly as the *shithole*.

My nostrils fill with the musty odors of three dozen men who have grown increasingly indifferent to salt-water showers. I must have bolted upright and bashed my head against the bunk of the man sleeping above me. I settle back onto my mattress relieved that, once again, I have experienced a disaster only within the confines of my own mind.

I manage to raise myself up on one elbow, reliving my reoccurring dream and lamenting that sleep on this voyage remains intermittent at best. I turn over on my thin wafer attached at the corners to poles extending from floor to ceiling. There are twelve stacks in our cramped cabin.

I hear a familiar voice. "Have you been dreaming again, Savoy?" Blue's bunk is next to mine, both of us on the bottom rungs of our respective stacks, separated by less than three feet. His deep Alabama drawl seems to fill the air available within the limited space between us. I look into brown eyes still bloodshot in the early morning hour.

Blue sits up on the edge of his precarious berth—no easy feat for a man with his girth. I imagine that sitting on his unstable mattress inside this pitching vessel must be like climbing into a hammock in a windstorm. It requires a degree of agility he has not yet mastered. In my first interview aboard the *Dix*, I learned that First Sergeant Isaac Blue, the ranking enlisted man in the segregated port battalion, has already served in the Army for over 25 years. After leaving Tuscaloosa, Alabama to become an Army stevedore, he unloaded supply ships at the Port of Bordeaux in 1918.

Since then, Blue has served in Army Service of Supply units, slowly earning tenure and promotions. Ordered by the Transportation Corps last fall to report to the new port battalions' training facility at Fort Indiantown Gap, he supervised trainees at the Pennsylvania facility.

Much to my appreciation, he is whispering. "Tell me again, Savoy. Why are you down here with us? I know what you told me, but since you can't answer straight *yes-or-no* questions, I don't really know anything. Why won't you just put on that little phony officer's uniform and move upstairs? Just let them hear you speak Canadian. They know there're plenty of people up there who should be down here."

Intrigued, I want specifics. He only laughs. "I should be spotting you upstairs drinking real coffee and eating real food. Just so you know, in 25 years I seen plenty of our boys in white face. I *never* saw one in black face. Hell, one of the officers on this boat used to pitch for us back in Tuscaloosa."

"Which one is he, Blue?" He laughs again and ignores my question.

"I swear, you must write for the society section of the paper." In the dim light of the crowded cabin, he looks down at his watch. "Damn, another hour before coffee and SOS." He monitors the movements of other soldiers dashing toward the places where they might find morning relief.

"I thought they said the *Dix* used to be a cruise ship, Blue. Every morning, a thousand guys look for a place to go at the same time." When I look up, Blue has already walked away, weaving through what has already become a crowded floor.

The big man gingerly negotiates narrow aisles, boulevards compared to the tight spaces in packed and poorly ventilated holds for colored privates. Often, the urinals overflow with vomit when the going gets rough in stormy seas. Men fall on perpetually slippery decks. In no time, complications from dehydration can reach epidemic proportions.

I remember Owen's warning. *There are more casualties from illness and accidents than from enemy weapons. For every soldier standing in the field, another is lying in sickbay. Yellow fever, dysentery, hepatitis, malaria—don't fuck around, Jack. Get your shots on both sides of the ocean. Above all, make sure they billet you with the white officers.*

Although I am in segregated quarters, the overzealous embarkation officer surely will claim ignorance of the Army regulation requiring him to billet war correspondents as Army officers. Rather than challenging his sleight, I opted to accept it and observe firsthand the ship's segregated facilities. The experience has been bracing. The ship is transporting two white and one segregated full-strength port battalions with identical support teams and capabilities. However, segregation of the units is absolute.

This morning, we pass, as always, through one fenced area on our way to eat what passes for breakfast aboard the small transport ship—tepid coffee and chipped beef on toast. The first breakfast shift designated for segregated troops is the third daily breakfast shift. While the segregated schedule clearly discriminates against colored NCOs, I have never heard my cabin-mates protest an arrangement that seems as natural to them as the horn that announces the shifts.

I step gingerly, avoiding wet spots and trying to maintain my balance as the ship rocks from stem to stern. While looking down to navigate a few traces of vomit, I almost collide with several soldiers standing on our side of the chicken wire exchanging threats with white soldiers standing on the other side.

Completely oblivious to the faceoff and with no interest in its origin, Blue and several in his close-knit group pass by just as one rather large white soldier returns a threat. "If we see one more pair of nigger eyes on those white nurses, I swear there'll be hell to pay."

"You ain't got shit to do with that, cracker," An equally large dark-complexioned soldier retorts, spitting through the wire to add an exclamation point to his defiant words.

"The devil is who I am, boy. I'm the one you gotta pay." The young man stretches his arm through an expanded hole in the wire inviting someone—anyone—to touch it.

I hear Blue's voice, but instead of restoring order, he is calling me. "Savoy, pull your ass out the middle of that and get in here." I still linger a moment longer, curious to see how long the precariously extended arm would remain intact. After an additional round of threats and verbal intimidation, both groups break off and go about their morning routines.

I manage to break in line behind Blue and ask why he did not intervene. "Are you shitting me? There's no need for them to separate battalions that have trained together. Separation is the problem. When my daddy wanted a good dogfight, he'd lash two big ones so they could barely touch. He'd keep um that way 'til they snapped. Man, when he untied those dogs, whew boy. This is a bad problem Savoy and it ain't mine to solve."

"I thought you would be the wise big brother on this voyage."

"Savoy. You all set to write about how bad the army treats these boys. Man, serving in the 480th is the best break some of them have had since the depression set in on us. Not too long ago, they'd have killed for a cup of Joe and SOS."

"I'm talking about you, Blue."

"Look, they all know I'd risk my stripes to take up for them—if they're in the right. I've preached to these boys that *the brass wants a reason to lock them up*. Savoy, we got four legit gripes: *We don't get second chances, we're guilty until proven innocent and our punishments are too harsh*. I know that makes the odds sound damned unfair, but they really ain't that hard to beat."

I venture to say, "But for some, they are impossible to beat."

"Yes, if you cross the line or allow yourself to get pulled across it—or you just get caught too close to it. Sure, they got towns all over the States where you can get killed just for being colored—you just have to know the lay of the land, and go with the flow."

Trying to drink our coffee before the last of the heat has dissipated, we watch the mess-stewards splatter their concoction of chipped beef over a slice of stale toast—known to all as *shit-on-a-shingle, or simply SOS*. The comments are the same every morning.

"Do we get this every day until we hit dry land?"

"I used to feed my hogs better than this."

"Do y'all feed this to everybody or just to us?"

"Is this what the first shift left in the toilet?" Once seated, Sgt. Johnny Mingo, a hatch foreman, asks about the verbal altercation I witnessed. "Savoy, what the hell caused all that fuss out there? White nurses, did you say? What white nurses are you talking about? There's nothing on this ship but grunts—as far as I know."

I try to avoid spreading misinformation. "All I know is that the fight is over colored soldiers looking at nurses." I still feel awkward using the word, but Owen was correct. It is far easier to say *colored* than to avoid it.

Sgt. Mingo whistles. "Oh shit. Now, that's a hell of a story for your newspaper. A white private and a colored private fighting over a female officer neither can ever have. Ain't that called irony—or something like that?"

I met John Mingo shortly after I arrived in the shithole. Before the war, he worked at a small hydraulics store in South Carolina where he learned about the equipment. Since enlisting in October 1942, he has received promotions quickly, scoring well on aptitude tests and demonstrating proficiency at Fort Indiantown Gap. Although he ended his formal education after grammar school, he has distinguished himself. His success is a rare example of a colored enlistee whose inferior education has not led to glaring deficits in his basic reading, math and testing skills.

I disagree with many of Blue's assessments and John's observations. "This is the result of confinement in this segregated pressure cooker, white and colored men imprisoned behind their respective sides of a chicken wire fence. But John, yes, it is ironic."

Chapter 6

· ·

Squared Away

S everal days into the voyage, a lieutenant and a sergeant, both wearing crisp khakis, pay a visit to the *shithole*. Mouths are agape when the lieutenant addresses me as *sir*. He tells me that I am to report the next morning to the ranking Army officer onboard the *Dorothy Dix*. Sensing my imminent relocation, my cabin-mates all agree that it is long overdue.

Blue admonishes the officer and the NCO, who show no appreciation for the raw humor I have come to enjoy. "It's about time y'all came down here to the bottoms. Get this damn white boy out of here. He's starting to act colored."

Reluctantly, I pack away the comfortable herringbone fatigue uniform that I have worn since we sailed from Virginia. In a week, it has been completely broken in. I take a shower, shave and dress in the *proper uniform* of a war correspondent—that of an Army officer minus rank, insignia and black piping. I also wear an armband with the block letter "C" that shows my press status. Considering the stench of our quarters, I cannot imagine that the Army will ever ask for any of it back.

The sergeant returns alone early the next morning. "Don't worry about breakfast, sir. I'll fetch you some grub when we get topside."

As we walk to my meeting with the ranking officer, I turn to the sergeant. "Do you know what I should expect at this meeting?"

Without looking at me, he speaks with the bearing of a career soldier concerned about the appearance of fraternization. "I think you've already guessed it, sir. You'll be moved to a different area of the ship."

"Don't call me *sir*. What if I don't want to move back, Sergeant Rawlings?"

He does look directly at me. "*Sir*, would you like some advice from an old hand?"

I become impatient. "I guess that's what I'm asking for."

Clearly unconcerned with my disposition, his tenor remains unchanged. "The colonel is used to getting what he wants. In fact, you might say that it's *his way or the highway*." He peers out over the vast ocean. "I don't believe I see a highway out there. Do you, sir?" I follow his glance, and understand his point. There is nowhere for me to go outside of the commanding officer's authority. On some days, the ocean appears to be trying to eject the ship like a foreign irritant. On days like today, the schizophrenic sea allows the transport to slice through it the way a sailboat cuts through an inlet cove. Still, there is only ocean beyond the Army's authority, with waves active enough to produce light foam at their crests.

It seems selfish to feel relief over the sight of other convoy ships finally providing a buffer for the *Dix*. However, my fear of attack at sea dwarfs the angst I feel about danger waiting in North Africa. Owen advised me before I left Washington that *German U boats sink a ship each day in the Atlantic*. Most have been bound for Russian or English ports. I suspect, however, that since the invasion, more have been on our southerly route.

Colonel Case, the ranking Army officer aboard ship, has staked out a spot in the corner of an area sectioned off into rectangular units. As I enter, he and two other officers sit smoking. "I'm not sure how this happened, Mister Savoy, but please accept my personal apology for your inconvenience."

The colonel rises from his chair to extend a hand to me. He conducts a sweeping appraisal with steely gray eyes that follow the length of my body and narrow as they fasten on mine. In contrast to the crumpled outfit I pulled from a duffle bag, his uniform is almost impeccable, considering the circumstances, clean and pressed with brass polished to a mirror finish.

A captain introduces himself as a member of the colonel's staff, responsible for, among other matters, public affairs. The third officer, who appears to vacuum rather than inhale smoke through his cigarette, does not get up and watches me intensely with unmasked derision.

Once seated, the captain apologizes again. "I think the fault lies entirely with me, Mister Savoy. I thought I had a complete accounting of everyone on board." I say nothing. Looking like a surgeon who has amputated the wrong leg, he continues to be contrite. "I have the matter under control now, and have taken the necessary steps to get you squared away correctly."

His words remind me of the junior embarkation officer at the control point in Hampton Roads. He had assigned me to the area designated for colored NCOs, stating with derision that someone in those accommodations *would get me squared away correctly*. Prior to yesterday, no one had tried to correct his lapse in judgment, and so my first instinct is to feign irascibility. "Actually, I'm fine where I am."

The colonel intervenes. "Now there's no need for that. We've offered our sincere apology and will take extra good care of you from here on out. We've got so many mongrel boys on board. I swear, it looks like a colored college homecoming around here. They're making it hard for us to get it right—on both ends."

His words are offensive, even in a war zone. I remain insistent. "No, really colonel, I'm not sure you understand. The people I need to talk to for my newspaper are down there."

"No. *You don't understand*. We're required to quarter you as an officer. I know you work for a colored newspaper, and I know what colored people like to read. We're the people you need to talk to, but you're right about there being things I don't understand. You'll be discussing those with Captain Daniels."

He speaks with finality, like a man unaccustomed to repeating himself. Hearing no more from me, he continues. "I know you didn't receive a press briefing. We won't defer it until you arrive at your next station—since you've been writing already. Where you provided with a *War Correspondent's Manual*?"

Before I can tell him how thoroughly I've studied it, he opens a pamphlet and begins paraphrasing: "Upon arrival, you report to the intelligence officer and the public relations officer. Register any complaints with the field force commander."

Looking up at me, he pauses before continuing. "I don't know why you haven't registered a complaint. That's the main thing I don't understand. The intelligence officer is Major Allan Wade here, and Captain Daniels oversees public affairs. As for the field force commander, that's me."

I decide not to press the issue further. Bunking with white officers will take me far away from the Negro troops, but I have a week's worth of copy on them. Moving may enable me to travel throughout the ship unrestricted. The colonel rises to signal the end of the meeting. "Captain Daniels, finish briefing *Mister* Savoy and show him to his new quarters."

They startle me with a flurry of razor-sharp salutes. Before I leave, Major Wade adds a parting shot. "As soon as you're settled in Savoy, I'll be happy to look at the stories you've written so far. I understand you're quite the prolific interviewer."

After we leave the other two men, the captain appears more relaxed, asking, "So you go by *Jack*?"

The sergeant has reappeared from nowhere, walking behind us with my bags. In this section of the ship, his medium brown skin stands out in sharp contrast. His uniform, however, is every bit as flat and his insignia as polished as those of the officers. When I offer to take one of my bags, he is insistent to the point of being annoyed. "No problem, sir. *I have them.*"

The captain continues to probe. "Please call me *Mike*, from a Midwestern town with one traffic light and four stop signs. The other intersections are negotiable. Is your family from France originally? Oh, you're *French Canadian*." That revelation always seems to help people *understand something* about me. He continues, "My only guess is that when they read your credentials and saw your employer, someone made an assumption."

Answering questions not asked is always optional. He scans my face before continuing. "I don't understand why you didn't immediately come up to complain."

Again, no specific question asked, and no answer given. "Well, there are no other correspondents aboard ship. The regulations establish your rank as captain and authorize me to put you in with company commanders. But I think you'll be a lot more comfortable bunking with me and a few others." He looks me over again. "So, you write for a colored newspaper?"

I understand all too well that his assignment is to *keep an eye on me.* I answer his direct question. "Yes, I'm a reporter for the *Washington Record.*" I have never understood how any American could, all things considered, determine my ethnicity as anything other than a Negro. However, people constantly guess incorrectly.

Mike waits *in vain* for a moment, probably hoping for a more detailed answer. "Well, I have to ask, Jack. How is it that you come to work for a Negro publisher?" He asks the question as if he has a right to an answer, a right to know. "Your folder notes that you were once at the *Chronicle.*"

I answer, "Mike, if that's something you need to know, the *Record* gave me a chance to get overseas right away." The sergeant continues to project practiced ambivalence. Mike leads me into a cabin with two sets of bunk beds and private lockers. There are two chairs pushed under a table.

"Just curious, Jack. No need to be defensive. I've got to go to the head. When I get back, we can get the rest of your briefing out of the way."

After Mike leaves, the sergeant, suddenly sporting a broad smile, drops my bags inside the door and walks over extending his hand. He is the first Negro soldier I have seen with the letter "T" below his stripes. I start to speak but he waives me off, presumably to make the most of our limited time alone. "I'm Technician Fourth Grade Joe Rawlings. If you need me for anything, find the radio room and ask for me."

"Thanks Joe. But why so quiet on the way up here?"

"I didn't know you on the way up here. Find me if you need me. I can go anywhere on this ship—as long as I'm carrying something." He chuckles and walks out though the cabin doorway before I can ask why a radio technician would be escorting me and carrying my bags.

Mike returns substantially later than I would have expected, allowing time for me to put away my gear in an empty locker. The small cabin seems cavernous in comparison to the cramped spaces below. "There are just a few standard items I need to go over with you, Jack."

He covers everything, including grounds for disciplinary action and prohibitions against inappropriate language. "That's important since you cover colored news, Jack. The colored reporters can be slick with their use of certain expressions." When I do not take the bait, his expression becomes pained. "Jack, how could you spend four days down there? You don't plan to write an expose, do you?"

"My job is to cover the war, Captain."

"So? I thought my job was leading a company of infantrymen. I wound up in a port battalion—but at least it's not a *colored* port battalion. I didn't know you were on board *since no one knew where you were*. So, imagine my surprise to find you down in that hole."

I am losing my patience with him. "It's the *shithole*, to be precise, Mike. I went to my assigned billet. Why're you surprised that a reporter accepted the billet to which he was assigned?"

He looks at me with a confounded expression, throwing up both hands. "*Surprised*? Savoy, it's the damnedest thing I've ever heard is what it is. I don't know what's going on here, but I hope you're not down there stirring it up a shit storm. If you are, please don't bring it my way."

Despite my uneasiness over a day of callous remarks, I decide to tell him what I have observed. "You won't get one that I start. I did overhear a heated argument that suggests you might already have a nig one brewing. There was something about white nurses."

He sits back in the chair. "Goddammit, they should never have put those women on a small integrated ship." I am amazed that Mike thinks this is an *integrated* ship. "We got a whole colored port battalion on a small vessel. If we get coloreds mixing in with white nurses, do you know what we'd have on our hands?"

"Captain, first, I have to ask. You do know this ship is as segregated as any place I've ever seen?" He does not respond, but appears particularly irritated by my comment. I change the subject. "Look, I'm here to cover the war from a different angle."

Still reeling from my observation, he leans forward. "And what angle might that be?"

Thinking that it will be better to have him helpful than defensive, I try to put him at ease. "I'm just here to cover the war—colored, white or red-white-and-blue. However, my publisher wants me to focus on Negroes in technical jobs, rather than on the ills of segregation."

The look of relief that settles over Mike's face nearly alters his appearance. He unbuttons his pocket and removes a cigarette from the pack. After a few draws, he explains that the Army Transportation Corps originally requested twelve additional all-white port battalions to support shipping operations in the Mediterranean.

"Under pressure to place Negro troops, they amended their request to ten white and two Negro port battalions. Then they changed that to ten Negro and two white battalions. I thought that change was extraordinary. What more do the Negro papers want? No, don't tell me, I know. They want colored infantry divisions."

I have a question. "Mike, I need to understand why that prospect creates so much angst. Why is it so hard to do? Certainly, there're enough colored volunteers."

He looks as if he cannot believe I asked the question. "Teach ten thousand colored guys to be proficient, in groups, with automatic rifles, explosives, machine guns, armor and artillery?"

"If that's what infantry divisions do."

"Tell me where we'll keep finding experienced *colored* NCOs to lead it. Since *colored* NCOs can't lead white privates, they can't get the proper experience outside their original divisions. The talented colored boys are in the Engineers, the Signal Corps and the Air Corps. If you ask me, the really bright ones are back home working in defense jobs."

I interrupt his speech. "But so many colored soldiers have been left stateside to stew."

"Jack, a few governments have asked us not to send any Negroes to their countries. Even struggling regimes are concerned about their darker countrymen seeing well-paid Negroes setting bad examples for the *less assertive* local people."

I fight the urge to pursue that topic further. "Since you raised the issue, what about those colored divisions training at home, and those armored units? Like it or not, they're coming."

"Are you sure about that? Look I know you're probably thinking that we don't have enough combat-experienced white leaders yet either—but we have ten times as many to work with and we can rotate them anywhere. Plus, now we have guys learning in North Africa."

Another question comes to mind. "Mike, did you know that the Negro papers asked the Army to create one integrated division where anyone, white or colored, could volunteer to serve? What do you think about that? Do you think they'd get any takers?"

"Never heard that, but why would anyone do that?" Mike's tone becomes conspiratorial. "We're off the record, right?" He waits for me to me to nod my confirmation. "Above the rank of captain, both those colored infantry divisions will be led by southern white men. There's no getting around that. What kind of leaders do you think they'll get? How much do you suppose they'll care about their men?"

His question goes unanswered. When other officers arrive, Mike relaxes, makes the introductions, and we table a sometimes painfully blunt exchange that, much to my delight, continues unabridged over the remaining days of the voyage.

Perhaps under orders from Colonel Case, Mike is generous with his time and accompanies me on several tours of the ship's facilities. He readily acknowledges the considerable thought the Army invests in carefully segregating troops but refuses to acknowledge the inferiority of segregated accommodations. "Jack, I'm honestly trying to see what you see, but I just don't. There is no difference in colored and white accommodations."

My interview with the Merchant Marine's chief steward provides even less of an acknowledgement. "Mister Savoy, it ain't my place to get into all that race talk. My granddaddy was a slave and my daddy worked as a laborer for a colored sharecropping family. Now I'm chief over *white and colored* mess men, traveling around the world." He adds, "Hell, I'm talking to a light-skinned newspaperman who eats and sleeps in the white officers' cabin. I ain't *never, ever* seen that before."

Chapter 7

· ·

Lost at Sea

I find out from several soldiers that unrest continues to spread throughout the *USS Dorothea Dix*. It is the result, despite my warning, of unchecked turmoil over Negroes looking at white Army nurses. Tempers cooled only after a fight between two privates ended in tragedy.

Witnesses said the combatants remained clenched even as they tumbled overboard. Others reported seeing two heads bobbing closely together on the waves until they disappeared on the horizon. Apparently, breaking away from the convoy to go back for them had not been an option.

Soldiers who had been promoting the fight moments before stood dumbfounded. Two facts were indisputable. There were two lives wasted over a taboo neither man was old enough to understand, and their tragic deaths probably prevented a ship-wide riot.

Just days prior to the encounter, neither man knew that nurses were aboard. In addition to arranging their separate accommodations, meals and recreation for two dozen nurses, Colonel Case thought he could somehow conceal their presence. On a ship the size of the *Dix*, the enlisted men discovered them immediately and established an observation perch. Pushing and shoving for time on the perch had been surprisingly limited, until someone discovered it during the Negro recreation period.

Mike had taken my warning to the colonel, who responded by posting a notice. He ordered soldiers to report any threats against them. Of course, no one reported anything. Eventually I visited the perch alone and gazed upon nurses bundled in coats and caps against the Atlantic wind. I watched as they smoked, read and passed the time, oblivious to the controversy their presence had inspired.

Certain that Major Wade would never clear a story about senseless deaths at sea, I write an account in my personal journal. When I attempt to obtain more background on events leading up to the incident, accounts are contradictory, yet consistent along racial lines.

That evening, I walk into the cabin and find Mike writing two works of pure fiction. They are letters of gratitude assuring two families that their sons *died honorably in the fight for freedom.* Initially I refuse his request for assistance, but later agree to proof his draft only to ensure that I copy his words accurately in my journal.

Like all the colored NCOs, Blue looks devastated by the news. "Savoy, that morning at the fence, I never expected anything more than a black eye."

During a private moment following an officer's call, Major Wade is in rare form. "I wish I could let you file a story on this one, Savoy. People need to know what happens when these damned social experiments fail. People die in war. But forcing white to live with colored will result in people dying, just like that young man." Before I can remind him that the races do not live together on the *Dix* and that *two of his men* were dead, the major reads my mind and becomes incensed. "Oh, go to hell Savoy, you know what I'm saying."

The entry in my log that night sums up my feelings. *I disagree with those who say the Army is not a laboratory for sociological experiments. The Dix is a floating laboratory testing a flawed hypothesis. Maybe it is appropriate to name this ship for an advocate of the criminally insane.*

"Okay, so let's round up all the usual suspects." Major Wade's feeble attempt at humor does little to alter the mood aboard ship. Some officers learn that they were destined originally for Casablanca but will be going on now to Oran, Algeria. The *Dix* will dock at Casablanca only long enough to discharge one battalion in Morocco before moving on to Oran with the other two.

I know that Tom James expects me in Oujda. However, per Owen, Tom *understands* that I may take a few extra days to report. With that in mind, I decide to spend more than a few days in Casablanca, willing to risk Tom's ire. Within just a few short months, I have traveled by train from California to Detroit and then to Washington, with an unexpected roundtrip over rough terrain to Nova Scotia. I have sailed, partially confined to a hold below called *the shithole*, from Virginia to the North African theater of a violent world war. I need a few days respite.

I plan to spend at least a day investigating Owen's personal concern. If Nurse Lieutenant Rachel Todd is still in Morocco, I can fulfill my commitment to Owen. It will be good to reconnect with her. Then, I can begin a new assignment that will put me in harm's way, covering the battlegrounds further east in Tunisia.

I take advantage of the atmosphere of confusion and uncertainty aboard ship to obtain Colonel Case's concurrence with my decision. "I'm not going to be posted in Oran anyway. I'd prefer to get off the ship now as originally planned, maybe cover the transition in Casablanca and work my way east later to Fifth Army Headquarters in Oujda, near the Algerian border."

To my surprise, both Colonel Case and Major Wade acquiesce. True to form, Major Wade leaves me with a parting warning. "Savoy, I'm sure you know how I'll respond to any uncensored articles that appear in your newspaper or elsewhere about the boy we lost at sea."

I prepare to leave the ship with even less fanfare than when I boarded. As I walk past the assembled colored troops, I salute Blue and chuckle when his pained expression laments my lack of discretion. When he struggles to suppress that big grin, I follow his gaze to a captain who appears older than most. With a wink, the former center fielder from Tuscaloosa finally identifies the pitcher on his childhood baseball team.

I walk down the gangway and walk quickly away from the dock before pausing again to get my bearings. I never look back again at the ship that has been my dysfunctional home for two weeks, even though it delivered me here safely across the Atlantic. With the sun now a little higher above the eastern horizon, I pick up my bags and walk toward a crowd of people in the distance milling around a line of parked cars.

Chapter 8

. . . .

Youssef

"**H**ey American war correspondent, I'm your man right over here." The voice comes from the driver's seat of a large black sedan. He does not offer the loudest proposition, but his familiarity with my uniform and military status grabs my attention.

I walk toward a late model English Rover to get a closer look at a driver astute enough to guess my status without seeing an armband or press patch. I wonder if he can also make an informed hotel recommendation for my stay. Dressed in a dark suit and tie, he gets out of the car. He bows subtly and loads my bags, without permission, in his trunk. His manner is respectful but not subservient. He opens a rear door and speaks in a thick accent I do not yet recognize.

"Welcome to Casablanca—such as it is now. My name is Youssef and, if it pleases you, I will be your driver during your entire stay. Some say that the Anfa Hotel is where a war correspondent wants to stay, where you will be comfortable and safe."

I slide into the plush leather back seat and look around at a rich interior inside a car I doubt I can afford—and doubt that Ted would ever authorize. "Okay, Youssef. My name is Jack Savoy. Your rates will determine whether you're my man. But you can begin by telling me what's so special about the Anfa Hotel."

Still wearing his black fez, he looks at me through the rearview mirror, responding with a shrug. "Good about the Anfa, Messier? Some say it was good enough for Roosevelt, De Gaulle and Churchill, so I think it should suit your needs. I can get you all over the city, inside the General's Compound."

"How do you know I can afford it?"

"Because you will pay what you can." He begins his own probe. "You wear the uniform of an American correspondent but I hear a little bit of a French accent—and I see a different kind of face. What country are you from? Oh yes, I should have guessed."

The city is only beginning to awaken as we stop in front of an imposing hatbox shaped building with gently rounded corners. The hotel is an off-white building of stacked balconied floors that rise gracefully above rustic surroundings.

I see what appears to be a lounge dominating the top floor over-looking the ocean. "Wait for me here Messier. I will be right back. But we will not talk about money until tomorrow after you rest." After a few minutes, Youssef returns with a yawning bellman who leads me inside through a lobby of mixed European, Arab and what I believe are Berber motifs. The registration desk clerk assures me Youssef has arranged a substantially reduced room rate.

Once upstairs, we enter a guestroom that cannot possibly be mine. Youssef instructs me to, "Just give Jamil all the clothes you have in that bag and take off those you have on. He will get the smell of the boat out, find you something else and alter your things to fit you better."

Thinking they are overstating their reach, I ask, "How can you get me an additional uniform, one that fits?" As Jamil estimates my measurements, they both smile good-naturedly as if indulging a precocious child intruding on adults.

Jamil remains respectful. "Okay, Messier Jack, we'll see what happens. Goodnight. Clean up and get into a deep sleep. You'll not be disturbed, and tomorrow you'll have something nicer to wear."

It is easy to follow Jamil's instructions. I take a hot shower and spend the rest of the day alternately eating and napping, but still manage to sleep through the night. Just over 24 hours after my arrival, a cheerful Jamil knocks on my door holding, dry cleaned, laundered and tailored, the same uniforms I stuffed into my duffle bag two weeks ago. He also has found an officer's uniform combination of tan trousers and olive blouse, polished brown shoes and a tan necktie. Paired on cool nights with a new waist jacket and garrison cap, the combination could become my outfit of choice in North Africa. Of course, I will still lounge around in my comfortable herringbone fatigues.

Mindful of the warnings I have received about the black market and the level of thievery on the docks, I decide not to ask about my new uniforms. I change and relax downstairs over a late brunch and Ethiopian coffee. As I devour my first good meal in weeks, I begin fashioning a plausible explanation for spending a week in Casablanca before making my way east.

After a half day trying to pick my own way through the bedlam of Casablanca, I realize that Youssef has correctly assessed my needs and proposed a reasonable fee for transportation and information. I decide that I am willing to pay him for three or four days. He turns out to be a stubborn negotiator but his information is as priceless as my introduction to the resourceful Jamil.

Youssef tells me, "The Anfa lies within a square-mile zone General Patton secured last December. The general had made improvements in comfort and security in preparation for the president's trip to the Casablanca Conference last January." With Winston Churchill and Charles De Gaulle also participating, the area was under heightened security. Some semblances of that level of security remain.

As promised, Youssef traverses the city freely and skillfully, darting in and out of traffic in a manner that would rival the skills of New York City cabbies—often to the dismay of other drivers and merchants riding or leading temperamental livestock.

Yousef tells me that word travels slowly between Morocco and non-government contacts in the States. Still, to head off any objections about my brief sabbatical, I ask him to mail a short stack of stories to Ted. They are my first official news stories, censored accounts of the voyage on a nameless ship traveling to a nameless port.

With memories of *the shithole* fresh in my mind, I constructed an account that Major Wade approved, with a few minor redactions. I omit the double drowning incident, aware that it would never have survived his censorship. I resist the urge to use Youssef to get an uncensored account of that tragedy to Ted. He would print it without regard to repercussions from censors. Walt would gladly forfeit the bond posted to insure my adherence to the rules.

Concerned that a nurse's unit could simply disappear at any time in the evolving environment of Casablanca, I quickly turn my driver's attention to searching for Rachel. At the exact time that we designate, Youssef arrives to take me to the hospital.

"It's just beyond this tent village the quartermasters built for the hospital staff." When we arrive, my first impression of the organized chaos within the morass of makeshift wards is that of a work in perpetual development. I sense that I could return in a few days to find that the Army has packed a quarter of the hospital in trucks and moved it to a new location.

As I walk through the main medical facility, reconfigured from two school buildings, I cannot deny the cascading adrenaline rush I get from thinking about a reunion with Rachel. I assured Serge and myself that I have long been over her. Yet memories of our short time together stir my emotions.

A civilian Moroccan nurse recognizes Rachel's name and points me in different direction. However, when I try to gather a little background on the colored Army nurses assigned to the hospital, she responds with a blank stare. Once again, I have that nagging feeling that Rachel may be in too much trouble for Tom or Owen to cure.

I walk into an open ward, and spot Rachel standing at one of three inoculation stations, administering shots to a long line of soldiers. However, after getting her to make eye contact, what appears to be initial surprise and excitement quickly fades to casual indifference.

I keep in mind that, while I have been thinking about this moment for weeks, Rachel has not seen and perhaps not thought about me for many years. However, I cannot help wondering how a woman preoccupied with civil rights, one who repeatedly questioned my commitment to racial justice, is pretending now to be someone she is not.

Although she has Owen's cheekbones and full lips, nothing else about her suggests that she necessarily has one drop of Nubian blood. However, considering the propensity of ethnic features among our troops waiting in her line, I see how she could get away with the subterfuge. I tread carefully.

All three lines of waiting GIs stretch to the back of the ward, but Rachel's is longest. From the back of her line, I observe her methodical, professional demeanor. She is comfortable enough in this sea of bursting testosterone to exude warmth to each soldier passing through her station. Now ten years older, her maturity and confidence are evident. She appears to have come a long way since she visited her uncle on campus.

I get a closer look at her as I advance toward the front of the line. She wears a man's utility uniform. I see the polished brass medical insignia of the Army Medical Corps and the silver bar of a first lieutenant. She is still a charmer, born to dispense human kindness, to practice medicine in some form. Her warm smile, the same smile that cast a spell over me long ago, puts each man at ease. Still, her steady voice commands respect and compliance.

When I am close to the front of her line, I roll up my sleeve. Catching my glance again, she smiles without giving a hint of recognition, while still working on the soldier ahead of me. She asks me, "Where're your records, and what kind of uniform is that, soldier?"

I have not changed that much. Assuming she has some good reason for not acknowledging me, I play along. "It's the uniform of a war correspondent. I'm Jack Savoy, on assignment here."

Her gaze remains unwavering. "That's a good name for a writer. You aren't a soldier at all then, are you? Well, just keep your eyes on the story, Scoop."

I say something pointless. "What kind of a hospital is this?"

She responds as though granting an interview. "You're in an army general hospital. If you were a real soldier and your wounds were serious enough, you might come here after you left a field hospital. Or you might be rushed directly here after being temporarily stabilized at a battlefield evac ward—which is my specialty."

"I see."

She laughs at my clumsiness. "See, all this was pieced together from what began as two evacs, but now we have real operating rooms and a thousand beds. Did you get all that?"

When a private walks away, my turn arrives. I freeze even as every fiber of my being compels me to ask her for an official interview, *for a date*. She rescues me by continuing the dialogue herself.

"It looks like you got almost everything you need before you left. You're still wise to get in here. What newspaper are you with?" She looks up at me again, this time her voice dropping to a whisper. "If you're a good reporter, you'll find me. You got some explaining to do, *Red*. Now, how did that feel?" The men behind me fidget impatiently but hesitate to challenge an officer's uniform—even one without rank or insignia.

Pleased to hear something that sounds like recognition, I playfully respond. "I didn't feel a thing. At least now I won't get malaria."

"Get the story straight, Scoop. We don't see a lot of malaria here. We see the full spectrum of battle injuries. Other than that, mainly reactions to medicine and the nasty local plagues—dust, heat and contaminated water."

She abruptly turns to the next person in line and continues employing her unique brand of comfort. In the States, people refer to her ruse as *passing for white,* an issue beyond my power to resolve. I remember her uncle's warning about the notion of *putting colored hands on white GIs.* He had made that statement with more conviction than anything else he said that day. I will do anything I can to overcome any problem that confronts her.

I stop before walking away, startled to hear my name again in that light bayou drawl. "Jack." When I turn around, she is pushing a needle into another outstretched arm. She looks up at me just long enough to say, "But only if you'll tell the truth."

Seeing her again has brought back memories. I cannot believe I am feeling the same pronounced infatuation I felt as a college senior. I walk away fully inoculated against North Africa's dangers but bitten once again by that most infectious of bugs. Later, when I hear myself asking Youssef where I might take Rachel for a very private dinner, I imagine Serge asking whether Owen, Rachel and I have all *lost our minds.*

On the next morning of relative comfort at the Anfa, I sit outside reading and listening to accounts from the few correspondents here, for various reasons, in Casablanca. A conversation between two reporters begins about signs of strengthened Red Army resistance against *Operation Barbarossa*, the massive German invasion of Russia.

However, their conversation, like their focus, trends eastward. They predict, based on the Allied bombing and harassment of Axis supply routes in the Mediterranean, that the Allied push is about to begin in earnest to take Tunisia.

One writer for a monthly magazine opines, "It's the last piece of the puzzle now that the Brits have been successful in Egypt. The Germans and Italians have invested everything they have left in defending Tunisia."

"You mean they're delaying the inevitable," corrects a reporter for a Florida daily. "The Nazis are trying to hold on to Tunis and Bizerte for as long as they can. Once we have those, it's no more oil for them and on to Europe for us."

Another correspondent flashes a smile. "I'm amazed at how simple we make it sound, sitting around tipping coffee cups. No matter though, with Patton and Omar Bradley in charge as of last month, it's only a matter of time now."

I volunteer, as perhaps only a French Canadian would, "If only the Vichy would just come around to making the right choice. They can't keep dealing from the middle of the deck. I know no one's concerned about the Vichy anymore. But by now, the right choice should be clear."

All three nod in agreement. One decides to interject what sounds like a mixture of envy and attempted humor. "Your paper only publishes weekly, right? My biggest challenge is getting stuff out over the wire. Hell, you can just mail it out."

Amid a chorus of chuckles, I retort, "If you're still hanging around here waiting for the FDR-Churchill conference, Roosevelt's back home now, so you can just drop your updates in a mailbox."

Over breakfast, Youssef walks up to me and whispers that we have a distinguished visitor in port. "Some say you'll want to interview this man for your newspaper."

He picks me up outside the hotel and spirits the Rover through a city that has changed markedly since the Allied amphibious assault teams waded ashore. Casablanca is located at a crossroads of three worlds. Diverse cultures have converged for centuries to fill this ancient mystical city with a plethora of customs, aromas and competing interests.

We drive along on one of the broader palm tree-lined boulevards that slice through the city. The broad streets appear to buffer, or section off, grids of numerous narrower thoroughfares, many resembling alleys more so than streets. The streets are in good shape, traversed primarily by cars, trucks and occasional horse-drawn conveyances. Yousef's knowledge of such a city is astounding. Throughout, areas formerly open spaces now accommodate military facilities constructed with wood and canvas. Many permanent structures house offices dedicated to Allied operations and logistics.

Youssef is chatty, speaking in a mixed dialect he has constructed of English and French. We head for my scheduled interview at the Port of Casablanca. He warns me that the hot temperate days will soon give way to cold chilly nights, and that the next six months could bring rain down in torrents on any given day.

"So Messier Savoy, you work for a newspaper owned by the blacks?" The sound of fighter planes overhead interrupts him. "Some say the planes protect Port Lyautey, Nouasseur Airport and ships moving past Gibraltar. They also protect the GIs on the docks and a thousand African and Arab laborers."

Through Yousef's contacts, I have located and secured an interview with the captain of the *USS Booker T. Washington*. The boat's skipper is the first Negro to captain a Liberty ship with an integrated crew. As I walk toward the ship, I recognize several veterans of the *Shithole* supervising members of the port battalion and hundreds of Arabs assisting them to unload newly arrived ships.

When I ask a hatch foreman for assistance, he extends a hand to his former cabin mate. "Mister Savoy, I didn't know you got off the boat with us, but it sure is good to see you again. No, this is just a trickle compared to the work they were doing here while we were still in the States. We see more bodies going out than we see people coming in. I'll tell Blue I saw you. Captain Mulzac? Yeah, I just saw him—a colored captain of a Liberty ship. Just walk up to the gangway and ask that man for permission to board."

As I walk away, Sergeant Mingo calls out to me. "You should do a story about the crane we fastened to a floating barge. Okay, just be sure to bring that camera."

At the top of the gangway, a chief petty officer introduces himself as Adolphus Folkes. The chief grants me permission to board and points me in the direction of a group of men. Looking down at my press corps armband, one of the more unassuming men asks, "Are you Mister Savoy? I'm Hugh Mulzac, ship's captain."

Lean and bespectacled with graying hair, he projects a quiet yet no-nonsense air of formality and competence. After confirming that I work for Ted Lomax, he issues a few parting instructions to subordinate officers before turning back to me.

After voicing his observations about the reduced volume of cargo coming into Casablanca compared to ports near Tunisia, the captain gets right to what he assumes is the focus of my story. "There're actually several Liberty ships captained by Negroes, but they have segregated crews. I refused to accept a segregated crew. You see, I earned my shipmaster's license way back in 1920. But only the desperate need for men willing to brave U-boats prompted the Merchant Marines to give me command of a liberty ship."

Born a British citizen, Mulzac speaks with a distinctive accent. He also speaks with the determination of a man who has held true to his convictions at great costs. He served on British schooners before immigrating to the States and earning the first master's certificate awarded to a Negro. However, despite his capabilities, he spent years limited to supervising ships' stewards.

"That was the most frustrating period of my life. When finally offered the opportunity to command, I wouldn't command a segregated ship." He pauses to ask me a question. "Where're you from Mister Savoy? Halifax? American slaves fled to Nova Scotia, didn't they? In fact, a lot of Negroes in Nova Scotia worked in shipping."

I add that they contributed substantially to the growth of Halifax, and mention the village of Africville. My reference appears to pique his interest but he looks at his watch and moves on. "I don't allow the Army to separate soldiers by race on my ship. Otherwise, the Army would segregate white and black troops as carefully as my crew separates munitions from flammable materials." It is an excellent quotable which he confirms is on the record.

Captain Mulzac goes on to cover issues related to training, licensing and risks. He shares several adventures at sea and a half hour later, the man who has been generous with his time and attention, indicates that he must return to his duties.

"As they get the eastern ports in shape, Casablanca will still have a role in moving salvaged materials, evacuating wounded GIs, and moving POWs. I'll only get here again a few more times. That's a pity. But I understand that things are really picking up in the Central Med."

I know he wants to ask me why I've remained in Casablanca, but is too polite to pry. I simply concur, "That's the way I hear it."

He turns me over to his chief petty officer with instructions to give me access to the crew for brief interviews. "You have been very gracious Captain. I wish you and your crew continued safe passages and a safe return home as well."

"I hope you have a very productive experience as a war correspondent, Mister Savoy. Maybe you'll also have an illuminating one, perhaps you'll return safely one day to Africville."

Chapter 9

· ·

A Night in Marrakesh

I hold my breath as I open my first message from Ted Lomax. Given the limitations placed on publishing by wartime paper rationing, I have already submitted enough copy to the managing editor to fill an entire edition of the *Record*. I have been confident that my extensive coverage of the Dix's Atlantic crossing and the deployment of Blue's port battalion satisfied his expectations. My Mulzac story had been significant enough to warrant transmitting.

Ted's note begins by telling me to *keep up the good work*. Still, I am certain that he wonders when I will move east. Since my last filing, I have transformed another bundle of notes into fresh copy. I have included articles about the pace of reconstruction in Morocco, always working in quotes and background on Negro soldiers in Quartermaster units and Moroccan civilians. However, I am still far away from the headquarters briefings provided by Tom James on the battles for Tunisia.

I had been fortunate to find an Army censor in Casablanca who acknowledges the intelligence and public relations briefings I received aboard the *Dix* and accepted my story about *not reporting directly to my assigned censor until I make my way to Oujda*. The officer has returned my copy promptly, noting that I have included nothing that would jeopardize an operation. However, I have nothing in hand that could compromise anyone.

Certain that Ted wants me to catch up to the real war, I feel relieve to read his short, cryptic appreciation for *working during my time off for rest and relaxation*. While his gentle dig brings a smile, he has echoed an observation made by several reporters I have met at the Anfa. They attest to the reputations earned by Negro correspondents for the *Courier* and the *Afro-American*, as they question my extended stay.

When Youssef suggests that I could use a short getaway within what is already a getaway, I instinctively resist. "But "I need to move on. I don't understand why I should travel to Marrakech."

Youssef is insistent. "Have I disappointed you yet, Messier Jack? I think you wish to have a quiet dinner with the Army nurse. You should stay a few nights at my family's hotel in Marrakesh. Then, it is settled. I will get both of you there. I do not think you will be back here ever again."

Youssef's connections are impressive, but his penchant for surprises is humbling. Marrakesh is an intoxicating town, once a fortress surrounded by the Atlas Mountains. The small inn and café are on an elevated plain tucked within clusters of palm trees. The foliage shields guests from the sun by day but allows glimpses of the moon and stars at night. Dinner in the outdoor setting is very much like a scene from an exotic motion picture. A Moroccan drummer, two men playing Oud guitars and lira flutists create a romantic mood with intoxicating melodies.

I compliment the owner on the venue, who could pass for his brother's twin. "Thank you, Messier Jack. It is not quite the villa that Roosevelt and Churchill had, but some say we do the best we can," he opines, sounding very much like his younger sibling.

As I look at the guest sitting quietly across the table, I easily sense her amusement with Youssef's obvious romantic trap. The sunset is the most beautiful I have ever seen. I try to distance myself from his plan and project my more constructive intentions. However, the woman looking back at me inquisitively no doubt wonders about my expectations for the coming evening.

I observe that the years have been kind to Rachel. Ten years ago, she was a reasonably attractive high school senior, generously endowed but not a woman most men would describe as *irresistibly attractive*—nor susceptible to *empty compliments* suggesting that she was. However, even then she had a haunting, earthy quality that time has molded into a stunningly gorgeous and intriguing woman. Her confidence gained from wartime service has sharpened her razor wit and honed an intimidating presence.

When she does not voluntarily share with me the source of the concern that burdens her uncle, I try to coax it out of her indirectly. "Rachel, I asked Youssef to select a place for us to talk, away from your work. I guess this is it. I was surprised that you agreed to accompany him to Marrakech. That shows a lot of trust."

Her tone is businesslike. "I know I suggested that you find me. I also mentioned something about telling the truth. Ten years have passed, but even though you continued to undress me, I thought you blamed me for what happened that night in Indiana."

Stunned to learn that she has felt as she has for so long, I part my lips to speak, but words do not come to me immediately. I stare at her in silence, hoping she has more to say.

"You never wrote to me. You never visited or called. Because of that, I really don't have a lot of trust in you. I didn't trust Youssef until two Moroccan nurses vouched for his family—people they've known all their lives. That's what made the difference."

She does not smile when she draws the distinction, which gives her words the effect of clearing the air about any misconceptions or preconceived notions. I say, "Okay. That's fair enough. Now, just so you know, I don't blame you or Serge for what happened at the rally that night—only the people who caused the trouble. You certainly did nothing wrong. When I asked Owen where you had gone, he became so infuriated that I never brought it up again. I thought he disapproved of me—as a match for you."

She is silent for a few minutes before speaking again. "Okay, Jack. I think you understand why I needed to hear that from you." I do not really understand, but continue listening. "Don't forget, you wouldn't have been there if we hadn't pushed you into it. And there would have been no trouble if I had not run away when they set fire to that cross."

I add, "Remember the way they lit that thing up? Hey, I was the oldest and I went along with the two of you. I'm so glad I did." I do not want to waste this beautiful setting rehashing things we cannot change. We can talk openly here, uninterrupted by distractions from people who might not approve of something they only misperceive. "So, without Youssef there'd be no trip, no dinner out here in this oasis?"

She appears reluctant to change the more unpleasant subject, but acquiesces. Suddenly she sounds playful, perhaps hearing that I have not held anything against her impetuous behavior. "I'm afraid not, Scoop. I hope that doesn't disappoint you, but why did you get Youssef to go to all this trouble to have dinner with me? I can't believe a weekly paper is paying for a car and driver for you." She is all business despite looking very much like a young woman on a date. I do not tell her that the whole evening is Youssef's idea entirely.

"Some say that we can talk privately about anything that might be on our minds." When she laughs at my imitation of Youssef's voice, instead of pressing for details, I concentrate on the ambiance. The night sky is beautiful—with huge stars against an indigo backdrop. Ours is one of six occupied tables in the outdoor café where doting waitresses serve local dishes. The other diners are a mix of Moroccan and European civilians who seem handpicked to enhance the evening's mystique.

"Maybe out of a sense of guilt, our very rich uncle paid generously for the properties my grandmother left us. He could have nickel and dimed me, but didn't. I'm just spoiling myself a little, but still paying Youssef well below his going rate."

I want to ask her bluntly if she needs help, but now that I am with her again, I do not want her to think that I am only here at the behest of her uncle. Over the next hour, I learn that Rachel participated in the Allied amphibious landings near Casablanca, wading ashore in Morocco under enemy fire. I try to picture her climbing into an assault boat with only a red cross painted on her helmet, an armband and her vivacious curves distinguishing her from the grunts.

She tells me that, "Once on the beach, our team found protection in craters blown out of the sand. We witnessed large scale mutilation and death for the first time. We found a lean-to shack and used it as the first of many makeshift hospitals."

Her team performed life-saving work and evacuations as the troops fought their way further inland. Like the fighting men who cleared the way, the nurses had access to only the equipment and supplies they could carry with them when they hit the beach. "All that first night, I stabilized wounded boys, cleaned and bandaged them by flashlights, Zippos and candlelight."

Assigned to an evacuation hospital, she has been near the front lines during the battles for key positions. During the early fighting, Rachel led a group of nurses in a narrow escape from a German armored column. Now she has a temporary assignment to a general hospital before going back east to provide evacuation training for incoming nurses. Perhaps tired of talking about herself, she says, "So tell me why a war correspondent is still in Morocco."

I do not want to talk about myself or explain, since I have no credible explanation, other than the truth, about why I remain here. Owen was clear that I should not press for any information she does not readily divulge. Instead, I flirt. "First let me say how stunning you look in that dress. I'm glad you decided to show up here in civilian clothes."

Rachel has on a beautiful long-sleeved kaftan dress that appears, based on what I have seen here, to be Arab inspired. It is simple in its elegance and form, perfectly draping the contours of her body and finishing with a floor-length flounce. She accepts my invitation to dance after our first glass of Algerian wine, leaving me lost in an exotic place from which I cannot fully return.

Seated again, she confides, "This dress was apparently Youssef's idea. I found it in my room. If you're telling the truth about not putting him up to this, he is quite the romantic."

"So, where's your room?" I feel embarrassed by the unrestrained excitement I hear in my own voice, which she neutralizes with her most stern look and serious tone.

"Don't let your imagination get the best of you, Scoop. You were about to tell me how and why you're here."

Without disclosing too much, I quickly tell her about my hectic schedule and the break I feel I deserve. "So, you see, a lot has transpired since going to work for the *Chronicle*. I've become a citizen and obtained press credentials, lived on trains, buried Mamie virtually alone, spent two months with Serge, two weeks breaking in at the *Record* and almost two weeks on the *Dorothy Dix*."

The mention of my brother's name brings a warm smile. "And just how is that handsome devil?"

"He's as impossible as ever, probably back in Detroit by now." I quickly change the subject, afraid that talking about my brother will distract her further. "Anyway, working at the *Record* seemed the only surefire way I could get over here before the war ends. How do you know about the *Record*?"

She scoffs. "Jack, I read several colored papers. People all over the South subscribe to the *Defender,* and my hospital back home made available dated copies of the *Record,* the *Courier* and the *Afro.* I've read them all. Connie Howard's series about the nurses treating the Tuskegee trainees is one of the best I've ever read."

She pauses to train her eyes directly at mine. "Jack, how long will you be here in Morocco?"

Since she has not yet acknowledged Owen's name, I do not tell her about her uncle's arrangements or his concerns about her. "I decided to spend a few days here, but that became a week. I've been working and hoping to get one interview. Now that I'm having it, I'll be going east in a few days. That'll be soon enough. Patton's still not out of Tunisia yet."

We are the last to leave, and as we walk in the moonlight, I limit contact to holding the palm of my hand against the small of her back. At the door to her room, I avoid an awkward moment by extending my hand. I am pleased that we touched on several points of interest but disappointed that she has shown no romantic interest.

"It's been a pleasure, Rachel. Since Youssef is taking you back in the early morning, I'll just say goodnight, good luck and goodbye."

She shakes my hand as she would a colleague, and opens the door to her room. "It was lovely, Jack. Thank you. May I ask just one more question? Am I wrong to believe that you're only working for Lomax because it fits into your plans?"

She sounds, once again, like the young activist I used to know. I answer honestly. "Yes. If my former editor had not gone back on his word, I'd be a war correspondent for the *Chronicle* right now. However, before you climb up on your soapbox, it's my turn to put you on the spot. My time in Casablanca is up and you've discouraged every attempt I've made to tell you what I'd hoped to discuss tonight."

Before I can speak further, she raises two fingertips to her lips and then presses them gently against mine. If she wants me to abort my advance, her gesture has the opposite effect—triggering my most primal instincts. Aware of the unintended impact, she retreats into the darkness beyond the open doorway. I follow her inside and begin kissing her softly, holding her tightly.

She is responsive, but I feel her hand on my chest, firmly pushing me back out the door. Reluctantly, I step back out. From inside, she says, "Jack, you know you were my first. I'm glad you still have feelings for me. I'm also going east to Algeria soon. If you found me here, you can find me there. I really hope you will. Thanks for everything though. Goodnight."

My remaining days in Morocco pass quickly, including one particularly long last night in Marrakech with a physically gifted Berber woman named Aya. Youssef makes the introduction, recommending an evening with the sultry belly dancer as *just the right cure* for my disappointing evening with Rachel. Awed by her energy and flexibility, I still decline her invitation to join her in a dance.

I awaken in her bedroom the next morning unsure of my obligation. She smiles. "No messier. Your friend has paid for my time, which I did spend with you—sex or not. You are still very young with a great adventure before you. Promise me you will try and find a way to release this great weight that you carry."

Back in Casablanca, I decide that it is past time I reported for duty at the newly established Fifth Army's Headquarters. Tom James surely expects that, by now, I would have made my way east to Oujda. Though I have used much of this time to work, I have delayed too long.

As expected, Youssef expresses disappointment that I do not accept his offer of a ride to Oujda in the comfort of his English Rover. Despite his invaluable assistance as a chauffeur and a resource, I am certain that Walt considers him and the Anfa Hotel to be unnecessary luxuries. I have employed Youssef sparingly, enjoyed discounted billing, and personally assumed some of his costs. However, I am convinced that we should end our arrangement. I will miss him, certain that he would be as helpful in Algeria as he has been in Morocco.

When I stop by the hospital to tell Rachel that I am leaving, I find her instructing an officer and his sanitation company. Our stilted exchange exhibits all the emotion of a street bazaar transaction. She behaves as though the night in Marrakesh never took place and we barely know one another. The charade is too much. I make an empty promise to look for her in a few months.

As we shake hands again like two colleagues, I wonder if I should tell Owen his niece is fine, even if precariously so, and resolve to forget the woman who has not left my mind—not even in the presence of the multitalented Aya—since I first saw her again in Casablanca. As I walk away, I tip my cap. "Good-bye, Lieutenant. I'm getting a one-way ticket on a train out of town."

Chapter 10

· ·

Fighter Pilots

"Take care of yourself Messier Savoy. Remember everything I've told you about doing business around the Mediterranean."

I respond warmly. "I'll never be able to think about my time in Casablanca without also thinking about you. Thanks for everything."

Youssef drops me off at the busy train depot in Casablanca on a cool April afternoon, with one parting tip. "A ship called the *Mariposa* made port in Casablanca and dropped off a precious cargo. I did not find out until today, and today, they are leaving. They are standing right now along the wall of the train depot. They are my gifts to you." He refuses to elaborate even as we say our last goodbyes.

I approach the depot to purchase my train ticket and notice a contingent of young officers milling about. I have never seen more than one Negro officer at a time, and would never have expected to see so many waiting outside the train depot. The young men smoke, laugh without reservation and engage in animated conversations, oblivious to numerous curious onlookers.

When I inquire, one particularly confident young man speaks, with exuberance, for the group. "We're fighter pilots fresh from the States—fresh off the middle passage, if you can appreciate the irony. We're the 99th Fighter Squadron."

According to them, they are the first squadron of Tuskegee-trained fighter pilots to deploy in combat. They sailed from New York assuming they would go to an undisclosed airfield in England. However, they have arrived in Casablanca instead, and are now on their way to an encampment near the French Moroccan town of Meknes, located about halfway between Casablanca and Oujda.

I can barely contain my excitement over the unexpected opportunity to file a story on the arrival of the first Negro pilots in North Africa. Ted has been adamant about the importance of covering them, and a coded letter from Connie suggests she was despondent over Walt's refusal to assign a second correspondent to follow them.

I suspect that, despite Walt's refusal to shadow them, both brothers will relish this story. To get my copy past the Army's censors, I will have to avoid references to their exact location, but my message will be clear.

I recall that the *Tuskegee experiment* was born of a flurry of activity during the last months of 1940. Congress authorized the enlistment of Negroes, promoted career officer Benjamin Davis, Sr. as the Army's first Negro general, and appointed Judge William Hastie as an advisor to General Marshall. Most surprising, the War Department announced that the Army would accept Negro pilot trainees in the Air Corps.

I present my credentials and immediately begin interviewing several of the young lieutenants before joining them onboard the train. Assuming they had been bound for England, these smart, engaging young men are surprised to find themselves disembarked in North Africa—but excited to finally *get into the war.*

They are different, in speech and manner, from any Negro soldiers I have met thus far. "Nice to meet you Mister Savoy. A reporter named Young sailed over here with us. He has all the stories. I think he's somewhere around here trying to file one now."

Their squadron commander is General Davis' son, now a lieutenant colonel, the first Negro to qualify for advanced flight training in January 1941. He has spent the last two years waiting for the Army to decide what to do with Negro pilots now that some have qualified. After the long delay, some of the young pilots carry the cockiness of young men on their way to an adventure. Others are more sanguine, perhaps contemplating the uncertainties, challenges and the rigors that still lie ahead.

I direct about a dozen general questions to small groups and con-duct extended interviews with the most talkative. Like most of the young soldiers I have encountered in North Africa, a few seem eager to get their names in the newspaper.

One talks about a trial in Japan for the captured participants of Jimmy Doolittle's air raid against the mainland. While these flyers will not be able to exact revenge in the Pacific, they promise to, "Do whatever we can to destroy the Axis powers in Europe."

I look around for Young, a reporter for the *Norfolk Journal and Guide*, but Colonel Davis agrees to give me his *second* overseas interview. I anticipate he will do hundreds more as other war correspondents write volumes about him and his untested yet highly visible fighter squadron. I decide to focus on a human-interest angle that speaks to their personal backgrounds and initial reactions to their first deployment.

Colonel Davis appears to be a very serious man at age 32, married and matured beyond his years. He seems surprised by my specific interest in his experiences as the troop commander aboard the *Mariposa* and his squadron's interactions with the white officers aboard ship. I tell him about my experiences aboard the *Dorothea Dix* with its troop commander, Colonel Case.

Without this opportunity to meet him, I would have difficulty imagining how Davis demonstrated objectivity and leadership over white officers during a truly integrated Atlantic crossing. After wit-nessing his no-nonsense approach, I accept his matter-of-fact assurance that he, "Simply exhibited the appropriate levels of professionalism and military bearing and expected white officers to do the same."

Davis is only the fourth Negro to graduate from West Point and, until America's involvement in the war, he and his father were the only two serving as officers in the Army. "I actually learned to fly as a barn-stormer before enrolling at West Point. What was the Academy like? It was an incomparable experience educationally, but socially, not so much. You see, I was never assigned a roommate—which really wasn't so bad—but only a few very brave classmates would even acknowledge that I was alive."

I state the obvious. "I guess that was a high price to pay."

His tone becomes professorial. "The price is always high, Mister Savoy. I've heard your publisher and my father speak about that." He seems amused that I cannot hide my surprise. "Don't look so surprised. Surprise isn't a good look for a reporter. At any rate, I still managed to graduate 35th in a class of 278. But yes, the price was high."

He approaches his responsibility with a seriousness that makes me question my own maturity. He also says the 99th Fighter Squadron is only the beginning. "Oh no, there are three other Negro fighter squadrons in varying stages of training right now. In Oued N'Ja, a name I can't spell and you can't to mention in your story, we'll train under a formerly segregated fighter group. That's right. An air wing contains groups, and a group contains squadrons. We'll make the most of that opportunity. In time, our ground maintenance crews and mechanics will catch up with us."

"Who will they be assigned to?"

"They will join us and additional fighter squadrons in the 332nd Fighter Group."

After nearly a half hour seated next to him, he extends a handshake indicating that the interview has ended, but before I get up, he has a parting favor to ask. "Mister Savoy, you are free to write your story any way you choose—and the censors will clear. But I'd hope the first article written after our arrival would not be some—if you'll pardon the expression—*sensational* piece that creates enormous expectations."

He waits for my reaction. I merely nod in acknowledgement. "You see, I know my men are a little cocky right now—as all fighter pilots must be. I also know their fight's just beginning and it's my job to lead them in the air—and maybe more importantly, lead them on the ground. Do you know what I mean?"

"I understand Colonel."

His eyes seem to pierce right through me. "You do? I hope you do. I really hope you do. I need to keep these healthy sexual beings alive in the air and on the ground, and I don't yet know which task will be harder. It's April. Come back to visit with us after a few months and I'll give you a comprehensive story—if you still want it."

"Of course, I will."

He asks, "So I'm sure you have your sources. What do you think we'll be doing here?"

I am surprised that he would ask my opinion on a military matter, but hazard a guess. "From the little I know I'd guess you'll be harassing the Luftwaffe and the Italian navy as they attempt to resupply the Afrika Corps in Tunisia. You'll be patrolling the sea lanes to back up any other moves Ike makes. My boss was right. This is a war of logistics."

"Lomax may be on to something." He surprises me again. "Other than your interest in the racial harmony on our trip over here, your questions have been surprisingly *less comprehensive* than I would expect from a man who works for the Lomax brothers."

I sense the weight of responsibility that Colonel Davis embraces, but his assumption that I should share it is disconcerting. Throughout the interview, he has subtly ascribed a portion of that responsibility to me. His words or, more accurately, the tone of his words stays with me a long time after I watch him and his young pilots leave the train and proceed to Oued N'Ja.

Although I regret missing the opportunity to compare notes with Tom Young, I marvel at my run of good fortune. I also wonder how much information about their deployment will survive censorship. Already I have written and filed at least 50 pages of original copy covering a range of people and topics, all undergoing very little censorship. However, prior to today none of my subjects performed in direct combat roles.

I have stumbled upon the arrival in North Africa of what could become one of the most covered units in the war. I hope I can do justice to this story in a way that will not violate the rules of censorship. Because the confident attitudes of the pilots have affected me profoundly, I want to write a story that captures the significance of the work they are about to do.

I close my eyes and envision Serge insisting that *I have a responsibility to frame a new dialogue on race from the perspectives of these combat pilots. People have judged them before they fire a single shot.* I can hear my brother demanding a voice for the next generation of advocates—to *press for new pathways through which we can one day tap into an enormous capacity.*

While I disagree with Serge about my *responsibility*, I understand that men like Benjamin Davis and his squadron will either confirm or shatter traditional stereotypes. If they fail, the Air Corps may not try again for another generation. However, I wonder if they will return home and become the men Serge expects them to be.

As I ride further east in the void that now exists without the young officers' animated voices, I feel every rattle and jerking motion of the old steam driven train slowly making its way toward the Algerian boarder. After a few minutes, I look up to see that a large army officer has taken the seat facing me. He lights up a cigar and begins asking questions without introducing himself or extending his hand. "What newspaper are you with?"

I extend my hand to him, trying to remember where I have seen him before. "I'm Jack Savoy, war correspondent for the *Washington Record*. And you are?"

The disheveled officer touches my hand with only his thumb and index finger, barely allowing his palm to brush mine before quickly releasing from my attempted grip. "Afraid I'm not familiar with that newspaper. From your interest in those boys, I assume it's a colored paper of some sort."

"The *Record* has been around for over 30 years. Where are you going? Did you just get on the train at the last stop?"

He flashes a smile. "No. I've been on since Casablanca. I'm at the Army general hospital there, trying as hard as I can to teach a company of colored boys one end of a mop from another. I just got on hoping we'd get a chance to talk, *Jack*."

Stunned to hear him refer to me by my first name, I sit in silence, waiting for him to reveal more about himself.

"I followed you out of the hospital, Jack, after you told your old girlfriend that you were headed to the train station. Then I got on before that group of colored lieutenants in Casablanca. I saw you taking statements from them. From a distance some people might not be able to tell." A curious smile curls in the corner of his mouth.

I remember him now. I did not pay close attention this morning to the officer talking to Rachel. "So, they're the colored boys in the Air Corps experiment? I heard they might be air controllers if they can learn the ropes fast enough."

I try not to sound defensive. "Actually, they've already trained at Tuskegee and other airfields in the States. Now, they're qualified fighter pilots reporting for duty."

He widens his eyes and feigns surprise. "Really, ain't that something? Flying fighter planes, you say—against the battle-tested pilots of the German Luftwaffe?"

"I steal a glance at his nametag. That's what I hear, Lieutenant *Matthews.*"

He snickers derisively, and shakes his head, his voice dropping. "Don't fret about my name, Jack. Let's just say I'm a friend of Nurse Todd." When he refers to Rachel, I sit up straight. "Oh, so now I got your attention. I wasn't sure it was you until I saw you with her this morning."

He waits but I still say nothing. "Then I see you with those colored officers, back slapping and such, looking just like one of the boys. That's when it all came together for me."

"I don't understand what you're talking about."

"The hell you don't, Savoy. I know she's the same gal—just a child back then—that went running from *a certain hilltop ceremony.* I've already talked to her about it. I remember everything from that night. When she ran down the hill to a car, a colored boy hiding on the floor popped up and took the wheel. A couple of *Hawks* followed them, just to scare them. We were in the wrong county to try anything else."

Certain that I know the only living eyewitnesses to the events of that night, I confidently continue to feign ignorance. "Saw me what night? I think you have me confused with someone else."

He is unfazed by my commitment to ignorance. "She watched the inductions with the women kinfolk who were allowed there as spectators. I was there to keep an eye on you. I had you pegged correctly as a reporter, but as a *white reporter.* I now know I was half-wrong about that, you fucking half black mongrel."

I become incensed. "Look asshole, I don't know you and you don't know me. You can call me by my name or nothing at all."

He ignores me. "You disappeared, *Mongrel.* I know you drove off behind them too. Lucky for you, my car was blocked. The next morning, they found two of our boys shot dead, lying next to their own shotguns—almost like they shot each other."

I sit almost frozen in fear, but struggle to project my innocence and indignation. "I'm going to ask you to find another seat, Lieutenant. I can just write up a complaint for your commander." As much as I would like to, I am unable to return his negative energy. However, I cannot take the bait, and give him the response he wants so badly.

He flashes that derisive smile. "But I know you won't do that, Savoy. You know, you could never understand the *force* that brought us all back together again over here. The force wants that gal to keep her hands off our brave white boys. You'd best believe I'm going to put a stop to it. And somehow, I'm going to make you pay for what we both know you did."

As he rises to his feet, I cannot resist a parting shot. "That was a remarkable piece of storytelling. I'm only sorry I can't use it—don't do fiction. But I'd love to interview a real live KKK *Knight Hawk*."

He ignores the jab. "It took me a while to remember where I'd seen her. Then, the closer I looked, everything started to fall into place. She's the same gal, and you're the same sombitch that helped her and that other boy."

After he walks away, I try to relax but I cannot. His ten-year-old memories are accurate, almost. He is correct about Rachel's panic and sudden exit from the rally that night. He does not know that Serge misunderstood why she ran toward the car. While his claims against me are speculative at best, he is certain about enough of his story to make trouble for Rachel. Her problem, the problem Owen asked that I investigate, appears to have found me.

I try to appear unconcerned, and take out a recent issue of the *Record*. I read the leads on the front page and the continuations of a few stories inside. Peripherally, I notice Matthews has returned to his seat next to another man in uniform. Their conversation grows louder and I can hear their impish laughter over the noise of the train.

Turning my attention back to the newspaper, on the inside fold, I see a reprinted wire service item naming the founding members of a new Chicago-based civil rights group. I recognize a few faces in the grainy photograph, including that of their mentor. Despite some distortion of several faces in the background, one familiar smile is unmistakable. Serge has been busy. I try to forget about Matthews, who appears to have gotten off the train, focusing instead on Serge, wondering what his role might be in this thing called CORE.

Chapter 11

· ·

Ron Maxwell

After checking in at the converted Girls' school that serves as Fifth Army headquarters, I enjoy a brief reunion with Tom James. I am disappointed to learn that I will share quarters temporarily with another correspondent.

The door to our room swings open after three soft knocks. A slightly older man opens the door. Even in military garb, he looks like a movie star or, at the very least, a bronze heartthrob of a jazz singer.

"So, you're Jack Savoy. Your reputation precedes you. The first colored reporter hired by a white daily—and the first to tell them where they could shove it. I'm Ron Maxwell of the *Harlem Advocate.*"

Placing a stylish cigarette holder between his teeth, he extends his hand. His army uniform is close to regulation, but has a unique drape and texture, accessorized with a fraternity lapel pin and a red bandana.

I had not expected to confront the man for whom I have a message to deliver. I try to begin our association on a positive note. "Pleased to meet you Ron, I read some of your coverage of the New York City council races last year. That was one hell of a coup, making Adam Clayton Powell the first Negro on the city council. What's next, a House seat? How long have you been in Oujda?"

He responds, "The real credit for Powell goes to the *People's Voice* and the *Amsterdam News.* My publisher, whose accomplishments pale next to the Lomax brothers, was only somewhat instrumental. Now, that's enough kissing each other's asses, though. They *pronounce* the name of this sand trap as *whish-da.* You know, as in *I wish-da hell I was anywhere else on earth."*

With an easy manner and a natural ability to put people at ease, Ron smiles like a commensurate politician—a personality that seems better suited for entertainment than gumshoe reporting.

"Thanks. Then I guess I've been mispronouncing the name of this place since I left Washington," I confess.

"Hell, everyone does. Some continue to mispronounce it. The locals don't think Americans care about saying it incorrectly. But hey, I guess we're going to be roommates until the crowd thins out."

"When do you think that'll be?" I ask, embarrassed by my obvious discomfort with our rooming arrangement.

Ron just flashes that smile again and says, "You might want to get used to it, Jack. At least it's a large room. Hell, we may have to share a foxhole in the sand one night. When the temperature plummets, you'll be thankful to snuggle up to a warm body that doesn't snore."

I try hard to block the image from forming in my mind. My second order of business, after reporting to Tom, was going to be locating Ron and initiating the conversation Owen wants us to have. Interestingly, Tom has made that task both convenient and inconvenient since I will have to live with the person I am here to admonish. I wonder whether it is entirely by coincidence.

Ron is still talking. "Anyway, I may leave for Sicily soon. Oh relax, Jack, everyone knows Ike's next move. Take Italy, not Greece, to control the Mediterranean. Clark's been pounding a new army into mountain climbing shape while Patton kicks the last traces of ass in the desert. He and Monty have figured out how to win, so people think they're going first."

"Then, you know it's Sicily?"

"Yes, I'm confident that I do. I can't decide whether to go with them or wait for Clark to invade somewhere on the boot, maybe Naples, if not Rome."

"If all that speculation is true, you must have a crystal ball—or a spy. If you're right, that will be difficult—guessing which lead to follow. But should you be so open with that kind of informed guess?" I ask.

He stares back at me in stunned silence and takes a long drag to finish the butt left in his holder. "You're really going to have to relax, Jack. News flows freely in this building—or any building in the world that houses correspondents. Don't take it out in the street, but we talk among ourselves."

"Any leads on locating Negro units?"

"Colored reporters are pretty competitive. Ollie Stewart's around here some place today. Ed Rouzeau might be anywhere. You might get a few from white reporters. They don't cover colored news. Some don't want it covered at all. Just find out what they like to write. Any tips you give them could make for a lucrative exchange—rather than sifting through an ocean of sand for a sand pebble of a certain color. But just think, in the last war, Negro papers printed letters from colored soldiers."

I imagine that other reporters take an immediate liking to this easy-going erudite and confident man. I have a serious message from a man Ron has refused to take seriously—and I do not know how he will react to hearing it. I decide to get it out of the way quickly so that we can get on with whatever kind of association we are destined to have.

I cannot wait for a proper segue from this talkative journalist—who does not know me, yet still appraises me *knowingly*. I interject clumsily, "Ron, I'm going to get right to it. I hope there'll be no hard feelings between us afterward. This has nothing to do with me. I'm merely the messenger—from Owen Todd for your ears only." I can see his posture stiffen. I tell him bluntly, "He's asked me to express his concern about news stories running in the *Advocate* without censorship."

Again, Ron sits for a moment in stunned silence. He does not deny the allegation but instead maligns my friend. "I thought that was Tom James' job. Owen Todd? I've heard my publisher mention that name. Isn't he the investigative reporter who turned lackey errand boy? I heard he sat on my accreditation application until we rewrote every word. What a jerk. Wasn't he putting out fires down South with Ted Lomax a while back?"

Unfortunately, I have come to expect the mention of Owen's name to elicit such disdain. Undaunted, I finish my message. "He risked his life trying to curtail lynching, and was nearly lynched, himself, many times. He just wanted me to tell you that the consequences to your actions could include revocation of your accreditation."

Hearing what apparently sounds to him like an absurdity, Ron laughs aloud from deep within. However, I have already seen the genuine concern in his eyes. "You are talking about the colored dollar-a-day man who settled for 25 cents?"

"He has always had his own money. He doesn't need the other 75 cents." Immediately, I regret saying it, even letting on that I know about it.

"What can he do to me, except tell the head messenger? Now I see it. That's how your outspoken bosses got a replacement correspondent for Chet Franklin. Just so you know, Chet didn't fear anything, certainly not what anyone thought of him. He was just too old for this war."

I appreciate his kind words about Chet, whom I have quickly come to admire. I ignore his baseless speculation about my credentials, and try not to take his accusation personally. I reiterate, "I don't have a dog in this fight, other than doing a favor for an old friend—maybe also for a new friend. Maybe Owen overheard something. I'm sure it's for your own good. Maybe he thinks it's for the good of the Negro Press Corps."

He is instantly incredulous. "The *Negro Press Corps*—these boys are going to get a hoot out of you, Savoy. What kind of accent is that, *Nova Scotia Patios*? What, they didn't beat that out of you at the Royal Acadian School? Look, we're just a handful of colored guys hitching rides through a million square miles of nothing, trying to find a handful of colored units to write about. There's always racism to write about but you'll have to save most of that for your post war memoirs. You're not at the *Chronicle* anymore, Savoy. They sent another guy—*a real white guy.*"

"No, they decided to wait until things wrapped up in North Africa." I sound defensive and regret stating as fact something I do not know.

He suddenly appears genuinely sympathetic. "No Jack. The *Chronicle* has already sent one guy to the Pacific, one to England and another guy who'll travel with Seventh Army. I met him last week."

My face probably reveals that he has opened an old wound.

Ron continues, "Look, they don't have to play fair. Do you think Ted Lomax brought lynch mobs to justice playing by the rules? We can't always *color inside the lines.* We have two jobs to do. One, we cover news about colored soldiers. The other is to draw attention to things that must change—for now and after the war. The real problem for us is that some of these Army censors understand that all too clearly."

I have not yet recovered fully from the information he shared. I mumble something just to fill the empty space. "There's still journalistic integrity, just giving the facts." I listen carefully to my voice, hoping my surprise has diminished.

He responds immediately, reveling in the banter. "So, when white reporters fail to mention a combat soldier's color—despite knowing how important it is to convey that to the people back home—do they exercise *journalistic integrity*? Here is a proven fact. When an Algerian woman accuses a white kid of rape, many—though not all—officers look the other way. With a colored kid, it's *off to the lockup*. Show me your integrity when you cover that. That is, if you intend you cover it."

Rather than wait for my rebuttal, he goes on. "If a white photographer shutters his camera when a colored unit arrives, is he exercising journalistic integrity?" I wonder if he can expand on that without using that patronizing tone.

I try to end the discussion and lick my wounds, "Look, I hope we understand each other, Ron. I've given you the message. That's all I was asked to do."

He looks at me curiously for a long moment, examining me as though I just arrived from another planet. I hope his intelligence is correct about the next invasion. *I also hope they save him two press billets—one for him and one for his massive ego.*

He continues to press on. "Why in hell are you *over here*, Savoy? I mean, what do you intend to do over here? Yeah, I think we understand each other clearly. I understand that Canada also has some serious civil rights challenges—and some serious freedom fighters. I've spoken at length with people like Wilson Head, and others—including an impressive young man named Serge Savoy. Do you know him? He certainly knows you."

Again, he has knocked me off balance. I say, "Then I guess you have me at a serious disadvantage."

He responds without a pause, "Actually, maybe not since I made some assumptions about you after speaking with him. No—he didn't say anything. I just assumed that the two of you would have *something* in common."

I go too far. "Yeah Ron, we do. We're both descended from a man who didn't wait for Americans to refuse to give him his freedom. When you blokes down under figure out that it's not something that anyone *can give you*, sign me up for the cause."

Ron places another cigarette in his long holder and lights it deliberately, sitting down on the edge of his bed and eying me carefully. "I see. Tell me Savoy, what is your relationship with Owen Todd? I'm trying to make a connection, but it's not quite working out for me."

"Well, you might understand the connection better if you weren't so dismissive," I respond, aware that I have said nothing really.

Ron does not give up. "I'd be more than happy to change my opinion of him considering where he works—or maybe more accurately, where he reports. But I'd like to know more and exactly where you fit in to the equation."

I am still indignant. "Have you ever wondered why the War Department is accrediting reporters for Negro weeklies? There's no real support for that in the government. They could have just approved a few and called it a day." I get personal, since that appears to be his context of choice. "Could you pull this *Duke Ellington* routine in that modified officer's getup if not for Owen? He has already made his mark in civil rights. Now he trades behind the scenes, willing to take shit from everyone—to help *people like you* get what they never would otherwise."

I begin to put away my things in the space he appears to have left available for me, as Ron stokes the fire in my gut. He retorts, "*People like me?* There're probably a couple million Negro men, and women, just like me who're ready to come over here and risk their lives for a country that is more concerned about keeping them out of the service, keeping them down, carefully managing their expectations. And by the way, your uniform looks professionally tailored."

When I remain silent, he goes on, "Savoy, I have a lot of respect for Negro publishers and editors, especially the people the government wants to try for treason and sedition. Publishers like Walter Lomax and heroes like his brother. Beyond them, look to people like Randolph,

White, Hastie, and DuBois, maybe a dozen others. But don't go around telling people you're a flunky for a bum like Todd."

"Oh, so you want to give those guys the credit for getting something done, over J. Edgar Hoover's objections, deep inside Marshall's public affairs bureau. Fine, go right ahead and believe that." It has been a long day and a long bumpy ride. I feel like I am losing my patience too easily and probably need a nap. I stretch out on the reasonably comfortable mattress and close my eyes.

I am almost asleep when I hear him speak again. "I guess you might have a point or two, Savoy. I'm going to have to get to know you better, find out what you stand for."

"I stand for the truth, and nothing else but."

"Oh, you *stand for the truth?* Let me know when you find that over here. In fact, here's a gift from me to you. Don't waste your time worrying about the truth. There is no truth—just different versions of the story. Just be true to yourself, Canada." When I awaken to the sound of my own snoring, Ron is still talking as though only a second has passed. "I've been told I look like Cab, but not like Duke."

Half asleep, I have forgotten the point of reference. "What?"

"I said I don't look anything like Duke Ellington."

The next morning, well before daybreak, I hear Ron's voice in my sleep. "Canada. Wake up. Come on with me if you want to see some colored artillerymen in action. We must leave right now to catch up with them, but I've got us a ride. Canada! Get out of bed. Your Moroccan vacation is over. It's time for you to get to work. Fifteen minutes."

Half asleep, I obediently dress, wolf down a little food and a lot of coffee. After hiking a mile, we climb on a truck loaded with sleepy GIs. Finding a vacant spot on the bench, I remove the helmet I am wearing for the first time, and try to catch another nap.

In the middle of a long hot ride through many mind-numbing miles of sand covered with layers of more sand, we stop for relief. As a highly competitive farting contest breaks the eerie silence of the desert, the men inquire about our status. Later, with a clear, and abnormally combustible champion selected, Ron and I are back in the truck, fully alert, jotting down names, ranks and hometowns.

Daybreak reveals that we are following the contours of what passes for a road. It is more of a compacted pathway, barely distinguishable from its narrow shoulders or the surrounding landscape. At a rendez-vous point that looks like a hundred places we have already passed; we join several jeeps and truckloads of men and material. Half-tracks tow what appear to be large canons of two sizes. Substantially later, the entire convoy comes to a stop.

Soldiers dismount and spring into action without prompting. Trying hard to stay out of the way, Ron and I get out later to observe the activity. I venture into the eventual line of fire, trying to capture a frontal photograph before they completely cover the howitzers with ragged shards of camouflaged netting.

A voice calls out to me with a warning that sounds both overly dramatic and premature. "I wouldn't advise you to stand in front of the guns, Mister. I'd hate to have one of those 100-pound shells carry you away with it for a few miles."

I sneak a few quick photographs from the business ends of the 155-millimeter barrels, but decide to heed the sergeant's warning.

"Good choice, sir. We don't want to lose a few seconds getting you out of the way when we get a fire mission. Also, save that water until you really need it. Let your body get the feel of going without it for a while."

I settle for a few side-profile shots before retreating toward the safety of the rear. The convoy of jeeps, trucks and tractors rests on an elevated plateau somewhere in the desert. The crews assigned to transport, set up, load and test fire four large 155-millimeter and four smaller, but equally menacing 105-millimeter guns work together in choreographed actions.

Munitions handlers prepare batches of shells for firing, lining them up in one area where others adjust and attach fuses. They work both with bare hands and fitted wrenches. Some carry the modified ordinance over to stack behind each gun.

Once the guns appear to be set up and ready to fire, I turn my attention to the soldiers in the command center, where the more senior men appear to plot points on maps, request and issue instructions by radio, telephone and voice communications. No one, including Ron, says anything more to me.

Just as the men of the battery begin to settle down, they react to body language inside the command area. Now participating in clearly distinguishable batteries, they spring into action with renewed intensity. Each gun crew begins their well-rehearsed choreographed motions. No one seems to notice that Ron and I are also out here in the middle of nowhere. I find their casual indifference to my presence both liberating and, interestingly, a little disconcerting. Still, I stay out of the way.

Somewhere far away, I hear war. Men position themselves within an ensemble of anti-aircraft weaponry, peering into the horizons for signs of Stuka dive-bombers. Each man clearly has a specific responsibility that is critical to these gun crews successfully sustaining effective barrages.

Men in the command centers communicate adjustments. Teams of four or more men begin a dance around each gun by raising projectiles and shoving them forward until they can push them deep into the breaches. White containers that appear to contain some sort of charge go in behind them before the breeches close.

After other less conspicuous adjustments, the dances culminate with one man pulling a chain on each gun that produces a deafening roar. Instantly, the movements repeat, sometimes after a few manual adjustments to direction and azimuth. They continue, with precise movements and timing, throughout the course of each fire mission.

Just as I realize that the replacements we accompanied here have blended in seamlessly into the performance, I hear Ron's voice nearby. "I'm thankful not to be on the receiving end of this. Did you ever think you'd see a battalion of colored men doing this?"

I confess that I had not. "I wonder if anyone will believe it, even when they see my pictures. Everyone tans out here after a while."

Chapter 12

· ·

Déjà vu

"**H**ey fellas, I'm trying to get to Algiers but I just missed the train. If one of you will just drive me down the road to the next stop, I can catch up with it—and you'll get back here before you're missed."

The drivers, both three-stripers, glance at one another, clearly amused that an ostensibly white Army nurse has asked them to risk losing their stripes, and maybe more, for her personal convenience. One points to the eagle on his jeep placard.

"No Ma'am. We can't do it." Even from behind, I can see the frustration in her body language. When she shifts her weight beneath the leather bag slung across her shoulder, the strap tugs her uniform skirt snugly, framing the protruding derriere beneath. Yet even that pose cannot get either driver to chance being away when two busy colonels reemerge from breakfast.

The nurse has my undivided attention. Although months have passed since I last heard it, there is no mistaking her crisp diction and light southern drawl. She naturally exudes warmth, the deliberate cadence of her speech suggesting that she is a person for whom clarity could mean the difference between life and death.

I sit at the wheel of a jeep that Tom allows me to borrow for weeks at a time, rationalizing that I should probably offer her a lift. My breakfast companions, whom have yet to emerge, can find other rides. However, I cannot decide. I had been certain I would never see her again. I think back to the cryptic telegram I sent Owen after that night from Marrakesh: *Visit over. Locals don't talk much.*

Almost involuntarily, I start the jeep. Startled to hear the engine turn over, Rachel spins around, hopeful that she has another possibility. I am mindful that I have not kept my promise to look for her. Doubting I would ever see her again, I had tried to put her out of my mind. I failed.

Now she is once again in my field of vision, in Oran, Algeria with bright sunlight revealing brown undertones within her thick black curls. She is wearing one of the newly issued nurses' uniforms, with an olive drab service jacket and skirt with khaki blouse and tie. Apparently stranded by the roadside, she needs a small favor I can easily grant. I hear myself ask, "Need a lift, Lieutenant?"

She peers into the glare of the morning sun that apparently has risen to a point directly behind my head. "Is that you, Scoop?"

She walks toward me looking even better than before, taking long deliberate strides that accent shapely legs beneath her uniform skirt. Even with this new substantially more professional attire, the Army places little emphasis on designing clothing for women. They try, usually without success, to project some semblance of individuality, of femininity. She walks up to the driver's side of the jeep and scolds me. "Okay, here we are in the middle of July. So, tell me why I haven't heard from you since April. And where have you been hiding?"

I try to sound collegial. "As I told you that day in the hospital court-yard, it was past time I left Casablanca to report for work. Nowadays, I go where the story takes me." Then, a lie forms on my lips. "Anyway, I just happen to be here in Oran, leaving for Algiers this morning."

Although my voice sounds detached, I jump out and deposit her bags in the back of the jeep. "I could use some company." Peripherally, I see the two young drivers looking on with interest. Mindful that she appears to be someone she is not; I look around to see if anyone else is interested.

"Who are you looking around for, Jack—a jealous girlfriend? Tell her I just need to get ahead of the train." I follow her hypnotically as she climbs into the passenger seat.

"I would have reached out to you, but wasn't sure that was a good idea. Anyway, what are you doing in Oran?" I am embarrassed that the officious tone I strive for sounds instead like a pouting schoolboy.

She just smiles and leans over to kiss me. Confused, I offer her my cheek, which she kisses lightly, but fully. I look around again, aware that we have much to discuss.

"They won't let me sit still, Jack. I like it that way. Look, that train makes a couple of stops nearby. So, if you ever get going, you should be able to catch up with it."

I stay with my lie, "Like I said, Rachel. I'm driving two hundred miles alone. If you want a ride, you can take it—or leave it."

"And I heard you." As she shifts to get as comfortable as one can in the front seat of a jeep, I struggle without success to keep my eyes on hers. She laughs, eying me with mock suspicion. "I'm up here, Scoop. You're thirty years old now aren't you, still with the instincts of a high school sophomore. And you know, I've been warned about you war correspondents."

"And everything you've heard is true," says someone climbing into the back seat of the jeep. Without turning around, I recognize the voice of one of my breakfast companions—both of whom could have easily hitched another ride back to our quarters.

Then I hear my other companion say, "But this one you can trust. Hell, the Army trusts him with his own personal jeep—on direct orders from General Clark, according to my sources. Jack has a lot to do over here. Who's your friend, Jack?"

Rachel still appears relaxed, sitting in a jeep with three Negro men—press credentials and officers' uniforms notwithstanding. I introduce them, wondering how much of our conversation these professional snoops have already overheard. "Lieutenant Rachel Todd, meet Ollie Stewart and Ron Maxwell." They both extend their hands to her, bringing with them a small cloud of tobacco smoke.

Rachel offers her brightest smile. "Oh really, I'm so pleased to meet you gentlemen. So, Jack has his own jeep. I didn't know he was so well connected." She takes Ollie's hand. "You write for the *Baltimore Afro American*, don't you?"

Ron answers for his thoroughly shocked companion. "Why yes, he does—the *Baltimore and Washington Afro American,* no offense to you Jack. And you must be the girl Jack has been telling us so much about." I shake my head in denial when Rachel turns back to look at me. "Jack and I used to be roommates. So, he knows I prefer my girlfriends to call me *Max*."

Rachel remains gracious, "Then *Ron* it is. But what has my friend told you about me?"

Ron manages to respond, "I'm afraid that whatever Jack told me specifically was in confidence—*journalistic integrity* and all. You know that's Jack's *raison deter*."

Ron is going too far. Ollie asks, "Jack, do you think we can catch a lift home? You need to stop by anyway to get *that bag you packed last night*."

It occurs to me that I have nothing in the jeep that suggests I am about to take a two-hundred-mile trip. I am always appreciative of Ollie. "Of course, you can."

Both men light fresh cigarettes and remain in the jeep after I pull up to our quarters and go inside. Wary of Ron's penchant for trouble, I quickly pack a leather *AWOL* bag. When I return to the jeep, Rachel is engaged in conversation with both men and two others now standing next to my jeep. I hear enough snippets to know they are discussing the eminent cornering of German forces remaining in Tunisia. "The Brits have Tunis and the Yanks have Bizerte. It's over." Ron and Ollie get out and walk toward me.

I say goodbye to Ollie and wish him well in Sicily. Ron whispers, "Jack, so her last name is Todd? That's an interesting coincidence." Then he speaks up louder. "Rachel, I look forward to our date when you get back in town."

I climb back into the jeep without a further comment. As we drive away, Rachel smiles at my obvious disdain. "Take it easy Jack. I made no such arrangement with that cat. I've already seen him try to bag half the nurses at the hospital. He's a flirt—very handsome but also very much aware of it. Y'all make quite a team though. Did you know Ollie was also from Louisiana?"

I acknowledge that I did not know, adding, "Ollie flew into London from the States. When Ike invaded North Africa, he and Ernie Pyle jumped on a steamer together. Ollie's going wherever Patton goes, and I hope he takes Ron with him."

She asks, "The way Ollie and Ron blend in with other reporters—isn't that unusual, even for men in modified uniforms?"

"Oh yeah, well they can be very likeable guys."

She says with mild astonishment, "Jack, I'm talking about *colored* men socializing so easily with white men—and vice versa. That is a little rare, don't you agree, even among educated men."

"I knew what you meant. Ollie and Chester Franklin were the first Negro correspondents overseas. The Army tried to quarter them in a separate building but they refused—*supported by the white correspondents.* Most reporters get along fine. Having worked for a white newspaper, I'm not that surprised."

She stays on topic. "And you? You could fall into a few categories—though I must admit you've tanned nicely in this sun. I like it." I change the subject to the weather and predictions of road conditions. After traveling less than a few miles, she is back on the topic again. "So how many colored correspondents are working in North Africa?" she asks.

I wonder if she is concerned that accompanying me all the way to Algiers will blow her cover. I think about the porter's advice on the train to Washington. I think about June Carter's words my first day at Lomax Publishing. I think about Matthews' threats on the train. I decide to find out where Rachel wants to belong before I drive another mile.

I pull the jeep over on the side of the road, and answer in a tone that reflects the anger I feel about a ruse she knows I have been onto from the beginning. "I don't know about all of them but I've only personally met Ollie, Ed Rouzeau of the *Pittsburg Courier*, and a guy named Tom Young from the *Norfolk Journal and Guide.*"

"And, of course, there's Ron."

"Yes. Ron Maxwell. An analyst at the War Department has been helpful in getting us over here as well as to the Pacific and the Middle East. I believe you know Owen Todd."

I say his name with emphasis, wondering why she refuses to acknowledge him. I continue, "We seem to get a pass over here when it comes to harassment. It may have something to do with the modified uniforms. Most white correspondents seem to see us as colleagues, but there are still plenty of people, *confused people*, who'd want to beat me up for trying to hang out with you all the way to Algiers. So, you need to tell me if there's anything you're concerned about right now."

She smiles at my measured indignation and, I suspect, my insistence on trying to get her to talk. "Cool down Papa, don't you blow your top. Get this jeep back on the road before we get stuck behind that convoy all the way to Algiers. It's bad enough that I'll be covered in sand by the time we get there." I pull back onto the road just ahead of a long line of trucks. "So, tell me Jack, what kinds of reactions do you get over here working for a colored newspaper? I want the whole truth and nothing but the truth."

Since she appears to be riding with me the entire distance, I acquiesce, and follow her lead. "And then, I'll get to hear your story, right?" She nods her agreement with my terms. I focus on my experiences in Norfolk, aboard the *Dorothea Dix* with Major Wade and Colonel Case. I mention the usual subtle and overt attempts to diminish me, "You know, all the usual misguided trash." I mention a few curious comments made by Captain Folkes, Colonel Davis and officers serving under Patton and Omar Bradley.

"And, as you say, most people don't know or can't decide how they should react to me." However, deciding that I do not want to wade into that morass right now, I try to change the subject. "As you know, I can't afford to be distracted by bullshit. This is just the first phase of my plan. I may want to try some broadcasting next, maybe work as a foreign correspondent for a major daily."

She says, "After all these years, Jack, you still don't talk like a Negro reporter."

I shrug. "I was never called that until I went to school in the States. If anything, I've always been *Noir Canadien, Caribbean Canadian* and more accurately, *Afro Canadian*. Like many of us in Nova Scotia, two generations separate me from my one Caribbean ancestor, and he just passed through Jamaica briefly in bondage before escaping."

"Funny thing is, I grew up referring to colored people from the States as *Americans*. But now I know that *one drop* is all that's needed— French and Cree blood notwithstanding. Besides, while I have obvious features for anyone who bothers to look, my brothers have a lot more. I don't have a choice and wouldn't have it any other way."

She is insistent. "But you've not mentioned segregation once. I don't hear any protest from you—no commitment to victory abroad and victory at home. You know, the *Double V*. I can't wrap my mind around that. Hopefully, there's more of old Papa Joe in you than you know."

I respond, "I and my brothers have experienced plenty. They just have a different brand of it in Canada. Even as a few things change, my grandmother made us promise to leave. Besides, it would be disingenuous for me to carry that banner in the States. I've witnessed it but only rarely experienced it. I feel strange, even phony, talking about it."

I am relieved that I must look straight ahead to negotiate this stretch of road. I am afraid my face may show how absurd her criticism of me sounds, coming from a woman who is passing for white.

Chapter 13

. . . .

Equestrian

I can almost feel Rachel's eyes piercing the side of my face. I decide to wait silently for her to explain the ruse I can plainly see. If she does not, I will deposit her at her hotel in Algiers and find a place to eat and take a nap in the jeep before getting back on the road tomorrow morning.

Several minutes pass before she speaks again. "So, I guess it's my turn. I've been in Oran training hospital evacuation teams for duty, I'm guessing, in Sicily. I can't imagine going back to Casablanca now when nurses are shipping out. Has your sleuthing revealed anything about that?"

After three months of open discussions in Oran, I still resist telling her what every correspondent there has concluded. The Allies have cleaned up the port of Oran and established new ports at Phillipville and Bizerte. After Sicily is secure, General Clark and the new Fifth Army will sail from these ports to conduct an amphibious landing on the Italian mainland. My hope is that Tom can figure out a way to get Rachel reassigned to the operation.

The activity easily visible out on the Mediterranean should offer her clues, and the heavy traffic on the road does nothing to belie the theory. Still I merely say, "Now even if I knew where you were going, I couldn't tell a nurse on her way to a hotbed of espionage like Algiers."

As we ride along further in silence, we alternatingly cruise and creep along with a seemingly endless line of vehicles. On most stretches of the road, we can make out sea traffic on the Mediterranean and the land that is home to a population still recovering from the devastations of occupation, invasion, liberation and reoccupation.

She reaches over and puts her hand on mine, holding it firmly as I fumble with the stubborn gearshift. When we stop alongside a truck going in the opposite direction, I wonder if she can feel the vitriol in the eyes of the driver—only one of several who have brazenly conducted close inspections of us today. She finally acknowledges Owen. "So, you've kept in touch with my uncle?"

I had expected to hear this question in Casablanca. I share with her all the things Owen has done for me since I first walked into his college lecture hall, since our time together there until the day she left without a word. I also decide to tell her he asked me to look her up.

Her voice becomes halting. "Then he still trusts you. You were in my line that day because he asked you to help me. That's why you stood behind a whole platoon instead of moving to a shorter line." She tells me about her life in New Orleans. After nursing school, she worked in various hospitals around the city, including one that provides 21 days of hospitalization a year to local Negro families for a penny a day.

"Jack, my father was in the 10th Cavalry. He had a quiet relationship with my mother in California while his troop served as rangers in the Yosemite Forest. Soon afterward, they redeployed to Mexico where he eventually became KIA chasing Pancho Villa. Several months before I was born, my mother moved to New Orleans, uncertain about how my complexion would turn out, and how people out west might respond to me."

As she imparts the information, she sighs with relief as though dropping a heavy bag. "I've been told my uncle always sent money, always seemed to have money. He even showed up for a few landmark events."

Her story is interesting, but I am far more interested in hearing about her current, dangerous ruse. Insidious racial discrimination is, by far, the worst of all the American traditions exported overseas by a segregated military. When people malign my mixed heritage, their words are of little consequence to me. I am a person of color, a Canadian-American reporter working for a Negro publisher.

On the other hand, the truth about Rachel's ethnicity could end her military service. Even in the best scenario, the Army would transfer her to Liberia, Tuskegee or Camp Huachuca. In the worst, she could be court martialed, her outstanding service record redacted.

She begins slowly, "I know you've wanted an explanation since you saw me in Morocco. Well, you're not the only one. You won't believe it but a man from that Klan rally 10 years ago has resurfaced over here. He's at the hospital in Casablanca. First, he criticized *my careless approach to segregating Negro blood*. Then one day he suddenly said he remembered me. Now, he says he remembers you too. He must have seen you at the hospital."

Stalled in a traffic jam, I fumble, white knuckled, with the stubborn clutch, and tell her that, "He approached me on the train to Oujda."

"Oh no, Jack."

"Oh yes, he rode just far enough to taunt me." Then, I must ask, "So, you don't know what he wants from you?"

Rachel lowers her head and answers softly, "No, Jack, I don't. But I think he is determined to hurt me any way he can."

Disgusted, I continue, "Hardly a day passes that I don't replay that night in my mind. I remember pulling up in my old car. Two men had already tied you both up and put Serge's neck in a noose. They left their loaded guns unattended. After I picked one up, I couldn't believe the way they just kept walking toward me."

"You had to make up your mind in an instant, Jack. They were going to overpower you, hang your brother and *take turns with me*." She averts her eyes when she speaks words she has probably never said before.

I shout, "I would have died before I ever allowed that to happen. How could I live with myself after that? How could I explain it to Owen? I've never understood why they doubted my resolve. I had a gun in my hand."

She says, "Maybe because they were drunk, I don't know. No offense, but under the influence, maybe they thought you were one of them, and thus were confident you'd hesitate before pulling the trigger."

I need to tell her about the lieutenant's assertion on the train. "You won't believe this, but Matthews maintains that the men were only going to scare you."

We drive in silence for another dozen miles. When the traffic stops again, Rachel looks both vulnerable and relieved. I feel as though I have put down a heavy bag, but have more to say. "Rachel, maybe it's true that I sought you out because Owen asked me, but the truth is I've never stopped thinking about you since our time in Ohio ten years ago. I know I should have told you this in Marrakech." Knowing nothing else to say or do, I lean over to kiss her.

A truck driver behind us has had ample time to assess my racial status, and leans on his horn. "What the hell are you doing boy? Hey boy, did you hear what I said?"

However, Rachel kisses me back, and I decide that the incensed driver can blow until his ears ring. Shortly afterwards, traffic is moving again. He pulls perilously close to the jeep, almost bumping us a few times. However, before he has a chance at real mischief, he turns off and proceeds on his route down another road.

We travel half the distance to Algiers without stopping. With a full gas tank and two extra *jerry cans* in the back, the trip is well within range of the jeep. When we stop briefly for coffee at an aid station outside the coastal town of Tenes, I notice that she is no longer the witty pistol exuding inner strength and confidence. Instead, she shows me a softer, vulnerable side. "Jack, why do you think I'm doing this, this masquerade?"

Relieved that we are finally on this subject, I voice the most positive assumption I can make. "You don't want to hand out quinine pills—or wrap bandages for prisoners of war. I get that."

Smiling now, she asks, "By the way, what made you think you could kiss me in front of all that stalled traffic? You could get into big trouble *kissing a white girl.* You could be killed and nothing would ever happen to anyone."

I look straight ahead again, showing no indication that I find humor in her words. Instead, I ask, "Do I need to apologize?"

She smiles and ignores my question. "Jack, you think I'm joking, don't you? I'm serious. Be careful. I needed to talk to somebody, but I need you to know I'm not *just trying to pass.* I joined the Army with two close friends, both white. No one bothered to ask and one friend referred to me as her *cousin.* They weren't taking any colored nurses, and they still aren't. We wanted to stick together for as long as we could."

I try to guess the rest of the story. "Now your silence has become the lie." Though it has no relevance, I hear myself clumsily ask an invasive question. "So, does this mean you've been involved with white men, officers, doctors?"

She feigns annoyance, and answers bluntly, "Jack, maybe you shouldn't ask for answers you don't want to hear."

When I say no more on the subject, she continues. "*Anyway,* next thing, I'm assisting surgeons, some of them gifted, working on every cubic centimeter of the human body. I've sewn together the slashed bodies of teenagers and waded through puddles of their blood on dirt floors. If I can get through this, everything else will be easy. After the war, I'll go to medical school, help my people, and raise my colored kids with my colored husband. You know what else, Jack?"

"What?"

Her tone is that of a conspirator. "There's a whole lot more of this going on than the Army knows."

I try to assure her, "No, Rachel, the Army knows. They can't just start rooting out people. Where would it end? Ted Lomax said it best in a famous editorial when he asked *how the melting pot could call the kettle black.* But when the Army gets a formal accusation, they probably investigate thoroughly."

We drive in silence again for a long stretch of road. I decide to try putting insanity aside, and address something that has begun to concern me. "I know that both you and Serge have always expressed concern about my lack of activism. Ron Maxwell says I hide behind a cover of journalistic integrity."

"And what do you say to that?"

"Just what I have already told you about the way I feel. Anyway, censorship limits the way I can tell the story. Then, there's my very recent citizenship. Some reporters try to use code words, but that's just a *cat and mouse* game—mostly mouse. I can say that *MPs arrested ten Negroes* but I can't say they arrested them without proof or probable cause."

She is thoughtful for a moment before saying, "I can't comment on your issues with your brother. I must admit to being impressed with Negro reporters who're committed to change. I look up to those who fight with censors, instead of avoiding confrontation. What our boys do over here will bring changes, and returning colored soldiers will look at things differently. Jack, for them, I think you have to stand for something."

I know she is waiting for an answer I do not have. Instead, I implicate others. "Would it surprise you to know that neither Walter Lomax nor your Uncle Owen want me to stand for anything but the flag?" I regret saying it and caution her, "You will have to keep being very careful Rachel, pay close attention to everyone around you."

Traffic slows to a crawl as we pass through Charchell and enter the outskirts of Algiers. She continues, "Matthews constantly makes his presence known. It might be just my imagination or coincidence, but lately, the chief nurse has twice noted her disdain for colored nurses treating white soldiers. I'm under enough pressure without dealing with paranoia. Do you think my uncle could really do anything to help?"

My mind is racing. "Owen has become a master at pushing buttons and pulling levers with an invisible hand. Do you think a transfer will fix the problem? You can't just keep running away from it."

Although I have proposed nothing, she responds to something in my voice that gives her the hope she expresses next. "I'm certain I'll only need to run once. The old bat is only afraid of the fallout from failing to act herself. If a transfer comes, she'll concur because I'll no longer be her problem, or potential problem, since there's only innuendo."

I am confident that Tom would assist with a transfer, particularly a request made by both Owen and me. However, to ensure he has plausible deniability, I could never tell him everything there is to know. As I plot a strategy in my mind, I inflate my own involvement. "Well, just let me try when I get back. When you settle in tonight, write down the names of your chief nurse and everyone in her chain of command."

She nods as if presented with a set of marching orders. I feel the need to stop talking before I promise more than anyone can deliver. Convinced that Owen will do everything within his power to protect Rachel, I try to lighten the mood. "So then, a girl scout has traveled alone to the city of intrigue and mystery—with spies rumored to be everywhere?"

She is upbeat and confident again. "Jack, I'm not a girl scout, and I'm not here alone. I'm here with you. I can wait until tomorrow to rendezvous with *my white cousins*. They refused to leave North Africa without a weekend in Algiers."

We stop abruptly, caught in a traffic jam that shows no signs of abating. We take a chance and turn down a narrow corridor that resembles an alley more so than a street. When that ostensible detour quickly becomes a bottleneck, we find ourselves stalled directly in front of a stable. We both look over to investigate a melee inside.

A stallion is out of control, snorting and filling the air with protests. The proprietor has tethered the powerful horse to a metal hook mounted on a stable wall. The wall is in danger of collapse. Speaking above the noise, a nearby voice explains, to no one in particular, that the stallion has not been fully broken.

A mature mare seems intrigued by the disturbance, but stands quietly in the next stall. With the benefit of two summers working at my Uncle Charles' stables in Quebec Provence, I understand that she is in estrus, calmly orchestrating the entire disturbance in ways that human senses will never evolve to detect.

To avoid certain destruction to his property, the proprietor frees the stallion, allowing the beast to clomp over and sniff the mare. I hear Rachel gasp as the giant beast rises on two legs, revealing his massive phallus. She stares wide-eyed as the horse's appendage continues to expand and independently probe for the correct point of entry. She grabs my hand tightly as he repositions himself and successfully mounts the mare.

That is where my relevant knowledge ends. I remember Uncle Charles patiently guiding young male horses into position, allowing them to acclimate themselves, and quickly tugging on the line to pull them back shortly thereafter. However, this beast requires no assistance as he impales the mare repeatedly, bludgeoning deep inside her with the instrument of his passion. The young female bares her teeth and snorts rapidly from deep within. Most surprisingly, the stallion literally bucks for what should be, for a horse, an unsustainable period.

Rachel unconsciously pulls my hand off the gearshift and squeezes it to the point of inflicting minor pain. I initially dismiss the notion that he could, but the stallion appears to be bucking at a steady, almost rhythmic cadence.

Sensing our fascination, the voice explains, this time in French, "That's how they do it after years in the wild." After a massive orgasm produces several full-body shudders, he deposits a voluminous discharge both inside the mare and all over her stall. With his personality significantly adjusted, the stallion dismounts and backs away. Like a passing thunderstorm, as suddenly as the chaos erupted, peace returns to the stable.

Largely because of heavy traffic on the road, our trip to Algiers has taken the better part of the day. When we finally arrive at the Aletti Hotel near the seashore, she asks me where I have arranged to stay. I give her the name of the only hotel in Algiers I know.

She laughs. "Jack, the *Kasbah* is off limits." She steps out of the jeep with all three bags, hers and mine, in tow. "This jeep is entrusted in your care, soldier. You need to find a safe place to leave it or the serial number will be the only thing left of it by tomorrow."

I try to temper my excitement, asking, "I just hope they have somewhere a soldier can grab a meal and a nap."

She smiles at my transparent quest for confirmation. "I'll see if there's someone inside who'll show you where to park. Tip generously. Come up to my room and I'll show you where to get some food and sleep, if that's really all you drove 200 miles to do."

After she disappears into the hotel, an attendant emerges and directs me to a nearby garage. Satisfied with his and other assurances that I will still have a jeep tomorrow, I tip as instructed. I make my way back to the lobby of the Aletti Hotel. I bound up the stairway clearing two steps at a time. A bellman moves quickly to avoid a collision. Knowingly, he directs me. "Her room is right there, Messier."

When I walk in, I latch the door behind me. The scents of the old city fill the air with spices, oils and incense, punctuated by the aromas of seasoned meats, breads, fruits and vegetables. In the dim light, I can make out Rachel's opened bags and the uniform she has already removed.

A sheer linen robe hangs on the bedpost. The sound of splashing water draws my attention to an alcove where I see Rachel stepping out of a tub. I gawk at her hourglass figure and powerful legs, chiseled by the hard work of lifesaving and endless hours on her feet. When she bends over, the motion juts out her round posterior. I inhale forcefully and audibly.

As she turns to investigate the sound, her tone is teasing and catty. "I thought I'd be finished before you got back here. Did you run back all the way?"

Suddenly, I feel dizzy, my breathing labored. Without comment, I sit down to collect myself, eat a bit of lamb, bread and dates, and pour a glass of wine. I cannot take my eyes off her naked form as she slips into the robe and cinches it with one hand. Her damp breasts and hips strain against the thin fabric, forming wet spots. She is no longer the bashful girl I once knew in Ohio.

She walks toward me, projecting sensuality with naturally provocative strides. After taking a long swallow from my glass, she bends down to kiss me, quenching my parched lips and tongue with the sweet taste of the Algerian red. The motion allows her robe to become undone and her breasts push through. She is unfazed.

"Thanks Jack, I needed this." She walks back toward the bed with my glass, pulling the garment taught again. I sit hypnotized by the rocking motion of her protruding derriere—its mounds alternately popping back against the dampened mold formed in the seat of her robe.

Suddenly feeling a close kinship to my equine acquaintance recuperating back at the stable, I struggle to resist a primal urge to snatch up the flimsy material and take her from behind. Instead, I pretend to be a human being socialized to feign restraint.

I search for something clever to say. I have nothing. When I open my mouth, my voice is coarse, almost foreign. "So, what happened to that girl scout I knew in Ohio?"

She chuckles and shakes her head at my clumsy attempt to appear relaxed. Sitting down on the edge of the bed, she crosses her legs and takes a few more sips of wine. I quickly remove my uniform. Aware of the dust that I have collected, I walk over, step into her tub of water and, standing, use her bar of soap to scrub my body from head to toe.

When I finish, I hear Rachel stand up and I feel a refreshing basin of clean water poured over my head. The residue from a day on the road rinses away as fine grains of sand collect around my feat. Unable to stay in the tub a second longer, I step out as she scrambles to dry me off.

As she walks back toward the bed, I watch her robe fall from her shoulders until just the seat of the garment clings stubbornly to her behind. There the damp robe pauses, suspended for a few seconds as though pasted to her bottom. When she raises the glass of wine to her lips once more, the last of the material reluctantly peels off and falls to the floor.

The sequence triggers something latent, primal and spiritual deep in the recesses of my psyche. I cannot speak. This very familiar woman now seems so unfamiliar, so desirable in this ancient world. The ten years since we first shared our youthful passions seems like a lifetime, a world away from the world we now occupy. I had assumed incorrectly that we would make love slowly and tenderly, newly reunited after so many years apart.

She crawls across the bed on her knees, pausing to look back at me. The steel frame squeals softly beneath her. When I follow her, I inadvertently step on the wet spot in the seat of her discarded robe. In an instant, the sensation travels from my toes to the back of my skull.

My mind is back in the alley, where it remains. She never turns to face me until she pushes me off and straddles me, with impressive dexterity, like a jockey. Obediently, I reach up to take hold of her outstretched hands. Each powerful lunge is more jolting than the previous thrust until, after an explosive moment, we both cry out in an undecipherable mix of English, broken French and something that sounds vaguely Algonquin.

Like the powerful storms that occasionally hug the American coastline all the way up to Nova Scotia, as suddenly as the chaos began, peace returns to the room.

Chapter 14

· ·

Tom Nightwalker James

Tom has detained me after a press briefing at Fifth Army Headquarters. The commanding general has just wrapped up his daily briefing on North Africa and the Allied campaign in Sicily.

"Sir, Jack studied journalism under Owen Todd. You may remember seeing Owen when you worked at the War Department in Washington. I believe you were then serving as an aid to the Assistant Secretary of War." Tom struggles to make a connection between the general, Owen and me. I assume he needs to explain to his commanding general why, after he has conducted his standard briefing with two dozen journalists, he remains behind to speak privately with a reporter from a Negro weekly newspaper.

The general quickly looks me over and glances toward a colonel standing nearby before responding to Tom. "Now that you say that Tom, I think I do remember Todd. Seeing a Negro around there was rare back then."

I resist the urge to add that seeing a Negro working in the War Department surely remains a rare occurrence. The general's voice has the bark of a combat veteran, belying his obvious education and socialization. His towering presence commands compliance and conflicts with my image of him climbing out the hatch of a submarine at night in the Mediterranean. According to the story, which has become legend, he rowed ashore in a raft at night to a secret meeting in preparation for the invasion of North Africa. To leverage the outcome he sought, he had stuffed his pockets with a perilously heavy cache of silver coins.

The colonel speaks up. "If I'm not mistaken, Todd runs some administrative errands at the Pentagon now, does he not?"

Tom rolls his eyes at hearing the senior officer trivialize Owen's job, but elects not to correct him. Instead, he turns back to the general and makes the introduction. "Well, sir, Jack Savoy is my old college roommate and Owen's favorite student of all time."

While I am impressed with the general's accomplishments as Eisenhower's trusted planner, I did not ask for an exclusive interview. His briefings have been sufficient for my purposes, given my doubts that a personal interview would produce a quotation, on the record, of interest to Ted.

I already write articles about the Fifth Army Commander in a way that suggests we have been meeting alone. Tom has assumed incorrectly that I look forward to this moment, and has arranged for a few minutes of impromptu conversation just inside the briefing room doorway.

Since the May 1943 surrender of German forces in North Africa, members of the press corps have been less interested in the commander. Even if, as the rumors suggest, he is *next in line* for a landing in Italy, the news spotlight remains on Generals Patton, Bradley and Montgomery, and on the conclusion of their campaign to liberate Sicily.

I have the general's background information, shared by a press aid prior to the earlier briefing. *Promoted to brigadier and named Assistant Chief of Staff under General Marshall. A year later, he was a corps commander, and currently, commander of allied forces in North Africa. Seven months after the victory at El Alamein and three months after the Axis surrender at Tunisia, he has welded together an impressive Army from units of active Army, National Guard and Army Reserve.*

He tries to offer something exclusively to me. "I didn't say this in the briefing, but here's a quote from Ike, on the record. Ike said *any soldier who goes through Fifth Army training is prepared for actual battle.* He referred to our training regimen as *comprehensive, thorough and efficient.*" My pencil races across the pages to get down the exact quote, but I know Ted Lomax will not be impressed absent a quote on the record about the performance of Negro troops in the successful Africa campaign.

I am surprised when the general sounds defensive. "I've helped to plan every operation so far, while relegated to entertaining sultans, potentates and pashas—prime ministers, expatriates and prima donnas." The colonel clears his throat.

I doubt either of them knows much about individual Negro units, and Tom may admonish me later for asking. However, I reason that they should expect a reporter for a Negro newspaper to ask questions about segregated Negro military units. I wait to see if the general provides the opening I need.

It occurs immediately. "So, Mr. Savoy, why don't you tell me something about your own background? Yes, tell me how you happen to be right here right now."

I spend a few minutes talking and answering a few questions before I decide to ask mine. "As you know, I represent a newspaper with a predominantly Negro circulation." I peripherally detect the colonel flinch. "I was wondering if you would comment, for the record, on the role that Negro troops have played in the victory in North Africa as well as in Sicily, and your expectations for them in the foreseeable future."

The general shoots the colonel a sidelong glance, which the colonel reenacts for Tom. Before he can respond, the colonel chimes in. "I'll start with what we'll say on the record. I believe the performance of colored soldiers in the Armed Forces Services Corps has been exceptional, but not appropriately documented in the Negro press.

"Between our efforts to take Bizerte and the Germans' efforts to limit our use of the port, the place was a wasteland. Sunken ships were sticking up out of the water everywhere and sections of the city were in ruins. Geographically, with its port and nearby docks, rail and highway capacity, Bizerte was our dart aimed right at Sicily. Harassed until the surrender of the Afrika Corps, Army support personnel helped restore and repair to facilitate loading and offloading cargo. They facilitated our progress in Sicily."

Seeing that I have written down nothing, he clears his throat again. "We're told that the squadron of Tuskegee flyers has been an asset to the 33rd Fighter Group—including some involvement in the fighting that cleared sea-lanes to Sicily. However, you might also pay more attention to Negro artillery units. Major James can direct you to those still in North Africa. I also wonder if you're familiar with the

45th Infantry Division. No? Well, we trained them from a guard unit and they've been in Sicily since July with Patton and Bradley."

When he pauses to take a breath, the general decides to speak, choosing his next words carefully—but also answering a question I have not asked. "What I think about the Army's policy of following established civilian protocols on segregation is of no relevance since that's in the Chief of Staff's wheelhouse.

"But I do fully expect a substantial number of Negro soldiers to be thrown into the fight—probably sooner than you might imagine. But right now, if you'll excuse me, I have to get a hundred thousand men ready for battle—wherever that battle will be fought." His words concur with a rumor that Fifth Army will get the Negro combat infantry division training in Arizona.

Later, Tom and I sit in his office, situated at the corner of a large bay area. Hanging above us on his wall is a wooden plaque depicting a golden thunderbird emblazoned on a red background. I sit facing his small desk, ready to remind him that there were no boundaries established for my chat with the general. While there is no reason for Tom to feel blindsided by my question, I am sensitive to his desire to shield his boss from uncomfortable surprises.

Since I arrived here from Casablanca, Tom has been supportive, crossing out only obvious compromising lines in my copy, introducing me to unit commanders and providing a jeep for my exclusive use. With his help, I have been able to file copy on Negro units and technicians from Morocco to Egypt, including a week embedded with the Tuskegee Airmen at Fardjouna. Tom also helped me get to El Guettar for the buildup to the German surrender of North Africa.

Tom has not changed much since we were in college. Our backgrounds are similar—including our early involvement in politics with former Vice President Charles Curtis. Even after we ran errands for the 1932 campaign, Tom and I were never close—not even as college roommates. We are both very private people but Tom's personality often trends toward introversion—an unlikely trait for a public relations officer. "Don't worry about your question, Jack. I would've been surprised—maybe even disappointed—if you hadn't asked it. By the way, I thought your piece on those Senegalese soldiers in Algeria was superb. How did you find them?"

"I heard them speaking French in a bar. We hit it off immediately." I become sanguine. "The *Tirailleurs*, as they're called, expect to join other Senegalese troops fighting for the liberation of France soon. Amazing, Africans giving their lives to save the colonial custodians of their homeland's wealth."

Tom clears his throat, signaling that I have been talking too loudly on a delicate subject. He changes gears for both of us, and spends a few minutes expanding on the colonel's references to the performance of the Tuskegee pilots, which he says are rooted in the mixed reviews they receive. "But now they've settled in, helped pave the way for the landings in Sicily, and bombed the hell out of enemy positions in Palermo. Even the most grudging descriptions of their performance now come in rated above satisfactory."

Tom knows that I have transmitted to Ted the most positive nonspecific accounts possible of their success in the shipping lanes and strafing ground positions on enemy-held islands, but the Palermo story will be new.

"By the way, Jack, they received a Distinguished Unit Citation for the missions over Sicily and a personal visit from Ike. I'll make sure you get the details. But you know they will probably move to Sicily shortly, and two other colored papers stay with them almost constantly."

My decision not to follow Seventh Army was a difficult one to make. My connections to Owen, Rachel and the value of Tom's commitment and support made the difference. "I understand why they would be moved to the new forward bases in Sicily, but I'll miss having them around."

Since my first encounter with the 99th Fighter Squadron at the Casablanca train depot, Colonel Davis has been true to his word. I have resisted the urge to write larger than life descriptions of them and accounts of their exploits. He has granted me several interviews, shared insights and identified the pilots with the most intriguing stories on any given day.

I turn to a more sensitive subject. "Tom, is it too soon to ask you about what's going on with Rachel's transfer? You have to admit her story is compelling."

He says, "It's impressive, but not just her record. I'm impressed with what I've learned about the Nursing Corps. I hadn't really appreciated the danger they face. However, I'm a little disappointed that you didn't trust me with *all of the pertinent information.*"

I look for cover. "It wasn't really my place to share too much of that."

However, Tom is insistent. "No, Jack, it *was your place* to tell me. I don't know why Owen thought I knew everything and I still don't know. Do you understand? No one will ever connect me to this. Oh, and for God's sake, could you two be a little more discreet? This sun is really roasting you. I hope you two have a good cover story."

Despite our long association, I am surprised to hear Tom take such license. However, given his exposure, I must be honest with him. "Actually, I tell people we *met in college while her father taught.* Even with that *platonic friendship*, we've been discreet, rarely ever seen in public. I understand that one time may be too many for some of your informants. But the man they've seen her with is actually Ron Maxwell."

Suggesting that Tom works with informants amounts to a cheap shot, but I take the license to do so, because he has been more than a little condescending. Perhaps because he knows that, he allows a cooling moment before continuing in a whisper. "Jack, the Army's position on segregation has left us with only a few colored nurses with bona fide field experience. I was thinking that, at some point, the Tuskegee boys will grow into a whole fighter group, but don't expect that to happen quickly. I'm not sure why."

"Well, I'd lose a lot of sleep thinking about her taking care of all those good-looking pilots." I smile but Tom's expression remains unchanged.

He says, "As the general alluded, we may need her ourselves soon enough. Rachel will go with our nurses when we leave here. I think we'll soon have a permanent place for her—where no one will give a damn—and she'll get all the battlefield action she can handle. Ron also may be going with us."

I do not react to that distasteful revelation. Tom reminds me to submit my drafts to him for censorship prior to transmitting or mailing them to Ted. "We get quite a bundle from you, Jack. I hope I'm getting them all." He taps the smoldering contents of his odd-looking pipe into an ashtray already overflowing.

When I choose silence over reacting to his implication, he continues, "Frankly, I was glad to see so many correspondents go to Sicily.

When I read some of the stuff these assholes write about the general, I want to go back under the War Powers Act. But Ike wants transparency and an *unbridled press corp.*"

To that, I respond, "Tom, you know the *Record* isn't trying to impact military careers—in news, features or editorials. You don't get anything from me other than stories about the war."

I stare into his eyes without speaking. He confides, "Just between you and me, I wished Maxwell had gone to Sicily. Things are about to get serious and we need to be running a tight ship." He rises to his feet behind his cluttered little desk and I stand, grateful to get away. "By the way, I have some mail for you."

Most of it is from Lomax Publishing. I am surprised to see a letter from Anne and a large envelope from Owen, which I open first. Owen's envelope contains, without explanation, a two-month-old copy of the *Detroit Free Press.*

I walk away scanning the newspaper and freeze in midstride. The edition reports a June 1943 race riot in Detroit sparked by tension over Negroes performing war industry jobs. There is a front-page photograph of a young man struggling to resist as an angry mob drags him from a bus. Although the man is unidentified, he is unmistakably my brother, Serge.

"Are you alright Jack?"

Chapter 15

· ·

Salerno

"**D**ammit, fire the big guns!"

Several correspondents swear repeatedly, afraid that Allied commanders might still believe that the invasion has been a surprise. Even the tidbits of intelligence we can gather aboard ship at three o'clock in the morning suggest otherwise. Most significantly, we have heard that the German defenders are not in disarray over Italy's unexpected surrender. They are not panicking over our arrival.

Even without weapons, in full combat gear, our group of civilian, Navy and Army war correspondents are barely distinguishable from the men in helmets packing into assault boats. Scuttlebutt continuously circulates among us. Under this three-quarter moon in the predawn hours, the entire amphibious invasion force could be vulnerable to entrenched German defenses.

When I take a turn peering into the darkness through powerful naval binoculars, I see nothing recognizable. Sidney Harris, a reporter for the *Cincinnati Free Press*, passes on reports of land-based German artillery trained on the beach, but no orders for naval guns to dislodge them.

Although he is careful to classify his information as rumor, Sid adds, "German trucks are ferrying ammunition along a road that parallels the beach and connects their artillery positions. If the Navy doesn't open up soon, the grunts will have to shoehorn them out of there. That diversionary task force fooled no one. It hasn't drawn a single popgun away from Salerno."

With less than an hour of darkness remaining, the order comes to launch the assault. As a group, we strain our eyes from the deck of the *USS Ancon* to watch minesweepers create sea-lanes for landing craft to follow. When the assault teams take off for the beach, Tom begins a running monologue on the action he expects to unfold ashore.

"The 45th Infantry Division will assault the center and make its way up along the river. The 36th Infantry will hit several objectives from the south, and the Brits and Rangers will hit the north end and drive toward Naples."

I watch the landing craft until they are out of sight, and through the pre-dawn haze, see an entire stretch of beach erupt from sustained explosions and automatic weapons fire. Finally, I hear the roar of naval guns followed by flashes from distant explosions, we hope are on the German positions beyond the beaches. As night gives way to day, fighter pilots begin their lethal dances in the sky.

We stay close to the command center, listening for clues about the situation on the beach. As dawn settles, waves of young men spring from landing craft and sprint across the sand through lethal horizontal storms of bullets and shrapnel. We hear that they are pressing the attack, seizing patch after patch of real estate grudgingly conceded by determined and entrenched defenders.

Thinking of going ashore whenever possible, I prepare myself for adjusting to the noise and vibrations from artillery barrages. In response to my inquiries, several combat veterans have attempted to describe their first reactions to the *flashes of blinding lightening, quakes that rattle your bones and cracks of thunder that seem to explode inside your head.*

"Maybe we should have persuaded more Italians to stay at their posts," mumbles one navy officer hurrying past us. "They've moved a bunch of fanatics—supported by fixed artillery and armor—into the positions vacated by the Italians. They're probably some of the same Nazis who escaped from Sicily."

As the troops quickly expend the ammunition, they carry ashore, I get my first glimpse of the amphibious trucks, or *Ducks,* in action. Tom explains, "The army hopes these vehicles will form a lifeline between *assault* troops and supply ships at sea. The Ducks use rear-mounted propellers to motor through the water, and then convert to six-wheel-drive chassis to drive on land."

Even as shipboard machine guns hose the sky with lead, German fighters dive for the 30-foot amphibs. Smoke from a small decontamination craft obscures my view to the south as soldiers lay smoke screens to camouflage the 36th Division's assault. Tom informs me that this is the first landing to employ such smokescreens to obstruct the view of enemy fighter pilots.

He shouts, "Tomorrow, that same colored support company will use smoke to conceal a twenty square mile area from enemy bombers. It'll make a good story Jack. It's not been done anywhere else yet."

Walking away, Tom stops and turns smiling broadly. "By the way, Jack, how'd you get that copy on the 45th Infantry Division in Sicily and the Tuskegee flyers clearing their way outside Palermo? I thought it was priceless."

"I got it as a gift from another correspondent from the *Chronicle*. Guess he couldn't use it. I never made a connection between the division's shoulder patch and the red Thunderbird mounted over your desk. So, the 45th includes Indian tribes from all over the Southwest, huh?"

Tom is beaming. "Yeah, they trained with General Clark, landed in Sicily and followed Patton all the way to Messina." I can hear a level of personal pride in Tom's voice I have not heard before.

"So, who else is telling their story Tom? They make up just a fraction of the whole division."

He looks at me for a long moment before answering in a lowered tone of voice. "If no one else does, Major Tom Nightwalker James will tell their story—and there're more Indians in that division than you think. Maybe Souwanas' great-grandson should tell their story."

Over the next few days, I hear reports that the assault is advancing slowly toward its inland objectives, and German panzer divisions are joining the fight. A few correspondents, including an almost gleeful Ron Maxwell, whisper that the mission could fail.

One morning, Tom approaches me with a proposition. "Here's your big chance, Jack. Several correspondents insist on going ashore now that the General has established his HQ. We're going today. Are you up to it? Good, I'll be back to tell you more."

I immediately regret the answer I felt compelled to give, and begin elbowing my way in earnest to take a turn peering through the binoculars. I can make out signs that combat activity is still underway near the beach, including enemy airstrikes. When I find out that both Rob and Sid have declined Tom's invitation, I feel ill.

Later, when I nervously join press officers and correspondents in the landing craft, it takes a Herculean effort to keep down what I have eaten and lock my teeth in place to keep others from hearing them clatter. The disconcerting sounds and smells of warfare are everywhere. Enemy attacks have damaged some Allied ships, including a few that appear to have turned back to African ports.

I do not think that, from the air, we would make for the most opportune target. However, I constantly look toward the sky, hoping that we can make it ashore without drawing attention. I feel more vulnerable than ever before, and the trip to the established beachhead seems interminable.

As our craft churns along the seemingly endless distance to shore, I think of ways to bolster my resolve. First, I suspect that Rachel is already ashore under far worse conditions. Second, I am determined that the memoirs written by these reporters will not refer to the lone Negro correspondent who became paralyzed by fear. Although Ted is not paying me to take this kind of a risk, I doubt that I can legitimately claim later to have witnessed the amphib without making this leg of the journey.

When we approach the beach, I see a few colored troops among those engaged in moving ammunition, supplies and the wounded—but I alone raise my camera to take a few snapshots. I also mentally replay Ted's persistent question: *If they can perform these jobs under fire, why does the Army exclude them from combat?*

I would argue that, like everyone else in this mile-long armada, they are in combat right now. Ted frequently charges the War Department with promoting a *white man's exclusive entitlement to glory*. However, the fact is, during an artillery barrage, race is irrelevant, and men determined to survive depend on one another to do their jobs under lethal conditions.

We step onto the sand amid a long row of landing crafts that have emptied their cargos of men and material. We pass drop-off points where medical collecting companies hide wounded men in plain sight, tucking some of them into the relative safety of hastily dug trenches and makeshift shelters.

Some wounded await transport to hospital ships and their eventual return to duty. Others, for whom the war is over, face lengthy periods of readjusting to disfigurement, retrofitted limbs or rediscovering sanity. There is another drop-off point reserved for those who already have made the ultimate sacrifice.

As we move quickly on foot, someone calls out from the *general's mansion*, a white opulent structure that has somehow survived intense bombing and shelling. "Why doesn't he just paint a bull's eye on his ass already? I'd rather take my chances in a slit trench." I turn to see a face I recognize from Oran but have not yet been able to match with a name.

"I don't believe we've met. I'm Jack Savoy, *Washington Record*."

"Pleased to finally meet you, Jack. Look, they're waiving us toward that house. Maybe we'd better hurry and get up there." We sprint up a long pathway toward the large house but someone redirects us to a bivouac area a few hundred yards away. "It appears the general has already had an epiphany."

"You two okay to share this one?" We respond affirmatively to a member of Tom's press staff and begin settling into a tent within a crowded group of camouflaged canvas shelters that cover a clearing of mud and stones.

I return to his introductory comment. "*Finally meet me?*"

"Yeah, I heard you were following Fifth Army and been meaning to look you up. I believe we have something in common. I'm Ross Carpenter from the *Oakland Chronicle*." He knows his introduction gives me pause, and waits an extended moment to allow me to process the information he has shared.

My halting response is not as free of emotion as I would have preferred. "So, you sent me the copy on the 99th Fighter Squadron and the 45th Infantry in Sicily. Thanks. We ran it. It's good to meet you, Ross. How long have you been overseas?"

He suggests, "Look Jack, let's just deal with the boogeyman in the tent? Okay. I asked for the correspondent's job while you were after it. They wanted a white guy and hired me officially the day you left. No.

No special qualifications, just a few years on a police-beat in Seattle. My first exposure to the military was aboard the transport ship."

I look down at my bag, pretending to look for something. I ask him, "So, did your editor tell you anything about me?" I am embarrassed that my question reveals that I care.

Yet he seems to understand, and answers me without hesitation. "Dave talked about you a lot. Let's see, you were born in Canada, descended from a runaway slave. You squandered the opportunity of a lifetime, and, oh yeah, you're an arrogant bastard working for a colored Communist rag. That about sum you up?"

The unflinching honesty in his dark humor is refreshing. "Sounds just like me."

His humor becomes darker, more personal. "Okay, now how about you and that nurse? Man, what gives? She really isn't white, is she? Don't worry. I won't spill it. I don't give a shit. Is that why you aren't scared someone'll kill your uppity ass?"

For a moment, I wonder whether Ross is crazy, perceptive, or just well informed. I wonder if Tom has been correct about my lack of discretion. I am surprised to hear myself joking about it. "She's as white as snow, but we're just old friends from my college days. So far, the only challenges to our friendship have come from Ron Maxwell one night in a dark alley."

"Is that what happened to him?" During the noise all around us, Ross laughs so loud that a soldier checks to make sure we are okay. After the concerned soldier leaves, Ross warns, "But just so you know, one look at you two together kill's the platonic friendship alibi. You probably should try to think of something else."

After a few weeks, Sgt. Blue and the 480th port battalion joins the others on the expanding beachhead. I write the invasion story broadly with sidebars about the contributions of segregated units. I make sure to give the lion's share of the credit for transforming the beachhead to the Navy Seabees, who have performed the critical and dangerous work of establishing a chain of depots from the beach to successive edges of the expanding battlefield.

I also write an article that hints at a thousand Indians from reserve units in New Mexico, Arizona, Oklahoma and Texas fighting in the infantry divisions committed to the invasion. For security reasons I cannot mention that the 45th includes a battalion of Navajo code talkers, trained in radio communications. Tom clears it immediately, but just as I send it, new developments overshadow everything I have filed.

Between briefings, observations and scuttlebutt I learn that General Clark faces armored counterattacks and a delayed link-up with the British 8th Army from the south. In response, commanders have adjusted in troop deployments, including arranging for the surgical deployment of the US 82nd Airborne Division.

During a trip to the forward area, I witness Clark directing armored and infantry battlefield tactics. Some accuse him of posturing, but I sense that he is a source of inspiration. In time, the Allies turn back the counterattacks and advance further inland and north toward the deep-water port of Naples, the operation's ultimate objective. While I must admit that I fear for my life, I find covering the fighting to be strangely liberating.

As is my job, I select and highlight contributions made by people of color. Yet, I cannot ignore the overwhelming sacrifices and heroism of the combat units. Wave after wave of young Americans have swarmed the beaches and fought their way inland one patch of ground at a time.

Against armor and entrenched artillery, they press forward while death and destruction occur all around them. If, in fact, the brass has improperly reserved the glory for them, they do everything required to earn that privilege. There is not enough space on the pages of America's newspapers and magazines to tell their stories adequately.

During one particularly hectic exchange of artillery fire, I feel a firm hand on my shoulder. Tom has bad news. "Jack, I need to speak with you for a minute." The graveness in Tom's voice sends a chill down my spine. "I don't have all the information yet, but the *Newfoundland* was sunk. She was carrying over a hundred nurses. They were supposed to go ashore once a secure beachhead was established. Rest assured, though, the Navy is certain all were rescued."

I have been wondering how Rachel and the evacuation teams are faring with the deluge of soldiers requiring care. I had assumed that she was ashore. Now strangely I feel relief—within Tom's slim margin for error—that she and the other nurses are safe for the moment either in Africa or aboard another ship sailing back to Salerno.

"I don't think the General really wanted them on the beach yet anyway. But, since we really need them now, he's shipping them back— and I suspect Rachel has been demanding it." The admiration in Tom's voice suggests his quiet investigation has revealed to him that Rachel has been nothing short of a genuine hero.

A week later, I receive a letter from Anne suggesting that Charles and the 761st Tank Battalion are now in harm's way. She also included a cryptic update on Serge. I had always imagined him more of a behind-the-scenes civil rights activist until I saw him trying to escape an angry mob in that photograph. Anne informs me that my headstrong baby brother has enlisted in the Army.

Chapter 16

Naples

"**S**avoy, I seen Stukas fly right past troop bivouacs to shoot up supply dumps. I guess cutting off supply lines can be more bang for the buck—especially since we got nothing to shoot back with."

Blue readily acknowledges that his battalion's casualties are minor compared to the losses incurred by the infantrymen who sprinted across the beaches of Salerno and took the fight inland. However, although his men followed them two weeks later, they too encountered stiff enemy resistance to their efforts to reposition ammunition and supply dumps closer to the front lines.

Blue had moved his men forward into the voids left by the advancing troops, setting up the rudimentary filling stations and makeshift warehouses that are now pit stops along the Allied supply line. Often, the temporary dumps are no more than rows of gasoline barrels and high stacks of boxes and crates, flanked by the narrow slit trenches where support troops seek hasty refuge from air raids and counterattacks.

Since coming ashore, I have been interviewing Negro soldiers participating in various support aspects of the invasion. Now, nearly a month after the initial landings, before I move further north to Naples, I spend a few days getting updates on stories already filed. I wrap up my Salerno invasion stories with the man who has become my friend during the lifetime that has transpired since I boarded the *USS Dorothy*

Dix in Virginia. "But I guess that's the way it is over here, Blue. You get to know people very quickly."

"And you never know how long they'll be around." He always insists on speaking plainly, particularly about the uncertainty of survival as the battlefront advances. "Savoy, you wouldn't believe how nice the ship was that brought us here from Bizerte. It was like an ocean liner compared to that bucket we sailed from Hampton Roads. Man, we had good chow. I guess I know now we were getting fattened up for the kill."

I laugh knowingly, painfully remembering our breakfast shingles. "I won't be seeing you guys for a while. I've decided to move further north to Naples now that they've cleared the surrounding hills and airfields. That's only 50 miles away and, the way things are going, you may be there soon."

"Well, I go where they send me, Savoy. You go wherever you get a damn fool notion to take off to." He taps the shoulder of the man sitting next to him who matches Blue in size and seemingly in personality. "Jack, this is Sergeant Hollis Cooper. This is the man you need to interview—soon to be cited for bravery."

I extend a handshake to Sergeant Cooper and he grasps it enthusiastically. "You mean this is going to be in a Washington newspaper?"

"Well, it'll appear in Washington's largest *colored* newspaper. Yes, I can guarantee that it will. Our readers will appreciate a story about a hero on Salerno Beach."

Looking embarrassed, his eyes drop. "No, Mr. Savoy, I'll tell you whatever you need to know, but the real heroes are the ones who came in with the first waves and met the Panzers head on in the hills.

"Put it in my own words? Sure, landing boats filled with men from the port battalions—white and colored—started pulling up, collecting equipment and setting up supply dumps. Man, whenever I heard Stukas whining down on us, I was afraid to look up. We'd have just a few seconds to dive for cover."

He pauses for reflection. "One day anti-aircraft guns blew a Stuka right out of the sky, but the damned plane crashed right in our work area. In a second, three men were dead and it scared the hell out of all the rest. We'd been under attack before in Africa but then they seemed to be aiming for railroad tracks and fuel depots."

He moves his hands expansively to emphasize his points. "Really, I was just trying to keep the boys moving. I had to yell above the noise, so it looked like I was making things happen—but so did others. I guess I just yelled louder while some big shot was around. It was no different from what we did in Morocco, Algeria, Libya and Tunisia."

His natural inclination to credit others is like that of almost every soldier I have interviewed since coming ashore in Casablanca. "And what happened to your group after you moved inland from the beach?"

He responds, "First, let me say that a lot of our boys want to join up with the combat troops, willing to take it on the chin and fight for every inch. We was also getting strafed and blasted. I heard there was 50 air raids on the beach. I lost count of how many times I got my face full of sand and mud. Me and this old country boy here, we pushed hard to set up a string of dumps from Paestum, to Avellino, to a place they call *Piano* or some such damned thing. Yeah, that's it—Piana di Caiazzod."

He appears to need an emotional breather, so I turn to Blue, who is never at a loss for words and fast becoming a familiar name to my readers. "If you just follow the path of the advancing troops, you see our dumps. Savoy, I can't tell you how many times we had to make something out of nothing—whatever we could find for fencing or walls—sometimes ceilings. The engineers provided a lot of ideas, and all the mechanical help. We worked with scraps of lumber, metal— whatever was lying around."

The 480th Port Battalion commander has established his temporary headquarters in the Temple of Neptune in Paestum, and we sit on wooden crates surrounded by the grand archways and columns of the Ancient Roman-Greco styled structures. The massive granite relic rises imposingly out of the rustic Italian landscape. The structure shows centuries of wear but continue to survive the test of time—and the expanding human capacity to destroy.

As darkness begins to settle, I terminate the interviews. As we say our goodbyes and make plans we hope to keep in Naples, Blue asks for a moment in private. "I was one of the last to leave on a ship out of Bizerte, and you know, the damnedest thing happened." Blue's voice drops to a low whisper. "A hospital orderly told me to report for a shot

I didn't need. When I got up there, a white nurse walked in and started a goddam conversation. Talked to me like we was kin."

Overjoyed to hear the news, I grab the front of his jacket. "What was her name, Blue? What'd she look like?"

"What do you think she looked like? She looked white. I wasn't trying to remember her name. I just wanted to get the hell out of there. I remember she said she was from Louisiana. Anyway, she wanted me to tell you she was okay."

He eyes me carefully at first, and then critically. "Just what in hell do you think you're doing, Savoy? I told you to play the game, not get lost in the game. Don't you remember what happened to those two kids on the Dix? I was scared shitless. You know I don't bring that kind of attention to myself. But when I looked real close, I saw she was really a light-skinned colored gal."

"And so, then what did you think?"

"Then I wondered what the hell both of y'all was up to. She was colored, right?"

"Well, maybe something like that." Other than Tom, Blue is the only person in the European Theater of Operations I would trust with Rachel's secret.

"I'll be a son-of-a-bitch. I don't want to hear no more. By the way, you need to be careful around her. I mean, you look different, Jack. No, it ain't the sun. It runs deeper than that. I think you might be hanging around colored people too much."

"Well, I'm always very impressionable around Americans."

"College boy, you know damned well I don't know what that means."

As the two men walk away, Blue yells back to me over his shoulder. "Remember to keep your head down. You know where to find me in Naples—anywhere there's something for a colored man to lift or load."

A few days later, just before leaving Salerno to travel north to Naples, I find out that Blue died in an air raid. The news leaves me numb. I have learned that, in war, a man can form a close association in an hour, and a lasting friendship can transpire in the span of a day. Though he was essentially a noncombatant, Blue's mission required that he transport the materials essential to combatants, making him and his charges constant valuable targets of interest.

Wearing test versions of the Army's new field jacket we got from Tom, several other reporters and public relations officers join him on the benches of a canvass-covered truck. The Studebakers move along the fifty-mile path of devastation that marks the road to Naples, bouncing over a month's destruction to the landscape from one checkpoint to another. To keep out the damp chill I pull up the collar on my jacket, not yet a general issue item, but clearly the most practical of all the clothing I have received. A heavy sheen on the thick cotton material acts as a barrier to cold, wind and moisture—making it an object of curiosity and deep envy.

Most infantrymen still wear the open collar wool shirts and trousers designed for modest weather conditions. They blouse their pants inside laced canvass or leather leggings called gaiters that cover their lower cut chukka boots. Many have scrounged insulated waistcoats that fasten to keep out some of the wind and chilly air. Few have high collar combat boots like Tom's—or mine.

Tom passes the time by continuing his passion for briefings. "English and American troops moved into Naples on D-Day plus 26 after capturing major rail and highway centers. Three Ranger battalions under British operational command began clearing the way through the Nocera-Pagani Pass as soon as they were ashore on the northernmost end of the 35-mile Salerno battlefront. You guys know what to leave out."

As the truck rattles along, ambulance drivers compete for the right of way. Now that Rachel and the other nurses have returned from Bizerte, I wonder how many carry wounded from her evacuation unit, which must be located within life-saving distance from the casualties of the 36th Infantry Division. The Texans had attacked Salerno at the southern end of the invasion map and secured objectives inland. Casualties had been heavy both during their initial thrust and in their stiff resistance to a determined German armored counterattack.

I had arrived at one of the last known locations of Rachel's evacuation hospital only to find it uprooted and moved closer to the advancing troops. I managed to interview wounded soldiers and medics who witnessed all the nurses' bravery. *Oh yeah, I do remember her. She triaged me, patched me up and left me here with these boys while she moved on up ahead. Man, that girl had nerves of steel, and she's pretty.*

As the trucks pick through checkpoints and traffic, my nostrils fill with the scents of burning wreckage and rubble, and something I have come to recognize as the persistent odor of animals collaterally destroyed in the fighting.

The thin layer of mud over the carnage and the intermittent staccato of rain herald the arrival of the rainy season. A month earlier than anticipated, the sound of rain pellets against the canvas top is just another indication that very little about the Italian campaign is going as planned.

When we stop for relief and coffee at a busy aid station, Tom walks over to speak with me. "Jack, I'm really sorry about your friend in the port battalion. That kind of news never gets any easier to take. I'm also sorry you never got a chance to find Rachel anywhere between Salerno and Foggia. I know this sounds terrible—but that was probably for the better. You know, some hospitals still separate white and colored wounded soldiers. How do you think they'd react to seeing a nurse in a passionate embrace with a colored man—even a Canadian Caribbean in a modified officer's uniform?"

Tom's timing could not be worse. I am having difficulty dealing with the news I just received about Blue, the first friend I have lost in the war. Now, I am increasingly aware of the possibility that Rachel could be dying as we speak. I also am certain that the people in her evacuation hospital are dressed inappropriately for the changing weather. "You're right about one thing, Tom."

"Yeah, I know. You're going to be a smart ass and say that I'm right that it sounds terrible. Don't go forgetting that the Army has brought with it all that is *good and bad* about America. I swear that girl causes you to have terrible lapses in judgment. That's why I've gone out of my way to make sure no one ever finds my fingerprints on this—and I mean nowhere."

Tom insists on believing that he can erase his intervention on Rachel's behalf by saying repeatedly that it never happened. I am in no mood for it today. "So, Tom, since European women fraternize with colored soldiers, are there any public relations strategies for dealing with that? I mean, other than giving white MPs carte blanche to settle disturbances as they see fit?"

He responds, "Yeah, I get it. It's not fair. I prefer to have the locals open two separate clubs. But, of course, there are no colored women to work or frequent the juke-joints."

So, their clubs are called juke-joints? I finish his thought for him. "Running two segregated clubs only solves half the problem."

Tom stands firm. "Would you rather we have race riots? More than once, civilians have found colored soldiers on Sunday mornings, clinging to life. *No one knows* the whereabouts of the perpetrators. You don't really cover colored news though, do you Jack? Come to think of it. We haven't had to censor a single race crime in your news copy. You talk a good game when you feel like it, but sometimes, I just don't know."

After a few miles of silence, Tom wants to explore still another controversy. "Since I've gotten on your bad side today anyway, there was something I wanted to ask you about your buddy Ron Maxwell. By the way, do you know what happened to his face?"

I feign ignorance. "What's wrong with his face?"

"I guess you haven't seen him since we sailed. He's okay, but he took a bit of a beating before he left Oran. My real concern is his article about the performance of the 99th at Salerno. I'm the first to admit that the Tuskegee pilots have done one hell of a job over here, but they weren't flying over Salerno, Jack." I say nothing. "The Advocate ran the story anyway, but as a feature with no byline. This sort of thing's going to leave me no choice but to make him the first Negro reporter to have his credentials pulled." Still, I do not say anything. "Jack, you don't want to talk to him first? Isn't his editor one of Owen's old buddies? Look, I know I don't need anyone's concurrence on this—certainly not Owens or yours. I'm just trying to work with two old friends here."

I still say nothing.

"Well, okay then, case closed."

I prefer to let Tom and Ron work this out between them. Asking me to intervene merely lends credence to Ron's whispering campaign. He has tried to brand me as an instrument of some *War Department public relations campaign to control Negro journalists.* After his public accusation at a bar in Oran, I quietly invited him to join me alone in a dark alley. However, Rachel incorrectly interpreted my moment of indiscretion as a lack of trust in her commitment. It has caused a wrinkle in our relationship that I have not yet ironed out.

After a few more hours of stops and starts, the trucks round a bend and the city of Naples comes into view below. Even from this vantage point, I can see half-sunken ships turned on their sides. The retreating Germans have rendered the port virtually unusable. The damage from bombing and the signs of tactical withdrawal are everywhere, but I can visualize the layout and architecture this jewel once had, wedged beneath the mountains on a curved coastline that opens like a quarter-moon into what was once a tranquil bay.

Before the war, this view must have been breathtaking. Dozens of interlocking slips, docks and piers reach out into the bay like jagged fingers. Narrow waterways transition into streets that crisscross, sectioning off dozens of large clusters of buildings. The ground slopes gently from the sea wall to the outskirts and the high points that wreath the town.

A sentry stops us with a sobering warning. "Y'all need to be very careful down there. Yes sir, it's true that the Germans are gone but they left behind some nasty surprises. Y'all should avoid entering any building that hasn't been cleared for booby traps—even if you see people in them."

He uses his hands for effect. "I need to warn y'all that civilians are everywhere, some just looking for something to eat. It's a horrible way to have to live but otherwise decent women will oblige you for your rations. Conditions have driven some of the men to do much worse.

"The Army is doing what it can, but you won't believe it until you see it up close and personal. The bombing *from both sides* has left some of them with nothing—I mean *nothing*. You can do what you want, but I would stay away from the women, and the girls, until you *learn the lay of the land*—no pun intended, sir."

As our drivers try to find our assigned quarters, we get a tour of the devastation. Along narrow streets, most structures remain intact. Still, many are uninhabitable and even reasonably intact buildings are in high demand. Most have suffered some damage, except for a gem on the water's edge that will serve as Allied Headquarters.

I see people foraging for salvageable materials and sustenance from hollowed out structures. Some welcome us while others appear unsure whether to view this newest occupation force with relief, suspicion or trepidation.

We receive additional warnings that the retreating Germans have destroyed key infrastructure and concealed detonators in death traps for the curious and the unwary. After an armed uprising by conscript laborers, Axis, guerrilla fighters and civilians lay dead, sometimes together, in plain sight.

When we finally arrive at our destination, I carefully make my way through the damaged building that will serve as our hotel. After climbing the last creaky staircase to the place that may be my home for the next few months, I toss my bags on the floor and pass out across an unmade bed.

Chapter 17

. . . .

Ahead of Ourselves

"**J**ack, I want to know exactly what went through your mind the moment you found out that my ship went down off the coast of Salerno."

Rachel's visit to Naples has coincided with a few days of clear skies and enemy fighter inactivity in the bay. Perhaps, lulled into a false sense of security by the absence of air raid warnings, we take a brisk Sunday afternoon walk. Near the tranquil waterfront, we find dozens of others who have also ventured out to enjoy the respite. However, eyes still squint skyward with the sound of any approaching engine and people walk by gingerly.

The deep tan baked into my skin by the North African desert has faded quickly in Naples. For the first time in my life, I find myself monitoring subtle changes in my complexion. It seems insane to feel relief that Rachel and I can stroll together without kneejerk reactions from indignant onlookers. With just a few hours of daylight remaining, and no idea how long she will remain away from her unit without guilt, I nudge her toward the direction of my hotel.

She laughs knowingly at our sudden change in direction, and leans against me. However, I refrain from the public shows of affection Tom has asked me to avoid. "Relax, with that Saharan tan almost gone, no one knows. It's the press corps officer's uniform. That's the attention grabber. You're back to that look of a hopelessly square French Canadian."

I try to add clarity. "Believe me, my restraint is not so much for me as for your own good—and the promise I made to Tom James. There is a terrible war within a war going on in the wake of the Allied occupation of Italy. Some of the Italians embrace everyone. Others view Negroes no differently than the racist soldiers who provoke violent acts against colored guys—just for sport."

Rachel responds, "You haven't seen anything until you visit an army hospital on a Saturday night. Some of the cuts and lacerations are clearly delivered with the intent to kill."

When we reach my hotel and climb the creaking stairways to my room, I am glad to close the door behind us. This is our first time alone since we sailed for Salerno. Memories of that last night in Bizerte two months ago have warmed me as I slogged through the mud of the Italian rainy season.

Those vivid memories of her body next to mine under warm sea breezes and cool bed linen arouse me even now. Yet instead of devouring one another with the usual abandon, Rachel entertains some abstract curiosity that I do not want to indulge or encourage. "You want to know what went through my mind when I heard you might have died. That's kind of a morbid game to play, don't you think?"

"It's not a game, Jack. Think about it." I know she will pout if I refuse to play along but I propose a solution that will not require my active participation, and my suggestion makes her face light up. "Really—you wrote it down where?"

"It's in my journal. No. It's not an official journal. I just write in this one when something is noteworthy for personal reasons. I guess you could say it's to record my feelings about things that affect me."

"Oh, please Jack. You know it's for the book you plan to write. Well it's nice to know I'm noteworthy—and that I can affect you. Where is it? Can I read it? No, I don't want you to read it to me. I want to see it in your own hand. Yes, I promise I won't read anything else."

I retrieve the small binder from deep in my duffle bag and thumb through it until I reach the last several pages of entries. I sit back against the headboard and hold the notebook flat against my chest—using it as a lure. "No. This is nonnegotiable." I have already removed and put away my boots and uniform, leaving on only my army-issued tee shirt and shorts. Eager to read what I have written, Rachel feigns exasperation and indulges me, removing her uniform.

"How's this?" She climbs into bed, sits up next to me and begins deciphering the words I scribbled on a battlefield outside Salerno. My shaky script reminds me of the destruction that was taking place around me. I pull her close and wrap us both in a blanket, thrilled that she has been able to make this short time available for us before she rejoins her evacuation team.

Just watching as she turns over from one side to the other challenges my will to resist exploiting any exposed angle. When she finally finishes, she is on her back looking up at me through cloudy eyes. "I guess I asked for that."

"You insisted on it."

"You could've warned me, Jack. Did you really mean all that? Especially the part you wrote once you knew I was safe. That you weren't going to *let another opportunity slip away to find out if we could reach compromise*—to see if we could both give a little to find some common ground."

"I meant every word of that. I guess everything moves fast in a war zone."

"Well, I don't think we can find common ground without mutual trust and respect. I am really concerned about the fact that you don't trust me." She feigns a pout.

"But I do."

"Sure, you do—just not with Ron. Is it true that you started a fistfight with him in an alley? Is that what you mean when you talk about *the Savoy brothers settling their differences?* I hope you're proud of what you did to his face. Why didn't you just talk to me?"

She sits up and scoots back against the headboard, I do not want to tell her about Ron's allegations against me if she has not heard them. When she places her palm under my chin to raise my head, I reluctantly look into her eyes.

"I'm up here Jack. You know, only people in special relationships are required to make those kinds of compromises. Where I come from, people are very serious about relationships. So, you need to tell me what you're talking about."

"Come on Rachel, you know what I mean. I want to find out if this thing is possible—a dedicated doctor in New Orleans and a foreign correspondent in Paris—with children yet? How does that possibly work?" Even as I ask the question, I stand and step out of my shorts. In the spirit of turnabout, I raise her head to reestablish eye contact.

She laughs and slaps my hand away. "We aren't really going to talk are we?"

"Not just yet. No."

"Jack, I want to ask you to do something before your mind is completely sidetracked. I want you to promise that you will write and publish my story if anything ever happens to me. I want you to have it written and ready to go before hand. Okay Jack?"

"Okay. I promise, though I hope I never publish the story, writing it will be my honor."

Standing beside the bed, I grasp both her ankles and pull her to me, sliding her on her bottom across the mattress. I bend her knees and plant the soles of her feet firmly against my chest. She expresses her desire clearly and without demure. "Now you know It's been a while."

It is approaching midnight when we awaken and sit side by side in the darkness, discussing the obstacles to accomplishing a goal we have not yet defined. Rachel tries to sum up our dilemma. "I guess the real question here is whether I absolutely have to practice in New Orleans and whether you absolutely have to work abroad."

I do not want to decide that yet. "Yes, I think that pretty much sums it up. Think about it some more and we'll talk later about compromise. Right now, it's hard to imagine myself doing anything else, but I have you to consider now."

As I feared, Rachel wants to reach some understanding now. "Well, I won't even be a doctor until years after the war ends, but I can say that it doesn't have to be New Orleans—though anything less than serving people in need is unacceptable. I'd hoped you'd see the need for colored reporters on national news desks—that your time with the *Record* and colored soldiers would affect you more."

I respond too quickly. "Look, just because I don't go on and on about it doesn't mean I don't care."

She does not react to my tone, refusing to be side tracked. "Have you ever thought about starting a paper yourself, even if you had to start out small and move up to weekly editions? You talk about the work you've done on the management side. You clearly like doing it. You could do just as good as, or even better, than anyone doing it now."

"And in the meantime, I live off my wife?" As I use that word for the first time, I feel both our bodies tense. Rachel does not pretend that it is inconsequential.

"We wouldn't be the first to ever do that, Jack." When I do not respond, she fills the empty space. "But there are some things I'll tell you one day about good old Uncle Owen and his stewardship of land held in a trust for my father, Garrett Todd. You're right. There's no reason for us to get too far ahead of ourselves."

We sit in silence for a long time, recognizing that we are already substantially ahead of ourselves. She is more relaxed now and her body seems to fit more snugly, more securely, into mine. "So, Jack, tell me what you were doing at the battlefront outside Salerno—not to mention in the middle of an armored counterattack."

I reluctantly respond, no more anxious to discuss this topic than the other one. "At first, Tom talked me into coming ashore—put me in a position that made his invitation hard to refuse. But after a few days, I guess I got caught up in the drama of it."

She asks, "Did Lomax print your stories? Did he appreciate what you risked to get them? I wouldn't think so."

Her assumptions are correct. "Ted thinks I should spend my time covering the colored pilots, like the guys at the *Journal*. Walt thinks I should be tracking down colored signal corpsmen. What do I think? I'd rather do whatever I want. And I don't want to explain to anyone later how I could come ashore at Salerno and only have stories about smoke pots, stretcher bearers and ammo dumps to show for it." Immediately regretting my choice of words, I add, "As I have written, the work of the Negro support units has been stellar."

She lets me off the hook. "I think the Lomax brothers expected you to sail with the Salerno invasion force, but they know you rushed ashore to further your own career outside of the Negro press. They know, and I know, that you're trying to make sure all your reporting is not exclusively *colored news*. There's nothing wrong with padding your portfolio. Just know that Lomax is nobody's fool."

"Then it's good that we all understand each other." I cannot stop digging the hole I am in even deeper.

The remark sends her on the offensive. "But you do agree that your first responsibility to the *Record* is to write about what Negroes are doing for the war effort—don't you? You covered the amphibious assault. Only secondarily did you target colored units."

I decide not to waste time denying it. "I send Walt and Ted plenty of what I know they want. Soon, General Clark will have my brother and his colored tank battalion and the 92nd Infantry in Italy. Then everyone will be happy."

"You think so?"

"Look, I could be somewhere warm and dry, but instead, I'm up all night scrambling to keep the ground from swallowing me whole, trying to keep explosions from snapping off my chinstrap, listening to metal fragments whizz past my head. I want to write about the men—of any color—who keep moving forward through that shit storm."

"Okay, Okay, Jack. Why not just stay in Naples. Wait until they move all the planes to Foggia. Cover the Tuskegee pilots for a while. You'll live longer." She suddenly looks as though she has misplaced something. "By the way, Jack, you know I meant to say something to you about Sergeant Blue. I'm sorry about what happened to him. I know he meant a lot to you."

I turn and stare at her in the darkness, wondering if my detailed article about him could ever be nearly enough, considering the requirements of censorship. I try redirecting her energy. "And when all those bodies come apart, you put them together again—and send them back. My God, how do you do it day after day, Rachel?"

She answers, "It's what I do, try to keep them alive. Most of all, I have no control over who goes home or who goes right back on the line. I can't bare the pain of repeat customers—boys we heal only to see them back on the table again. Did you read Ron Maxwell's article about that in the *Advocate*?" She stares at me directly as she asks.

I cannot understand why my acceptance of Ron is so important to Rachel despite her many efforts to explain. It is as though he is the eccentric father, I must tolerate to win her affection. I ignore the question. "By the way, I've asked over a hundred white infantrymen if they would care if colored men fought alongside them. I've found that most of the men who've experienced real combat couldn't care less if we take a few live rounds."

She allows me to avoid talking about Ron but shakes her head in a manner that suggests her patience with me is wearing thin. "Look, Jack, I just have a three-day pass. I'm leaving tomorrow. It only gets worse from here. It's a long way up to the top of the boot, busting through one line of defense after another."

"So, I'll see you when?" I ask for an answer I know I cannot have.

"As often as I can get to where you are. Tom is right about you not looking for me, unless you're going to start calling yourself French Canadian again—but the fact that you don't may be the one saving grace that allows me to love you." I hear her words clearly but do not comment. "Didn't you tell me once that your uncles tried to make you abandon your brothers and cross over to the other side?"

I do not answer, refusing to have that conversation. Her voice is pleading. "White nurses, including those thought to be white, are off limits to colored men. There's no greater transgression, punishable by any means at hand—usually with zero consequences. "I don't like this, Rachel. I'm a Negro in love with a Negro. Yet, I sneak around as though I'm crossing the color line in the Deep South. Relationships are hard, but we're dealing with factors that go far above and beyond." When it occurs to me that I have made the ultimate statement of commitment, I say it again, less there be any misunderstanding or equivocation. "I love you Rachel."

Ordinarily my words might have stunned her, but we have already said so much today. "I heard you the first time, Jack, and I'll be glad when you understand that I love you just as much—or more." We embrace tenderly and passionately, well into the night.

Chapter 18

· ·

Anzio

"So, then you're saying once was enough for you?" Vigorously, I nod my head in the affirmative to Tom's rhetorical jousting. "And you're not even going ashore after the beachhead has been established?" I shake my head vigorously. "No? Why Jack? I thought you had become a real trooper after Salerno—a regular Ernie Pyle."

I flinch at Tom's crass reference to the pioneering correspondent, but still respond with all the sarcasm I can muster. "I especially enjoyed the fireworks."

"You're not even wearing combat gear." Tom is aware that Ted Lomax has warned me in the strongest terms not to risk my life again on a *segregated battlefield*. In his last letter, Ted clearly described—within the confines of censorship—the type of coverage he prefers. *"Limit the big picture stuff. Leave that to big budget papers. Until our boys arrive, send colored engineers. Send more on Ducks. Also, hang out with flyboys."*

Ted underscored his instructions by electing not to print a few censored combat stories that did not specifically mention Negro soldiers. With my portfolio in mind, I submitted them, including a few about the 45th Infantry Division, to a Southwestern newspaper under the pseudonym, *Joseph Domingo*.

Walt has suffered a severe stroke, and Ted's power has grown. He insists on coverage of the 99th Fighter Squadron, now based in Foggia. I have learned that three new squadrons will join them soon and a Negro ground-support unit will provide operations, security, and ground support. Despite saturated coverage of the fighter squadron's participation in the air war, Ted insists our readers want more.

I make plans to visit Colonel Davis after I cover one more landing, this time from the safety of a Liberty ship that has been committed to resupply the invasion. However, I have decided not to risk my life on this assault, which everyone suspects will take place somewhere up north. The Army has met yet another formidable German defensive, the *Gustav Line* anchored by a huge abbey at Monte Casino. General Clark plans an end-run somewhere north of that line, maybe near Rome.

Tom continues to chide me about not going ashore after the operation establishes a beachhead. "Well, you're going to miss a hell of a show."

I assure Tom I will have plenty of news copy. "No, I can see all the show I need to see from a supply ship. If I really get crazy, I can climb down the side, jump on the back of a Duck and hitch a ride to the beach. Good luck, if I don't see you back here in Naples—maybe I'll see you in Rome. That's where we're going, right?"

Tom smiles at my attempt to get confirmation of today's destination. "They don't tell me stuff like that. It would be nice to stick it to Kesselring that way. He's been a royal pain in the ass, but I don't think Rome is our objective. By the way, I'm sorry to hear about Walter Lomax suffering a stroke—I've never agreed with his journalism, but I hope he recovers."

Walking out to board my designated Liberty ship, I pick my way through the controlled chaos along the docks that line the harbor. Along the way, I reflect on some of my favorite news stories about the work that engineer, quartermaster and port battalions have accomplished since October. The men, still working in strictly segregated units, have transformed a massive obstruction of mangled steel and concrete into a productive port facility.

I feel certain that my stories about the colored port battalions' role in the aftermath of the battle for Salerno and their work during the Naples' cleanup have appealed to the *Record's* readership. I wrote a story about one sunken vessel lying in the harbor on its port side. The 480th Port Battalion helped to transform the hull into the foundation for a bridge ramp rather than lose the precious time required to have the wreck removed. Now, ships simply moor against its capsized aft and unload their cargo on trucks that drive back and forth from stem to stern across the makeshift ramp to the docks.

Another story describes Sergeant Mingo's recommendation to remove the superstructure of an upright sunken vessel in shallow water and build a wooden platform over its deck to create a new dock—again saving precious time and resources. These and other initiatives have turned challenging obstacles into productive assets.

Mingo's men are now building a causeway and will operate a boat repair yard—skills they have acquired on the job. Recently, however, the battalion reassigned the versatile sergeant to a special transportation company of Ducks. According to scuttlebutt, the company will support the invasion of Southern France. For the first time since they sailed from Hampton Roads, Mingo is away from his friends, and they have lost one of their best leaders.

At the end of the pier, I present my credentials and board the Liberty ship that will take me to a location off the coast away from the amphibious assault. While I know the story will be on the beach with the other correspondents, I have worked through Tom to make this arrangement. However, I discover right away that the Liberty ship carries a volatile cargo of fuel and ammunition the assault teams will need once they are a few hundred yards inland.

After boarding and finding an open mess, I am sipping a cup of remarkably hot coffee when I hear the voice of the man who has slipped into a chair on the opposite side of the table. He begins talking without greeting or introduction.

"I've heard two things about you, son. One is that—like me—you're from Canada. The other is that you're a newspaper reporter." He chews on the end of a cheap cigar and speaks in a rude tone that is purposely void of the respect due the uniform I wear.

"Both are true." I extend a hand to a merchant marine warrant officer whose thick salt-and-pepper beard and mustache give him the appearance of a man born on the high seas and out of place on solid ground. He wears his uniform casually and lacks the spit and polish of most non-combatant officers. "I'm Jack Savoy with the *Washington Record.*"

He disregards my collegial energy. "I'm Chief Warrant Officer John Davis. Isn't that one of those Negro newspapers? Oh, I see. Look, I was just wondering what you expect to observe from a Liberty ship."

Not in the mood for banter, I moderate my tone. "I think this is where I'm going to get a story that'll interest my readers. A lot of action will take place tomorrow around this boat. Taking a beachhead is a waste of time and blood if the boys don't have enough ammunition to hold on to it. They'll be thinking a lot about what's on this ship the second they realize they're down to their last bandoleer."

"You sound like an old hand at this."

"I've never thought of myself that way, but maybe I'm becoming one—strictly from a reporter's perspective. I don't pretend to know what it's like to fight in battle." I struggle to maintain my collegiality in the face of his obstinate tone.

"Yeah, about that—I've been aboard this ship since before there were any Americans in this fight. We've been hauling supplies to ports in England and Russia since 1938—dodging U-boats and fighters all the way."

"I know. I've interviewed several Liberty ship captains and crews. Articles about your work have appeared in newspapers and magazines—broadcasts have aired on radio, spots on newsreels. The whole world knows and appreciates you."

"That all sounds good, Savoy. But we're a little concerned about being a part of an amphibious task force." He apparently sees confusion on my face. "I didn't say I was scared, Savoy, I said I was concerned. We're doing our part. We know what to expect in a convoy—but taking orders from some hotshot admiral in the middle of a fight? I just don't know about that."

I understand but cannot empathize. "Ike had to redefine your mission. He's fighting on multiple fronts in multiple theaters. He needs every swinging dick on point—committed to doing whatever he needs them to do." I regret that my words sound like an admonishment, but I cannot always moderate my tone to avoid ruffling sensibilities.

He adopts a sudden change in posture that immediately confirms my thoughts. "Young man, I don't need anyone like you to tell me that." Perhaps recognizing that I have said nothing that should cause him to lose his composure, he lowers his voice. "I didn't mean it that way. Look, I'm just a little frustrated—okay, very frustrated—with this arrangement. If everyone carried his weight, this whole thing might be over sooner—if you know what I mean."

I smell bullshit astern. "No, I don't. What's that supposed to mean?"

"Well, I mean the colored boys do a good job working on the docks, and I'll admit we do have a few good ones among our crew, but I don't see them doing their share of the fighting."

I pause a moment before responding to this often-repeated misconception. "Like everyone else who joins up—whether white, yellow or red—and I mean everyone, a colored man raises his right hand, steps forward and follows orders from that day on. Like everyone else in the Army, he does what they order him to do. Get my point?"

"Sure Savoy. I get your point. The Army puts them where they can be of some use. I just can't believe what they've done to Naples. When we used to dock there before the war, it was one of the most beautiful cities in the Mediterranean. Now, it's a cesspool of colored men and destitute Italian women, mothers and sisters, who take money for doing unnatural and filthy things with African and colored soldiers. It's disgusting."

He shows no indication that anything I say will change his sad perspective on this volatile issue. Fortunately, an announcement over the intercom interrupts him. The message sounds routine but, apparently, he must leave.

Abruptly, he stands up and grabs his pea coat off the back of a chair and his cap from the tabletop. "We'll be getting underway soon. But I hope we never come back here again." He begins speaking before looking back to see that my chair is now empty. With no interest in hearing his parting patronizing remarks, I have already gotten up, grabbed my life jacket and walked away.

Our ship gets underway later. The armada of liberty ships, tankers, transports, light cruisers, destroyers and minesweepers move off the coast of Naples and into deep water. We set out to the west before heading north. After catching a few hours of sleep later, I awaken to shouts of *Anzio!* That confirms the press corps' best guess.

I gulp down another cup of coffee and walk up on deck, raising my appropriated naval binoculars to peer into the darkness at nothing. Hours go by. With dawn approaching, stories reach us about thousands of troops transported to the shoreline with token resistance. There has been a general reluctance to utter the word *surprise* within the context of a planned military operation. However, there appears to be none of the violence on the beach that I saw in the Bay of Salerno. We also seem to be much further out on the water than I would have anticipated.

Reacting to a tap on my shoulder, I turn to see a familiar face. The merchant marine is wearing a navy pea coat, enjoying a smoke and making log entries. I instinctively reach for my small leather-backed journal. Though still a young man, he appears to have quickly aged somehow since I last saw him aboard the *USS Dorothea Dix*. "I'm glad to see you still alive, Mister Savoy. Nice lifejacket."

"You're Madison, right? I see you're now *Petty Officer Second Class* Madison. So, is that why you aren't still on the *Dix?* It didn't go down did it?"

"I guess only in your nightmares Sir." Remembering my uneasiness during that voyage across the Atlantic, I join in with good natured, self-deprecating laughter.

I tell him, "Quiet now, I thought that was a closely held secret."

He becomes serious. "It was as much a secret as the one about two men in a fist fight going overboard—which I never read about in the newspaper. Did you ever do a story about it? I'm not surprised. Your work is censored isn't it?"

I respond, "The story is alive as long as my notes are intact. I'll write it when I go home."

Madison's voice lowers to a whisper. "Are you ready for something else you probably won't be able to write? This ship's Captain doesn't want to move in closer to load the Ducks. From here, it's too far from the beachhead for Ducks to operate. He doesn't want to take orders from a Navy task force commander without a guarantee that the Navy will assume liability for the ship."

"That sounds very strange, Madison."

He says, "It sounds like the craziest thing I ever heard. I haven't sailed with this man long, but this will be the last time." Madison leaves to resume his duties, and I make my way to the bow to get a look up at the body language on the bridge.

This is not the only ship carrying ammunition. Still, the men ashore will soon desperately need resupply. An excruciating two hours pass before I hear the now familiar sounds of a ship getting underway.

Soon several Ducks, some piloted by members of a Negro amphibious transportation company, appear on the waves. As soon as our ship arrives at a manageable distance, they flock to its sides like hungry ducklings anxious to consume the life-giving ammunition and fuel on the mother ship.

By the time the cargo transfer activity begins in earnest I have a compelling story to write for the *Record*—but only half of which will withstand the scrutiny of Tom's censors. The Ducks pull alongside and the soldiers begin pointedly advising the merchant marines on the most efficient techniques for packaging and lowering down to them measured nets of wooden crates.

Some members of the ship's crew, led by Davis, initially resent the frustrated Duck pilots shouting up to them. The process begins grudgingly, but they soon establish rhythm. I begin snapping photographs of Ducks pulling, one after another, up under a crane and receiving premeasured cargo. The men operating the Ducks disconnect the entire loads, and quickly motor away to make room for the next craft. The merchant marines raise the empty netting cables, attach a premeasured load and lower it onto the next waiting Duck.

The Ducks travel toward the shoreline under fire from the few persistent fighters that manage to avoid the blasts of hot lead sprayed by naval gunners and Allied fighters. Near sundown, the Ducks have unloaded half of the explosive cargo. I recognize one of the last to arrive, and shout down to him. "How's it going on the beach?"

"Mister Savoy, they dropped off the grunts without much fuss. The quartermasters drove loaded trucks onto the LSTs in Naples, and drove them off on the Anzio beach. Then drivers can head straight for the dumps."

He waves once more after detaching his last load for the day and takes off again toward the beach. The urge to get in with him is almost overwhelming. "Sir, you know what Blue would want me to tell you."

"Yeah, keep my damned fool head down. Good luck."

As I watch the loaded Duck make its way, darkness falls. I make my way toward a mess area where I know hot coffee and sandwiches await. Without warning, I hear the gut-wrenching roar of an explosion ripping into the deck and igniting the volatile cargo below. A sailor shouts something to me before bolting toward the bow. I run back toward what I have come to know as the port side.

In the intensity of the moment, time slows to reveal a level of detail one perceives in the seconds prior to a collision. It is as though a movie projector has malfunctioned, showing a sequence of individual still frames rather than the continuous film of a motion picture. Members of the ship's crew scramble to their pre-assigned battle stations, reacting with varying degrees of calm and hysteria. Most instinctively follow their training, but some stand frozen in panic.

No emergency lifeboat drill can prepare anyone to deal with impending death. I hear the harrowing sound made by tons of steel ripping from a superstructure. The terrifying sounds reverberate through the marrow of my bones, and the force of a blast catapults me over the side.

The salt water smells of fuel and I do my best to remain calm. There is no fire yet on the water, my arms and legs still function despite sharp pains. I struggle to maintain consciousness, watching the ship drift away with the current beneath a tall column of billowing black smoke. My lifejacket easily keeps me afloat and I continue to tread water until I hear a smaller craft headed my way. I turn to see someone pick up a distressed merchant marine, who advises the rescuers to assist others more seriously injured. Just when I cannot keep my eyes open a second longer, a pair of sure hands pull me onto the boat. "Don't worry, Mister Savoy. I've got you."

The last thing I remember is asking, "Who are you?"

Chapter 19

. . . .

Leadership and the Negro Soldier

"Hop on in Jack."
"Thanks a lot."
"Sure."
"I really appreciate the ride, Major. It's been a long time since I've ridden in such a comfortable car."

"No problem. Glad to be of assistance. Besides, it's a long way back to Naples in the back of a truck—and with that leg. My driver doesn't talk much, so I could use the company. How'd you get here?"

"I hitchhiked. Reporters ideally travel with Army personnel, but we'll jump on a hay wagon if need be." A sudden burst of activity on the grounds and the distinctive sounds of approaching airplanes distract us. The driver instinctively delays his departure so that we can take in the activity. We both look up to see several P-51 Mustang fighter planes approach and, one by one, land on the single long runway at Ramitelli Air Field.

They taxi past clusters of farmhouses and barns on the fringes that were once the property of Foggia residents. The now repurposed structures serve as maintenance, quarters and operations buildings for the 332nd Fighter Group, located near the Adriatic Coastline.

"I've been here before, Major. No, I don't mean previous visits to interview the Tuskegee pilots. I was here shortly after Salerno when the Brits linked up with elements of General Clark's invasion force.

I saw them fight for this real estate. Even then, the strategic value of these flatlands was obvious."

"So, you have been around."

"I've been around."

With the brief impromptu air show completed, the driver pulls off and makes his way through the various 15th Air Force fields clustered in and around Foggia. After a long muddy winter of war, the summer sun returns muddy roads to the reasonably navigable thoroughfares they were last year. The quality of the ride along smoother stretches reminds me of Morocco and the comfortable rear seat of Youssef's English Rover.

"We can take you all the way to Naples. Jack, just call me Ed, from the Service Forces Training Division in Washington. So, what happened to your leg? Oh—you got hit at Anzio."

I want to temper any expectations Ed has for hearing an actual combat story. "Before this gets to be misleading, I was on an ammunition-laden Liberty ship that got blown to bits. Luckily, someone fished me out of the drink. I woke up on a hospital ship with a fractured foot and a twisted knee."

"Jack, you sound like an old veteran describing a day at the beach. My God man, you're hopping along with a cane. I'll bet that read like one heck of a news story."

One of only a handful of Negro officers I have seen above the rank of captain, Ed speaks with a pronounced southern accent, enunciated like a badge of honor. The interior of the car is pristine, reminding me of the disregard I have come to show for the care of my uniforms. Both he and his young Army driver wear crisp Class A uniforms. Their low-cut shined shoes could not have touched the mud that covered Italy during the long, cold rainy season.

Out of respect for the men and women who routinely put their lives at risk, I try to downplay the sequence of engagements that sound more impressive than they are. "After covering the mop-up in Tunisia, going ashore at Salerno and traveling by truck to Naples, I jumped on a convoy headed for Foggia and later saw the mess at Casino. I was going to follow that story to the end when I got wind of another amphib ginning up. It has all been through the eyes of a reporter—not a soldier. The highlight was an extended house call from a doting Army nurse."

"An Army nurse, huh?" The driver glances curiously into the rearview mirror, and Ed looks confused. Over two thousand Negro volunteers have joined the Nurse Corps since the president dropped the quota system last month. However, without knowing how many are in Italy, I have made the kind of errant slip of the tongue Tom has asked me to avoid.

When Ed does not ask a follow-up question, I change the subject. "So, Ed, what were you doing in Ramitelli? I'm trying to guess why a DC-based editor for the Army would be here."

"Jack, you mean a *Negro* editor. I'm here for reactions to a new training publication we dedicated to better understanding *Negro Soldiers*. Someone had the bright idea to get comments on the draft from colored offices—stateside and abroad. Naturally, that pointed us to Italy. We flipped a coin to decide who would travel over here. I lost. Once back in Naples, I'll begin the trip back home—by sea."

It is an interesting story that I take a few minutes to digest. I decide to flesh it out with him later as we ride, certain that a story about it would easily survive censorship. He breaks the silence with a question for me. "So, then you were in Ramitelli to do a story on the *Tuskegee Airmen*?"

I chuckle. "I see that label's going to stick. It's catchy enough. Yeah, I've been waiting for the whole fighter group to deploy together under the command of Colonel Davis."

"That's interesting Jack. How'd you know?"

"I visited with the Group here in June after all but the 99th Squadron was still serving in the 15th Air Force. It was just my luck that the group flew its first bomber escort mission while I was here. Then the next day, they escorted more bombers to Munich. Colonel Davis was awarded the Distinguished Flying Cross."

Ed appears to be weighing his next question. "Why did it take so long to bring the colored squadrons together under one command—headed by Colonel Davis?" He has asked a question about an issue on the minds of several reporters.

"A lot of people have asked about that, but they'd never get Davis to bite on such a question." I continue, "Let me try to put what I actually know in perspective. I reported their arrival when the first Tuskegee squadron docked in Morocco 16 months ago. Then, the

Journal and Guide began a tag team that started with Thomas Young, who left in short order. He handed them off to Lem Graves and John Jordan. We've all spent some time with them, including Ron Maxwell, Art Carter and Ollie Harrington, but the *Journal and Guide* has the edge in coverage."

Ed reacts to hearing Ron's name. "Oh yeah, I've read Maxwell's stuff. How well do you know him?"

"I don't really know him at all," I lie. Before he can inquire further about Ron, I continue. "A year after they arrived, the other colored squadrons of the 332nd started arriving in Italy. The brass assigned the new pilots and the experienced hands of the 99th to Davis' Group. Still, they weren't all placed under *the young old man's* complete operational control."

He shrugs and tries to abort the conjecture he initiated. "Maybe it was just something to do with preparation and training—you can never know about the Air Corps. In fact, forget I asked. By the way, have you heard about the Negro bomber crews training stateside?"

"I'm sure you know that's going nowhere." I answer his question bluntly. I still want to hear what he clearly wants to tell me about Davis. I egg him on. "I believe Davis may still be up against people who don't want him to succeed. Last year a two-star condemned the 99th for its so-called inferior performance. Six months later, an objective report vindicated the squadron. I was there when they celebrated their first year of combat—and their 500th combat mission. They became more determined than ever."

"So, I heard at Ramitelli." He quickly tries again to redirect my energy. "They also told me they were flying over Anzio during the battle. Did you get to write that story—16 enemy planes shot down in one week."

"No. I found out too long after the fact, in addition to the job they did harassing supply lines. It's good to hear that the rest of the 332nd Fighter Group is coming together. They'll be workhorse bomber escorts. It's the way to demonstrate undeniable success. Either the bombers come home or they don't. There's very little room for subjectivity or exaggerations."

Ed agrees, as though the simplicity had not occurred to him. "I guess that's right."

I continue, "My publisher believes service units form the backbone of the Army, and will be best prepared for jobs after the war. While the Air Corps has been training colored pilots, they've also been training the men of the 96th Service Group—the colored technicians who keep the 332nd flying by handling maintenance and repair, ammunition and ordinance, medicine, transportation, communications signals, security, quartermaster services and so on. They may be my main story this week."

Ed is reflective. "You know, I saw colored guys working everywhere and doing everything at the airfield, but I guess I just thought, well, I don't really know what I thought."

I give up my quest for the tip on squadron deployment I am certain he almost shared. We ride in silence for a dozen miles watching the landscape that has improved markedly since the British and Americans first linked up here. Ed breaks the silence with a surprising question, given his reluctance to share what he knows about the deployment of the pilots. "Do you know anything about what happened after the beachhead was established at Anzio?"

He has asked about one of the most controversial series of decisions of the war. I have only discussed with Rachel and Tom the landings or the aftermath. I want to avoid talking about it now. "I was hospitalized without ever going ashore. I heard later that General Truscott replaced General Lucas. Then, Clark ordered Truscott to take Rome instead of cutting off the Germans retreating north from the Gustav. That's it for me."

I sense that Ed once again wishes to weigh in with his own opinions but again demurs. Presumably, to fill the awkward silence, he asks another question that I have been expecting. "Jack, you sound like you used to have an accent. Where are you from originally?"

It has become an often-repeated question for me, but as structured, it will not produce the information he really desires. I take a few minutes to tell him about my journey from Halifax to study at Oberlin, and on to the San Francisco Bay area. After another awkward silence, he asks a more specific question that still leaves room for equivocation. "So, your family is originally from Canada?"

I smile knowingly, and answer the question he will not ask. "My great-grandfather arrived in Canada as a runaway slave from a Jamaican sugar plantation—no more than a boy, with no real recollection of his origins. I was born and raised by my grandmother as a Caribbean Canadian and by other relations as French Canadian. But, of course, Americans have their own labels."

"Jack, as soon as you started talking, I realized you probably answer that question far more than anyone should have to. I apologize for prying." I anticipate—and catch—the young driver's glance into the rearview mirror.

"It's okay. Now that we're on the subject, maybe you could help me with something, Ed. We absolutely have problems in Canada, but Canadians rarely ever ask me about race. On the other hand, Americans feel *entitled* to know. Americans feel I'm *obligated* to tell. Why do you think that is?"

He responds immediately as though I asked about the weather. "Well, I wouldn't presume to speak for everyone, but I'd bet most—like me—just want to know who *you identify with*, since you appear to have options in that regard. I mean you no offense, Jack. If you had not said you worked for the Lomax brothers and spoke about the Tuskegee Airmen with such passion, I might not have assumed. Now, with my foot firmly in my mouth, I may as well ask my other question."

He turns away, looks out the window, and turns back. "I'll bet there have been three dozen Negro correspondents overseas. Most work for papers with limited circulations. People ask me how just a handful of civil rights editors sent so many. But I'm new and no one seems to know, even though the Bureau accredited them."

"Ed, I can only give you my best guess. To remain competitive, the largest Negro papers need the eyewitness coverage, and to show the policy of segregation works, so does the War Department. Really, a few dozen reporters are not enough to cover all the Negroes in uniform. I've only met people over here from the *Journal and Guide*, the *Afro* and the *Pittsburgh Courier*. The *Chicago Defender* has a couple of guys on the other side of the war, and I haven't met Ed Toles. Compare that to the thousand white reporters who've rotated back and forward.

"Are you the only guy over here working for the *Record*?"

"The Lomax brothers just hired a guy to work in the Pacific Theater. The *Advocate's* Ron Maxwell, whom I left out, says FDR passed on a great opportunity. With one bold stroke of the pen he could have begun the end of segregation as we know it."

"Do you believe that, Jack?"

"Ron can be a bit of a sensationalist, but experience has taught me that he may be on the mark with that one. Put black, white, brown, red and yellow recruits all together, shake them up vigorously with Army drill sergeants, and you can bet that an olive drab army comes out the other end."

Ed replies, "Well, going into the fall election, FDR can't really afford a public relations problem with Negroes. The best way to resolve bad PR is to counter with good PR. But Jack, surely you don't think that even he could ask the country to agree to swallow a gigantic shit sandwich like integration in 1944."

"I don't know, but that's why we're over here. Our readers open newspapers and magazines to read compelling stories and see pictures of colored soldiers preserving democracy. They feel a part of it. Most don't think about them serving in separate units. Hell, the Army gets to censor every word in advance."

Ed interjects, "The more activist publishers can still run negative editorials."

Suspecting that we are both saying the same thing, I end he exchange by adding, "Who cares? Our photographs are each worth a thousand words—and maybe ten thousand votes. If activist newspaper publishers write opinion pieces about discrimination, so what else is new?" We ride in silence for several miles.

I break the silence by asking about my old friend. "So, have you met Owen Todd in the public affairs bureau? How's he doing these days?"

Ed smiles broadly. "He's doing fine. They brought in a couple of young Negro officers to work in the public affairs press section. Owen's still holding on." He laughs. "But if things ever become uncomfortable for him, he could go back to teaching."

"I have no doubt that he can," I add. He nods as a gesture of appreciation, and I take out my pad. "So, Ed, what else can you tell me about this *Negro Soldier* publication?"

Chapter 20

· ·

Buffalo Soldiers

"Say, that's a colored regiment with colored officers—and guns! Is that why they're coming ashore at night?"

Realizing that neither Ron nor I share his amusement over the scene playing out on the Naples docks, the photographer walks away. His high-resolution camera and flash remain shuttered down at his side.

Peripherally, I watch him join a group of other correspondents who, except for Ross Carpenter, share his lack of interest in the images I eagerly raise my small Medalist to photograph—though I doubt that in this darkness, my pictures will develop.

Of all the port activity I have witnessed in North Africa and Italy, nothing generates excitement like infantrymen stepping smartly off the gangway of a troop ship. An entire Negro port battalion jubilantly cheers their arrival. As junior officers direct platoons of enlisted men, the dockworkers roar as though the home team has just won the World Series.

Stunned by the loud reception in honor of their arrival, the men of the 370th Infantry Regiment emerge from the holds of the troop ship, some with backpacks and rifles. They make their way in the semidarkness, packing into barges that ferry them and their baggage to a line of trucks waiting on a road near the shoreline.

Once they are closer, I can clearly see their divisional shoulder patches depicting a black buffalo on an olive background. The design of the patch is a tribute to the segregated regiments that once served on the American western frontier. Only Tom has guessed correctly they would come here, rather than join the advance that has begun in France. This regiment is a component of the 92nd Infantry Division, the *Buffalo Soldiers*.

Ron dampens the mood with a brief soliloquy. "So, we finally get to see the 370th. They aren't the first colored combat troops in Italy. That distinction belongs to colored artillery and antiaircraft batteries. Plus, the 366th regiment arrived last April and got scattered all over to guard airfields." Ron's editor roundly criticized the reassignment of the 366th Infantry Regiment to security duties instead of engaging them in combat.

Ron remains in Italy, deciding to stay close by rather than traveling to France. While I regret our physical altercation in the alley, it appears to have ended his preoccupation with Rachel—an interest that I still believe was born more of his dislike for me than his attraction to her. Our brawl, while juvenile, settled our differences on several issues, including his whispering campaign to brand me as a War Department informer.

"But Clark should reassign the 366th to combat with t*he Buffalo Soldiers* now that the 370th has arrived." Behind me, I recognize the voice of John Jordan, a reporter for the *Norfolk Journal and Guide*. John freely employs the nickname of the 92nd Infantry Division.

"And don't forget the colored troops mixed with Brits in Task Force 45." John is Ron's match in erudition and advocacy and is skilled in expressing blunt criticisms of the Army's policy on segregation. "The 370th is just the first installment—the vanguard—of a whole division. At some point, they'll have their own colored artillery, armored, quartermaster and medical units."

Needing to have the last word, Ron limits the false expectations he assumes we have. "The men in the division don't even know one another John. They trained separately all over the States—any place with enough buildings to house them away from white soldiers. They only spent a few months together at Huachuca after the 93rd shipped out to the Pacific Theater. If you ask me, the Buffalo Soldiers should be in France. And I'm going to say as much in my coverage of this arrival." I must acknowledge that Ron is correct. "Of the three infantry regiments that comprise the 92nd Infantry Division, the 370th Regiment trained in Kentucky, and the other two trained at separate installations in Indiana and Arkansas. The headquarters and support units were in Alabama. But forget it, Ron. The way you'd write it, it'd never get past the censors." Instinctively I caution him, but I have forgotten to whom I am speaking.

Ron shoots me a sideways glance and responds dourly. "There're other ways to get it in print, but that's right Canada, let the Army censors decide how the world remembers what we're witnessing. I'll tell you one thing. When the local Italian Leagues and our own homegrown Klansmen see these boys, it's going to be open season. Do you mean to tell me, nobody else is going to cover that? I don't know why you're even over here, you goddam buck-dancers."

Before I can reply, another correspondent chimes in. "I sailed with the 366th. If given the chance they could've helped push the Nazis out of Italy. If, on the other hand, it's true that we're just here to keep Kesselring in the boot, the Buffalo Soldiers will help to hold him in check. History will remember them for it."

Ron is dismissive. "Art, we'll call you if we need the baseball scores. No matter what the brass says, don't ever assume that the 92nd will get to succeed. We should all maintain that healthy skepticism about everything that goes on over here. It's essential to the job of a Negro war correspondent."

Art Carter is a reporter for the *Afro American,* a replacement, so to speak, for Ollie Stewart. While Stewart takes a deserved trip home, despite an affinity for sports writing, Art has established a record of his own during several months in Italy. He also needs no assistance to handle Maxwell.

I am tired and intend to make my way back to my hotel room. If they develop, I have enough photographs and observations to weave into the official release and backstory from Tom. With just a few interviews, I can file a comprehensive first story on the arrival of the unit.

Since it is Sunday, I consider splurging on a wire service so that it makes this week's edition. After that, I can mail any updates and follow-up coverage of the combat troops and the stories that bring Ted satisfaction. As I begin to make my way over to request a few moments with the arriving troops, a hand reaches out to hold me back. I turn to face Ross. "Is it always this way, Jack?"

"Is what *always this way*, Ross? Do you mean the disinterested white correspondents or the arguments among colored reporters?" For someone who is not afraid to speak his mind and take personal liberties with me, Ross sometimes shows me a naïve side. This persona is so startling that I question its authenticity.

I continue walking toward the trucks, answering him matter-of-factly. "It's just like it is in the States, Ross. The big dailies don't cover *colored news* unless it's about the commission of a crime. The *Chronicle* has no interest in running a story about a couple thousand armed colored men marching off a troop ship."

"Don't talk to me like that Jack. You know the *Chronicle* is a better paper than that. Not perfect—but better than that. They'll run the story. I know the score. I just feel like this is important. Fifth Army is just a shadow of its former self. Neither Clark nor Truscott have much left in the tank. They just need Kesselring to run out of running room. If these guys can play a big part in that, then I'll write it up."

Ross walks with me toward the formation. "Ross, I have a brother in a Negro tank battalion that I believe is rolling across France as we speak. It's hard to tell from the vague wording he must use in his letters, but I doubt that the 761st Tank Battalion has one white reporter interested in the unit. I'm not complaining—that's our job. I'm just saying the same thing I would say to him—this is the way it is and the way it's always been."

Ross has just returned to Naples after spending time with an infantry battalion operating north of the Arno River. The combat fatigues he still wears are those of a GI who has done a fair amount of crawling and sleeping in holes dug deep into the ground. He stares with eyes filled with the images he has collected since Tunisia. He has earned the right to push for quotes. "And the way it always will be Jack?"

However, we are too close to the formations to continue this conversation, so I do not indulge him. "I don't allow myself to think like that." I joke, "What would it do to my objectivity? If you'll excuse me Ross, I've got some questions for these newcomers."

I watch as Ross walks up to an officer, perhaps determined to file a story his editors may not publish. Other correspondents have already quickly staked out a few officers and noncoms. We are all cognizant of the hour and anticipating the departure of the entire regiment by truck as soon as practicable.

"Hello Lieutenant. I'm Jack Savoy, a reporter with the *Washington Record*." He shakes the hand I extend and states his name and home-town in Wyoming.

"Lieutenant, I'd like to ask you a few questions and speak with some of your men. Thanks. First, let's start with a straightforward one. How was the voyage over?"

I hear instructions making their way toward us. "It doesn't look as though I'm going to get anything more tonight. I'm going to find out where you guys are and, after you're settled, look you up again. In the meantime, please tell your men to stay alert. Non-combat related trouble looms everywhere, and from all directions."

Chapter 21

· ·

Brawler

"**C**ome here you goddam mongrel nigger."
Even as I refuse to acknowledge that I have heard the words, I cringe as his shout pierces the noise at the bar and silences the buzz of the restaurant's patrons. My instincts tell me to do nothing that would escalate the encounter, which still might pass without violence.

However, Sidney Harris is both inebriated and intrigued by the ignorance. Somehow sensing a need to add clarity, a need that exists only in his mind, Sid calls over to me from the bar, "I think he means you, Jack."

"Thanks Sid, I never would have guessed."

Speaking from a peculiar depth of hatred, the drunken soldier confirms, "Yeah, I'm talking to you, mongrel boy with the sweet tooth for white nurses." Now he has my attention.

When I turn to investigate, a half dozen red-faced drunken GIs glare at me from across the room. However, distracted by the group, I miss the soldier who has already repositioned himself next to me. When he grabs my arm, I shout, "Take your hands off me!"

Peripherally, I see patrons head for the door. Although I make my demand with all the conviction I can muster, he has other plans. He is big, and accompanied. Considering Sid's state, I am alone, and outnumbered. He remains within striking position.

Sid demands to know, "Why didn't you assholes speak up a half hour ago, when all our friends were still here?" Sid has a point. Six other reporters had abruptly *called it a night*, and left less than a half hour ago. As a rule, correspondents of color avoid walking the streets alone at night. I remained behind to accompany the guest of honor, watching his *one more for the road* become three *more added to his load*.

Sid was at the bar collecting what we both agreed would be his final double whiskey. I had been waiting for him at our table, more than ready to begin the mile-long stroll back to our hotel from this venue he chose for his sendoff.

Seeing me detained, Sid starts, in earnest, moving in my direction, but a large fist appears out of nowhere and jams into his face, sending him crashing to the floor. Like a spunky prizefighter, Sid pops right back up, but inspired by seeing how easily his companion has knocked down such a large man, my assailant takes a swing at me.

I roll with his roundhouse punch enough to limit it to a glancing blow. Though I still walk with a noticeable limp, I counter hard, and he stumbles against the wall. A second man smashes his fist flush against the side of my jaw.

Facing multiple fighters with limited support, I decide to reduce the odds. I wrap my fingers around the neck of an empty champagne bottle and smash it against the nearest forehead. I hit him harder than I intended. He is unconscious before he lands on the floor with a disconcerting thud.

The group's anger subsides for a moment and a few GI's hurry over to help the fallen assailant. I make a dash for Sid, looking back at the body slumped on the floor. Someone yells, "Come on Skip, snap out of it." When I have Sid in tow, I assure them that *Skip will be fine*, just as he awakens to find a large knot on his forehead.

I pull Sid. "Come on. It's time to go."

Before we can make it to the door, they are after us. "No Jack, don't run. We can take them."

Bedlam resumes just inside the doorway. Several soldiers are all over us, flailing and kicking, yelling out an assortment of demeaning epithets. We swing back, such as we can, but give far less than we receive. Sid is back down on the floor. I can see that his mouth and nose are bleeding. My ears are ringing and a few of my ribs feel bruised. I keep trying to get Sid up and out the door, hoping that salvation awaits us outside.

With heels and soles stomping me, I look around for another weapon. I spot a broken bottle with the neck still intact. However, I decide against picking up a deadly weapon, mindful that no one has knifed or clubbed us, even as fists and feet rain down on us. I am not too many blows away from passing out, but this is surely not the kind of assault that has hospitalized many young servicemen attacked for perceived transgressions.

One soldier jumps into the fray. It is a mistake. I grab the back of his neck and snap his face down into the filthy tiled floor. He seems surprised by my continued spirited defense. Blood streams from his mouth and nose. He rolls away, mopping his face with his sleeve. I discover my second wind.

Through all the swinging and kicking, Sid and I manage to crawl through the door and fight our way out into the street, right into four waiting military policemen.

"How long have you been out here?" They ignore my indignant question. I suspect they have been here the whole time, allowing the lopsided fight to go on inside. Sid and I both have minor injuries, though I suspect he will not feel his until tomorrow.

"Well, that was kind of stupid. You boys picked a fight with a whole squad." That comment from one MP tells me how much support we can expect from them.

Even bleeding, Sid is indignant as always, "Oh, so we started this? I guess I drank even more of that cheap shit than I thought."

One of them flashes a demonic smile and sneers, "Yeah, that's smart. Get me riled and your long night has only just begun, big boy. I just love to whip on a big old colored boy."

"So, this is the Army's finest," I mutter, just as someone walks out carrying our bundled jackets and caps, and tosses them out into the street. "Oh. We're going to have to shut that mouth, ain't we?"

However, as he examines the uniform items, the sergeant notes our press armbands and patches. The buffalo insignia patches I suspect he hoped to find are not here. Sid and I both chose to wear a Class B shirt and wool trouser combination that was popular in temperate desert weather. The rules, which Sid generally ignores, allow for open collars. We had removed the olive *Ike jackets*, the only items we wore tonight with stitched-on correspondent's patches.

The MP's crooked smile evaporates and his voice softens. All four men become visibly uncomfortable. "You two okay? You really need to get the hell out of here and don't come back. This is a rough club, even for people who're welcome here."

"So, declare this dump off limits."

He hands over our stuff. However, I know that he will not be able to dismiss Sid so easily. Sid assures him that, "I'm leaving tomorrow to go back to the States. I'll make sure General Clark gets a copy of the *uncensored* article I'm going to write about your involvement tonight. Oh no, *Sergeant Pike*, I don't need to write anything down. Even drunk, I have total recall for faces, names, units and ranks. Since Jack writes for a Washington DC newspaper, I'm sure his story will get read over at the Pentagon."

The sergeant appeals to me. "Look, we pulled up and got out of our jeeps just as the two of you were coming through the door. Now, I've seen boys carried out of places like that. I don't know if these boys were just picking on you or if they took it easy on you for being reporters. I don't know what started this."

I respond with sarcasm. "And you haven't yet asked, have you? Maybe that's because we're still alive. If we were dead, I know you'd be writing down our side of the story."

I manage an audible chuckle. Sid laughs from deep within. The face of one MP has an expression of hate unlike any I have seen on this side of the ocean. His hand has not left the handle of his 45-automatic seated in its unsnapped holster. In his steel gray eyes, Major Wade's eyes, a fire burns out of control. I sense an innate need for retribution. "Why?" I ask without explanation, startling him for a moment.

As is often the case, Sid and I are on the same page. "Jack, he has no idea why he wants to shoot us so badly. A voice in his head tells him he's supposed to." Though I taste my own blood and see someone else's on my uniform, I feel no long-term injury, no lasting pain. I focus most of my attention on Sid, who has covered armored units and infantry without a scratch. Now, he has been ambushed in Naples at his going away party.

The news story Sid promised is no idle threat. Sounding much more sober now, he demands to know, "Why haven't you tried to find out what happened?" I wonder if the MP knows that everything he says will appear in print.

The MP appears to be losing the modicum of patience he has thus far been able to muster. He says, "Because we already know what happened. Will you accept a ride or would you prefer to walk back to your hotel? If you're where I think you are, it's at least a mile."

Sid supplies a blunt answer that works for me as well. "You asshole, we wouldn't be caught dead in the back of that fucking jeep with you or any other night rider. And who are you glaring at you cat-eyed sombitch?"

I decide that my companion has said more than enough, and point him, somewhat battered and bruised, toward the relative safety of our hotel. I ask, rhetorically, "Can you walk okay, Sid?"

His tone is mildly indignant as we begin our journey. "I told you, I can always make it home. I have a question for you, though. Why is it that people assume that she's white, but examine you like a lab rat?"

I have never thought about it that way. "That's a good question."

"So, Jack, did the events of this evening help you with your big decision? Oh, come on, you know what I'm talking about."

"This is a hell of a time to ask me about that, Sid." I had not anticipated another conversation tonight about my meeting with a senior editor from *Free,* a new internationally focused magazine published in New York. An editor had been in Naples visiting his publication's wounded war correspondent. The injured reporter, who has paid far more attention to me than I would have guessed, arranged the meeting.

Sid is insistent. "I think this is the perfect time, Jack. Besides, I won't be able to ask you about it after I leave tomorrow."

I have spent much of the latter part of the evening using Sid as my sounding board, certain that he would not remember most of the conversation. I had needed to talk to someone about what amounted to a post-war job offer from the well-financed magazine. As my relationship with Rachel progresses, I focus less on the allure of global travel. Thus, their search for a national news reporter caught my attention.

However, the editor's matter-of-fact honesty had been bracing. *Jack, we think you could be our guy to bring some objectivity, some reality if you will, to covering this emerging civil rights thing. Oh yes, it's gaining traction. You know, we'll need someone who'll keep events in their proper perspective.*

I look over at my co-combatant. "Sid, if I had to give an answer tonight, I just don't think it's a good fit for me."

"Okay, good. For what it's worth, I agree. You're a helluva writer, Jack, and clearly were the *Chronicle's* loss. You'll get plenty of good offers."

As we walk along in silence for a while, I wonder if Sid is correct. I also wonder if it is sensible to factor Rachel into my decisions. I had thought that listening to her obsession with race and mimicking the *Record's* activist style had shifted the tone of my copy markedly away from objectivity. I am surprised that the magazine editor thinks my point of view still aligns with his stated *editorial direction*.

As though he is reading my mind, Sid interrupts with a timely question. "Jack, of course I don't know nothing about nothing. However, have you asked yourself why they thought the job would be the perfect fit for you? I mean, for you in particular?"

"It doesn't add up, Sid."

"Call me crazy, my friend, but suppose I said that ass whipping may be the best thing that's happened to you?"

"Oh Sid, I wouldn't say you were crazy."

"No?"

"No. You're just drunk."

Chapter 22

· ·

Christmas in Florence

"**S**o, let me make sure I have this right, tough guy. You're brawling in bars. You've all but dropped the accent. You talk like a cat from the East Coast. Did I mention that you were brawling in bars? You're going up on the front lines, crawling through the mud with infantrymen. Let's see, if memory serves me, your boss *and I* asked you to stop doing that."

"Stop right there, Rachel."

"No, Jack. Was that your fifth extended visit to the front? You're wearing a heavy Mackinaw combat coat and a pair of real leather gaiters. Is that a helmet with camouflage netting? Now, that's impressive."

"Slow down, Captain Todd. It's Christmas. You sound like a GI in a bar itching for a fight. I hitched a ride to Florence from some cold, battered place called Calomini, nearly freezing in a truck bed. I came here to spend Christmas with you." The convoy driver dropped me off in Florence two hours ago. My feet have not completely thawed and I fear that my patience with Rachel's sarcasm will be short. "What's all this about?"

Rachel knows I am no stranger to battlefield coverage, including the copy I filed on the 92nd Division's efforts to nail down Fifth Army's left flank along the west coast of Italy. She knows I lived with Rifle Company C his past fall near the Serchio Valley. I am confident that the work published under my byline reflects my commitment to the truth about their experiences and challenges. Still, the person whose opinion I allow to mean most insists on marginalizing my work.

No matter how often I risk bodily harm, *against my publisher's instructions*, to document these Negro infantrymen in combat, I fall short of her *ideal*. I ask, "You do know that censors will never allow anyone to write the stuff you want to read?"

She ignores my question and continues to skim through my uncensored copy, offering unsolicited comments as she reads. "Rachel, my best uses of ink and rationed paper are printing real stories about segregated units in action, fighting and taking prisoners and casualties. Isn't that the real point we need to get across?"

"But Jack, where is your defense of the criticisms against the division? You write a ton about them being present, about them fighting hard, even about earlier reports of inferior equipment, but nothing to counter the lies."

I do not want to spend Christmas Eve having this conversation. "That's a job for editorialists. If other correspondents choose to do that, that's their choice. My job, *my responsibility,* if you must, is keeping positive war news flowing about Negro units. Besides, the criticisms you speak of are coming from inside the Army."

She pouts, "Then, challenge the Army."

I cannot decide if she is serious. I ask, "How do I get that past the censors? Besides, what makes you so certain all the stories you hear are false? There are some things about the division that do need fixing, with plenty of blame to go around."

She sighs impatiently and continues reading. I welcome the silence. A chance meeting with another reporter resulted in a tip about this intact little hotel. I had hoped we could spend our short time quietly, lost in ourselves, ignoring the cold weather and the endless rumbling of rolling vehicles and convoys. However, while I am thrilled just to be here with her, she has not yet told me how long she intends to stay.

Soon enough, she will be back at one of the evacuation hospitals of the 317th Medical Battalion. They will become overwhelmed with wounded soldiers. When they finally break the Gothic Line, the Allied front will shift north once more to overwhelm the enemy, resulting in thousands more casualties.

She may not be able to see me again until the Allies blow the remaining German defenders into submission. Still, Rachel and I are sitting in the same room, worlds apart. As I lay in bed longing for the warmth of her embrace, she alternately sits and paces, fixated on the deficiencies she perceives in my reporting.

"Jack, do you honestly believe they were given a fair chance to capture those towns along the west coast? I've heard dying men complain about the quality of their senior leaders. What about all those southerners who've convinced the Army that they know how to *handle colored boys?*" Rachel looks over at me and back at my short stack of drafts. "They certainly send us plenty of business."

I do not want to invest the time required to explain what has doomed the Buffalo Soldiers, including unmotivated white officers coming in with low expectations rotated out before they get to know their troops. Besides, she already knows all that.

Speaking softly, I read from memory an editorial I keep deep inside my personal journal. *The 92nd was doomed to fail. If you ask ten thousand colored GIs to die for people who hate them, you can't send them officers who feel duty bound to ensure their failure. Someone with the best intentions may have planned the division, but the Army picked people with the worst intentions to implement the plan.*

Rachel stands staring at me in silence, shaking her head. Finally, she asks, "Now where's all that coming from suddenly and where's it been? You aren't just talking that way to get me in bed, are you?"

"It wouldn't be the worst idea."

She had walked into the room earlier with her hair a mess under a dented red-cross helmet, her soiled uniform faded to a light shade of olive drab, her brand-new captain's bars already dulled by exposure, her boots worn from rocky terrain. Still, she was the most beautiful sight I have seen since I last saw her in Naples. I embraced her tightly, unwilling to let go until I awakened from a nap to find her reading.

I have cherished every minute Rachel steals from nursing wounded soldiers in a seemingly endless battle against a stubborn enemy. I am concerned about the effects of having human carnage delivered to her hourly from battlefields. Hearing Rachel refer so routinely to the mauled bodies arriving at her evacs, I sense thick calluses buffering her emotional responses. I have feared the impact it will have when she returns home and does not develop new scar tissue.

I do not know how she will be able to shut out images of mangled teenagers. I do not know how she will ever reconcile memories of the young men they could not save. She will have to live with the inevitable second-guessing no person should ever have to endure, and it will all be the sum cost of victory.

While I have grown accustomed to her glib assessments of my commitment to *her and Serge's movement*, I am unprepared tonight for her unrelenting salvos. So far, I have given her a wide birth, in deference to the violent deaths of her good friends near Anzio. I attribute much of tonight's abrasiveness to that tragedy, but I have limits, increasingly resentful that our fleeting moments together devolve into pointless debates.

I groan audibly as she walks further away, over to the window, clad only in my last clean undershirt. I want to restore some cordiality, but instead hear myself saying. "You're in rare form tonight. Your sarcasm cuts like a knife, Rachel. In truth, Lomax never wanted foxhole-to-foxhole coverage. I go to the front to add more depth to my stories."

"You mean more depth to your portfolio, don't you Scoop?" Despite her obvious determination to darken the mood, I am willing to try anything to keep our reunion from stalling out completely.

I try changing the subject. "Since we got here, the Italians have called every rainy season *the worst ever* and every winter *the coldest ever*." The thought of it chills my bones and makes me hunger even more for the curved silhouette standing in the window. "You really should get away from that drafty window. We'd both feel a lot better if you came back to bed."

When she steps away from the window, the headlight beams of a passing vehicle sweep through the curtains and bathe her in filtered light. My pulse is racing. "Now, that's the image that got me through sleepless nights in the mud."

I inhale involuntarily as she crawls back into bed and backs her now chilly bottom into my lap. Wrapping her in my arms and legs, I warm her skin and try to rekindle the fire we shared earlier in the evening. When my body reveals my intentions, she giggles for the first time tonight. "Come on now Jack, don't you ever get enough? I want you to tell me what the other colored correspondents are saying."

"What?" Though I cannot imagine how I could ever get enough of her or why we are pursuing this subject, I reluctantly sit up straight. I lean back against the headboard, speaking slowly and deliberately. "Normandy was always the real show. Ike redirected half of Clark's muscle up there. They'll get past that nasty little surprise in the Ardennes, provided the costs won't be too high."

She responds, "They tell us the casualty rate is off the charts around Bastogne. I'm surprised you haven't run off after that story."

I flinch, reminded that I will have to tell her I plan to leave for France soon. I continue with my answer to her question. "People say Italy has become a sideshow. However, there's still that 500-mile river of blood that runs up the boot. Maybe they should just keep Kesselring pinned in until this thing is over."

Rachel's focus has not budged. "So, you don't think the 92nd was ever going to march into liberated Germany?"

"March into Germany?" I remind her that, "The 92nd is only one division. The whole Alliance is here in Italy. I haven't heard a single person talk about *marching into Germany*. They want to get this over with and march back into their homes."

"Okay, fine then. So, what's next, Jack?"

I correct her. "You mean, *what's now, don't you?* The 92nd isn't getting Christmas off this year. Clark has lined them up against the anchor of the Gothic Line. Kesselring has big, nasty coastal guns he can use to lob shells on any troops trying to sneak up the west coast to dislodge his anchor. He'll move back and forward along other parts of the Gothic, but he won't budge from there."

When she remains silent, I continue while gently stroking her hair. "Rachel, a lot has happened since last summer when the guys in the 370th Regiment were the only colored soldiers on the line. They picked up two colored regiments, exchanged plenty of fire but just couldn't take the strongholds. The army will judge them for that no matter what else lies ahead. When those guns started opening tank sized craters in the ground at Massa, their retreat was *less than organized*."

Rachel lowers her head. "They sure were regular customers for us. Sometimes it was hard to tell what color anyone was. All I saw was blood red and olive drab. But I also saw some guys who shouldn't be here, several who shouldn't be in the Army. I was hoping you guys found some good stuff to write, somewhere."

I try to assure her that we did. "Trust me, a lot of it has run in the *Record.* A lot is still in that stack you just went through. One day John and I witnessed a firefight led by a colored lieutenant he started calling the *River Raider.* They sent him up a hill reinforced by a colored tank crew. Did you know there were colored tank battalions in Italy? It really was quite a show—but only five out of 42 guys that went up that hill walked back down."

"Good God, Jack. Is that what it's going to take?"

I paint the picture that is in my mind. "To do move up on the left flank, the boys need to be ready to take on a casualty rate of 50-70 percent. I confess that I was surprised when Clark asked all that of men who think they're *dying for second-class citizenship*. But the job is theirs now, regardless.

Rachel takes a few moments to digest what I have shared. Then, without warning, she breaks a bit of bad news to me. "Jack, with all this going on, the 317th is going to be swamped soon. I can't leave them shorthanded to play house with you. I'm going back with a convoy at first light—in about five hours. In fact, I can see the line of trucks from that window."

I protest, "No, you can't leave so soon, Rachel."

"Oh yes, and you need to get back too. You owe them that." Since I have no reason to hide my disappointment, I do not. She pulls my arm down around her bare shoulders. She has casually announced that our Christmas together is over before it begins.

Instead of addressing those concerns directly, I express annoyance over her references to *my obligations*. "*Owe them what?*" I respond impulsively, instantly regretting my dismissive tone.

She pulls further away from me. "You owe them your news coverage. You work for a colored newspaper's colored readers, for America's colored readers. Get in there and get the truth just like you have been. You need to tell the story the way Ron would have."

There's that name again. I respond, "And here we are once again. I hadn't heard his name all night. What's he doing that's so important?"

She is ready for the question. "Ron *was* looking into allegations that the 92nd was ordered to bring 800 unfit soldiers with them from Huachuca, men with poor attitudes and psychological issues, but with high test results that bolstered General Arnold's claim of 31 percent Class II scores."

I am skeptical. "That sounds suspiciously specific. How does he dig up this stuff?"

Her tone becomes condescending. "Ron was an *investigative* reporter, Jack. He just did it. He told me those 800 guys became morale liabilities—troublemakers, repeat offenders and malcontents." Listening to her, I wonder when and where she and Ron held this discussion.

I do not know why, but I jealously respond, "Trust Ron's findings if you wish. If any of this is bullshit, everyone's work loses credibility. That would be the real injustice to every colored GI I've interviewed from here back to Casablanca. I go the extra mile for facts. I crawl around and sleep in rain and mud—for facts. I come under bombing, strafing and artillery fire while taking pictures that I'm never sure will come out, for the facts."

Sometimes I forget that, as a daughter of an original buffalo soldier, the kinship Rachel feels for the 92nd Infantry Division is absolute. However, I have said nothing against them. Still she aims low, saying derisively, "Oh yeah, that's the only reason you're here, to build that resume of work, amass a repertoire of personal war stories."

I remain defensive. "My work advances the same cause that pre-occupies you. Accept that as truth or not, it is so."

Rachel continues to malign, even more pointedly than usual. "But it's just all a part of your grand plan, Jack. One day, you'll be wearing a French beret and telling war stories, in French, around Parisian bars. Sure, you take a few calculated risks, you with your connections. Tell me Jack, were Ron's press credentials revoked because he attacked segregation head on or because the two of you were after the same girl?"

Surprised to learn of that development, I think back to my conversation with Tom James on the road to Naples. Distracted, I unintentionally share more than I should know. "That's the first time you've ever said that to me. I only knew that he was under the microscope again for fabrication and for bypassing Army censors."

Her response is immediate. "So, you knew he was in trouble and you didn't warn him?"

"I've been warning him since my first day in Oujda. He never listened."

"So, you knew even before you left Washington. Then the rumors are true? Someone sent you over here to spy. Was it my uncle? Well, it's too late now. On the first leg of Ron's trip home, the plane crashed into the ocean leaving no survivors." In an instant, tears flow from her eyes and she begins to sob openly.

I pull her back to me and wrap my arms around her again, uncertain what to say next. She is shivering. I tell her, "Despite our differences, and our apparent commonalities, I'm genuinely sorry to hear this. The truth is that, before I left Washington, Owen asked me to remind Ron to cooperate with his censors—for his own good. That's all he asked me to do. Ron was dismissive as always. The last thing I heard about was trouble over an unsubstantiated story he ran in the *Advocate*, something about the air support during Salerno."

She is determined to connect me with his death. "Did you warn him about that, Jack?"

Annoyed by the absence of fairness in her assault, I dodge. "He knew what he had done. I couldn't have stopped him after the fact."

"Did you warn him, Jack?"

Angry that our brief holiday is already over, my voice grows louder. "No. On that particular occasion, I did not."

Her body goes stiff and rigid, coiled as though ready to spring from the bed any second. "You're talking about the dispute over Ron's coverage of the Tuskegee pilots over Salerno, right?"

Again, Rachel has caught me off balance with her knowledge of the details. "I think you're doing the talking, so why don't you just tell me what you're talking about."

"Ron didn't make that up. The 99th did fly in support of the Salerno invasion. He just had better information. The press office, your friend's press office, just didn't know about it. So, you see, you should have stood up for him."

"If what you say is true, he could have easily stood up for himself. There had to be something else. I heard a few brief remarks last year in the back of a truck on the road to Naples. Look, if you choose believe Ron's rumor that I have any kind of authority I can assure you, I do not."

"I *choose to believe* you could have stood up for him more."

The argument has become circular. I allow a few minutes to pass before shifting to survival mode. I try changing the subject, hoping to persuade her to stay. "I'm not talking about this anymore. I never spied on Ron or anyone else, and I sure as hell am not responsible for his death."

We both remain quiet for a long moment. I decide this is as good a time as any to share my news. "A letter's going out tomorrow inviting colored soldiers to retrain and fill combat vacancies created by the mess in the Ardennes. I'm going to follow the lead—to France for a few weeks."

Her terse response is immediate. "How would you know that, Jack? Is it common knowledge or inside information? Even if it's true, it's just bullshit. The war will be over before they could get them retrained and reassigned. You know someone will put a stop to it. But if you're saying *goodbye*, just say it Jack."

"You've already said *good-bye*. And the letter is from Ike, tacked up on bulletin boards all over France. It's not inside information."

Her voice is eerily calm. "You already have a colored division that needs you here, but go ahead and chase bullshit. Just drop everything, *including me*, and go to France where you always wanted to be. Maybe I was just a sideshow too."

I feel my remaining composure slipping away, and struggle to remain in control of my emotions. "You know that's not true. There's nothing more important to me than you. You know this story could mean integration. It's easily the biggest civil rights story of the war."

She remains silent. I continue, "Rachel, there's no authority to create another colored division nor are there any colored troops to reinforce the 92nd any further. I hear Clark's had it with them. They're not going to die to take those guns out, and Clark's going to scatter them to the wind. Other reporters can stay here to cover that."

"And which one of them is going to *cover me*, Jack?"

The cheap shot is more than I can stand. "You mean, *cover you* now that Ron's gone? I don't know. But if I can't *cover you* in Florence, how can I do it the Po Valley? And for God's sake, stop telling me about *my obligations.*"

Finally getting the argument she wants Rachel pushes away the blanket. "Lomax was just your ticket overseas and my uncle made your job a cakewalk."

"Sure, he did Rachel. Think whatever you want."

She steps out of bed, turns up the lamp and starts putting on her uniform. "Hey Scoop, how about a story on all the colored soldiers Pierrepoint hung in that jailhouse in England? That's the biggest *civil rights transgression* of the war. Jack won't write it though, because Jack wants to keep getting the inside track. Jack gets his own jeeps. Jack writes anonymous letters about how good the Army treats colored reporters. Good old *Jack Crow.*"

Incensed, I offer the worst retort imaginable. "Jack kills two men to save your young impetuous ass. Then, Jack saves your ass again when, an ocean away from home, you go passing for white." Strange, my words sound nastier than anything she has said. However, I cannot pull them back out of the air.

Rachel looks at me as though this has been a case of mistaken identity. Her tone blankets the room under a layer of frost. "That's right. Ron bends a few rules and has to leave, but not Rachel because she's Jack Savoy's girl."

I want to wake up and find out this has all been just a bad dream. "You know I didn't mean it that way. Let's talk this over. Why don't you turn that lamp out and at least stay here until daybreak?" In desperation, I try to deflect to a topic we have not discussed for a long time. "So, whatever happened to that crazy Klansman anyway?"

She looks around the room as though making certain she leaves nothing behind that would require her to ever return. She looks coldly into my eyes. "He died in my arms in triage."

Her words cause my body to go numb. "What, really, when?

"Lieutenant Matthews, of all people, ended up in the 317th. He was directing a collecting company when they hit them with an artillery barrage. By the time they got him to the evac, he was too far gone to save. Trying to save the vegetable that was left of him would have denied resources to too many salvageable GIs."

Forgetting my foot, I try to jump up and stumble onto the floor. She instinctively moves to assist me but catches herself, remaining in front of the door. In pain, I pull myself up and place my hand over the doorknob. "My God, Rachel, you had to make that decision about his life? Now, I know I can't just let you walk through the streets at night all by yourself."

The ice remains in her voice. "Really, Jack? Are we walking past those white reporters down in the lobby? Don't forget, one day someone may ask them whether you knew how to stay in your place."

It is the proverbial last straw. The comment saps my remaining energy, my capacity for reason and compassion. Our dialogue has become a dangerous forum for vile exchanges we can never take back. Dressed with arms folded, her eyes are now dry and clear, riveted straight ahead.

"So, in death, Ron wins what eluded him in life." I release the knob. She opens the door. The light in the hallway is out. She steps out into the darkness. When she turns back toward me, I slam the door in her face before she can speak. Then I turn the latch hard so that it locks with a loud metallic clap.

A second later, I turn off my room lamps, dousing even the sliver that would have been visible under the door, the only source of light in the hallway. Almost a full minute passes before I hear the thud of her combat boots as she walks away haltingly, feeling her way down the dark corridor until she reaches the first creaking step.

I hear her stumble in the darkness but catch herself in time to prevent a nasty fall. I wonder if she will ever speak to me again.

Chapter 23

. . . .

Bad News

I am sitting alone in my room in Florence. I hear what sounds like a New Year's Eve celebration going on downstairs in the hotel lobby. I dress and hobble down to find a festive party has ensued. Around the dining room, correspondents mill about with Army officers and civilians. Through the thick cloud of cigarette smoke, I spot a familiar face and walk over to him.

Though engrossed in a pointed conversation with a woman I recognize as an Army photographer, Ross Carpenter eventually notices me next to him. His smile fades and his face drops, as he takes on the posture of a man bending under the weight of tragedy. He begins by apologizing for failing to offer his *condolences sooner*. When he discovers I have no idea what he is talking about, he turns ashen, and his head drops again. Ross hands me his tall glass of whiskey. He, however, appears to need it more so than I might.

After composing himself, he leads me out of the noisy lobby and down one flight of stairs toward the entrance to a storage room. Ross rests a hand on my shoulder and tells me that, "during an offensive that began in the Serchio Valley on Christmas Day, your Rachel was killed while supervising an evacuation of wounded soldiers."

My mind and body go numb. She had repeatedly cheated death and escaped retribution for cheating the Army's policy of segregation. Rachel died while trying to do the job denied to Negro women, that of saving others. Ross adds that, "I was there because I'd been meaning for some time to do a few stories on the battlefield hospitals. A unit of the 317th was close by. As fate would have it, I hitched a ride and found myself right in front of Captain Todd's evac."

I do not know what to say, I know nothing that I would say of any relevance. I hear myself ask, "What happened to her? Had you already interviewed her for your story?"

As though concerned about his best friend, Ross continues to speak softly and deliberately, "Yes, and she asked *if I had seen you around*. I took the liberty of saying *you were miserable without her*. After the first few shells landed, I made for a shelter. I heard several rounds hit close by, but didn't know how close until I climbed back out." He hesitates as though he does not want to go on, as though he wished I would stop him from talking further.

I do not want to stop him. "And, then what happened, Ross?"

Ross is shedding tears. "Everything looked so different than it had just a few minutes before. I walked over to a tent that had suffered a near direct hit. Several bodies lay together as though hit by a single round. Rachel was one of them. Right after that, we hightailed out of there."

He need not feel ashamed for making that decision, but I understand his embarrassment, given the context. I do not know why, but I ask for confirmation. "Ron, are you certain?"

He responds with certainty. "I'm very sorry to say that I am, Jack. Taylor liked the story idea and went with me to take photographs. I saw her body again in a tasteless photograph taken right after the barrage. The reference scribbled on the back read, *killed by a single shell*. No, you don't, Jack. It was censored out, and you don't ever want to see it."

Ross takes the drink that is about to fall from my hand, and finishes half of it at once. I have feelings that will not manifest, tears I cannot shed. On each occasion that Rachel returned to the front, I feared for her safety, but always remained confident I would see her again, be with her again. She reminded me on so many occasions to be careful that I began to see her as invincible. Strange, I had never verbally expressed my fear, as though giving a voice to my concerns would make them come to be.

I consider the irony of helping her out with her problem in Casablanca. If I had never bumped into her again in Algeria, right now, she might be Stateside or working at a hospital in Liberia, perhaps England. Instead, after surviving air raids and artillery barrages from Morocco to Tuscany, the woman I love, perhaps the only one I have ever truly loved, is dead.

From a distance, I hear Ross say, "You know, you should do her story, Jack. Do her *real story.*"

I think about how alone I have felt since the harsh words Rachel and I exchanged a week ago. I have loved her since the day I saw her in Casablanca, perhaps since the day I first met her as a teenager near Lake Erie. However, for some reason, I cannot yet respond to Ross or express my grief.

Now, rather than feeling alone in Italy, I feel alone in the world. I have frequently imagined Rachel joining Anne and the Savoy brothers, and now I know she will not. The thought causes my empty stomach to cramp and sends an icy chill up my spine. Suddenly, I cannot imagine life without her. As I replay in my mind our senseless argument, the disturbing truth is that I may not want to contemplate life without her.

Chapter 24

· ·

My Brother`s Keeper

"I blame that colored general. What's his name, Davis? I hear they put his kid in command of those colored flyers. Hell, if Marshall hadn't reined in Ike, Davis Senior might've convinced him to integrate the whole damned ETO."

"How is that, Lieutenant?" *I think I have a live one.*

"With stunts like this letter right here on my desk, that's how." The newly minted press officer speaks as though he can read the mind of the Supreme Allied Commander. In truth, I doubt he has witnessed anything beyond the deck of the ship that brought him across the English Channel or the short road he traveled between the French port of Cherbourg and the town of Valognes.

I indulge him, just in case he knows anything that might lead me to Serge's current location in France. "Just out of curiosity, Mister Savoy, have you covered any actual combat action?"

I summarize a version of my standard response. "I've witnessed a lot of shootouts. While Fifth Army was training, I covered some operations in Tunisia. Later I went ashore at Salerno and followed the Allied linkup in Foggia with British Eighth Army. I arrived in Naples during the German retreat to the Gustav Line. I covered a week at Casino. I was wounded at Anzio and, after recovery, spent a month at the front with a rifle company in the Serchio Valley."

"Oh." He is probably thankful when I do not embarrass him with a similar question about his service. "That's impressive, Mister Savoy. There're reporters around here who haven't ventured beyond the briefing rooms. How'd you get hit at Anzio?"

I do not know how much time I have, and want to keep him focused. "Just fractured my leg and foot-nearly healed already. But I don't want to use up our time talking about that."

He continues to engage in small talk. "You said you traveled up here by ship and train—hope that was uneventful. You know, I have some leave coming up. How was the countryside between the southern coast of France and Paris—considering it used to be Vichy after all?"

I give him an overview, hoping we will soon be getting back on topic. "There's still some damage from the opening action in '39 plus the *Champagne* landings. The Germans retreated from San Raphael and Toulon north to Dijon before scattering. South of Paris remains largely intact even after Patton swept through with Third Army. I stayed in the city a few weeks before coming here. I'm interested in getting back to those letters. Will the Colonel be joining us?"

I do not mind speaking with a junior level press aid if he can assist me, but this one has not yet been of much help.

"Reporters always think you need a higher-ranking officer, and the Colonel will drop by if he can. But I've got enough information to provide good background for your story, plus I, as much as anyone else, understand the intent of the first letter and the reason for Ike's retraction." He talks like a man underestimated by a string of correspondents with the same assumptions about his reliability as a source of credible information.

If he has internalized the sleight, nothing loosens lips like a bruised ego and the impulse to soothe it. He begins speaking with authority. "After the German breakout through the Ardennes, several divisions were short a total of 20,000 riflemen. With no replacements coming from the States, Ike decided to use support services men to pitch in and fight at the front. A committee was supposed to work out the details. You know what that meant."

I try my best to look impressed and leave my notepad closed to suggest that we are off the record. I also indulge him, with a stale joke.

"In North Africa, they say a camel is a horse that was designed by a committee."

He laughs from deep within. "I'll have to use that one, Jack." He leans forward attempting to confirm what my body language is trying to suggest. "Now this is strictly off the record, right."

"Hell, frankly, I'm surprised the whole thing isn't marked with a higher classification." It is an old ploy, responding to a question without answering it.

"So am I, though it was supposed to be kept *Confidential.* By the time Davis and the committee finished, instead of a plan to retrain new infantrymen, we had an integration plan—another *goddam social experiment.*"

He shakes his head and stops to collect his thoughts. "But I'm ahead of myself. Let me explain." I listen as he takes ten minutes to describe ADSEC, the Advance Section of the Communications Zone. It is a canned pitch. "ADSEC moves information, supplies and people between the front and rear echelons. We advance behind the combat troops. We maintain everything still standing. We provide everything from field hospitals and blood banks to ordnance and munitions. We invented the Red Ball and all the other color-coded transportation runs, so we've got a lot of colored help."

I try hurrying him along before I become visibly annoyed. "And so ADSEC was expected to recruit Negro volunteers, retrain them at replacement centers in France and then send them to units depleted by the Bulge?"

I already have a lot of background. After we read a bootlegged copy of the first letter, Ted concurred with my trip to Valognes to report on the retraining program. Tom gave the trip his tacit approval and established this contact. As I prepared to leave Naples, a letter Anne wrote about Serge altered my mission to one of a more urgent and personal nature. I ask an obvious question to keep the Lieutenant talking. "But wouldn't that also deplete ADSEC's resources?"

Sensing that I have already done some homework, he continues with specificity. "No. Meeting Ike's need for 20,000 retrained riflemen only depletes ADSEC by ten percent. We were looking for men who wanted to experience real-life combat before the war ends—you know, something to tell their grandsons. General Davis is ADSEC's *special colored advisor.* He wanted to make it all about the coloreds—that's what stirred up the pot. Davis wanted coloreds to *fight shoulder to shoulder* with white infantrymen—to integrate combat units. He drafted a letter, Ike concurred and copies of it were on bulletin boards by Christmas."

He clearly remains incredulous about the notion and searches my face for concurrence. I try to feign an expression of mild exasperation, just to fuel his fire. I ask, "Did Negro soldiers read it as a change in policy?"

"Hey, please don't ask me what goes on in a colored guy's head—I swear, I know nothing about that. But almost 5,000 signed up right away."

He emphasizes the number as though awed that Negro servicemen traded the relative safety of rear echelon duties for the dangers of front-line deployment. "Half were truck drivers and laborers. Colored sergeants signed up knowing they'd have to accept reductions to private—since no combat replacement can hold rank above private first class in his new unit."

Almost unconsciously but still audibly, I complete his thought. "That way, no retrained colored soldier could issue an order that any experienced white combat soldier was compelled to obey."

The comment appears to give him pause and I regret adding a hint of sarcasm. He wants to be sure he sets the record straight. "That rule holds true for both white and colored retrained infantry."

I respond truthfully. "I wasn't aware of that—hadn't heard it. It makes good sense. What did you think about the second letter?"

Now he becomes expansive, gesturing with his arms. "After we posted it, we got instructions to take it down and replace it with a second letter, back—dated to December 26. Off the record, the second letter caused so much confusion it set us back a month. They should have stuck with the first letter and issued guidance. You know what I mean?" I merely sit in pokerfaced silence.

He no longer needs my encouragement and begins to rant. "From what I've heard, someone told Ike to tone down the first letter—that ran counter to General Marshall's thinking. So then, the second letter extended the invitation to retrain without regard to color. In fact, it mentioned colored soldiers only as an afterthought, stating the Army might assign a limited number of Negroes to existing colored combat units. Only if there was a surplus would any of them integrate white combat units."

It is new information that may lead us to the breakthrough I seek. Since I know he will not be as candid if a senior officer arrives, I decide to give him a nudge to see how far he will go. "Oh, I see. But tell me Lieutenant, what prevents an officer from seizing this opportunity to get rid of bad apples?"

For the first time, I detect suspicion. After glancing toward the door and leaning forward, he confides. "Well, this is the first time I've gotten that question. That would be a punishable offense, Savoy. But since you ask, I will say that the second letter does say that commanders *should survey services units to see where redeployments make the most sense—and be prepared to document how a replacement's duties will be fulfilled in his absence.*"

Since I have not seen the revised letter, I make a simple request that might reduce the amount of time he makes available to me. "Do you mind if I take a few minutes to read the two letters side by side? Thank you. I'll only need a few minutes."

As I read them together, I come to understand the confusion. I am intrigued most that so many sergeants have volunteered for reductions in grade. These men came of age during an economic depression, and as Blue used to remind them, military service increased, for some, their standards of living. I am about to ask him if their pay remained the same when he jumps to his feet to acknowledge the arrival of a senior officer.

"Colonel Evans, this is Jack Savoy, a war correspondent." I stand and extend my hand to the Colonel who extends his to form a tight grip and releases. He looks annoyed that the Lieutenant tells him what he can plainly see. "Jack is writing a story about the combat infantry retraining program at the reppie-deppies. He's a reporter for the *Washington Record*—which I don't believe I've heard of."

The Colonel's tight smile fades. "You haven't heard of it because it's one of those colored weeklies, John. Of course, I can understand why there'd be a lot of interest from the Negro press."

The young Lieutenant looks at me, mouth agape. He searches my face for the clues he clearly missed. He begins to stammer, but regains some composure. "Sir, I was explaining to him that we received two communiques."

His superior becomes very annoyed. "What do you mean you were *explaining*? What's there to explain, John? We received a letter that superseded an earlier letter. ADSEC has done its part to implement the program as ordered and transferred the volunteers to their new command. What happens next is up to the Army Group commanders—and of course, the individual soldiers themselves."

The Lieutenant looks down at his hands searching for the right words that might free him from his boss's ire. When the colonel asks if the briefing is over, he again responds with the wrong word. "Yes sir. I was just *explaining* to..." The colonel abruptly cuts off his subordinate.

"Mister Savoy, I see you have both letters in front of you. Do you require anything further? Good. Do you have any further questions?"

Suddenly, I appreciate every moment I have spent alone with the Lieutenant. If the Colonel had been present, the briefing would have been far less useful. I decide it is time to get to what has emerged as the real point of my visit. "Well, actually, I'd hoped for another meeting, next time in ADESC HQ—and if I might interview a volunteer. There is one, if you can tell me where to find him. He was with the first group and I understand they haven't completed retraining."

"Where've you been Savoy? That was okay when I got the heads up from your Army press officer, but as of March 10, 1945 the first 2500 colored volunteers completed the first phase of their retraining. They were at the 16th Ground Forces Replacement, or *Reinforcement*, Command Depot in Compiegne. That was over two weeks ago. They're in new infantry platoons now. Their records followed them and ADSEC's authority ended with their delivery to the reppie-deppie."

I feel that familiar sudden sharp pain in the pit of my stomach. Between the lines, Anne's coded letter suggests that Serge, an ADSEC truck driver, was retrained against his will. Now, it appears that losing track of the days during my unscheduled sabbatical in Paris has cost me an opportunity. My eyes burn slightly as I stare at these obtuse bureaucrats. Frustrated, I begin rambling.

"I'm just really surprised at how quickly the Army formed and deployed these new platoons. It took two years to get a colored infantry division to Italy. Although there are no replacements for casualties or transfers for that established division, within the space of a few months, dozens of new colored infantry platoons have been sent to the front lines in Germany."

Colonel Evans, clearly an experienced press officer, has heard no question. He offers no response to my emotion-charged diatribe. He asks his own question instead. "So, Mister Savoy, did you say that you wanted to interview one particular volunteer?"

"Well, it sounds like you wouldn't be able to help me with that now. But maybe you could answer a question for me." I've already overstretched the bounds of propriety, and my next thought may cause them to snap. "Were all of these reassignments strictly voluntary? That is, did all soldiers come forward on their own accord? Let me ask the question another way. Are there records of the requests for transfer?"

The colonel is far past the point of even modest cordiality. "Standard forms have always existed for requesting and approving transfers. The guidance for processing those forms is clear and incontrovertible."

I am certain the colonel's answer is merely a gatekeeper's dodge. "Then if I wanted to see a particular request, how would I get it?"

"Mister Savoy, before this goes any further, why don't you spit it out. What are you getting at?"

In my exasperated state, I decide to do just that. "I believe that at least one company commander saw the retraining initiative as an opportunity to move someone out of his unit—against his will."

Recognizing now my previous attempt to implicate him, the Lieutenant is livid. "Hey, come on now Jack. That's a serious allegation. Do you have any concrete evidence—other than hearsay—to substantiate that? If not, you might want to tread carefully."

His stance is now aggressive. His eyes dart back and forth. The colonel can probably guess now that his subordinate has been much too talkative. He comes to the Lieutenant's aid. "Mister Savoy, are you pursuing this as a story for your newspaper? Do you have permission to investigate this, this preposterous allegation? Tell me, who exactly are you looking for—what's his name? If you can't give me a name how can I help you?"

"Prior to retraining, he was a truck driver. Prior to landing at Cherbourg and moving here to Valognes, he was stationed in Bristol.

His name is Sergeant Serge Savoy." Both men flinch at the sound of my brother's name.

"Serge Savoy—Jack Savoy, geez, that's what this is about."

The colonel waives him off. "So then, this is personal."

I stand my ground, shaky though it may be. "Whatever it is, it's pretty obvious you're familiar with it."

Chapter 25

· ·

Charlie Drum

"**M**ister Savoy, I don't know how you can assume you can hitch your way through a shooting war to find a regiment on the move." Despite agreeing to drive me to the west bank of the Rhine, Corporal Charlie Drum appears to be having second thoughts.

I try to lighten the mood. "Well yeah, but you have to admit it's a beautiful day for a drive ain't it, Charlie?"

Ignoring me, he continues, "If and only if the road is clear, I'll take you as far as Remagen. If the road's not clear, you can ride back with me or stay out here on your own. It gets dark early." For the third time since we left Compiegne, Charlie has repeated the terms of our arrangement. However, he has not once mentioned the 100 dollars he is charging me to make the extended trip.

Despite the end of hostilities in France and Belgium, Charlie keeps a wary eye out for lingering threats. He constantly surveys both sides of a busy stretch of road that should take us peacefully across the Muse River into Belgian. Much too old to be a corporal, in just the right light, he looks like a thinner version of Isaac Blue. Unlike Blue, I am certain that the mere sound of gunfire will cause him to waver on his conditional commitment.

I replay in my mind Colonel Evans' parting warning: *I can't imagine what you hope to accomplish at this point. Trying to find your brother's outfit, which might be anywhere in Germany, is a damned fool's errand.*

As we cross into Belgium, Charlie prods me to clarify the same set of facts I have given him several times in varying iterations. I patiently repeat myself, understanding that I may present something of a curiosity. Unlike a soldier under orders, I am in a hurry to get to the front, armed with a notepad and an unauthorized camera. Still, reporters have been hitchhiking across Europe since D-Day. Charlie has no legitimate reason to question *my authenticity,* as he has been since I walked into his ADSEC motor pool.

"So, Mister Savoy, you say you landed in Italy September 1943?"

Unwilling to rehash that again, I ask, "Can't you relax, Charlie? I don't want to dig through my stuff for press credentials. Who else would be trying to do this?"

"Yeah, okay. Maybe you are who you say you are. I know you've heard that everything's been quiet in Belgium since January. You think the Germans are all hiding in Berlin, waiting for us to come in on them from all directions. Well, everyone had better keep his powder dry. There are still plenty of fanatics."

Crossing the bridge at Remagen, Germany is my best chance of locating the headquarters of the 9th Infantry Division and getting in contact with the division's 60th Regiment, and Serge's new platoon. I have no plan, no maps and no other source of intelligence. I know only that they are actively engaging German forces and putting my brother, an ostensible volunteer, in harm's way. I am prepared to continue without Charlie, wherever he leaves me. Giving up on finding Serge is not an option, now that I have missed him in France.

My meeting at ADSEC took place two weeks later than originally planned because I had not grieved properly for Rachel in Naples. Instead, I focused on getting aboard a ship sailing from Naples to Toulon. Later, on the train north to Paris, I began feeling guilty about my excitement over returning to the beautiful intact city.

By the time I arrived in Paris, the short distance to Valognes seemed like an impossible odyssey. Instead, I checked into a small hotel on the West Bank. For two weeks, I slept into the afternoons and frequented bars late into the nights, replaying every moment with Rachel from Casablanca to Florence. It all ended the night I awakened atop a bridge with no mental record of my purpose there.

After my meeting in Valognes, I hitched a ride to Compiegne. There, through persistence, I learned that the 60th Infantry Division had absorbed Serge's retrained platoon. That same day, I met Charlie Drum, a driver with a regular route that takes him as far as Liege, Belgium.

"You still expect trouble west of the Rhine, Charlie? Look, I'm to report to the press liaison in 9th Division HQ." While the statement is a lie, it is within the realm of possibility, and I need no prior authorization. No one knows I have gone east beyond Valognes, and the ADSEC colonel in Compiegne assured me that he would deny any knowledge of my whereabouts or plans.

"I just need you to get me to Remagen Charlie. I'll find a way to get across the Ludendorff Bridge."

He eyes me with renewed suspicion. "You mean get across one of the temporary bridges, don't you? The old one collapsed last week, crashed into the river without so much as a jeep on it. I would expect a war correspondent, *even a colored one*, to know that, just as I would expect the Army to arrange for a war correspondent's transportation."

"Actually, most of the time, we just show up." He has already expressed doubt that any Negro war correspondents exist. He also raised suspicions about the combat uniform I wear rather than the *sniper's-bait* officer's Class A outfit. "I'd bet only a few people west of the Muse know a damned thing about that bridge, Charlie." I quickly change the subject. "Tell me what you know about the infantry retraining program?"

He becomes animated. "I know all about it, but I never gave it a second thought. I've done my share. I landed right after D-Day with my gun crew. We laid down fire wherever they said, right where they said." I take out a pencil and notepad. "We got assigned to the 333rd Artillery. We were already in the Ardennes when the Tigers busted through. We never stopped shooting for anything until we ran low on ammo.

"Just before Christmas, colored truck drivers started dropping off paratroopers near Bastogne, and so we supported the 101st Division. Another colored gun outfit, the 969th, was there. We kept firing, kept playing Tiger and mouse for days. Ain't nothing like a German 88-millimeter gun in the right hands, ooh-wee boy. I caught some shrapnel in both my legs and went to the hospital.

"I heard later that General Taylor recommended us for a citation, but when all the smoke cleared, they transferred most of us out. In the hospital, I heard they were looking for other places to send the colored guys. I couldn't wait around for that. I jumped at the chance for a motor pool job. I wound up in ADSEC, and there I stay, until that slow boat home."

I am still writing. "That's a hell of a story, Charlie."

I hear emotion welling up as he continues. "When you get over the river, remember to look for the colored gun crews. I lost friends in those woods. One good friend in the 333rd and his whole battery just up and disappeared out there, likely dead or captured. We hung in there from the first day the tanks broke through in the forest."

We arrive outside Liege without incident. After a brief stop, Charlie continues with renewed confidence. "I ran into a buddy. He thinks I've lost my mind, but we should be fine the rest of the way. He says any Germans we see on this road will probably want us to feed them."

The countryside is a series of hills, rock formations and forests. Signs of fighting are evident, some towns and villages along this route of the Allied advance lay partially destroyed. However, I can still imagine the splendor of the world the Nazis put at risk and the German people have now lost. Charlie seems to read my mind. "Man, have you ever wondered how better things would be if he called it quits after the Czechs?"

I do not want to get Charlie started on a stale argument I have heard many times before. "Not so good for the Jews. Hitler, or a successor, would've consolidated power. Some think he would've eventually gotten *Poland anyway with just a slap on the wrist.*"

As we approach our destination, traffic slows to a crawl. Charlie, aware that my plan ends with him, finally looks relaxed as he tries to maneuver. "I'll say one thing, Jack. You got a pair. They may be in a firefight when you get there. Those boys don't fool around. I wouldn't worry about your brother. I'd be amazed if he's doing anything more than digging latrine holes."

Much of Remagen is very much the destitute wasteland I anticipated. However, in many areas, civilians struggle to resurrect the lives they had six months ago amid a mass of Army tents, commandeered buildings and temporary structures. Following suggestions, he received

COLOR INSIDE THE LINES

at our last stop, Charlie continues until we are near the river, where he finds the transportation outfit he had hoped to locate.

There, Charlie quickly announces that he *found me walking on the side of the road*. A young sergeant casts a wary eye. "Just where are you going, sir?"

"I'm trying to cross over the river and get through Erpel to catch up with the 60th Infantry Regimental HQ."

He laughs, apparently at the absurdity of my plan, yet walks over to inquire at a makeshift structure. Through the window, I see him inside conferring with an officer. A few minutes later, he returns shaking his head in disbelief.

"You must have a golden horseshoe up your ass. Damned if there ain't a small group going out at dawn, headed to the 60th. You'll have to stay lucky. Those boys could move out of there on a moment's notice." Immediately, I slip the bills into Charlie's hand and wish him all the best. I climb out of the truck before he can respond.

Dropped off where I need to be, I am reluctant to tempt fate. "If you don't mind, I'd like to wait in there. In fact, do you have a spare corner where I could stretch out? Where's the convoy headed tomorrow? The Harz Mountains—no, I've never heard of it."

Serge, or someone resembling my brother, is guardedly ecstatic to see me in Germany. "Don't tell me. Let me guess what you're about to say." I try to say something but I do not hear any words. "Go ahead and tell me that this is the last place on earth you ever expected to run into your baby brother."

After some effort, I manage to say, "Serge, if I listed a million places, I thought I might find you in April 1945, a bivouac in the heart of Germany wouldn't be on the list. What in hell are you doing here? No, let's start with what the hell are you doing in the Army?"

Mindful that the slightest spark of controversy between my brother and me can ignite a bonfire, I have been turning over in my mind several ways to approach him. However, nothing—including my knowledge of his deployment—could prepare me for the circumstances under which I have found him.

207

Earlier this morning, I crossed the Rhine with two trucks carrying green replacements and rehabilitated wounded returning to the 60th Infantry Regiment in trucks. As fate would have it, a senior NCO directed me to ride with returning veterans.

When they found out they were traveling with a war correspondent, the men told me they suffered their wounds expanding the initial beachhead on the east bank of the Rhine. I was surprised to hear words of praise for retrained colored infantry platoons that helped clear the heights on the east bank and reinforced a depleted company just when it needed help most. Then, rather than the non-stop exchange of war stories I had hoped would follow, the men engaged primarily in small talk about families, hometowns and girlfriends.

Given Remagen's location on the Rhine, I had anticipated a short ride to the 60th Infantry Regiment. However, throughout the morning, we moved deep enough into Germany to hear sporadic firing. Further into the interior, the soldiers began to talk less and listen more, relaxed yet poised, ready to respond to force with force.

After passing through several checkpoints, I began to see larger clusters of soldiers and makeshift shelters. When we finally arrived, I found a lieutenant responsible for press relations. He was remarkably casual in his acceptance of my request to cover the battalion's new colored rifle platoon. "Have fun."

Soon, I was riding on the bench seat of a jeep behind a sergeant wielding a machine gun and a corporal who drove with a carbine mounted at the ready. Both carried holstered 45 caliber pistols. Fortunately, once we arrived at our destination, the men of Company E were still close to battalion headquarters. I covered the remaining distance easily on foot.

"What am I doing here? Red, what in the hell are you doing here? If you came this far to cover the new colored platoons, why don't you look happy to bump into me here—hell, anywhere? Do you realize that it's been two years?"

I am overjoyed to see that he is still alive. "What do you expect from me? The last time I saw you, you were on Page-One of the *Detroit Free Press*. An angry mob was trying to peel you off a bus. Now, after traveling halfway across Europe, and rather deep into Germany, I find you in a colored combat platoon on the razor's edge of the American advance. Do you realize where we are?"

"Oh, come on Red. Take it easy." My youngest brother only laughs at me the way a salty combat veteran might amuse himself about the fear in a raw recruit.

I defend my honor. "It's not like I haven't seen plenty of combat—I have, just not at Hitler's front door. Don't you think you need to start off this conversation with some sort of explanation?"

He takes a moment to collect his thoughts. "That seems like a whole lifetime ago now. The police didn't arrest anyone else in that photo. I was the only colored guy and the only noncitizen there. They locked me up without stating a charge—under the threat of deportation. Much to my surprise, they allowed me to make a phone call. After a few hours, they released me and strongly advised me not to leave town until they finished investigating. I knew that if I so much as sneezed it would trigger another arrest."

"So just like that, you decided to join the Army? And when did you start describing people as *colored*?"

"Well, when did *you*?" I had not realized I was saying it. Serge continues, "Don't try to make it sound like that. You know I had already aced their aptitude test. I took it as part of our investigation into Army placement practices. They said it was *my path out of trouble and my path to citizenship*. "Before I shipped out, I got on a C-47 bound for Bolling Field. Charles and Anne came home and found me napping on their front porch."

"So, then he still hadn't shipped out yet at that point. I don't suppose you've seen him over here."

"No, but some of the men say they saw colored tankers attached to a 3rd Army armored division. They've fought through France, went with Patton on that crazy assed hook shot to Bastogne, busted through the Siegfried. That's who you should be trying to find for an interview."

I must agree that the correspondents have not written enough about the 761st Tank Battalion, raising little awareness about the unit. However, just hearing the good news that both my brothers are healthy raises my spirits.

"I'm glad to hear you saw him before he left and I hope you behaved yourself in their home. Now that I'm up here, maybe I'll try to find out where he is. Things change quickly now. You describe this stuff like a day at the beach. I'd like to know why the Army had the family genius driving a truck."

"I didn't make a lot of friends, Red." Serge begins to laugh and talk as though we are standing in Charles' back yard rather than on the smoldering business end of a violent push into enemy territory. I hear shells exploding close by. Serge and the soldiers around us ignore the sounds as they would a distant thunderstorm.

"Well, it's like I told you. These men will form the civil rights vanguard one day. I just wanted to be wherever *Afro-Americans* would be. You should have seen that frustrated classifier, Jack—a man under pressure to find a lofty place any Negro scoring in Group I. But somehow, He finally gave in and assigned me to basic duties."

"Okay, we can fill in the other blanks later. Let's get to how you ended up in a combat unit. I'm familiar with the initiative and I've read the letters that were posted."

"Then you know everything I know, except that when the list of volunteers was posted, my name was on it. When I asked, my *First Shirt* said they were given a quota to fill and added several names to the list of volunteers."

I cannot accept his nonchalance. "And just like that, you accepted that explanation and marched off to infantry training? That doesn't even sound like you, Peanut."

Serge is still smiling. "I know, it's crazy, ain't it?"

"Crazy? It's insane. Do you fully grasp where you are right now— where we are? Tell me honestly. Why do you think your name ended up on that list? Why do you think the ADSEC senior press officer immediately recognized your name?"

"How do you know that? What were you doing at ADSEC? And are you saying someone in ADSEC HQ knew me?" Serge seems more impressed with his notoriety than concerned that people may have conspired against him. I struggle to maintain my composure as my brother answers my questions by telling a story.

"Back in Alabama, I went to a segregated movie house to see a Crosby movie. When he sang *Dixie* in blackface, the locals stood up, clapped in time and sang along. I left and came back the next week in whiteface and white gloves. I tell you that to say that any man who loves to poke the bear as much as I do expect to get his ass chewed. I poked the bear a lot—every day. I poked an officer with a pedestrian of humor to match his narrow sense of right and wrong."

His acceptance of the situation has caught me off balance. "Even if I can get you out of this, you have to understand that no one's playing games over here. Promise them you'll straighten up and fly right. But we need to act quickly."

He is incredulous. "*Act quickly to do what*, Red? I'm not going anywhere, other than to move out tomorrow and shoot every Nazi I can find in some place called Lengenbach."

"What—you mean you want to stay here?" I look around at the men who make up the newly trained colored platoon assigned to this battalion. My contact in Compiegne said that the 9th Infantry Division has *taken an impressive approach to reassigning and preparing its Negro platoons*. Rather than grouping several platoons into new, inexperienced Negro companies, the regimental commander has attached each new platoon to one experienced company within each battalion.

This evening they move about with a serious, focused sense of purpose and professional demeanor that is somehow different, not more disciplined but *more focused* than men I knew in Italy. I wonder how much motivation they get from the quality and reputations of their new leaders. The division commander's commitment to fairness is encouraging. Unlike Serge, the others genuinely volunteered to come here. Many are risking their lives to prove they are capable of frontline combat.

"But even if I didn't want to stay, what in hell do you think you can do here? This ain't Washington. What are you going to do—put in a call to Owen Todd, go talk to Taft's people? Are you finally going to claim an instance of discrimination? As much as I'd love to witness that, I'm staying. Day after day, we go out on patrol—that's right, I'm usually on the point—knowing that somebody won't come back. Once you're here, there's no walking away. I hope you intend to interview some of them."

I take a long look at my brother—perhaps for the first time since I walked into the small bivouac area that serves as a temporary home for the colored platoon assigned to Company E.

A layer of grime covers most of Serge's faded, neglected uniform—even the stitched outline of his previous sergeant's rank. His hair has not visited comb or brush. Stubbly whiskers cover his sallow, deadpan face. His eyes are hollow, looking out into the distance at something only he can see. He is not the free spirit I expected to find here rebelling against every link in his chain of command. I barely recognize him.

"Red, I wouldn't leave here even if you had a plan—which you clearly don't. Look at the men in my platoon and tell me what you see. Tell me they aren't the proudest, most confident *Mandingo warriors* you've ever seen. No bent-over coons, no mush-mouths up here."

I whisper through clenched teeth. "That doesn't change the fact that you were duped into this."

He is speaking in a course, hushed whisper now. "You damned right I was—at first. For a week, I spent every day planning ways to go over the wall. Then, every day I spent with these guys changed me. Jack, I finally understand why they never wanted us to be a part of this kind of thing."

I nod, but say nothing. Sweeping his arm around in a circle, Serge includes everyone here. "Do you see all these white guys? They are the famous fighting 60th Infantry Regiment. They invaded Morocco in '42. They invaded Sicily in '43. They landed on Utah Beach in '44, and fought their way across France just to wind up spending Christmas on the Bulge.

"They were among the first to cross the Rhine, catch hell in the Hurtgen Forest and helped seal the Ruhr Pocket—capturing 300,000 Germans. Now we're pushing through the Harz Mountains. A few of them grudgingly mentioned hearing about a few companies of Sherman tanks in the Roer operated by colored guys. No Jack, they said it was the 784th. Who are the 784th? Go find that out, please."

"Who cares if they grudgingly admitted seeing them? Who cares if they got their unit number wrong? Hell, they give white replacements the blues until they get their feet wet. You want to be useful. Go and find those colored tankers, Jack. No one else will. You know what these boys are asking each other tonight: Why'd they put *all these damned coons in the 60th and what will they do tomorrow when they step in the real shit*?"

"So, if you're so sure you know what you're going to do, I guess I'll just turn around and leave empty handed." I can hear the frustration building in my own voice.

Serge places his palm on my shoulder as if to steady me and probes my face with those new dark, hollow eyes. "I am sure. What do you mean *empty-handed*? Are you okay Red? What's with this impetuous dash across Europe? It's not like you—this impulsive, irrational behavior. That's my forte—and it's just occurring to me that you came all this way just to find me and set me free."

"I did it because I love you, knucklehead." For a moment, I think I see that familiar sparkle in his eyes, Mamie's eyes. For the first time in our adult lives, we embrace—in front of warriors. However, I have been around combat enough to know that they all have brothers, fathers and sons whom they wish they could hug today.

As I am about to speak, I push my index finger into his chest for emphasis, but as though indulging an impetuous teen, he grabs my wrist and gently pushes my hand away from a grenade. I keep it brief. "Okay tough guy. Just keep your damned-fool head down."

"I can't do that Red. Around here, they depend on my head being up and my eyes open. Tell Anne I love her, and tell that big-headed middle brother of ours to get back home and take care of his family."

Because I have witnessed death in Italy, honoring his request, which suggests that he may not survive, is too difficult for me to contemplate. "You tell them yourself."

"Cut the bullshit Red. If I can, and I'll try my very best, I'll tell them myself, but you may have to tell them for me. Can you promise me you'll do that, without all the emotional bullshit?"

I do not know this man that I instantly admire, the man my bother has become in two years. He leaves room only for compliance. "Yes, I will Serge."

Then he asks a question for which I am ill prepared. "And whatever became of you and Rachel? Did you find her? Tell her I still love her. I know you haven't told her that you do yet. Hey, Jack, what's wrong with you?"

Chapter 26

· ·

Buffaloed

I confirm that Charles' battalion is still on the move and that a few
Negro companies of Sherman and Stuart tanks are in another sector
supporting the 35th Infantry Division. I hear about the introduction
of a few larger, safer American tanks with 90-millimeter turret guns. I also
get confirmation of a colored 784th Tank Battalion that trained alongside
the 761st and arrived in France right after D-Day. However, after much
thought and soul searching, I weigh the odds against finding Charles
among a million Allied soldiers poised to invade Berlin.

I feel guilty, but rationalize that I must return to Italy and get my
own version of how the Buffalo Soldiers' story ends. After hiking with
Serge's platoon on two missions, I hitchhike back across the Rhine,
and retrace my steps across Belgium and France. I resist the urge to
detour toward Paris, and instead sail from Toulon back to Naples for
a rest before hitchhiking north again for the final showdown in Italy.

However, when I hear that the final Allied offensive to end the
fighting in Northern Italy already has commenced, I hitch rides on
three different trucks, piecing my way north toward the Po Valley.
With Rachel's admonitions still fresh in my mind, I do not want to
miss any significant contribution the Buffalo Soldiers' might make
to Fifth Army's campaign to close the door on the stubborn German
forces in Italy.

Upon my arrival in the valley, I find that much has changed in the 92nd Infantry Division since last Thanksgiving. The battalions of the 370th Regiment are the division's only remaining Negro combat infantry components, and there's talk of taking them off the line.

"That's right, Mister Savoy. Although, we've been anchoring the west flank of the Allied push, they may pull us. I know you were with us last year. Still, I'm asking you to keep your head down—unless you can do a lot more with that dull-edged bayonet than I think you can."

I ignore the sarcasm, and do not react defensively to the sergeant's joke about the bayonet that has been my useful digging, trenching and hacking tool since Salerno. "I'm not a combatant but you won't need to babysit me. So, I'd appreciate it if you could just tell me about today's mission and whatever's going on."

I am surprised to hear the normally somber Chicago native laugh. "Relax. I heard about you, Savoy. They tell me you can hold your own— that you were in the mix last fall with your face covered with mud. I just think you can be a little reckless at times for a non-combatant."

When I do not respond, he continues. "Okay, okay tough guy. To answer your question, my regiment is all that's left of the all-colored 92nd Infantry Division. Today we're executing a pincer movement. We're supposed to connect with members of our other combat regiment, the Nisei, the Japanese Americans. That way, we cut off the escape route for the remaining Germans north of this area. HQ thinks they'll try to give us the slip through this place on the map they call the Cisa Pass. We are on the point of one pincer."

He pauses for a reaction, but I have none. This is exactly where I want to be. I can sense that the mood among the men is positive but cautious. These troops have survived on the line for a year, and now dare to entertain thoughts of victory, even thoughts of going home alive. "Sergeant Smith, I just got back from the fighting in Germany. I'll go with you wherever you're headed."

He appears both impressed and confused, but has a different issue to explore. "Okay, Savoy, I may hold you to that. You asked my men how they *feel* about being here. Let me tell you plainly. When we got to Italy last year, they sent us to guard airfields. I went to Sardinia. I got used to that. Then y'all newspapermen prodded Ike to fight to *the last Negro standing.* So here we are—the last of the buffalo left on the Italian Prairie.

"Over 12,000 of us have served in this division. After casualties, reassignments and the latest round of *asshole reductions*, the numbers dropped fast. In no time, the 370th was all there was."

As Smith takes a long drink from his canteen, I add, "So, the Army's trying to preserve some semblance of the Buffalo Soldiers." I hear derision in my own voice, and Smith appears to be accustomed to hearing it from colored reporters.

He nods his concurrence, and says, "In January, the brass rebuilt other combat units in Italy—not just us. We were the only colored guys left to make into one Regimental Combat Team." He slowly claps his hands together, accordion-style. "To that, the Army added the regiment of *Nisei* and a third white regiment of retrained artillerymen."

It occurs to me that the strategy must have proved effective. Supported by its existing Negro 758th Tank Battalion and artillery battalions, this new *Rainbow Division* has advanced up the coast liberating the stubborn German strongholds of Massa, La Spezia and Genoa. Smith's performance has been stellar. He is the senior NCO of a platoon that frequently has been without an officer.

Before the platoon moves out again, I try to get a quote from one of Smith's squad leaders. "So, what are your expectations for today's push?"

"We expect to stay alive, Savoy—and get these boys home. I hear Germans are surrendering further north. I just hope nobody dies today—*not even you.* Look, we know some white regiments have been bleeding since they invaded North Africa in 1942 but they didn't invite us to that party. I'm just dying to see these Germans surrender to us colored boys."

I understand why both survival and retribution dominate his thoughts today. According to their company commander, if all goes as expected, this operation will be their last. In an offensive front stretching from one Italian coast to the other, French, British, American, Brazilian, Indian and South African infantry, artillery and armor are all advancing north simultaneously. The tested 10th Mountain Division is right next door. With the end so near, no one wants unnecessary casualties.

One of the division's longest tenured squad leaders, Sgt. Jay Phillips, chimes in. "I've watched our boys die liberating towns only to see Jim Crow signs go up declaring those same towns off-limits to colored soldiers. Who wants to die for that? I remember when we had to fight with practice mortar rounds and secondhand rifles."

Abruptly he stands when Smith puts on his helmet, and rejoins his squad. "All right, get on your feet and get ready to move out."

Phillips' experienced squad moves to the front of the formation, reminding me of Serge's eerie nonchalance in Germany. The others fall into their usual positions in two single file lines on either side of the road. I step into the middle of one line, pick up their pace, and start making mental notes about my approach to telling their story.

Against this dreary landscape, these soldiers are like any others photographed or drawn on the pages of newspapers and magazines spread over breakfast tables across America. They wear the same dirty uniforms, carry the same lethal weapons and move in the same formations. They share the same fears of any grunts described by the late Ernie Pyle or any reporter trying to mimic his style.

However, among these tanned Yanks are no first or second-generation European immigrants, no lone Indian to call Chief or big cowboy to call Tex. They do include the same kinds of Midwest townies, fast talking city toughs and southern farm boys. Just like every other reporter's heroes, they find solace in their passions and memories of wives and sweethearts.

Nations win or lose wars with armies on the ground. The combat infantryman is the fundamental building block of an army. He is the symbol, the essential component of an infantry division. There is something special about the sight of a platoon of soldiers, each man wearing his nation's uniform and organizational patch proudly on his shoulder.

I do not yet know what Americans will feel when they see the photographs and sketches of these men of color with their buffalo emblems. I do not know how Americans will react to Negroes moving in formations carrying M-1 semiautomatic rifles, carbines, Thompson machine guns, Browning automatic rifles and side arms. A few tote components of machine guns and bazookas.

Treading with both confidence and trepidation, they have traversed ground in Italy that has exploded from death that rains from the sky or lurked silently beneath their feet. Like all other GIs, they have stared many times into the death that awaits them over the next ridge of Italy's jagged spine or anywhere along its coast. Like their counterparts in other divisions, they have survived hazards that could have buried any one of them at any moment.

However, there are concerns about the ridicule and criticism levied against these men and the very notion of an effective colored infantry division. Now, I walk along with them on what could be their final mission. I fear that no success achieved nor blood shed nor words written will ever remove the stigma now affixed to the Buffalo Soldiers. Perhaps for the first time, I understand why Rachel believed that constantly nagging me was worth antagonizing me. She was correct. Neutral press coverage will never be sufficient to vindicate these men.

From behind me, I hear the voice of the young man they call *Patches*, one of the Platoon's medics, and one of two other unarmed men in the column. "Mister Savoy, do you think this will be the last of it like they say?" I shrug without turning around, keeping my eyes on the ground ahead of me. Because he believes that information is my trade, I must be careful not to confirm or deny rumors that can spread through a regiment like wildfire.

Three years ago, Patches was a blissful hospital orderly. His focus, appropriately, was only on life on his strip of the California coast. Since he arrived in Italy last year, he has become proficient in stabilizing his butchered friends and buying precious hours for wounded men, some who desperately cling to their last gasps of life. On numerous occasions, Rachel has attested to the lifesaving work medics, like Patches, perform.

After several miles, I see the point man raise his arm, followed by Phillips and then Smith doing the same. As the formation assumes a defensive posture both men scramble forward. After several minutes, two men pass us marching disarmed German prisoners in the opposite direction. Our advance slows as the scene repeats again until Smith calls a halt to allow his escorts to drop off their human cargo and rejoin us on their return trips.

Anxious to hear the latest, I hurry up the line to see Smith reluctantly settling in and posting guards. I wade right into an exchange
with his squad leaders.

"From what I can make out, Germans, including some wounded SS
men, are surrendering—but the main body has moved east. Recognizing
the implications of the news, the mood of the leaders turns dour. "If
they've moved east, that makes us baby sitters now. We come all this
way just to feed Nazi stragglers?"

Another asks, "You mean the same people who've been blowing
holes through our friends?" They sense that two remaining German
divisions have eluded capture *by them*. I almost express my relief that
the Germans are going elsewhere, missing the significance these men
attach to being present for the surrender of the main force.

I look into the eyes of men with friends who did not survive nasty
booby-traps during house-to-house searches. They are men who have
watched members of their platoon killed by lethal projectiles from
explosions ricocheting among jagged mountain rocks. In the eyes of
these men, I can sense their disappointment and feelings of disrespect
when the German garrisons at La Spezia and Genoa elected to surrender to Italian partisans rather than to the Buffalo Soldiers.

"The old man says we did our job, and the regiment will link up as
ordered. No one cares if the Germans don't want to surrender to the
Untermensch—the *niggers, mongrels and nips* of the Rainbow Division.
They're moving away from us, and we can't tell whether they're trying
to run somewhere else or run to someone else."

Smith's perceptions are more than just a figment of his imagination.
Thus far, he has shown no imagination. When he speaks today, his
eyes dart from one man to the next, gauging their reactions to his
next words. Normally, he addresses his men with eyes fixed and steady.
"We're to wait here for others to join us in holding this position."

"I don't like it Sarge," Phillips weighs in, clearly annoyed by the
change in circumstance. Another squad leader speaks up for the
first time.

"Yeah, me neither. But at least it's just about all over."

As the men dig in for the night, I overhear the usually pedestrian
Smith appeal to the squad leaders with the unimaginable. "But if
we could just be there when they walk in under a white flag, I'd do

anything just to see the looks on their faces." He has ostensibly spoken in jest. However, his men owe their lives to correctly interpreting his every word.

Phillips chimes in on queue. "I'd love that."

In the morning, I receive word that, *out of the clear blue sky*, they have new orders. Sergeant Smith has finished selecting and briefing the men who will accompany him to a location where a Brazilian force is facing off against German infantry and armored regiments.

I see right through his lie. He refers to this planned escapade as an *assignment*, but I am certain the ruse is obvious to everyone. "So, tell me Sarge, how did you ever convince a tank platoon to take you with them through hostile country—just so you can witness a German surrender?" I ask in a moment alone with him, trying to open his eyes to the insanity of his overt disobedience. However, Smith does not respond to my appeals to his better judgment.

In fact, I reach up to clasp the hand he extends down to assist me as I climb aboard the lead half-track. "Are you coming or what, Savoy? I don't care either way. Don't tell me how to watch my ass and I won't tell you how to watch yours." Speaking louder, he passes on the latest report. "It's confirmed. The remaining Germans are trying to break through a Brazilian Expeditionary Force."

Behind us, I hear the tank platoon commander mumble intelligibly into his radio and four powerful dual Cadillac engines turn over. "Alright, last chance Savoy—this is it." I pretend to ignore the advisory, and forfeit the last chance to change my mind.

I know that, in truth, Smith is supposed to hold this position and wait with the rest of his battalion, possibly for relief from the converted artillerymen of the 473rd Regiment. But what began as a harmless fantasy last night was throttled toward reality when the Stuart's and half-tracks from the Division's colored tank battalion stopped on their way to support the Brazilians dug in around the town of Collecchio.

Smith alleged that his platoon was to serve as their infantry support, which apparently sounded plausible enough. The tank platoon sergeant did not seek confirmation of Smith's alleged orders, and had no reason to doubt them. So, whether complicit, indifferent or naïve, he agreed to take along his new infantry support.

This time, Smith does not equivocate. "Savoy, are you sure you want to be a part of this?" This time, rather than showing concern about my safety, he seems concerned most about my complicity in his scheme. However, no one will perceive me as complicit in the mutiny he has inspired. Rather I am an investigative reporter who merely found himself in the middle of a fascinating breaking story—one that any good journalist would have followed. With other units under the watchful eyes of reporters from the *Courier, the Afro-American* and the *Journal and Guide,* I am determined to get this story.

I assume Smith has promised his squad leaders that he will take full responsibility for ignoring his real orders. He has mounted Negro infantry *volunteers* onto two M-3 halftracks and a Studebaker truck behind four tanks.

When I do not respond to his question, he presses for an answer. "I'd really like to know why you're going with us. It makes no difference to me. I just need to know. Are you here for us or for our story?"

I do not have an answer. "You think the question should be easy to answer, don't you? I know you think you have a cause. Truth is, my mind is probably split fifty-fifty, for the story and for your men." Smith, one of the most straightforward men I have ever met, nods his appreciation for my honest response. Still, if I had to choose a tank platoon to accompany on this adventure, the four M-5 Stuart Lights would not be my first choice.

Appropriately, the riflemen of the 370th always cheer the arrival of the 758th to neutralize fortified machine gun positions. A few incoming 37-millimeter explosive projectiles absolutely will clear out a building, saving precious lives. However, the 37-millimeter turret guns will be no match for any panzer, or man carrying a panzerfaust that may target the sweet spots inside their thinly armored skins.

However, as I think longer about his question, I believe that if Rachel was going home with me, I might be no further north today than Rome. I would be on a balcony above a plaza, enjoying vintage wines and what passes these days for an impresario meal. This morning, I should have watched the sun come up over the Tiber River, sipping espresso and catching up on the news.

Instead, because of her ghost's constant needling, I have been hiking through this valley of lingering *Armageddon* with a platoon of buffalo soldiers. Now those soldiers have decided that they must support a man who may have become delusional. I cling precariously to a side of the halftrack. This unauthorized mission, if it does not end in death, could produce prison sentences. We stop briefly after about 15 miles, and I shout above the noisy engines. "Do you know how far we have left to go?"

"Collecchio is about 50 miles east. Over this terrain, these tanks will range over two hundred miles—even if they maneuver a little. If we can keep at 25 miles per hour, we'll be there in no time." I listen to the sound of his calm and rational voice. "I don't think we'll stop again—unless they have to."

I look over our small renegade column. The tank platoon is merely following orders. The Infantry volunteers are following the leader with whom they entrust their lives—a man who seems to have lost, or surrendered, his capacity for rational thinking.

I am concerned that he may be, driven by a perceived sleight, reacting to a mere slap on his already calloused face. I wonder if the shift in the enemy's strategy should be no more insulting than the everyday occurrences of bigotry to which he should have long ago developed immunity. However, now he and his men are committed to their plan. Any opportunity I may have had to reason with him has passed, so I do not mention that I suspect the main German force does not want to surrender at all. As we rumble along, I pray for a miracle to intervene.

Then out of the corner of my eye, a miracle appears around a bend on a wide opening at the base of a hillside. The mass of green and black uniforms packed into the confined space is unmistakable. As the lead halftrack and the command tank roll to a halt, Smith slaps my helmet gesturing for me to jump down as the tank turrets pivot toward the group.

I hear the whine of ball mounted machine guns turning and bolts pulled back on 30 caliber weapons. The disciplined German soldiers leave their weapons on the ground and do not react, as though they have been waiting patiently for someone to come along. I feel relieved, certain that apprehending the survivors of a company-sized force will satisfy prevailing lusts.

As I begin to move about snapping photographs, I see through my lens faces expressing humor and arrogance toward these Negro soldiers.

Although they outnumber us, many in the company of infantry and several SS men lie in obvious pain or sit nursing wounds.

Because they do not hide their disdain for us, I pray they do not underestimate the resolve or the lethality of Smith's angry battle-tested warriors and the experienced tank crews. These are not the initial crop of Negro soldiers cobbled together with inferior officers leading a division plagued by roller-coaster morale.

Smith's men have jumped out of the trucks and positioned themselves along the road mixed in and behind the line of vehicles. Guns train ominously into the surrendering crowd. The Germans appear to have selected a spot where any Allied formation traveling along the highway could spot them. The closest among them are no more than thirty feet from the road, clearly in a posture of surrender. Only a cluster of SS troops hold fast to their weapons. Smith, with his Thompson slung over his shoulder and his 45 in hand, steps out in front. "Who's in charge here?"

An arrogant response from an officer who remains seated in the middle of the cluster evokes snickers from his English-speaking subordinates. "Actually, we were just wondering which one of you could possibly be in charge."

It is the wrong answer in the wrong tone on the wrong day, but his expression turns serious as Smith chambers a round in his sidearm and walks menacingly toward the speaker. I am concerned that the German is trying to provoke the resistance that will surely result in the deaths of dozens in an instant.

"Okay funny man, step out here." The situation becomes tense as the officer rises and waives off a person I cannot see. Several American gun barrels follow his ill-advised gesture. The officer with palms outstretched steps forward followed by two others. Smith addresses the three of them. "I want to see your hands at all times. We don't have a problem killing every goddam one of you right here, right now. Does everyone *sprechen sie*?"

I quickly use up a roll of film. One of the tank commanders shouts to them in German, presumably repeating Smith's admonishment to the whole group, many of whom respond with a show of hands. The German major still does not mask his derision and his speech is still mocking. "Don't worry sergeant. We are clearly surrendering. Some of my men need qualified medical assistance. I would appreciate your calling for *qualified* medical support. There is no need for threats."

"Just tell your men to get ready to go to prison."

Smith's instructions bring a mocking smile, and the German officer laughs as though he has heard a joke. "We are going to prison? You are the ones going back home to prison. In a few years, you'll be mowing lawns and waiting tables at our weddings when we marry those same southern girls you get hanged for ogling."

Again, I hear chuckles from a few of his men. I flinch at the major's words, aware of how much they have probably enraged Smith and his men. Still, no shots ring out. "We had not expected to see you here. We thought you'd be at the Pass with the Japanese regiment they sent to bail you out along the coast. But, at any rate, I guess you have captured us—a whole band of walking wounded. Congratulations, *buffalo men*."

As I snap in a new roll of film and begin walking closer to the German prisoners, I see a barrel followed by a flash from within the group of surrendering Germans. As I collapse on the road, I wonder why anyone would give his life to shoot a man armed with a camera. A soldier atop the halftrack literally hoses him, riddling his body with a long high-velocity 30-caliber blast.

After brief yet concentrated salvos of similar gunfire, the senior German officer, the shooter, and at least a dozen men around them lay dead. I do not know whether restraint or proximity has prevented the tank gunners from killing a hundred more with 37-millimiter guns fired from point blank range.

Leaders on both sides frantically restrain their men, shouting to restore order. I hear Patches telling me to hold on as he pulls open my uniform to gain access to the wound that feels as though it is on fire inside me. Smith also appears at my side and remains until he hears that the bullet has passed right through my side.

"Okay. Put him on a halftrack and get him out of here." I want to tell him that I like the sound of his plan, but I cannot speak.

Chapter 27

· ·

Rehab

"If it's all over, when can we go back to Tulane?"
Drifting in and out of consciousness, I cannot be certain about the words I think I just heard. Each time I awaken, exhaustion sets back in, quickly sending me back into deep sleep. During this extended lucid moment, I seek confirmation from a doctor standing with a clipboard at the foot of my bed. "Did someone just say the war was over?" I am surprised by the effort and discomfort required to produce my hoarse whisper.

The doctor appears tired and distracted but spares a minute to indulge me. Despite the long-awaited news he shares, his voice is void of emotion. "Let's see here, you're a civilian war correspondent? Well here's the news you may have missed. The Germans in Italy surrendered today, but the Russians still haven't taken all of Berlin. What's today? It's May 2, 1945 and you're in a 24th General Army Hospital recovery ward in Florence...Italy."

I had not noticed a nurse ay my bedside. I think I've heard her take-charge tone of voice before. "That's right, Mister Savoy. You're in Florence this time." When I try to turn toward her, my right abdomen feels as though it is pulling apart at the seams, and she firmly pushes me back down on the mattress. Catching a glimpse of her, I realize she does not fit the image I have envisioned of the nurse who has handled me so gently and lovingly during my occasional lucid moments.

"Be still young man." Her commanding tone demands compliance. After giving me just a few sips of water, she slips a thermometer under my tongue and lifts my wrist with her thumb and index finger. "I remember you from before, in Naples with the first batch of wounded from Anzio. I don't usually see war correspondents once, let alone twice. That puts you in a pretty select group."

"Yeah, I'm in the group that doesn't know when to duck." The quip is costly, every word scratching my throat. I struggle, with some success, to clear my throat.

As she gives me a few more sips, the doctor interjects his prognosis. "Well, just so you know, you're fine but you need to relax. Don't talk so much yet. Your gunshot wound was not severe—although the bullet tore through some lateral muscle tissue. The wound was clean but you had a rough trip getting here and lost blood. Just follow the nurses' instructions and you'll be fine."

As he strolls away to another bed, I roll my eyes in the direction of the nurse. I do not see a transfusion device. "Do you know how I got here?" The water has helped. My voice is stronger, the discomfort less pronounced.

"Well that story has followed you up here. A colored medic delivered you to a hospital in a halftrack, and you bounced around a lot. Instead of taking you to the nearest medevac, they dropped you off at a field hospital in Genoa—with no explanation. You were ambulanced here a few days ago, once you were properly stabilized."

Using limited neck movement, peripheral vision and sound, I get a clear sense of my surroundings. I am in a large bay area filled with beds occupied by soldiers in various stages of consciousness and rehabilitation. Almost all lay wrapped in bandages over limbs or covering the places where limbs once were. Men on either side of me have their faces and heads bandaged, unable to see the scene unfolding around them with nurses moving through dispensing medicine and encouragement. There are no Negroes.

"I've been covering the 92nd Infantry Division in the northwest. Do you have any information on them?"

"Do you mean the colored boys? No, I don't. But I think we might have some patients in another ward that can help you." She lowers her voice to a whisper. "They almost put you down there, but like I said, I knew you were a correspondent, even though you came here in those filthy rags."

Her posture suggests I should thank her. I do not. "Now if you get some more sleep and let your body heal, you can go down there in a few days and ask around. I'm guessing they're all breathing a sigh of relief today. It's all over in bloody Italy and the Brazilians bore the brunt of the last fight. They've been coming in here by the dozens. Why is that—do you know?"

Perhaps because I feel compelled to add clarity to what may be a misconception, my response sounds defensive. "The Brazilians were handy. The Germans chose them as their path of least resistance." I regret speaking words that seem to downplay a surely violent encounter and probably a heroic stand.

She continues, "If so, they were wrong. The Brazilians, who have a lot of their own colored, fought back and took thousands of prisoners. I guess our colored boys were just doing whatever it is they were doing."

I feel an urge to get my stories written and published as quickly as possible. "How long do you think I'll have to stay here? Do you know if there was a small camera with my stuff? Where is my stuff?"

"Just relax. It's all here. You need to rest. That Lugar slug tore through more than just a little tissue. Don't worry. All your gear has been stowed away for you."

"I need to get back to work." Frozen in fear, I can only helplessly watch her fill and clear a large hypodermic needle. "I said I need to get back to my job."

She whispers softly in my ear. "And I said, you need to rest. In a few days, you can sit down and write all the stories you want about how the colored boys singlehandedly won the war. Today, you need to sleep."

For the next few days, I fall in and out of consciousness. The medical attention I receive is not only superb, but also emotionally supportive. On several occasions, while I drifted in and out, she has been by my side. She held my hand after changing compresses and dressings. Though the picture I now have is far less appealing than I have imagined, I appreciate the tenderness with which she has cared for me.

As she takes my hand this morning to check my pulse, I am still only semiconscious but cannot resist a tease. "Oh, nurse, I'm feeling some tenderness on my chest. I was wondering if you could rub it for me a little."

As I await her snappy response and terse rejection of my advances, her hand lifts my undershirt and gently massages the center of my chest, working its way over my pectorals, and abruptly down underneath the covers. My entire body stiffens at her inappropriate response to my equally inappropriate request. I open my eyes, suddenly much more alert.

"What's the matter? I thought this was what you wanted. Scoop, what's wrong? You look like you see a ghost. Did you read my letter?"

After a week, I begin taking daily afternoon walks using crutches, venturing a little further away each time. This afternoon, I make my way outdoors through the complex of brick buildings and surrounding structures that comprise the General Hospital. The complex is stately, compared to other facilities I have seen. In many ways, it resembles a stateside hospital with its circular entryway and tennis courts in back. I had assumed Patches would take me to some hastily constructed shelter for a field evacuation hospital to treat severely wounded soldiers.

I am certain that I will always remember watching men groaning and screaming as they lay dying or fearing death—scenes that medical personnel would never have witnessed at home—absent some unimaginable calamity. In addition to the horror stories that Rachel continues to share with me, I have seen men agonizing in front of triage teams who make instant life and death decisions. I can still hear teenagers praying to hang on long enough to get to a place where they stand a chance for recovery.

I learn that doctors from Tulane University Medical School run the 24th Hospital. Since arriving in the Mediterranean just before the invasion of Salerno, they have become increasingly proficient in responding to daily occurring disasters

The mood among the patients and staff soar as news filters in of the Allies tightening the noose around Berlin. German units surrender to the Americans en mass to avoid capture by the Russians. We hear rumors of Adolph Hitler's suicide. Skirmishes persist in Germany and flare-ups continue in Italy, even as Benito Mussolini hangs by his heels from piano wire.

When I seek out the location of the colored ward, I find no one recuperating there who is averse to patient segregation. The mood is reflective of the strange duality of many Americans on the issue of racial integration. All want unlimited access to housing for their children yet, with few exceptions, cherish the differences that distinguish them.

Other than being in a different location, medical personnel appear to be present in proportional numbers to the shifts that attend my ward. The equipment appears to be no less functional. Its occupants appear indifferent and no one inquires about the location of my bed.

In any event, concerns about fairness here in Italy have dissipated, trumped by a general elation over the news from Germany. The promise of home fills the air with a collegiality that bonds men contemplating journeys home. Some confide in me that they hope conditions at home have improved. Others are doubtful. No one intends to accept business as usual, and I must admit to sensing a contagious determination to affect change.

As I wander among them in an ill-fitting Class A officer's uniform and press band, I encounter the usual curiosity and assumptions that I am here to both chronicle the military victory and advocate for a social victory.

After another week passes, I have a visitor. Unaccustomed to seeing one of the infantrymen in a Class A uniform, I almost fail to recognize David "Patches" Murray.

"First, we got you the hell out of there fast. I thought there was going to be a fight between us and the tank platoon right there in front of the Germans. Smith was going to have that halftrack for you—one way or the other. Those dead Germans—ripped apart. We had a mess on our hands." Patches speaks in hushed tones even as we sit outside a hospital building on the periphery of the complex.

I ask, "Since we weren't even supposed to be there, do you know how that part was resolved? And did Smith press on to Collecchio?"

"By the time I got you squared away and returned, the tanks and the other halftracks had left. They tell me that Sarge got that damn fool idea out of his system after all the shooting. Phillips said we were to stick to a story about a report of a German force waiting to surrender. We were to say that we found them further away than expected. I wondered how we would explain how over a dozen got ripped at close range. But no one asked, and I don't think G-2 cared at that point."

He looks down at his hands searching for answers he will not find there. "I don't know what the German prisoners will say. Lord knows that enough colored soldiers have been court-martialed, jailed and executed over here."

I try to console him. "You don't need to try balancing one against the other. They fired first, Patches. Smith stopped the killing immediately. I would never have believed it if I hadn't seen it with my own eyes, the way they all held back. How many Germans did you say died?"

"A dozen were KIA on the scene. Others surely died later. Luckily, the tankers also had a medic with them. The confusion I see on Patches' face reminds me of the insanity of the encounter. "How did they expect the guys to react, Mister Savoy? That SS man *chose to die* rather than surrender peacefully *to us*—couldn't stand the *thought of you* taking those pictures."

It occurs to me that this young man has seen too much carnage as an Army medic. He has come here, to me, seeking closure, in addition to checking on me. I am just as pleased to share this moment with him. It has allowed me to put aside my fears about the fate of Sergeant Smith. It is also a chance to talk to an eyewitness about an avoidable tragedy that also has haunted me for weeks. "Patches, we understand. We just don't like *what we understand*. I doubt anyone involved will ever forget."

"Are you going to write it up, Mister Savoy?" He asks.

I give him a ponderous answer to a question he has not asked. "It's complicated. The Nazis Party is synonymous with racism. Yet our own people tolerate racism, within *limits*. Patches, I plan to write it all up."

Chapter 28

· ·

Extra, Extra

O ur regular readers are familiar with Jack Savoy's chronicling of the Allied advance from North Africa to the victory in Northern Italy. After licking his wounds suffered at Anzio, our prolific war reporter stowed away aboard a liberty ship, hitchhiked across war-torn Europe and bivouacked with an all-Negro combat platoon as it battled on toward Berlin. Our man almost died in action after rushing back to Italy to cover the Buffalo Soldiers and their role in the German surrender. In this Special Edition of the Washington Record, he brings us, as only he could, vivid images and untold stories of our brave young men and women.

The sensationalized introduction that only Ted could have written belies the initial outrage he must have expressed about my adventure across the Rhine. His exaggerated opening notwithstanding, I must acknowledge his instincts for marketing. I must admit that Ted has tastefully laid out this special edition of the Record.

I have spread out several pages of uncensored articles over a small dining table in my hotel. Ted has filled it with captioned photographs, news accounts, journal entries, features, interviews and opinion pieces. It includes my detailed account of the ADSEC Negro infantry retraining initiative and accounts of my journeys through France, Belgium and Germany. The issue includes my eyewitness coverage of Serge's platoon in action, including photos and interviews with both colored and white soldiers of the 60th Infantry Regiment. I include assessments by non-commissioned and commissioned officers.

I have written a detailed chronicle of my time spent with the 92nd Infantry Division and the 758th Tank Battalion, as well as a series of articles on my personal experiences with and observations about Colonel Davis and the 332nd Fighter Group. I also include two informative articles on Negro artillery battalions. Of course, there is a large photograph of Sergeant Smith instructing surrendering German SS officers. I almost paid for that one with my life.

The edition also includes stories written by the *Record's* stateside reporters and two articles by Jim Peterson, our correspondent in the Pacific Theater. All my stories in the issue violate adherence to objectivity, all marbled with subjective references to the origins, effects and dangers of maintaining segregated armed forces.

However, Ted has expertly framed a lengthy story, with photos, about an anonymous Negro woman who, despite the Army's strict enforcement of its quota, amassed an amazing record as an Army nurse. There is more than enough information to identify her. I am certain Tom will revoke my accreditation. Still, I am at peace and Walt can afford to forfeit the money he put up for my bond.

I began this morning late, managing to ignore the stack of unread mail upstairs in my room that represents three months of correspondence. I have newspapers, notes from Ted, letters from Anne, and one from Rachel dated December 26, 1944.

"Are you ready Signor?" Tom is late and the Sunday breakfast crowd has dissipated, providing privacy but unnerving Raphael. He has grown frustrated with trying to keep the last of my food warm without drying it out. Like everyone else in Naples, he still places a high premium on fresh food, and considers waste offensive.

"No. Let's give him just a few more minutes. When he shows up, bring it all out at once, please."

The Allied victory has transformed the mood of the people in and around Naples. The celebrations have dissipated. While depression persists among the most victimized, there is a new feeling of hope in the air. Before briefly passing Tom on the street a few days ago, I had not seen him since we boarded separate ships bound for Anzio. Most correspondents are either homebound, looking east to the Pacific Theater or Germany.

A few of the Negro reporters remain nearby covering the Tuskegee Airmen at Rametelli, just in case the pilots and ground crews will transfer to bases within striking distance of the Japanese mainland. I doubt that will occur, and no one speculates that the Buffalo Soldiers will redeploy. Rumors persist that the Army has issued them brooms, mops and shovels. The segregated port battalions remain busy in the major shipping hub of the Mediterranean that Naples has become.

I finally have a comfortable hotel room with a view of the waterfront. As I wait for Tom to arrive, I sip dark roasted Ethiopian coffee and look out over a harbor that still bears some ugly scars inflicted by both sides, but is recovering even as a few unsightly rusting hulls still dot the water line.

If the Army has not yet gotten around to revoking my accreditation, I plan to spend one more official week in Rametelli to bid farewell to Colonel Davis and the 332nd Fighter Group. If my revocation is final, I will spend an unauthorized week at Rametelli. I simply do not care about the consequences anymore.

Tom's voice intrudes on my rebellious thoughts, and I stand up to shake his hand. "Good morning, Jack."

"Congratulations on the promotion, *Colonel* James."

"Thank you. It is overdue and then merely a wartime brevet rank. I guess they'll only bust me down to captain in peacetime. How's your recuperation?" He asks.

"Sometimes I forget it ever happened *again,* Tom."

His voice becomes acidic. "Glad to hear it, especially after your unauthorized tour of Europe and that 25-page social commentary you have spread out in front of you. Unless you plan to wrap some leftovers in it, can you take it off the table please?"

I am accustomed to Tom's blunt language and his preference to get unpleasant business out of the way before preempted by pleasantries. "Any one of my officers would've redacted almost every line you wrote—and yanked your credentials for a stunt like this."

"And you? What would you—or more importantly, what are you going to do now? I went to find my brother in Valognes. I had no idea I would travel as far as Germany or generate this kind of copy."

A waiter comes over and confirms that we are ready. "But my trip was transformational, and I refuse to apologize for doing what I feel is right." If we are being frank, I also want to get right to the point.

He eyes me curiously. "I'm not asking you to apologize—at least not for that. I have two brothers in uniform. I understood the trip to Compiegne—maybe even across the Rhine. I don't understand why you took a shit on that ADSEC colonel's floor in Valognes." Tom's eyes widen and his lip quivers. "And opining that the Army set up the 92nd to fail? Jack, you can't really believe that."

I do not respond. "So, then my credentials are revoked?"

"Revoked? Hell yes, they're revoked. If anyone asks, I don't even know where you are right now, Jack. I can't find you—so get your ass out of here, say by Wednesday morning." Satisfied that he has blown off sufficient steam and done his duty, he pauses as the aromatic smoke from several plates waft up from the table.

I manage a smile. "So, then you're staying for breakfast?"

"Yeah, I'm staying for breakfast. If anyone sees me here, I'll say I was shocked when you walked in and sat down *at my table*. How much food did you order Jack? We can't eat all this."

"Oh yes we can. On my way back to Italy, I stopped in Paris only long enough to board the next train south to Toulon. After making my way back to Florence, I heard about the Fifth Army's offensive and headed for the action on the coast. I got back here from the hospital, and hospital food, three days ago. Then I moved out of that fleabag and into this hotel. The chef clued me into an unusually large delivery. So, this is my first real meal in a long time." Without another word, we dig in, oblivious to social grace.

"So, you didn't like anything I wrote?"

"I liked your piece on the colored artillery battalions—first rate stuff. It's about time one of you hacks really focused on them. When you guys tell the real story of Negro contributions to this war, it has to include them."

"I admit I've overlooked them until Valognes—over ten battalions in the ETO, each with 12 guns and 500 soldiers. That's a pin prick compared to the total gun crews, but they made a difference."

Tom confides that, "If you take out your unsubstantiated claims, editorializing and pandering, your writing is first rate Jack, but your accreditation is out of my hands."

"It's okay. Really—I'm spent, Tom. But I was thinking of going over to Rametelli for a few days before I go home."

"No Jack. Oh, why should I care? Do whatever you want. I'm cutting your orders today. Remember to replenish your survival bag. I don't want anything to happen to you now."

"Already have—cleaned up my waterproof compass and watch, picked up extra batteries for my flashlight, replaced bent sunglasses, packed full cans of foot powder, water purification pills, aspirin, anti-acid, new medical kit. Need I go on?"

"If you need to go on you may have too much." We both laugh when Tom recounts a story about an unfortunate correspondent who left a few critical items behind. After we have eaten every scrap, Tom sits back in his chair and takes out his pipe. "So, you caught up with Stewart again?" Tom has always been fond of the gregarious Ollie Stewart whose natural charm belies his determination to expose racial injustice wherever he finds it.

"Yes. I met several interesting people in France including Ed Toles and Rudy Dunbar. I ran into Ollie in Paris and spent an evening with him and a fellow from New York named Roy Ottley. He's a literary-styled correspondent, a regular Harlem Renaissance man. He called the Tuskegee flyers the *Dark Angels of Death*."

"Did you say the *Dark Angels of Death*?"

"I know—real moody stuff. Both he and Ollie should be back in the States by now. Oh yeah, I went to a mock wedding ceremony at Josephine Baker's house in Paris. She pretended to marry Ollie."

Do you think he'll be in France after the war? What do you plan to do next?"

Despite assumptions to the contrary, I have not given much thought to that since I sailed for North Africa. "Just a few years ago, I would have answered without hesitation that I wanted to be a foreign correspondent for a major daily. So much has happened since that I'm no longer sure. I've been so affected by the things I've seen, but mostly by the way nothing has really changed."

"I think I understand."

I respond much too abruptly. "No offense Tom, but I'm not sure you do. I didn't myself three years ago."

I have offended him. "Well then enlighten me, Jack. Please tell me what you believed three years ago that you no longer believe today?"

"Call me naïve. I thought America's obsession with preserving white entitlement would take a backseat to victory over Germany. Now I'm sure some would rather not win if it means they must share that entitlement."

"Yes, I would call that naïve. Tell me you didn't have to cross an ocean to discover that discrimination everywhere is rooted in the preservation of entitlement." He becomes professorial, as though there is a real difference in our ages. Tom continues before I can speak, "That brings me to your thinly veiled expose about Captain Todd—you know, the colored girl you and Owen, through you, asked me to help do something *she was not entitled to do*. I suspect you never realized how screwed we all could be right now. Jack, don't ever lecture an Indian about entitlement."

"But Tom, no one knows you're a Kaw Indian unless you tell them."

His rebuttal is immediate. "And most people don't know you're a Negro unless you tell them—which I notice you rarely do. I've watched you hide behind that French-Canadian mask since high school. In fact, isn't that what this is really about?"

Long before I was born, Papa Joe had explained to my grandmother that the planter class in the South depended on average white citizens to correct or report any Negro who did not behave like a slave. It was their civic responsibility. Failure to report the offense was as egregious as the offense itself. Thus, Papa Joe developed two personas, two complex masks—one to survive and one to maintain his sanity. This was but one of many survival skills that were his legacy.

"Tom, I'm not conflicted about who I am, never lied about it. People choose to see a French Canadian or choose to see a Negro. I simply did not care. Should I have instructed them by embodying some colored stereotype any more than you should paint your face and tuck a feather in your hair?"

Rather than responding in kind, he lowers his volume and continues in a calm steady voice. "I have two brothers in the 45th Infantry who were entitled to be killed but not entitled to enjoy a cold beer downtown on a hot day. Yes, I know the Army didn't build separate barracks, chow halls and hospitals for Indians. Jack, your discomfort stems from not having convictions of your own. That's what you're finally coming to grips with."

I stare through the window in silence for a long moment, weighing similar words that I have heard from Serge and Rachel—from Sid and Ron Maxwell. Tom waits before continuing. "I know we've exchanged some harsh words about your relationship with Rachel. I was afraid we'd all regret you dating the same woman I got people to cover for. Now I know I was right. I just don't understand what you two hope to accomplish with unmasking this. After all I've done, this so-called expose feels like betrayal—a thankless, arrogant thing to do."

I feel that I owe him the benefit of clarity. "Tom, Rachel made me promise that I would publish her story—if anything ever happened to her. While it was true that she never identified her race, technically, she never actually pretended to be white. Admittedly, she had to lie outright a time or two. However, she has been my biggest critic. She thought all my work should have read his way."

He looks confused. "Jack, I don't get either one of you on that score. A person is who they are. Anything else, whether verbalized, implied or assumed, is just a lie. It's passing, nothing more than a masquerade—plain and simple."

Rather than counter his argument with a comment about the number of Americans who often choose to remain silent about their Indian ancestry, I say, "Well, just so you know, much of my behavior earlier this year was due to Ross' erroneous report of Rachel's death."

"Killed? Wait a minute, Jack. What are you saying? She went back on the line on Christmas morning, and you heard that on *New Year's Eve*? No, I don't know where Ross got that."

"I do now. Rachel was doing light duty at the hospital in Florence while waiting to ship out. She filled me in. It wasn't entirely Ron's fault. She suffered a concussion, knocked unconscious by a bomb dropped next to her evac. Ross saw it before he left, but she recovered, rested a while, passed muster, and continued working. She had done enough. They reassigned her to Florence for a while and then sent her Stateside. Who knows if they annotated her service record after my story ran, and who cares?"

"Okay, I see it now. That's how you got this copy and the pics to Lomax. How about Serge, is he okay?"

"Yeah, he somehow made it through without a scratch. Of course, he still must get his big mouth out of Europe unscathed, so I'm still *playing it by ear*." I almost forget to ask, "How about your twin brothers, Tom. Are they okay? I heard the 45th went all the way."

His response comes with a combination of relief and pride. "Those knuckleheads are just too onerous to die, Jack. They served in North Africa, Sicily and on the peninsula, and then marched through France to the outskirts of Berlin. I don't know what history will say about native peoples in this war. I only hope it's fair."

After breakfast, I hobble upstairs and catch up on my mail. An outdated letter from Owen expresses regret about Ron Maxwell's tragic accident. In the next paragraph, he also thanks me for my testimonials about the close collaboration between Negro correspondents and Army press officers. He employs coded words that give weight to Ron's accusations of my arrangement with War Department's public affairs bureau. Last year I would have been indifferent. Today, reading it makes my skin crawl.

An old letter from Anne includes a photograph of her beautiful baby girl, the spitting image of Charles. I laugh about their choice for the baby's name and about my middle brother's threat to go AWOL to see her.

Then, I pick up the envelope containing a note Rachel must have scribbled as she returned to the line the morning of our argument in Florence.

Jack,

Thanks for not reacting even more impulsively. I apologize for my behavior and hope you can understand the stress that caused it. You mean the world to me. I hope there's still a future for us. I know I said some horrible things that I can never take back. We have something well worth salvaging. You know how to find me—so find me.

The Love of Your Life, Rachel

In Florence, Rachel and I talked for hours at a time over several days and nights before she sailed. However, we spent too much of our time together explaining and clarifying, writing and editing. Now, rather than further tempting fate, I decide to head straight for home to get my girl.

Chapter 29

. . . .

Stateside

"Hey buddy, is there a place nearby where a guy can grab a good hearty breakfast—somewhere a little *less crowded*?"

I had noticed the man hastily leaving the diner but, self-absorbed with getting together with my old friend for breakfast at his favorite place, I did not sense the exasperation in his body language. I point out several empty tables and counter stools available in the establishment he just left. He merely becomes annoyed that I have not instinctively recognized the root of his frustration. However, I do now. "Oh."

"*Oh?* Do I need to spell it out?" Two young Negro men walk past us, dressed in the summer uniforms of Washington's career bureaucracy—light summer fedoras, short sleeve white shirts, thin dark ties and slacks. They join two young Army officers seated amid a predominantly Negro breakfast crowd.

The stranger's face flashes some nonverbal passcode, but I do not know the universal countersign. Since returning to Washington from Naples, I have realized that I remain unfamiliar with some of the capital city's most deeply rooted traditions.

This morning's primer continues to be instructive as the angry stranger spits out his next words plainly. "I'll be glad when they take off those goddam uniforms and get back into their Pullman clothes."

He grows angrier, possibly from not receiving the support he expects from me. "I see you can't decide whether to go in either."

A few years ago, I might have responded with an indulgent nod— perhaps even a recommendation of an alternate venue. Now, a few years ago seems like a lifetime. I speak only loud enough for him alone to hear. "During the war, nearly a million colored men wore *those goddam uniforms*. Thousands died, thousands are still recovering, thousands will never fully recover—and you still can't stand to eat bacon and eggs in the same room with us."

The look of confusion on his face morphs into one of betrayal. "Well, I'll be damned, boy. You could almost go either way. But I can see the difference now." I hear *the difference* in the collegial quality his voice held a moment ago and the acidity it holds for me now.

He continues, "Yeah, I heard something about coloreds in the war, but I never saw any outside of truck drivers and laborers. I was wounded badly at Kasserine Pass—then I came back home. I thought our biggest concern was job safety, you know, now that coloreds are getting all the work. You don't expect to see this kind of thing so far south. I tell you it's a time bomb. So, tell me, boy, did you serve with any of those thousands and thousands?"

I extend a hand that he does not take. "I'm Jack Savoy, and I'm no one's goddam boy. I was a war correspondent. I reported from battlefields in Tunisia, Italy and Germany. I saw colored soldiers with guns everywhere I went."

He retreats, somewhat. "Take it easy, Jack. Well if you say you were and that you did, I guess I must believe it. Since you're a reporter, maybe you could tell me something. I heard about some colored boys trying to fly airplanes down in Alabama. Whatever became of them?"

Owen appears virtually out of nowhere, and interrupts. "Not much. They just compiled one of the best bomber escort records in the ETO." He smiles and extends his hand to the stranger. Getting no response, Owen catches on, laughs from deep within, tips his summer hat and walks inside. His favorite table becomes available. When I turn back, the man has already walked away.

Once I join him inside, Owen says, "Jack, I assumed you knew that guy until he looked like he wanted to beat me up." He laughs again, but does not ask me for the explanation he does not need.

I have not sat down with Owen since returning stateside. I have news for him, but I hold out. "Ted wants to commemorate the first Independence Day in the city since war broke out in the ETO. It looks like people from everywhere have converged here. I would have thought this a little too soon, with the war still going on in Japan."

"No. The country needs to celebrate the victory we have." Then he asks rhetorically, "When is the Pacific War going to end? How many families will the Emperor allow to burn alive in bombing raids? It ain't going to let up."

I am equally sanguine. "I don't know, Owen. I asked a similar question after Dresden, only to see the war drag on for months afterward. I know the militarists have committed some unforgivable things, but man oh man. They don't want to wait until Curtis Lemay gets through with them."

I want to change the subject and make my announcement, but I also want to know why Owen asked for this breakfast meeting. We can barely hear one another above the corridor noise mixed in with the clatter of stainless steel, glassware and plates. The usually serene dining room is buzzing with animated conversation. Every time the door swings open, the noise from travelers passing through the cavernous lobby renders hearing impossible. As a particularly loud throng of passengers walk by, I am not certain I have heard Owen correctly. "What did you just ask me to do?"

He waits for the noise to subside before explaining his request. "By VE Day, over two dozen colored war correspondents had been accredited by the War Department—with a few, like your guy Peterson, still covering the war in the Pacific. I want you to write my story as an exclusive to the *Washington Record*."

I agree without deliberation. "Well, of course, my answer's yes. Tell me though, why give it to me exclusively? Everyone will pick up the story." Since the war began, Owen has appeared content to work in relative obscurity deep in the bowels of the War Department. Despite being a celebrated investigative reporter, he has been the brunt of jokes about his acceptance of a position so far beneath his stature. I have heard no one else defend him in public.

Owen misunderstands my question. e misunderstands my hesitation.HH"If you think anyone is concerned about your revoked accreditation, think again. No one cares. In fact, you should wear it like a badge of honor. I guess you belong to us now."

I ask, "Who are *us*, Owen?"

He responds with a burst of pride. "Why, the Negro press Jack Savoy, who do you think?"

I am confused. "It's been a long time since I've heard you associate yourself with the Negro press. In fact, I expected you to be annoyed today about what I wrote during those last weeks—my critiques of the Army's policies on race. I came here this morning expecting to get a whipping."

His smile exudes genuine warmth today. "You won't get one from me. Something happened to you over there, Jack."

I cannot resist stating the obvious. "Owen, I think something has happened to you over here."

He does not respond, but continues, "I read every word you wrote and I saw how the Lomax brothers framed your news articles with their own editorials, analyses and domestic coverage. I could tell you never scribbled anything. You always took the time to organize your thoughts and write them out—like you were trying to build a portfolio for the *New York Times* or something. I couldn't believe you took so many chances to cover those campaigns."

Owen's tone has an almost fatherly quality as he goes on, "But somewhere between Casablanca and Berlin you found your voice. You never really tackled the tougher issues like unfair imprisonments or executions. But you found your voice—maybe even found yourself. Now your editorials are solid gold."

"I can't say what changed exactly. Since others are sure they know, I'm rarely pressed for an explanation. I'll admit that a few thoughtful reporters offered criticisms from time to time that hit home. Even Sid railed into me one night after I pulled him out of a barroom brawl."

After Owen laughs at a picture he has constructed in his mind, I continue. "Then I couldn't ignore the unfair assessments almost gleefully leveled at the Buffalo Soldiers. There's a lot of truth in those claims that they never had a fair chance."

Owen leans forward in his seat. "That's quite an accusation, coming from you. If Sid had said it, I wouldn't even notice."

I am sanguine. "Traveling with the 60th Infantry, I witnessed the near total lack of bullshit in their deployment of Serge's platoon. Maybe I had to see integration done right instead of segregation gone wrong. I saw black and white GIs move out in separate platoons only to have that distinction blurred under fire. Then all I saw were shades of green, all bleeding the same shade of red."

"I think it was then that I really began to struggle with reconciling objectivity with being a Negro reporter. Every colored man I met overseas, without exception, shared at least one account of a racially motivated violent confrontation or reprisal." I have unpacked a lot before breakfast, and decide to break it off there.

Owen looks into my eyes as though he sees something different in them. I am pleased to see that he has removed that bureaucrat's mask, as though coming home after a costume ball. With his masquerade ended, he appears to be trying to reclaim the alpha persona I knew in another lifetime. I feel sorry for my old friend. He may never be able to recover the personal costs he has incurred to accomplish whatever he believes he has achieved. I know that no matter how compelling the story I write about him, people will never again see him as a champion of civil rights.

I need to return to the topic he has asked me here to discuss. From my heart, I ask, "Owen, you know I'll do whatever you ask, but why don't you tell your own story? I'm not sure I can convey the subtleties I think it requires."

His smile, which I now recognize as Rachel's smile, has regained some of its former magic. "Jack, right up to the end, the War Department doggedly enforced its policy of strict segregation. At the same time, they approved 30 colored civil rights reporters to go overseas to observe it firsthand. They approved guys like Frank Bolden, Ollie Stewart, Leroi Ottley, Sid Harris, John Jordan, Tom Young, Ed Rouzeau, Rudy Dunbar, Ron and, hell, you Jack. Why would the Army transport you guys all over the world so you could stir the pot? How do people think that happened?"

I must admit to being thrilled to hear my name included on that august list. I also regret the blunt answer forming on my lips, but I want Owen to understand how people will perceive his version of the story. "They think the War Department painted itself into a corner with segregation, and couldn't afford a further erosion of Negro supporters. People reserve all the credit for Negro publishers and fighters like Hastie, Randolph or Walter White. It's been my experience that even the implication that you deserve credit is met with doubt—if not outright derision."

Unfazed by my blunt force honesty, he says, "I know, Jack. That's why I need an actual correspondent with a reputation for unmitigated honesty. Look, I'm not inferring I did it alone. That would be ludicrous. I did take care of details, the horse trading, coaching and rewriting. I didn't need a fancy title to do what I did. I'll give you everything I have—on the record. Just write it your way."

"You already have my answer."

"Thanks, Jack. Now I must confess that I have an ulterior motive. In full disclosure, I should tell you that I'm writing my autobiography. Do you have a problem with that?"

He has removed the mask, but he is very much the Washington dealmaker. I chuckle and shake my head, though unoffended by his public relations scheme. "No, no problem, but I can't be your press agent. The story can't read like a press release. Don't contradict what you tell me. I'm writing a book of my own that includes my interactions with you. So, I may *kill two birds*."

After breakfast, Owen reaches for a pack of cigarettes. For the first time, I notice his polished lighter's engraved White House seal. After a few long draws from a cigarette, he asks, "Do you remember how certain I was that there would be no integration of combat troops? I've never been happier about being wrong, even if only half wrong. I would never have believed it was possible, even on the limited scale which it occurred."

He will eventually discover that the ADSEC retraining and redeployment initiative will be a primary focus of my book. "People don't know about it. People like *our friend* this morning prefer to talk about truck drivers, though there would be no victory without them. The public will never know about the dangerous work of amphibious transportation companies or artillery battalions. Everyone will talk only about colored laborers in the warehouses and on the docks, but not getting strafed on the beachheads.

"They'll know about sanitation companies and stretcher-bearers, but only grudgingly acknowledge the nurses and fighter pilots. The colored tank battalions seem already to be well-kept secrets. The colored infantry, well, I think the word *ridicule* captures it."

"You have heard that the mainstream press doesn't cover colored news, haven't you Jack? You guys have to tell those stories, just as we always have and maybe always will."

Something reminds Owen that Charles did not come home from the war. "Oh Jack, I haven't said anything to you about Charles. I am so very sorry for your family's loss and apologize for not saying it right away."

"Thank you. But pardon me if I don't want to talk about it." We are silent for almost a full minute. A few months of mourning have not been sufficient for me to deal with losing Charles to a fanatical *Hitler Werewolf* youth *after the official surrender*. The Army told Anne her husband died in combat. Charles had been sitting alone atop the turret of a parked tank, not far from the Gunskirchen concentration camp in Germany.

I strongly suspect that my brother refused to fire his weapon—probably assuming the teenager was not aware that the war was over. Knowing Charles, he might have hesitated, after witnessing 180 consecutive days of killing across France, Belgium and Germany, to fire a 30-caliber burst into the body of a brainwashed child, even one toting a panzerfaust. I cannot shake the guilt of going all the way to Germany without trying harder to find him. After all, I found Serge when no one thought I could.

From my vantage point, I see Negroes boarding and moving to the back seats of buses in this genteel southern town. Very little has changed around Union Station where middle-aged porters answer to the becks and calls of adults and children alike. Charles served here as a porter when law clerking opportunities were not available. I picture my brother as a married man, a two-year law student, wading through a throng of travelers much like the ones departing and arriving in the Capital today.

Owen searches for something else to talk about. "How about Walter Lomax's colored technicians—does he think you helped him prove his point? Can we expect a new generation of Negroes to emerge from the war with technical skills?"

I am pleased to talk about *anything* else. "Actually, I believe we can expect some of that. I interviewed as many as I could find—maybe many more than Walt ever imagined and surely more than I expected to see in the air, engineering and signals corps. I couldn't have found them without help from Tom. I have not properly thanked you for arranging that collaboration."

Owen brightens with the mention of Tom's name. He says, "Tom stopped by to see me just last week on his way back home for a spell. He's going to remain in the Army. He couldn't say enough about you Jack. I think getting to know an older version of you had a profound impact on him."

With my mind still dwelling on my recently deceased brother, I struggle to engage in small talk. Compared to what my family has lost, everything else seems trivial. Perhaps because he understands my state of mind, Owen keeps the conversation going alone. "It will definitely be up to you to help shape history's depiction of the Buffalo Soldiers. Keep reminding them that the Axis killed, wounded or imprisoned one in four. Stay on Truman until he integrates. Don't let up."

After another half hour, Owen turns his attention from his impromptu lecture to the Lomax brothers. I sense that it will be his last attempt to engage me on the issue, and force myself to speak to my old friend. "Stay tuned. You'll see Walt back in the saddle soon enough." I tell him that I have never really watched anyone go through rehabilitation following a stroke, but Walter's recovery has been remarkable. "He's relearned ways to do everything."

Looking relieved, Owen says, "That's great news. I agreed with him on many things, just disagreed with him on so many others. But tell me honestly, Jack, how is Ted dealing with all this?" It is an astute question, and perhaps one that only someone who knows the brothers well would pose. Unfortunately, I can only give Owen the answer censored for public release. "They get along as well as they've ever gotten along before."

He recognizes my dodge and resists questioning the party line. He shifts the focus back to the impact their relationship may have on my professional career. "Are you still doing the work of a managing editor? It's none of my business, Jack. I don't need to know the details. Just remember that you're part of a small community and eventually the obvious becomes obvious to everyone."

The Lomax brothers' ability to coexist is key to my long-term status with the newspaper. In truth, although my compensation has been more than fair, I work on the slippery slope of a minefield. The Lomax brothers have never been able to function as a team. At times, the diplomacy required to remain neutral becomes taxing for the entire staff. Thinking about it reminds me of the hour, and I direct our attention to the elephant that I alone see in the room.

I begin with a distraction. "So how is Muriel?"

Smiling broadly upon hearing the name of the woman he loves more than life itself, Owen responds, "Muriel is doing well, Jack. She asks about you from time to time. She'll be thrilled to hear you inquired about her well-being. She's working for the city, in health services administration."

He is still smiling when I ask, "Owen, do you ever think about your niece?"

The question catches him off balance and his charged emotions are apparent. He rambles, "Jack, I tried to get closer to her back when you were both in college. However, as my detractors seem to have forgotten, I was still very busy risking my life to expose hate crimes across the South. I never pretended that we had a real family relationship. I don't think she would have ever written to me from Morocco if not for her problem. I was glad you were willing to help her, and glad Tom James intervened."

When I try to warn him never to speak of Tom's involvement, he cuts me off. "The war's over Jack. No one is going to pursue that or Tom. He's just paranoid. I figured you would never have written that story without her permission. Do you have any way of finding out how things are going for her now?"

Before I can answer, he continues. "I've only seen her twice as an adult but I do feel a kinship. I was pleased that she trusted you. To be honest, I always hoped she could find a guy like you."

"Well, Owen, in that case, you may want to reach for another smoke."

"What do you mean?" For the first time, I see the anguished face of an uncle who would be devastated if I had bad news. I smile to allay any fears, showing him the face of a man who is much closer to his niece than he thought. "So, you know where she is, Jack? Did she go back to New Orleans?"

I must end his agony. "No. Actually, she's living in Northwest—trying to decide whether to work or attend medical school. So, you two may run into one another very soon."

"You mean my niece, Rachel Todd, is right here in town?"

"No Owen—I mean my wife, Rachel Todd Savoy, is right here in town."

Chapter 30

· ·

Dreams

I awaken to find that, although my wife is still asleep, she calls out from a place deep within the recesses of her mind. I have difficulty making out the words. I cannot tell whether she is reliving the carnage of North Africa, the explosion that killed everyone around her in Italy, or everything in between.

Like so many of the Army's brave, indispensable nurses, Rachel spent four years a world away from home right at the battlefronts of the war. Often covered in their blood, she stood between life and death for young men, sometimes saving the lives of soldiers long before they ever saw a doctor. Mostly, I suspect that she remembers those who gasped their last breaths while in her custody, sometimes in her arms. I do not know how many years must pass before she fully recovers.

I do not know whether awakening her rescues her from the misery or merely postpones the cleansing process required to wash away a thousand unwanted images. Since our first night together as husband and wife, some of her late-night outbursts have been startling. Though I have no professional knowledge of her problem, I note that she calls out far less frequently now than just a few months ago.

After reading her last note in Naples, I immediately began the long journey back to Washington. I found out that, after she hand-delivered my last batch of uncensored copy to the *Record*, Rachel followed up with daily phone calls taken by June Carter. When I returned to DC,

June informed me that the woman I was prepared to search the country to find had been anxiously awaiting my return at Anne's house.

We checked into the Whitelaw Hotel after being married in a small, quiet ceremony. She vetoed my suggestion to invite Owen. Each time I felt her stir during that first night, I awakened her with a kiss. For two weeks, we lost track of the blurred transitions from night to day. Three months later, the nurse I married informed me I was going to be a father. I expressed my deepest feelings of joy and absolute faith in her prognosis.

I nudge her. She awakens with an expression of bewilderment. I behave as though nothing out of the ordinary has occurred. "Don't even try it, Jack. I must've been talking in my sleep again. I just had another dream about Lieutenant Matthews, from Casablanca."

In the space of a second, I recall the rumpled lieutenant who had vowed to get revenge. "That's the guy who threatened to give you up, who later died in front of your evac. I had almost forgotten him. What do you mean when you say you had *another* dream about him? He can't bother you now."

She stretches as she responds with a tight smile, "Well, it seems he got to torment my life after all. It's not funny. We couldn't save him. I'll never forget that day. He spent his last day on earth in front of that tent. He could only get a few final words out. After that he could no longer speak."

I must ask. "What were his last words to you?"

She offers her best imitation of his inflections. *"Now you look here little nurse Missy, don't you give me no colored people's blood."* We both smile at her attempt to mimic his voice, though we keep his tragic death in perspective. "He was clearly dying, but he was still concerned about that. Jack, he kept following me with his eyes, as though I was going to slip him a pint—you know."

"Would you have done that?"

She shrugs. "I had it ready a few feet away, a vintage bottle of dark red, perhaps direct from the cellars of a Harlem donation center. But now the joke, which really isn't funny, seems to be on me."

"Rachel, let's not even speak of this again. I know you. You'd never do such a thing as to arbitrarily condemn him to die. Don't let your mind play tricks on you. I don't care how long he took to go."

"Of all the evacs he could have come to—why mine? Jack, I held him close for a long time, even after he slipped away." Clearly, she has been feeling guilty, irrationally so, over the incident, relieved to unburden some of it. I hold her close, knowing she is a long way from reconciliation.

"Jack, can I ask you something? Why did Charles join up and volunteer for tanks?"

I answer the question only because I need to purge as well. "I wish you had known him. He was the best of us, but nothing ever worked out well for Charles as a kid. He was the textbook *middle child*, quiet and moody, caught between an underachieving boy genius and a bossy big brother who never got a chance to be a child.

"Charles never hit his stride as a young colored man in Canada, but as soon as he was in the States, opportunities just seemed to unfold. He met Anne and believed meeting her had been his *Destiny*. I couldn't argue with that. He became, simultaneously, hopelessly monogamous and devilishly handsome. So, my brother felt as deeply indebted to America as anyone else who volunteered to serve in the Army.

"While he was a law student at Howard, he started talking about a guy named Owen. No, not your uncle, this man's name was Chandler Owen, a guy who wrote something called *War and the Negro*. I won't say that he persuaded Charles, but his thesis echoed almost everything Charles came to believe. My brother had two heroes at Howard. Owen and Charles Houston, Thurgood Marshall's mentor who had served in the first war as an army artillery officer.

"Anne, Serge and I all tried everything we could to talk him out of it, or at least, into finishing his law degree first and serving that way. Once he had his mind made up, we could be supportive or risk him going away feeling alone. An issue with his vision kept him out of Tuskegee, and I have no idea where he got the notion of being a tank platoon commander, but he forged some great friendships in the 761st. Several alums have been over here to pay their respects, particularly an officer from DC named Lightfoot who was apparently a close confidant."

I feel my composure slipping away. My wife is already out of the bed with both arms around me, pulling me close. "Just think, Rachel, all three of us almost made it back. He just needed a few more days.

Then there was the day I thought I lost you." Tears stream down my eyes, and though I have cried twice before in the past few years, I cry now like never. My tears are for Charles, Anne and Charlene. They are for Blue, and Ron.

A long time passes before we speak again. We hear tiny footsteps that begin in a small bedroom, run into Anne's bedroom, and finally make their way downstairs into the kitchen.

I try to refocus Rachel's attention on one of her favorite people—a man whose plans I am anxious to hear. "Okay, so tell me. What does Serge plan to do next? I know you two have talked. I'm only asking because I'd rather not hear about it for the first time over dinner."

She confirms my suspicions that Serge has been in contact with her at least once since he arrived back in the States. While I envy the love my brother shares with my wife—instead of his older brother who tracked him across Europe, I am grateful that he now has a sister in whom he can confide.

"Geez, Jack. Okay, I'll tell you, but promise you won't start with him tonight. Anne will have enough mixed emotions from seeing both of you safe at home for the first time since she lost Charles. She doesn't need to compound those emotions with you two going after each other."

I try to keep her focused on giving me the details I want to know. "I agree with you, Rachel. Although, if he's been in the States since August, why is he just now deciding to visit us—only to leave us right away? I haven't seen him since I followed him to Germany last spring. I was hoping he'd stick around at least long enough to ring in 1946, a new year without war, with his family—for Anne."

"Sure Jack—*you're doing it for Anne*. Well, I know Serge's plans involve some sort of a demonstration—something about Bayard Rustin, and about a Supreme Court case." Her voice trails off, indicating that all she has left is conjecture.

Since she has unknowingly answered all my questions, I interrupt. "Oh, got it. They think Bill Hastie and Thurgood Marshall have the Justices boxed in on *Morgan versus Virginia*. Rustin must be planning *to poke the bear*. As soon as the Jim Crow seating rule is overturned, they'll test the ruling by going down south and daring the locals to arrest them. I've got to hand it to them, they don't waste a day."

My wife becomes coy. "Do I detect a little admiration, a little jealousy, in your voice? What about you, Jack, do you ever have any regrets—a sense that you're wasting days you should be spending doing something else?"

With my palm resting on her bare stomach, I feel a well-timed kick from my unborn son warning his father to tread carefully here. I think he already senses that his ostensibly self-assured mother exudes confidence when making difficult choices but mires in insecurity when the appropriate course of action seems clear. As I look at her thick disheveled hair, ever expanding midsection, and temporarily oversized breasts, she is by far more beautiful than I have ever seen her before. "And miss all this? No, I don't."

"You know what I mean Jack. Answer the question." As has become her habit, she runs her index finger around the small circular ridge left on my side by a bullet wound. She also tries to keep away from my sight the small burn scaring still visible on her lower back.

I take a moment to phrase a response, but I still fail. "The only thing I am conflicted about is whether to feel thankful that the war brought us together or regretful that it so often kept us apart." My words sound straight off a greeting card. I roll over and kiss her stomach, embarrassed and afraid I will not be able to suppress a smile.

"I didn't ask you for a greeting card. Don't manage me. I thought you were supposed to be working on that annoying habit." Fully expecting me to try again, she slides back against the headboard, waiting patiently with her arms folded.

Under no illusions about the length of time she is prepared to wait, I decide to try harder. "Look, we both have made adjustments, but we've been talking about this ever since that night in Naples. As it turns out, we were right. You won't be a surgeon practicing medicine in New Orleans and I won't be a foreign correspondent reporting from post-war Paris. Like you, I've moved on. That's it, plain and simple."

She is prepared to rebut that answer. "But I'm just as needed in Washington as I am in New Orleans—regardless of whether I work as a doctor or a surgical nurse. I wasn't asking about me, Jack. My options don't vary much at all. Now, yes or no, would you be turning down job offers and waiting around for Lomax to promote you if you didn't have a pregnant wife? And answer me honestly."

Though it will only fuel her anxiety, I want to tell her that Walter Lomax is making a complete recovery and my chances of becoming managing editor of the *Record* are slimmer than she suspects. If Ted continues to delay his decision, he will lose all authority to name me as his permanent successor.

Before I can share my trepidations with Rachel, my salvation arrives announced by three light knocks on the bedroom door. I get up and slip on my robe as my wife ducks under the bedspread. "Come on in honey." Shaving case in one hand, I scoop up my nearly three-year-old niece with the other and watch as my wife's expression morphs from concern to unbridled joy.

"Put her down Jack, so she can give me a big hug."

Charlene scrambles across the bed and jumps into waiting arms. "Aunt Rachel, mamma wants to know if you're going with us to the market."

Just after nightfall, amid squeals of delight, warm embraces and streaming tears of joy, Serge arrives. After the initial excitement has subsided, I take his hat and coat as everyone listens intently to his answers to a flurry of questions. He patiently brings us up to date on everything that has occurred since his last letter to Anne.

Fortunately, Anne retreats into the kitchen with her helpers in tow, and I have a chance to ask him what happens next. "So, if Marshall wins in court, you're going to stir things up by taking bus trips through the South? I may want to send a reporter down there with you, but I need to understand how this tactic is supposed to work."

With Charlene still bouncing on her newly discovered uncle's knee, Serge responds reassuringly to comfort the ladies who pretend to work silently in the kitchen—yet hang on his every word.

"We're still working everything out. W*hen* Marshall and Hastie win, we'd love some news coverage. There's no telling where the fire might start. Our plan is simple—we'll purchase bus tickets in Washington, sit wherever we damned-well please and ride until we're arrested by some backwoods crackers. But we have to be ready to strike before the bus companies find a way around the ruling."

"Well Serge, if you ride far and long enough, some cop is bound to violate the Court's ruling. If not, vigilantes will. I can predict that with absolute certainty. What about physical security?" I know this is a sensitive topic to address today, but I wonder if Serge has prepared for all the possible dangers.

He simply looks at me as he did in Germany, patiently indulging his overly concerned brother. "Well, I hope you don't plan to hitchhike down South to save me like you tried to do in Europe. Did Jack tell y'all how he went all over the continent accusing army officers of kidnapping his baby bother and sending him off to fight? Then, he found me and realized there was nothing he could do about it."

We can all hear the affection in Serge's tone. I want to be sure they know the truth. "But then I'd also have to tell them how I found you. Instead of a smart-assed kid, I found this hard-core battle-tested dogface, walking the point with an M-1 in one hand and the fate of a platoon in the other."

He retorts. "And what I learned over there is also true back here. *Freedom ain't free.* We know that some of us are going to get a rough reception down there. As the buses roll out, some of our people with bail money will follow us in cars. They'll be taking an even bigger risk. But we can't bring security guards along on a nonviolent protest."

The kitchen door swings open releasing a symphony of aromas and Rachel stands glaring at me. "That's right Jack. After I push your baby out, I may go along with them." Watching her standing defiantly in the doorway with hands on hips, I remember—despite her current bulge—of the day I saw her hitching a ride to Algiers. Unable to resist, Serge fuels the fire.

"There's still time, Rachel. We don't have a ruling yet and Bayard's in no hurry to organize the protest. That baby may be old enough to come along for the ride."

Despite knowing better, I take the bait. "You won't be going on any kind of bus ride for freedom, and certainly not with our son in diapers."

My wife is ready, as usual, with her rebuttal. "What are you going to say when he—*or she*—asks what we did while Uncle Serge worked for our civil rights?" Far more intrigued by the conversation in the living room than her limited role in dinner preparations, my wife stands defiantly, chomping on a carrot that Anne surely intends for some other purpose.

Before Rachel can swallow her last mouthful of raw vegetable, her uncle tries to deflect our spat. "Jack surely you were impressed by the brilliance of Hastie and Marshall to tie the *Morgan* case to the Interstate Commerce Clause. If they win, there're too many established precedents for inaction. Who the hell would've thought they'd be able to build a Supreme Court case around a colored woman refusing to move to the back of a bus in 1945?"

Serge chimes in, believing that Owen's distraction has provided a proper segue for him to speak on another matter. "That reminds me Owen, I'd say that a lot of people, namely me, owe you a debt of gratitude—and my apologies. I read Jack's story about your work at the War Department. It created quite a buzz. Yes, and very artfully written. It was honest and forthright—and it helped that you thoughtfully shared most of the credit. Yet, after reading it, I suspect you took far less credit than is due."

"Thanks. But, as I like to tell your brother, you can get a lot more done when you share the credit." Owen has a point of his own to make. "Serge, you know I will stand with you shoulder to shoulder—go to jail with you. If you don't mind someone from the old guard asking, how many civil rights organizations do we really need?"

I sit up straight, pleased that my wife and I are not arguing and that someone else has *launched a rhetorical rocket*. However, rather than the defensive salvo I expect, Serge offers thoughtfully, "I know how you see it. The thing to keep in mind is that just one medicine will only cure one symptom of the disease. All the groups have their own remedies, different cures. We're all trying to eradicate a killer virus that comes in many different strains and manifests itself through radically different symptoms."

Owen can only mutter something mildly coherent in response to an answer Serge obviously has given before. Rachel looks down at her hands trying to find something to do with them, finally reaching over to cover up Charlene, who has fallen asleep.

After she returns to the kitchen, we continue talking about Serge's plans, giving far more thought to our questions before asking them. I had expected to see my brother in uniform today. Instead, he is wearing a dark business suit and tie, looking like an impeccably groomed professional. The dirt and grime of combat is gone, but traces of that distant stare remain in his eyes. Of interest to me is his new relaxed persona, the confident intellectualism of his mentor, in contrast to the outspoken brashness that singled him out for combat duty in Germany.

Anne steps out of the kitchen followed by Rachel and Muriel Todd. "Well, sorry for the wait but dinner is finally served." They carry large serving dishes, leaving haunting aromas in their wake. Then they go back in the kitchen and reemerge with three more vessels. "Serge, since you're our guest of honor this evening, you and Jack take the seats on the ends."

We stand in unison and drift into the dining room where the table has been set with china and silver carefully passed down through four Savoy generations. The sale of Mamie's house had drained me emotionally. However, it was lucrative enough to divide into three substantial portions, and to eliminate the need to sell off housewares and antiques that we wanted to keep in the family.

Anne adjusts the comforter over the first member of the fifth generation. Serge picks out a seat at one end leaving me with the place usually reserved for Charles. From my vantage point, I see a cluster of images on the wall, including Charles and Anne, the only surviving image of Joe and Souwanas Domingo, and a portrait done from an old photograph of my grandmother surrounded by her three teenaged grandsons. Now, there is a professionally enlarged and framed photograph of the adult brothers Savoy and Anne.

I take a few minutes to give thanks using a mental outline I have prepared in advance, and Serge, Owen and I sit mesmerized by the feast that has been prepared under Anne's tutelage and watchful eyes. Rachel and I moved in temporarily months ago We both attest to the contrast between Anne's meals and cold rations, scraps from abandoned villages and the so-called hot chow dished out by mobile mess units. They have banned me from invoking memories of the SOS served aboard the *USS Dorothy Dix*.

Even the usually conversational Owen is singularly focused but also careful to include Muriel's participation in his own expressions of appreciation. About ten minutes transpire before Muriel speaks the next coherent words. "So, Rachel, have you decided what you're going to do?"

Rachel, who has been assisting Anne with the now wide-awake and re-energized Charlene, shakes her head—no doubt reflecting on the conversation my niece interrupted this morning. Wiping the toddler's mouth, she responds with uncertainty. "A year ago, I would've said a medical degree and surgery without hesitation. I still might. I'm just going to put in this first year of med school and see what happens. Jack and I have a lot to talk about, and a lot of planning to do."

Because he is aware of the situation unfolding between the Lomax brothers and the possible ramifications for my continued employment with the *Record*, Owen tries to change the subject, but Muriel, a hospital administrator, is on a mission. They have already discussed the possibility of Rachel interning at a hospital for the city's poor and indigent, located in the Northeast quadrant.

Serge, surprising me yet again, rescues us with a civil rights soliloquy that ends with a pronouncement. "I've been telling people that we're in a new age. People of color all over the world just fought and bled in a world war to end oppression. We haven't made it back home just to keep putting up with it."

In truth, I would have to confess to my wife that I envy Serge's freedom to go and do as he pleases. I also detect an air of assurance in many of the returning soldiers that was not there before. Of course, equally determined detractors will challenge them. "If we're really seeing a sea change in attitudes Negroes have about their power to end segregation, this'll be an exciting time to be a newspaperman. But, I've gotta admit it'll be an extraordinary time to do what you plan to do."

Serge does not miss a beat. "There's no difference between the two, Red." I am surprised to see Owen nodding with Rachel in agreement. After desert, Anne and Muriel begin removing the vestiges of the feast, and Owen reminds us of the bourbon he brought. Serge speaks up first. "To Charles, if I may, the best of the Savoy brothers and a man who always knew exactly what he wanted, and the woman who was exactly what he needed. Finally, here's to beautiful Charlene, for the moment anyway, the newest Savoy."

The Todd's clink their glasses together and Anne starts to cry. Rachel reaches over to grab my arm, startling me by the intense pressure of her grip. As she looks down in the seat of her chair, her expression tells me everything I need to know. I take a big sip from my tumbler and allow the smooth bourbon to play over my tongue. Anne meets our gazes. I get up to collect the bags packed for this contingency.

Muriel catches on and starts to applaud as though the second act of a play is about to commence.

Charlene suddenly no longer seems so little. "Well, it looks like your cousin has decided to crash the party. Now we know. It must be another big-head boy. Get me to Freedman's so I can pass this melon."

Chapter 31

· ·

Walter Lomax is Dead

"**H**ey, Walt, can you hear me? Can you hear me?"
I want to stop Ted from talking, from asking senseless questions of a man who can no longer answer them. However, I do not know how to suggest that he should give up on his brother's life.

I want to remind our employees, as they stand around wondering what to do, that they already have something pressing to do. We have a newspaper to get out. "Jack, is he still breathing?" I am neither qualified nor willing to answer the question, let alone confirm that businessman, publisher and civil rights activist Walter Lomax has died.

Despite her limited understanding of chest compression, Connie Howard continues to work on Walt's lifeless torso, in lieu of professional medical intervention. I tilt the conference room fan toward them. Increasing airflow is the only contribution I feel qualified to make. When Connie finally collapses, Ted cradles his older brother's head in a gesture that seems appropriate. Doris, who broke Walt's fall as he crashed to the floor, nervously fidgets with the publisher's shirt buttons.

Everyone else is whispering, crying or praying quietly. I need to make a managerial decision. "We probably need to clear the room and limit the number of people around the doorway." I direct my observation to a production supervisor, unable to muster the audacity to do it myself. I know that I should tell the employees crowding around the doorway to get back to finalizing tomorrow's edition, to clear the front page for Walt.

If Walt could speak, I know he would roar his disapproval of the deafening silence that has fallen over the newsroom floor. He would rail against his managing editor, ordering him to update the *deathwatch* stories assembled last year after his stroke. However, I have been the managing editor for less than thirty minutes.

I simply cannot tell the people who served him loyally for so many years to disregard the man sprawled out on the conference room floor. The mere suggestion would be much like desecrating the body of the man who just promoted me. So much has occurred on this day that began like any other publishing deadline, except for an unexpected visit from Ted.

Ted had arrived to the office much earlier than usual. "Good morning Jack. How're you doing?"

I looked up from the galleys spread over my desk to see him smiling like a jack-o-lantern, a man with too much time on his hands. Still, I answered him with far more acidity than I intended. "That's a good question Ted. Why don't you tell me how I'm doing?"

Ignoring the impatience my voice conveyed, he said, "What can I say? You're a natural. You've exceeded everyone's expectations. I'm sorry you've spent a whole year in limbo. If it were up to me, you'd already be managing editor. But as you can plainly see, it ain't up to me anymore."

However, a year ago it would have been *his decision to make.* I hear impatience in my voice as I remind him, "Ted, it's actually been 16 months since I took on these duties. Remember?"

I remember reading a letter in January 1944, stating that the prognosis for Walt's recovery from a massive stroke had been doubtful. Most observers had expected Ted to lighten his new workload by dropping the second weekly edition his brother had imposed on the staff. However, Ted surprised everyone by refusing to write off Walt's initial cash outlays or the advertising commitments.

When I had returned to Washington in June 1945, Ted had lightened his workload by giving me the national news desk. He also assigned to me a foreign news desk that scarcely existed beyond wire service reports and Jim Peterson's coverage of the Pacific war. Later, two key mangers resigned over uncertainty about Walter. Barely able to maintain the production schedule, Ted shifted even more management functions to me.

Two daily newspapers had proposed to send me back to Europe as a foreign correspondent. While that had once been my goal, it was easy to decline both offers. I had a wife. A substantial raise from Ted eased my trepidations and helped me look beyond the bruised egos of longer tenured editors.

I knew that Ted had hoped I would be the capable manager who served him as loyally as he had served his brother. I buried myself in work and earned Ted's trust with my embrace of each additional delegated task. Meanwhile, Ted and Doris doted on Walter during his slow, painful recovery. However, I knew Ted was ecstatic about his chance to run Lomax Publishing with the latitude to invoke his own personal style.

Then, for no apparent reason, Walt had started beating the odds. His speech and motor skills improved markedly, and he began approaching his recovery with fever pitched intensity. Walt's doctors accelerated his recovery timetable and revised milestone dates to accommodate each surprising step forward.

By late fall, he had reclaimed swaths of his old turf. In front of dozens of Christmas party guests, Walt had left little doubt as to who was in charge—*and who was not.* Owen had walked over to me during one of Ted's particularly embarrassing moments. "Now I see why Ted never gave you the managing editor's job. He left it open for himself. So now, what do you get for working late every night?"

However, my salary and workload remained unchanged. Rather than reclaiming his former management duties as predicted, Ted merely repackaged himself as an in-house consultant of sorts, behaving like a man not long for the exit door.

Earlier this morning, as I sat indulging Ted in my small office off the newsroom floor, I thought about how my plans and priorities had changed over the last two years. Instead of reporting from Paris or

Rome, I sat buried under a pile of paper and photographs, listening to Ted, the consultant, intrude on my limited time.

"By the way, Jack, how's Joe? Like a weed, huh." Ted took a seat on the other side of my desk, insistent on interrupting what was quickly becoming a busy morning. "How's Serge? I haven't heard you say much about him for a while."

With effort, I maintained my patience and composure. "Rachel hears from him occasionally. She says he's in Chicago working at CORE for a guy younger than he is. They're probably cooking up another *Freedom Ride*." I try not to sound dismissive. "Look Ted, no offense, but my dance card is filling up real fast this morning."

He remains nonchalant. "I understand, Jack. Bring Serge in some time. He should hear some of our firsthand accounts of what they used to do to *race men* down South. By the way, the other guy at CORE is James Farmer, a young prodigy from Texas. He should know there's a big difference in getting arrested at a Chicago sit-in and getting stopped on a dark road down South."

I tried giving him something to do. "Have you read the latest submission from Pete?" As he read Peterson's censored story that just arrived from Tokyo, I returned my attention to work. I looked up again when I heard his familiar low whistle.

I speak up for my correspondent, "I know it runs long. Pete's done a good job for this paper, chasing down the 24th and the 93rd, running behind colored units scattered over the Pacific—a lot of territory to cover, on bumpy flights and over rough seas."

Ted agreed, "We sent Pete over there but McArthur never threw his colored infantry into a fight like Clark did. I should've moved Pete to France after Normandy, instead of him following ghosts through the jungle, looking for *Monmouth Marines*. Maybe it's past time to call him home."

Knowing such a decision once again rested solely with Walt, I ignored his musing but tried to make productive use of time. "Maybe since the 24th never left Okinawa, Pete thought they deserved a little press. He even updated the Aka Island angle."

Peterson had written an extensive article about the Japanese on tiny Aka surrendering their outpost to the 24th Infantry during the battle for Okinawa. Though the action marked the first time an island garrison chose surrender over suicide, the event had paled next to the fighting for the main island.

Ted's response comes as no surprise. "Well, you can probably get it into the paper without Walt seeing it. Still, you know how my brother feels about that ugly episode in Houston over 25 years ago."

I take the hint and kill the story idea. "Yeah, I know. I've heard him talk about it. On one hand, he says he understands why they armed themselves against the cops and civilian vigilantes. But then hell quickly add that their bloody retaliation in Houston was the reason for much of his regiment's harassment in Europe. Forget I mentioned it."

"Yeah, I just don't think this is a good time for it, though you've got to hand it to Pete. He makes the surrender sound like a really big deal." Ted adds, "Walt's all caught up in that fair employment practices bill. It won't ever get a vote. But that won't stop Randolph and White from trying." We heard several people walk past us on their way to the conference room. Ted asked, "Jack, can I sit in on this morning's meeting? Great, let's walk together."

I was annoyed further, knowing that, in addition to wasting my time, Ted was demonstrating a lack of professional courtesy by making me wait to find out what he had to say to my staff. Ted was committing the same kind of sleight that Walt routinely perpetrated against him. As we took the short stroll, I gauged the pace of newsroom activity and my curious gazes met several *thumbs up*. When we walked into the cloud of tobacco smoke already forming in the windowless conference room, I turned on the floor-mounted fan, sending some of the thick smoke billowing out through the open doorway.

"Hey boss, I'm surprised you didn't pick up smoking in all those rain-soaked foxholes." I ignored Connie's thinly veiled sarcasm since asking her to cease and desist would only inspire more of the same. Besides, I understood her frustration. While unfair, neither of the traditionalist Lomax brothers had promoted her. However, in addition to directing the city news reporters, Connie had always been a prolific writer, crusading for women's equality in employment and housing. I simply nodded in her direction and, as always, took the first available chair.

I immediately turned the meeting over to Ted. "Thanks Jack. I don't need much time. I know how busy everyone is today. First, I want to thank Jack again for taking up so much of the slack around here." People who never warmed to the notion of reporting to me visibly flinched. "Also, I want to let you know that I won't be involved any more. I've decided to take a teaching position at a Negro college's newly formed journalism department."

For a long moment, everyone sat in stunned silence. Then, Ted waved off a flurry of questions and expressions of sadness. "Don't worry, I will be speaking with each of you individually, but suffice to say now that it has been a privilege to know you and work with you." I pretended to have known about Ted's announcement all along.

Just as Ted was about to excuse himself, we heard a familiar bass. "June, where is everybody?" People grinned and reached for cigarettes and pipes in anticipation of the entertainment. With growing anxiety about my looming deadline, I cocked an ear toward the open door to gauge any lull in newsroom activity.

The buzz of work continued unabated even as Walt walked in followed by Chet. Both appeared to have aged substantially during the war years, with Walt going completely bald and Chet's remaining hair turning completely white. Walt greeted each person individually before turning to me.

"I'm sure Ted told you he's taking a job elsewhere, so there's nothing more I can add to that. So, Jack, is there any real estate left on Page One?" Out of respect or force of habit, I cast a wary glance at Ted before answering a question ordinarily reserved for him, and responded only after getting his subtle nod of concurrence.

"We've got two local stories and the piece on the Employment Practices Committee, Randolph's remarks and his letter to Truman, and a lead in for an update on the bus riders. There's a little space still in play—if I take out photos for those two local stories. But those stories will make us look like a daily when we hit the stands."

I regretted my last comment, knowing it revealed my desire to publish even more frequently while most still struggled to produce our two weekly editions. I also wanted to expand, like the *Afro,* into other markets. Well past the end of paper rationing, we could now improve the paper's appearance and increase its space times four. "Other than that, I'm giving priority to anything good about GI readjustment—jobs, medical, education. And of course, court rulings and anything significant on employment practices."

Walt continues. "By the way, I want everyone to join me in congratulating the *Washington Record's* new managing editor, Jack Savoy." The publisher made his statement as though announcing the lunch menu. After a moment to absorb the initial shock and awe, hands extended around the table and I accepted a round of hearty handshakes, congratulations and pledges of support offered with varying degrees of sincerity.

I wanted to suggest that we all take a short break, but Walt quickly moved on. However, I detected a sudden change in his posture that also suddenly manifested in his speech. A frown formed on Ted's face and concern, perhaps fear, registered in Chet's eyes. Connie rose to her feet.

In the apace of a moment, Walt's speech became halting and slurred. "Since Pete obviously never wants to come home again, I think we should send him to Pusan, Korea." The room was silent. The elder Lomax frowned at their blank expressions. "Is anyone following this thing in Korea?" I hoped he might leave if no one encouraged him to linger.

However, Ted had a different notion. "Okay Walt, I'll bite. *What thing* in Korea?"

Walt struggled to pronounce the challenging phonetics. "Two young State Department staffers have drawn a line through Korea, separating American and Russian spheres of influence." Eyebrows raised as Walt struggled with the phonetic constructions. "Rather than invest the time to divide Korea logically, they just cut it in two. That was the real scoop when y'all were around here buck-dancing over McArthur's theatrics in Tokyo Bay."

No one seemed to understand. Ted tried to summarize. Walt flashed a grimace and glanced down at his watch. He reached for a chair but stubbornly remained standing, holding on to the chair back for support. He turned toward the wall, looking at nothing. "I need a nap."

Connie and Doris bolt toward him to assist. "Sure Walt, let's get you back to the sofa in your office."

"No dammit, I said *map* not *nap*. Doris, where's that big nap of Asia?" Now an indispensable copy editor, Doris gestured with all the respect she could muster to the map that had hung in the same spot since the attack on Pearl Harbor. Undaunted, Walt insisted on continuing, struggling stubbornly with each word. "Here's young Dean Rusk's arbitrary line that Stalin has accepted. The damn line makes no sense to the Koreans."

Walt looked around the table for concurrence but proceeded even though he received none. "Look, my guess is that Stalin's man will run the northern half and we'll install some greedy asshole in the south. Pete will be safe in Pusan." As Walt became agitated, he lost even the diminished composure he had been able to summon. "I've been right before."

Ted concurred as he stood and walked over to stand next to his brother. "Yes Walt. You made all the right calls."

Although Ted tried to calm his brother, Walt released the back of the chair and attempted to take a step toward the door, but keeled against the wall and collapsed on the floor, with Doris extending her arms to break his fall.

A medical emergency crew arrives and clears the conference room. Still, neither Ted nor I order the staff back to work. Rather, we both try to comfort a few people who appear to be devastated by what has occurred. When I follow the gurney downstairs and outside on the sidewalk, I see figures standing in windows and doors all along our section of U Street.

People watch as they place the motionless body of Walter Lomax gently into the back of an ambulance. The attendants do not hurry. One of our photographers begins taking photographs and, after running down from the other end of the street, two photographers from the *Afro American* remain respectful but cannot shirk their duty to photograph a fallen civil rights icon. Someone has fetched Ted's car and he remains in the driver's seat, parked behind the ambulance. As he slides into the passenger seat, Ted motions for me to walk around to him. Looking over at several women and men crying openly, I speak before he does. "What do we do now, Ted?"

He answers me sternly, void of the emotion that surely overwhelms him. In fact, he sounds very much like his older brother. His first words are for June, spoken loud through the driver's window for the benefit of everyone within earshot. "Get Jack moved into my office today, but don't disturb anything in Walt's office." Pack my personal things and stack them in the storeroom.

He turns back to me. "You've got to get these people back to work and put the paper to bed. You must write this story for Page-One, banner header above the fold. You have all the photos, the obit and prepared copy. June will know how to find me if needed. I'll be back as soon as I can get away."

I bow my head as I consider the places he might be later today. "Get your head out of your ass Jack—these people need leadership. Walt put you in charge with his last official act. I'm ordering you to promote Connie Howard to City Desk Editor as your first official act. I'll be calling in as soon as I have updates, so stay close and get it done, Jack. I know this has been one hell of a day."

Chet slips into the passenger seat and they drive off behind the ambulance, which cruises at normal speed down U Street toward Freedmen's Hospital. Everyone watches until the vehicle is out of sight. Then, all eyes fix on me as I climb the stairs to the newsroom. I reach the landing flanked by Connie, and, without saying a word, we lead the entire staff back to work in a solemn atmosphere of quiet reflection.

"This call is for you, chief." June points toward Ted's office. The phone is ringing by the time I get to the desk where Ted has sat for a decade.

A woman—unaware of the sudden turn of events—laughs on the other end, trying to disguise her voice. "Hey soldier, we missed the last streetcar downtown, and were wondering if a colored driver could take us to the next depot."

I have not yet processed nor do I want to speak of the tragedy that has just occurred. "Well, that's quite a coincidence, Captain. I was just on my way downtown myself. Maybe you could ride with me—you know, keep me company."

"Actually, I would just pass the time reading my copy of a new book that just arrived in the mail today. *The Triple-V,* written by a new author—some cool cat named Jack T. Savoy. By the way, I don't even know your middle name."

"It's *Toussaint.*"

"Boy, your mamma named you *Toussaint*? Oh, Junior, it was your daddy's name. No wonder two border-line colored people ended up with a son who looks like, well tell me Toussaint, just who does our boy look like?"

It is impossible to describe the love that fills her voice when she talks about young Joseph Garrett Savoy. Even now, Rachel obsesses about a physical characteristic that should be the least significant, though it will surely be the most consequential. Then I hear him gurgle, and forget just for a moment about the things I will have to tell him about the world he must be prepared to face.

I forget about a long terrible war that has changed every corner of the world, I forget about how much the country has changed and how much, stubbornly, the country remains the same. I forget about the Lomax brothers and eulogizing Walt in tomorrow's edition.

I forget about the war and Walt's dying preoccupation with where the next one might begin. I forget that America has emerged from a terrible war as racially divided as ever. I think only of the woman I almost lost and the son who bears the names of a runaway slave and a buffalo soldier.

"So, Mister Savoy, what does your son look like?"

"I don't know. I think he looks like *change*, Rachel."

"Oh, no, don't say that, Jack. That's the thing that scares people most."

ABOUT THE AUTHOR

W ith a degree from Howard University's School of Communications,
I worked 35 years as a researcher, writer and consultant for several
defense and civilian agencies. Moonlighting over those same years,
I ghosted speeches and presentations on African American history—
mainly to supplement educations for my two legacy Americans. My eight
years of Vietnam era and active reserve service pales in comparison to
those who answered the call to duty in 1941. But I'll mention it just the
same. And, oh yeah, *Color Inside the Lines* is my first published novel.

For over 25 years I solicited stories from veterans, particularly
African American veterans of the Second World War. Like my father
and uncles, most served in segregated Army services units. My father
moved supplies and piloted *DUKW*s in the North Africa, Foggia,
Rome-Arno, Southern France and North Apennines campaigns. Several
of my other veterans served in air corps, artillery and armored units.
A few were Tuskegee Airmen and a few others were on the beaches
of Normandy.

However, I did not find a unifying storyline for this novel until I
began researching contemporary African American newspaper articles.
The publishers, editors and reporters of the pre-war *Negro Press* stood at
the vanguard of the Civil Rights Movement. Their war correspondents
chronicled the contributions of African American soldiers, sailors and
Airmen, sending back photographs and news stories read eagerly in
barbershops, on porches and around dinner tables across the nation.